Star Dreams

June Flaum Singer

CORGI BOOKS

STAR DREAMS
A CORGI BOOK 0 552 12418 4

Originally published in Great Britain by
Judy Piatkus (Publishers) Ltd.

PRINTING HISTORY
Judy Piatkus edition published 1984
Corgi edition published 1984
Corgi edition reissued 1984
Corgi edition reprinted 1984
Corgi edition reprinted 1985
Corgi edition reprinted 1986
Corgi edition reprinted 1987
Corgi edition reprinted 1989
Corgi edition reissued 1991

This book is set in Palatino 10/11 pt.

Corgi Books are published by Transworld Publishers
Ltd., 61–63 Uxbridge Road, Ealing, London W5 5SA, in
Australia by Transworld Publishers (Australia) Pty. Ltd.,
15–23 Helles Avenue, Moorebank, NSW 2170, and in New
Zealand by Transworld Publishers (N.Z.) Ltd., Cnr. Moselle
and Waipareira Avenues, Henderson, Auckland.

Printed and bound in Great Britain by
Cox & Wyman Ltd., Reading, Berks.

For Daddy
and
In memory of Mama

When Nessa is bumbling around the world and making each thorn blossom, what room is there for me?
— VIRGINIA WOOLF

PROLOGUE

Hollywood
1970

It's Oscar night in Hollywood once again, and tonight Beebie Tyler is being honored – a special award for her contribution to the movie industry. For over forty years she has been writing about the stars, reporting on their doings, befriending them, advising them, occasionally castigating them. In many cases she has elevated them to stardom, all with her mighty pen. For years she's been queen of the Hollywood scene, and tonight she is going to get her official reward.

She reminds herself that she has yet to choose a hat from her collection to wear this evening. Every star has a certain signature, as it were, and she has always been noted for her hats.

The maid interrupts her thoughts.

'There's a young lady at the door, Miss Tyler. She says she's a journalist and would like to interview you about your award tonight.'

She considers. Why not? It's not often she gets to be the interviewee. 'I'll give her a few minutes. I'll receive her in the drawing room.'

The girl tells her she is from Omaha, Nebraska, and is working towards her degree in journalism, and that her dream is to follow in Beebie's footsteps – to become a chronicler of the stars. Beebie cannot help but recall the plump young girl from New Orleans, grown up poor and certainly not pretty, who came to Hollywood determined to reign over filmdom's beautiful and famous.

'I was at that first Oscar presentation in '28, you know. Janet Gaynor won the Best Actress award. She

3

was a sensation in *Seventh Heaven*. I still get goose bumps thinking about it.

'I was merely a child then, a cub reporter, no more than an assistant to Ed Peterson, who was the regular movie reporter then. Well, Ed got sick that night – I suspect that he was drunk – well, by the time the next Oscar night rolled around, *I* was the regular movie columnist and Ed was back in New York.

'That year – 1928 – all the reporters and columnists went to the Motion Picture Academy Awards, and they all reported on who won what, but I was the only one who made a whole other thing of it, described the magnificent gowns, who was with whom, and what secret romances were going on behind the scene – not to mention all the little scandals the Awards had precipitated. And after that . . . well, it was I who always saw the dreams that were there in movieland, captured it on paper for everyone to see. Oh, others came along – Louella, Hedda – but none were ever as influential as I. Maybe it was because I really and truly loved the dreams that were the movies . . . and its stars.

'Yes, I've seen a lot of stars come and go. I've seen a lot of Oscar nights. I was there when Mary Pickford won for *Coquette* and when Shearer won for the *Divorcee*, when Clark and Claudette and *It Happened One Night* took the top prizes. In all modesty, I take some credit for that. I can't tell you how many arms I twisted – gently, of course – to get people to vote for the King, a dear sweet man. Oh yes, I was there to see Tracy and Davis win, Joan Fontaine and Vivien Leigh, Cagney and Garson and Olivia de Havilland. I saw sweet little Olivia turn away when her sister, Joan, came up to congratulate her. Brando, Taylor, Bergman . . . I saw them come on the scene, took them under my wing if they behaved themselves, saw them go on to take their Oscars. But tonight I get to go up on the stage and get *my* Oscar.'

'And that Oscar is long overdue, Miss Tyler,' the girl compliments her. 'Why, you're a shining example of

4

American journalism. Why, you practically *invented* the career of movie journalist.'

Beebie is not taken in by the girl's flattery, but she feels magnanimously disposed towards her just the same, so she tells the maid to bring in some tea and some little sandwiches and cakes and says, 'You wanted an interview. What exactly, my dear, would you like me to talk about?'

'I think everyone would like to read about Beebie Tyler's most favorite movie star and why—'

Beebie smiles. 'That's a tall order. To pick one out of so many. I knew them all, you know – Pickford and Garbo, Dietrich and Fairbanks, Tracy and Hepburn, Gable and Lombard, the Bennett sisters, Joan and Connie, and their handsome father. What beautiful girls they were. Barrymore and Cary . . . John Garfield and the Lane sisters and some I'm sure you never even heard of. I knew Liz Taylor from the time she started in the business. I had to give her a slap on the hand when she married Eddie Fisher, breaking poor little Debbie's heart. Some of them were extraordinary actors, and some were great personalities. Some were beautiful and some were just darn good copy. Like Rory Devlin. He was always fun to write about. Offscreen he was probably Hollywood's greatest lover. The stories I could tell you about him!

'But you see, I never told *all*. That's one of the secrets of being a great columnist, knowing when to tell a story and when to repress it. But Devlin was one of the handsomest men that ever came to Hollywood, even though he wasn't that photogenic. Not really.

'And then there are Devlin's daughters, Kiki Devlin and Angela du Beaumond . . . that was their mother's maiden name, you know. Both of them, coincidentally enough, are up for awards tonight – both of them nominated for Best Actress. That happened once before, you know, when Joan Fontaine and her sister, Olivia, were up for awards the same year.

'Kiki Devlin was my neighbor, you know, for quite a

while. She lived in that great big white house right across the street there . . .

'We were always great friends, the Devlin girls and I, and I always tried to guard them . . . in print . . . tried to protect them even when they got themselves into a bit of trouble, like when Kiki . . . Well, I looked on them almost as daughters. Maybe it was because they were from New Orleans, just as I was. I knew the whole family, you see. Even Rory Devlin. Or I should say I knew *of* him. Everybody in New Orleans knew of Rory Devlin in those days. He had quite a reputation. He was a few years older than I, of course, but I thought he was the most beautiful man I had ever seen. And I knew Marie du Beaumond, the Devlin girls' mother, and Marie's sister, Desiree. We were the same age, me and Marie. But of course we weren't friends. *She* was royalty in New Orleans. Everybody knew the du Beaumonds. And I . . . I was just a poor girl from the other side of the bayous.' Beebie laughs. 'Well, if anyone knows the *real* story of the Devlin sisters, it's me. The outward things – their glamour, their beauty, the men that they married . . . well, practically everyone knows about those things. But *I* know the whole story . . .'

'Oh, Miss Tyler, will you tell me about them, the Devlin sisters – the whole story?'

She pauses to think for a moment. She has some time. 'Why not? Have some more tea, my dear, and some of these dear little cakes. They are my very favorites.'

PART ONE

New Orleans
1927–1937

'I think this story has to start in New Orleans – before the sisters were born, when Marie du Beaumond first determined to marry Rory Devlin. It was the same year that I left New Orleans myself – 1927. But I know all the details. Even then I knew how to snoop out a story. Well, Marie was a deep one. Nobody really knew what she was about. Everyone said that when she met Rory Devlin every bit of a brain in her head went out the window, she was that crazy about him. And who could blame her? He was the handsomest, most dashing man – a lot like Clark, but even better-looking. Clark did have those ears. And Marie, well, *before* she met Rory she was a cool one. And quite a beauty. Her hair was so pale it was almost silver, and her eyes . . . well, they were pale too. A strange pale green.

'Well, the first reckless thing Marie du Beaumond did in her whole twenty years was to become engaged to Rory Devlin, who bore his father's Irish name and his Cajun mother's olive-skinned beauty. And it wasn't an easy decision for Marie. She was very much under her mother's influence, and her mother, Eugenie Manard du Beaumond, was one of those blood-proud, fiery Creoles and she forbade Marie to marry him. She told Marie that he was no good. "All New Orleans knows him for what he is – a common Irish gigolo hiding behind a cheaply handsome face with clothes to match."

'When Marie insisted he was an architect, Eugenie responded, "An architect whose office is always empty. No clients, no clerks. Which isn't surprising,

9

considering that the architect himself is never there. Everybody knows that he makes his living gambling, and when he loses he makes good his losses by getting the money from his women."

'They argued back and forth endlessly. Marie told her mother that if she didn't marry Rory Devlin she would die, and her mother bitterly responded that one did not die so easily. But months of argument, threats, and cajolery on Eugenie's part failed to bend Marie's newly found iron will. Nothing budged her. Finally Eugenie had no choice but to give in and make a formal announcement of the engagement. Once that was done, she proceeded with her typical energy and dispatch. With her aristocratic arrogance, she simply ignored all the gossip and innuendo that circulated and arranged for the wedding to be held in the Manard–du Beaumond house in the Vieux Carré, the house where French royalty had once been entertained.

'Most of Eugenie's old friends were settled by then in the Garden District, which, despite Eugenie's denials, was the more fashionable neighborhood. But she had stayed on in her old home through her marriage and subsequent widowhood, and always started sentences with "when the Duc d'Orléans dined here . . .", as if she herself had joined the eighteenth-century future king of France in the *salle à manger* to eat glazed wild duck, or danced a minuet with him in the *salle de bal*.

'Yes, revamped and renovated through the years, the great Manard–du Beaumond house was the only suitable place for Marie du Beaumond's wedding.'

1

The food was served on the first level of the house, while in the *parterre*, the enclosed garden, a string quartet played. Liveried servants brought out silver-domed platter after platter of pungent Creole dishes. There were those in New Orleans who believed in only a *collation* following the wedding ceremony – wedding cake, pastries, tarts, and champagne – but Madame du Beaumond insisted on a complete banquet, a reception comparable to that given the Duc himself.

Crawfish Cardinale, Oysters Pierre, Shrimp Rémoulade, Lobster Bisque, Maque Choux, wild rice with oysters. And still the butlers issued forth with ever more aromatic smoking dishes. Trout Véronique, Crêpes de la Mer and Chicken Duxelles, Cornish hens in Cognac sauce decorated with grapes, turkey redolent of brandy and stuffed with pecans and oysters. The wedding cake was preceded by chocolate rum soufflé, homemade ice cream, orange crème brûlée. And the radiant bride was toasted repeatedly with French champagne from the prodigious du Beaumond wine cellar.

Upstairs in the old ballroom, the guests danced the Charleston as well as the more formal waltzes, while the orchestra played from the open gallery that surrounded the front of the house. Marie, lovely in her century-old gown, looked up misty-eyed at her new husband as he held her in his arms and whirled her about the room, while her sister, Desiree, looked on in envy. Desiree considered Rory Devlin the sexiest man in New Orleans. When she saw her brother-in-law with his incredibly beautiful blue-black hair bend over to kiss her sister's ivory throat, then brazenly descend to the swelling where the breasts met, it was almost more than she could bear.

That night as the newlyweds boarded the ship leaving at dawn for Le Havre, Desiree masturbated in her bed, fantasizing that it was *her* wedding night; that the swarthy face with the gleaming black eyes and wicked black mustache was buried in her bosom; that his male organ was piercing *her* maidenhead. And tears of some undefined emotion coursed down her prominent cheekbones.

Marie's wedding night was everything she had imagined it would be and more. Rory Devlin made love to her as eloquently as he had done hundreds of times before to ladies who could better appreciate his expertise.

Marie had read in a marriage primer how the ritual of deflowering was to proceed. It seemed the bride readied herself for the marriage bed while the husband conveniently retired from the room, ostensibly to smoke a cigar or perhaps to enjoy a snifter of brandy. When he returned the bride was already under the covers. But while Rory Devlin did not leave the room, his skill was such that Marie was not even embarrassed when he undressed her himself, then showered her with kisses on areas she hadn't realized were so receptive to caresses. She didn't even feel pain at that precise moment when she became a woman. As her body shook under the waves of orgasm, she felt her heart quicken with both love and gratitude. And Rory Devlin was pleasantly surprised by his wife's fevered response. He had hardly expected such passion from this cool, innocent girl-woman.

2

Only hours after the ship left port, Eugenie du

Beaumond dressed for the lawyer's appointment she had made weeks before, when the wedding plans were first being formulated. Outside of a few pieces of unimportant jewelry and some inconsequential bric-a-brac, she was cutting Marie out of her will completely. The Rose Plantation, which had been in the du Beaumond family long before the Louisiana Purchase, and lay on the River Road between New Orleans and Baton Rouge, was already her son Julian's, left to him in his father's will. But the Manard–du Beaumond house was still hers, as was the bulk of the du Beaumond fortune. She would instruct her lawyer to divide everything between Julian and Desiree. She was going to be sure that the only thing Devlin would get out of this marriage besides Marie herself was the fifty-thousand-dollar dowry provided for in her husband André's will. (She was certain that it was the dowry that was paying for the French honeymoon.) There was the Napoleonic Code to consider, after all – the Code, the law of the land in Louisiana, giving control of the wife's worldly possessions to the husband. She was going to see to it that Marie had no possessions.

She considered telling the couple about the disinheritance as soon as they returned, so that she could relish Devlin's despair. But the *bâtard* might then disappear on Marie and then perhaps Marie would have a breakdown – she *was* delicate in both body and spirit, had frequently taken to her bed over the slightest disappointment or slight. No, Eugenie finally decided, it was best to say nothing at present and wait to see how things developed. She hoped she would not live to regret the decision.

When Marie and Rory returned they took up residence in the du Beaumond townhouse. Marie was already pregnant. It suited Rory perfectly to live in the well-staffed, elegant house. It was exactly what Eugenie wanted, too – to be in a position to watch over her

13

poor child, especially during her pregnancy, and at the same time to keep a sharp eye on her shady son-in-law. It would be a joy to thwart him in his private pursuit of happiness.

As for Marie, she could not care either way. She had experienced two months of marital bliss and now she would pay the price. The doctor ordered her to bed and forbade physical exertion of any kind, including sexual.

Marie and Rory settled in – Marie to her bed and he to his routine of office, then home. Eugenie du Beaumond decided to *hint* at a possible future disinheritance in order to keep him in line, to make absolutely sure he remained a faithful, loving husband throughout Marie's confinement.

Marie's days passed in endless, stultifying torpor. She lay in bed preparing an extensive layette, each article meticulously embroidered. Eugenie sat at her bedside much of the time. Although her eyes could no longer adjust to the fine needlework, there was nothing amiss with her strong voice, and she read to Marie as her daughter sewed – first the newspapers, and then the Bible.

Marie demurred. '*Maman*, I beg you. I never considered the Bible very fascinating reading, and may I remind you, I've heard it all before. Many times. I would like something a bit more stimulating.' Her mother was nothing if not practical. She put aside the Bible and laid in a stock of romantic novels, which they both enjoyed.

Desiree also put in her daily stint of amusing her younger sister. Although she and Marie had both attended the convent school and been instructed in embroidery as well as all needlework, she had resisted mastering the art. So while she was of no help in preparing the layette, she did possess an intimate familiarity with all the latest gossip. She was extremely gifted at mimicry, and she imitated everyone they knew in grotesque exaggeration, from old lady Grégoire squeezing tomatoes in the French Market to Consuelo Le Mans, a notorious flirt, making up even to the fusty old clerk in Lazarus's Pharmacy.

She kept Marie in a constant state of giggles.

'Desi, without you I think I'd just curdle up like a spoiled custard.'

'What about Rory? I hear the two of you giggling all night,' Desi said, striving to keep her tone breezy. She was always trying to extract the details of wedded bliss from the reticent Marie. 'Was it heavenly?'

Marie conceded that it was.

'Was it pure ecstasy?'

'You've been reading the trashy novels *Maman's* been bringing home!' Marie countered accusingly. In the end, she was forced to concede that it had indeed been ecstasy.

Desiree settled herself, cross-legged, on Marie's bed. 'Tell me exactly how it was – from the very beginning.'

Marie refused to elaborate, which inevitably led to much pinching and tickling and pleas for relief from her sister's quick fingers. 'When you get married you'll find out!' Marie gasped between laughing fits.

'Oh, but if little sister would tell me, I'd be all prepared.'

'But it's *Maman* who's supposed to tell you how you must prepare for your husband.'

They both went into a paroxysm of laughter at the notion of Eugenie du Beaumond describing a wife's marital obligations.

'Listen, Marie, I read in this book of Genevieve's that the bride awaits the groom in bed in her long nightgown, which she has donned while he's outside freezing his chestnuts off—' Laughter interrupted the recital. 'Please, no interruptions! The groom returns all robed and pajamaed. He flings aside his robe. He gets into bed. Now he must lift up the hem of her nightgown and gently fold it up – but *where?* That's the part I don't understand – they don't say *where.* Does he fold it up to her heaving bosom? Below it? Tell me!'

she demanded, her eyes wide, trying to keep her face straight. 'And what does he do about his pajamas? On? Off? When? *Before* lifting the hem of the nightgown or after?'

Marie held her heaving abdomen. 'Stop, Desi, or you'll make me lose the baby.'

'But you haven't answered me,' Desi persisted. 'How am I ever going to have a wedding night if no one tells me what happens to the damn hem of the damn nightie?'

'What would you say if I told you I didn't wear a nightgown?' Marie asked slyly.

Desiree's mouth fell open. 'Marie Devlin, I don't believe you. Not *you*!'

Marie whispered in her ear.

Desiree's eyes popped.

'Did the earth move?' she asked. 'That's what that stupid Hélène Palcier told Genevieve – she said the earth moved and heaven fell right into her bed!'

Marie smiled enigmatically.

3

So cowed was Rory Devlin by his mother-in-law and her unsubtle reminders of a possible disinheritance that he remained completely faithful to Marie in the first months of their marriage, aside from the three times he had managed to give his bride the slip in Paris. In New Orleans Eugenie kept such a close watch over his activities that he was forced to stay away from his former friends – the city's gambling, drinking, carousing, fast set.

Instead, he spent long drab hours in his office reading publications of the kind found in barbershops, ones that he wouldn't dare bring into the house. Now that he was pinned to his desk, a few clients even materialized, mostly as a result of his mother-in-law's influence. Perhaps in her heart of hearts there flickered the glimmer of hope that maybe, just maybe, he might still be rehabilitated.

Except for his lunch hour, he didn't dare leave, since he was frequently visited by emissaries of either sex sent there on some pretext by Eugenie. And was there someone actually spying on him from a window across the way? Was it a shadow or a figure he saw in the doorway diagonally across from his office door? When he left the office to use the men's room in the hall he imagined he heard muffled footsteps behind him.

At first he had ambitious plans for his lunch hours – so much could be accomplished in an hour or two by a vigorous young man in his prime – but these high expectations had also been quickly dashed; Eugenie du Beaumond made it quite clear that he was expected to take his lunch at home at his wife's bedside. At these command appearances he exerted himself to be entertaining, regaling Marie with whatever gossip he might have heard. Of course, he complained that his nose was kept so close to the grindstone, that scant amusing stories came his way.

The evenings were, naturally, completely given over to his bride. He liked Marie, was proud of her, and considered her the ideal wife – if only he weren't forced to spend so much time with her, *all* of his free time. His tastes had grown jaded by years of indiscriminate rutting and he needed spicier fare than his wife could offer, even if she had been at her best. Under the circumstances, he found the quiet evenings a deadly, insufferable torment. He imagined his hands actually shook from the strain of self-denial.

After a single abortive attempt to leave the house one evening after concocting a story about a business appointment that sounded incredibly lame even to himself, Rory gave up on all efforts to break out. On that one occasion, Eugenie allowed him to leave after extensive questioning but then quickly dispatched Absalom, their houseman, to trail him. The elderly

Negro had been instructed to let his presence be known while only pretending to keep out of sight. As a result, Rory had been so completely unnerved that he returned within the hour, after having dallied at Antoine's restaurant, alone, and reported that his appointment had not materialized.

Even on those occasions when there were guests for dinner and he anticipated a small break in his monotonous routine, Rory was told decisively that it would not be fair for poor Marie to be deprived of his company just so that the guests could enjoy his presence. These occasions were especially hard on him when it was Desiree who was entertaining and he could hear the laughter and conversation of mutual friends floating up the staircase.

With the local news and gossip quickly used up at lunchtime, Rory was hard put to entertain Marie and himself through the long evenings. He taught her every card game in his extensive repertoire and they played for hours, alternating with chess and backgammon, interspersed with word games.

On those occasions when Desiree joined them, at either Marie's or Rory's insistence, the evenings became less tedious and interminable for Rory. Desiree was gay, lively, flirtatious – providing stimulation he needed desperately. While fashion decreed dresses short and skimpy, Desiree's were the shortest and flimsiest. And though boyish figures were all the rage, Desiree didn't fret if the curves of her small but pointed breasts showed more than a trifle. She was the quintessential madcap flapper, and Rory felt the old familiar thrust in his loins when she was present.

It was really out of total ennui that Rory introduced Marie to the delights of digital sexual gratification. Just as on their wedding night, she surprised him. He had expected protestations of shock and modesty, but Marie took to the ways of the finger quickly.

It started one night as they were playing honey-

18

moon bridge. Rory suddenly swept up the cards and flung them on the bedside table. Without a word he got into bed with Marie, his white shirt opened at the neck, his tight trousers still on. Lying beside her, he kissed her convulsively – her mouth, her temples, her neck, her exposed bosom. He pulled off her nightgown and attacked her breasts with his mouth, sucking the swollen nipples until they stood hard and erect and her breath quickened.

He ran his hands over the feverish, milky skin, trailing down across her as yet only slightly extended belly, into the mass of pale, silky hair that covered her Venus mound. His fingers played with her as he watched her face, her mouth slightly open as her breathing intensified, and he felt the contractions agitate within her as she heaved in a long, drawn-out orgasm.

As she lay there breathing more softly with her eyes closed, he undid his fly and let his hardness emerge. He put her hand around it, showing her silently how to milk its length until it grew even hotter and more engorged. He then took her other hand and taught her how to massage the bulging testicles.

After a few minutes she was able to carry on without any further prompting. She felt a new, different kind of thrill seeing him lying there so subdued under her touch, eyes closed, body writhing.

'Now,' he breathed urgently. He grabbed her hand roughly and showed her how to clasp him for the climax. 'Harder . . . Faster!' As his manhood came to froth he encircled her body and allowed the milky fluid to spurt onto her soft, ivory-skinned belly.

As he lay there exhausted, he marveled at how quickly prim Marie had picked up the fundamentals of the game. Every whore a lady and every lady a whore, he thought just before he fell asleep. Lying beside him, Marie smiled smugly in the dark. She felt a vague sense of victory, but over whom she was not sure.

*

A pattern evolved, as the evenings became more tolerable for Rory. He and Marie dined from a tray a servant brought up, then played cards. Each night the card-playing time grew shorter as they hurried to get on with more stimulating amusement.

After several weeks, when the manual sex began to pall as well, Rory felt it propitious to proceed to more sophisticated practices. He began as usual – kissing Marie's mouth, her throat, her breasts. He gauged the state of her arousal before moving his head down. He kissed the lips of her pubescence, her clitoris, thrust his tongue deep inside the heaving opening as she groaned and involuntarily drew his head closer to the core of her excitement.

As he felt her exploding under his mouth, he gave a final, harder thrust, then withdrew. As she lay quietly regaining her breath, he sat himself on the edge of the bed and said to her commandingly, 'Get out of the bed.'

Eyes still closed she lay caught up in the slowly declining concentric waves of her rapture. 'What?'

'Get out of bed!' he ordered, his voice louder.

She clumsily rose and stood there, awaiting his next order.

'Down on your knees.'

She still didn't understand what he wanted, but she obeyed. After she knelt and saw his red, throbbing organ staring into her face, she realized what was expected of her. She opened her mouth, more in protest than in acceptance of the enlarged member, but soon she moved voluntarily, working gently at first, then harder. It did not take her long to learn her role. Teasingly, she let it slip from her mouth until he caught her by the hair and regained purchase. She ate at him until he commenced to spill into her mouth. When she tried to withdraw from the acrid, unsavory fluid, he wouldn't allow her the privilege. He held her head fixed, his hand entangled in the mass of white-gold hair, his legs around her shoulders, locking her in place.

Finally he let her go. He followed her into the bathroom and found her on her knees before the toilet bowl. He helped her to her feet, washed her face tenderly, and carried her back to bed.

He was excessively cheerful and charming to his mother-in-law in the mornings now, which annoyed Eugenie no end. She felt that somehow he was besting her at the game they both knew they were playing. How could he possibly be outsmarting her? she wondered. She was certain he wasn't sneaking out of the house in the evenings. What was he up to?

As the weeks slowly dragged on, even the new sex games with Marie grew tedious. At times he would look at Marie's adoring face and feel a desperate urge to flee. And then he would look at Desiree. He knew what was on her mind – she was a bitch in heat.

For weeks Desiree had listened at Rory and Marie's bedroom door, trying to learn what it was they did to substitute for lovemaking. What she heard was enough to make her run to her room and bring herself to climax, but often without satisfaction. At other times she would join them for the evening and linger for hours, perversely delaying the sex play she knew would follow once she left.

She would sit cross-legged on the bed so that only Rory could see she was bare beneath her dress, see the garters holding the stockings against the white thighs and the thatch of curly black hair cushioning her triangle; he alone could smell the perfume of her urgent desire. It was a scent he well recognized, and one that aroused all his primal urges.

Desiree felt no animosity toward her sister. Aside from the fact that Marie had the man she wanted, she loved her. But the void within her could be filled by no other man. If she could have stopped herself from desiring Rory by simply willing it, she would have done so. But she could think of no one but him.

*

Ever since Marie's confinement, Eugenie rarely left the house in the evenings. She sensed that the moment her back was turned some dreadful calamity would befall the family. But an invitation to dinner came from an old friend, one that she simply could not refuse, and so she went. Before leaving, she warned Rory – by emphasizing that Absalom and Celie would be on call all evening to take care of their needs. Rory knew exactly what this meant – that if he dared leave the house, Absalom would trail him as he had on the previous occasion.

But the moment Eugenie left the house, with Marie's door closed and Absalom and Celie in the kitchen below eating their dinner, Desiree stood poised in the doorway of her room like some Bourbon Street hooker. She had anticipated her mother's departure and had prepared herself. She was nude and heavily perfumed, and she waited for Rory to come up from downstairs. When he appeared at the top of the stairway and looked down the corridor, no words were necessary. He was fondling her flesh even as he kicked the door of her room shut behind them.

Desiree, unlike Marie, needed no instruction. She had his trousers open before he finished pulling her to the floor. And even as his lips sought hers, her mouth sought his hardness and found it. He clasped her head as her mouth enveloped him, her lips pulling on him incessantly, and he screamed softly as he felt her sharp teeth bite into him. She had waited for months for these moments – she had practiced time and again and again in the recesses of her mind, all through the empty nights alone. And she was expert. They finished on the floor, barely beyond the closed door.

Later that night, as Desiree drifted off to sleep she thought, At least I will keep Rory at home for Marie . . .

22

4

Almost exactly nine months to the day following the wedding, Marie gave birth to a little girl. The child was small and delicate, and after a few weeks it became clear she would be a carbon copy of her pale, fair-haired mother. Over Eugenie's violent objections, Rory and Marie named her Kilkee, after Rory's father's birthplace in Ireland, a name that Rory associated with romance and beauty. It was quickly transformed into Kiki.

Two months later Marie was once more with child. She had hardly been out of bed at all. It had taken six weeks of bed rest for her to recuperate from the delivery of Kiki, and she was still depleted when the doctor informed her she must take to her bed again. The second pregnancy was altogether more difficult than even the first. She felt much sicker this time, and was cranky, something she had not been during the earlier pregnancy, and resentful of the members of the household who were free to come and go as they pleased. Dr Heureux, fearful that she would miscarry even though bedridden, prescribed drugs that left her sedated and lethargic.

Rory made a halfhearted effort to be amusing in the evenings, but now Marie expressed no desire to be entertained. She spent most of the day dozing, which only intensified her torpor. She could hardly manage to keep her eyes open at all in the evenings. But as she yielded to her own state of semistupor she could feel her husband's eyes upon her, impatiently waiting for her to drift off. Then each morning when she awoke, and before she received her ration of pills, she was consumed by emotions that were new to her – vague anxieties, feelings of disorientation, alienation from the rest of the household, indefinable twinges of rejection and betrayal.

Eugenie took over the bulk of the care of the new baby.

There was sufficient help in the household and excellent nannies were available, but she felt it was her duty to look after Marie's colicky child personally. A wet nurse had been obtained for the baby, who cried day and night, but other than that, it was Eugenie who saw to Kiki's needs. Mentally alert as ever, she was rapidly losing her prodigious physical energy. Taking care of the difficult child, on top of maintaining the burden of a large household (her old-country French blood prevented her from handing the keys of the *châtelaine* to servants), was not an easy task for a woman of her years.

As a result, Eugenie had neither the time nor the spirit now to supervise her son-in-law's actions – his comings and goings. So while Marie lived in a kind of mixed half-world of dreams and distorted reality, Rory joyously threw himself back into his old life. Now, during long lunches that dragged on for hours, he held court in fashionable restaurants surrounded by old cohorts. Afternoons, he found his way back to places where his presence and money were welcomed with relish, or visited boudoirs of ladies he had too long neglected.

The evenings were even better. He would eat a quick dinner with Marie, murmur a few endearments, bestow a few perfunctory kisses, watch as she fell asleep, and then he was free, Mme du Beaumond having collapsed into her own bed with the fervent prayer that her grandchild would allow her a few hours of uninterrupted sleep. As an added bonus to the newfound freedom, there was Desiree, whose door was always open for him when the rest of the household was fast asleep. It was true that *she* kept a jealous account of his comings and goings and threatened every once in a while to tell her mother and sister what all New Orleans already knew – that Rory Devlin had returned to his life of delicious debauchery – but he only laughed at her.

'You won't tell Marie. To begin with, you don't want to inflict any unnecessary pain upon her. And if you did say something, it wouldn't take her long to realize that if I do take lovers, you are among the most cherished, *chérie*. As for your *maman*, she might just come to believe that you were not all that innocent yourself. She's an old *chienne* but she's not stupid. And then her stiff-necked Creole pride would force her to throw you out with the garbage, along with me.'

He had gauged Desiree correctly. She decided that it would be better, rather than try to keep him for herself alone, to join him out in the open, where no one could possibly condemn them. What was more natural, after all, than for her brother-in-law to escort her to functions to which they were both invited, in place of his poor bedridden wife?

After the birth of her second daughter, Angélique, Marie grew almost totally withdrawn. Rory, Eugenie, Desi . . . each pondered the reason. Rory speculated whether she knew his secrets, Desi worried that she knew hers, and Eugenie wondered how Marie could show so little interest in her babies.

Only Marie knew the answers, but she would not verbalize them. It was a matter of pride. Her pride and her daughters were the only things that mattered to her now – all she had left. At first she used her physical weakness to avoid facing the truth and having to confront it. She could barely summon the strength it took to get out of bed, much less to care for her daughters and deal with the sordid thing that was her marriage. It was easier to let her mother take charge of the babies and avoid the realization that her marriage to Rory Devlin had been an act of self-destruction. But gradually she faced the knowledge that her husband was being unfaithful to her. It wasn't that he didn't try to make love to her but it was such a passionless effort. He was easily turned away, his relief almost showing. Of course, she had no proof, but still she *knew* in her heart of hearts. Her mother had been right after all. Rory Devlin had only been after an advantageous marriage – her social position, but mostly the money, her inheritance. Therefore, she had to conclude that he had *never* loved her, *never* desired her as she, to her shame, still loved him, still desired him.

When she looked at him her blood still surged, her heart still pounded, her foolish body still yearned for his touch. She still wanted him. But she *couldn't*, wouldn't try to win him back, lure him into her bed. Her pride was as strong as her desire. Still, she couldn't divorce him. The whole world would know and would sneer that Marie du Beaumond had married a man who was unworthy of her, a man who shamed her by sneaking around on her. She had only one choice for the present; to ignore his presence. She would let him live in her mother's house, sleep in one of the two beds that had replaced their large one, allow him to be a father to his daughters. But she wouldn't touch him, or allow him to touch her. She would have that single satisfaction for the moment – the pretense that it was she who had rejected him.

There were the babies. Although they were the fruit of his loins as much as of hers, and a pointed reminder of her own weakness, she loved them fiercely. Still, she did not have the strength, the mental and physical energy, to care for them herself. Someday this situation would be resolved and she would, she promised herself, tend them and express all the love she felt for them. But now she could not do it. For now her mother would have to look after them, and they would keep her very busy indeed. Kiki was difficult, given to tantrums, and Angélique, while of seemingly placid temperament, was a finicky eater, and caught cold so easily that she required constant vigilance. Poor *Maman* would have her hands full.

Yes, in withdrawal from the world lay her only chance for salvation. For the time being . . .

5

Eugenie's burden had grown no lighter with the years. At seven and eight respectively, the girls were no easier to handle than they had been as infants. And still Marie showed no more than a fleeting interest in their development. Rory and Desiree continued to fulfill the family's social obligations, and every now and then Eugenie, weary, would remind herself that Desiree was not getting any younger and that *someone* had to be looking for a man of suitable means, character, and family. She made a mental note to speak to her son about finding someone. Maybe Julian had some ideas, although, heaven knew, he had his own troubles trying to hold on to the Rose Plantation in these difficult times. Although it was already seven years since the crash, the depression was still deepening, no matter what that awful man in the White House kept asserting. And poor Julian. He also had to put up with his wife, Audrey, who was constantly after him to sell the plantation. She was determined to get off the River Road and settle in New Orleans, and gave Julian no peace.

No, it was not fair to burden Julian with this additional weight. She would have to do something about Desiree herself. Her elder daughter was well on the other side of twenty-five, and although she was still a beauty, the crop of eligible young men was fast running out. And as she had frequently told Desiree herself, eligible young men gravitated toward docile young ladies who had an eye to their future and did not, despite the frivolous times, live for the moment only.

If only Marie would take a greater interest in her own children, she, Eugenie, could concentrate on Desiree. Perhaps she should take Desiree to Europe. A girl . . . a woman . . . of her breeding and beauty could easily attract a count, a duke, even a prince. But it would have to be soon. Everyone said trouble was brewing in Europe. She should really take Desiree and go quickly, before Europe erupted, before Desiree got any older. Soon it might be too late. Thank God she was still able to afford it, despite the depression.

But before she could go off to Europe, she had to find a way to rouse Marie from her apathy. But how? The way things stood, she could hardly leave the house and Kiki and Angel to an oddly indifferent Marie and her husband. Maybe she could find a doctor – in New York or Chicago – who would be able to help Marie, restore her interest in life.

Much as she hated to admit it, Rory Devlin seemed a better father than Marie a mother. He played with the girls, supervised their music and dancing lessons, encouraged them to read poetry and commit it to memory, wrote little plays for them to enact, took them for walks and had them name all the different varieties of trees and flowers, took them each morning to the convent school after he inspected their daily grooming. He often took them to visit his mother on the Bayou Teche, and there they would ride together, the activity the girls loved the most, after the play-acting. And heaven knows, Eugenie had to admit to herself, she welcomed these respites when Devlin took over – she needed the rest. Angélique was a docile child, but Kiki was a caution.

Of course, the girls behaved much better for their father than they did for her. Even Kiki was a little doll when it came to Rory. But at other times it was incredible how strong-willed such a young child could be. That mouth! *Mon Dieu!* Even the nuns couldn't control it. How many times they threatened to expel her! And they surely would have if it hadn't been for her own influence and the glib tongue of Rory Devlin, who could beguile any woman, even a bride of Christ.

Still, she didn't like the relationship that existed between the girls and their father. Something made her uneasy – the girls competed for their father's attention almost as if they were his sweethearts. Kiki, as was her nature, was more aggressive, even to pushing Angel out of the way to get to her father. But Angel, who was shy and not aggressive at all, also used tricks to get his attention away from her sister – her delicate health and her standing as the 'baby' in the family. It was too bad, Eugenie thought. If this rivalry for their father did not exist, the two girls would have only love for each other. Kiki watched out for her younger sister, and Angel adored and looked up to her big sister. To give the devil his due,

Rory Devlin played no favorites – he called Angel 'my littlest Angel' and Kiki 'my big girl', and showered both with affection.

It was all Marie's fault, Eugenie decided. If she took more of a hand with them, they would have less of this obsessive need of their father. If they had more attention from Marie, they would be more secure in themselves.

Perhaps that was the answer, then. She would just up and take Desiree to Europe, *forcing* Marie out of her apathy, forcing her to act more the mother, thereby lessening the girls' constant need for their father's attentions. And hopefully it would all end well, with Desiree making an appropriate match on foreign shores. Two birds with one stone. Yes, she would do it almost immediately. The following week the four of them, she herself, Marie, and the two girls, were going to visit with Julian and his family at the plantation. They would stay for a week, and then, on their return, she would make arrangements to leave right away.

Eugenie told Marie of her decision while they were driving back to town from the plantation. Marie was at the wheel of the Hudson, and when Eugenie said she was planning to leave for Europe as soon as arrangements could be made, and that she might be away for nearly a year, Marie did not blink an eye, and Eugenie could not tell what she was thinking.

When Marie said nothing, Eugenie persisted, wanting a reaction. 'You do agree, Marie, that I must do something about Desiree?'

'Whatever you think best, *Maman*.'

'And you will be able to care for the children?'

'I dare say they won't starve.'

'I didn't expect that they would. My point is, will *you* manage?'

'Absalom and Celie will take care of the house and do the shopping. Joni will do the cooking. Rory will take the girls to and from school.'

'There is more to taking care of the girls than that,'

Eugenie observed with some resentment.

'Rory or Celie will hear their prayers at night and will take them to Mass. Kiki will settle down once she knows her *grand-mère* won't be around to go into a tizzy each time she says a naughty word. And Angel will most likely eat all her vegetables if no one watches over her every bite. Go, *Maman*, and Godspeed.'

Then, glancing sidelong at her mother: 'Does Desi know about this trip?' Perhaps she will not wish to go?'

Eugenie did not answer. She only speculated as to what lay behind her daughter's cool, placid exterior.

The drive had been hot and uncomfortable; the air hung heavy and moist.

'We will have to take our baths at once!' Eugenie told the girls in the back seat.

'We?' Kiki asked innocently. 'Are you jumping into the tub with us, *Grand-mère*?'

Both girls giggled and jumped from the car, running ahead of their mother and grandmother, each eager to be the first one in the house to find their father.

Angel was first, and she raced up the stairs. Kiki ran into the library and, finding it empty, sprinted across the hall into the salon. Finding that room empty too, she came back out into the hall just as Angel emerged in view again at the top of the stairs. As Marie and Eugenie entered the house, she yelled down to her sister, 'Daddy and Aunt Desi are both sick. They're in Aunt Desi's bed together.'

Marie and Eugenie stood as if frozen in a tableau of eternity. Kiki mounted the stairs quickly and, followed by Angel, raced down the hall to their Aunt's room. She found her father trying to wriggle into his trousers as her aunt cowered under the sheets, revealing bare shoulders.

Kiki laughed crazily. 'Ninny!' she yelled at Angel. 'They're not sick. They've been doing what Bobo and Fluffy do out in the yard! They've been making babies!' Angel wrinkled her forehead, confused, as Kiki punched her shoulder. 'I told you all about that, you ninny!'

Kiki ran back into the hall, to the top of the stairs, yelled down to Marie and Eugenie, who stood motionless, silent, their faces turned upward. 'They've been making babies!' Kiki shrieked triumphantly, proud that she knew about such things. Angel hung back, not understanding but disturbed.

Marie started up the stairs as her mother looked on. *Yes. This time Marie has to do for herself. Perhaps some good will come of all this. Maybe Marie will come alive. Feel something! Do something!*

Marie pushed past the now crying Angel and the gloating Kiki, who was jumping up and down in excitement, sensing that something very dramatic was imminent. But Marie didn't turn to the right, toward Desiree's room, but to the left – to her own. She walked into the room, shut the door, turned the key in the lock. And still Rory Devlin did not emerge into the hall and still Eugenie made no move as the house lay swathed in a great silence despite the sounds of the two girls.

Finally Eugenie began to climb the stairs, leaning heavily on the wrought-iron railing, placing one hand over the other and hauling her body up after them. She ordered the children to their room. Angel went at once, but Kiki resisted. Her grandmother pushed her along with what seemed the last remnants of her strength. She locked the door behind the girls. Next, she went to Desiree's room, where Devlin stood at the mirror brushing his hair with Desiree's brush. As Eugenie appeared in the doorway, he smiled at her quite charmingly and cocked an impudent eyebrow. He was completely dressed now and immaculate. Eugenie's gaze shifted from him to Desiree, who lay huddled in bed with the covers over her head. Eugenie found it an effort to breathe. She would deal with Desiree later, but she knew what she had to do about Rory Devlin.

'Well,' he said. 'I can understand your embarrassment, your loss of words, *Maman*. And I sympathize with you. I think it's time to take my graceful leave and spare you any further discomfiture. Ladies!' He bowed first to Mme du Beaumond and then to Desiree. He had heard the click of the lock on the door to his and Marie's bedroom. He would have to leave without his clothes. It could not be helped. And he would have to leave without saying good-bye to his daughters. And while that was very upsetting, it also could not be helped. He'd get in touch with them as soon as he could.

'Perhaps we'll meet again, Desiree,' he called out to the form in the bed, sidling past his mother-in-law's bulk in the doorway and still smiling pleasantly.

Eugenie hurled herself at him and hammered at his body with her fists. He laughed and sauntered down the stairs. He heard the scream, *'Cochon!'* and the sound of a revolver being cocked. He whirled and felt a sting in his side as his mother-in-law collapsed at the top of the stairs, her husband's old cavalry pistol in hand. It was one of an exquisitely worked pair that had been in the family a long time.

He took out a clean, white initialed handkerchief and held it to his side where a trickle of blood seeped out. 'Old bitch!' he said dispassionately to the motion-less figure on the floor upstairs, turned, and walked out of the house.

The only sound now was that of the children – Angel's mournful howling and the percussion of Kiki's fists pounding against the locked door. Marie reclined in a bath of perfumed water. Her bathroom door too was shut and she had not heard the sound of the pistol. Desiree came running from her room, a hastily thrown-on dressing gown drawn about her. She ran past her mother's prone figure and down the stairs, looking for the fallen body of her lover. Not finding it, she threw open the door and screamed out into the heavy-laden late-afternoon air: 'Rory! Rory! Wait for me!' But there was no answer. The street was deserted.

She ran up the stairs and past her mother's still body once again. As she passed the children's door she didn't even hear the shrieks of the hysterical girls behind it. She dressed in minutes, threw a few things into a bag, and was down and out the front door. She would find him. Where would he go without money and without clothes? Most likely he would head straight for the Bayou Teche, where his mother lived.

It wasn't until an hour later, when Celie came back from the Old Quarter, where she had spent a leisurely afternoon talking softly, laughing, and drinking lemonade with friends, that Eugenie du Beaumond was discovered lying unconscious; Kiki and Angel, exhausted, sleeping on the floor of their room, close up against the locked door; and Marie, locked into her room.

'*Mon Dieu!*' Celie said over and over as she called Dr Heureux, then Julian at the plantation.

6

Eugenie du Beaumond came home from the hospital paralyzed and unable to speak. She was not expected to regain the use of her body or the power of speech. 'But her heart is very strong,' Dr Heureux observed. It was not clear if he meant this as plain fact or as consolation. She would have to be hand-fed and kept clean, dressed and undressed, and, if the time could be found, spoken and read to. From the bright look in her eyes it was apparent that she knew what was going on around her despite the slightly deranged look caused by the collapsed facial muscles.

Julian could draw scant information from Marie, but with the help of the children he was able to piece together what had happened. He wondered if Marie

33

too had suffered some kind of physical or mental aberration. She barely spoke, and conducted herself as if she were no longer of this world but not of the next either. Actually, he was forced to admit, she had been behaving this way for years. She would not even rouse herself to look after her own brats.

He heard that Devlin and Desiree had hied themselves off to California. That son of a bitch, Devlin, had strapped him with his half-idiot wife and his two spoiled, whining daughters. But Julian was even more furious with Desiree, who had saddled him with a burden of which he would never be free, the paralyzed Eugenie. He considered sending detectives after the pair. At least he might be able to do something about Devlin, who had, after all, deserted his legal offspring. But when he mentioned this to Marie, she came out of her half-comatose state, flew into a wild rage, and forbade him even to consider it. She swore that she would kill herself and leave Julian with her orphans on his hands as well.

'I never want to see either of them again,' she spat out. 'I'm only sorry *Maman* didn't kill them both!'

After Eugenie had been settled into a routine, Julian told Marie that he had to get back home.

'Are you going to leave me alone in this house with *Maman*? You can't . . . I won't—'

'I have to get back to my own family and the plantation. I can't stay here indefinitely. There's nothing more I can do here for *Maman*. But I'll be back every few days or so. After all, you don't have to take care of her yourself. The servants will do all that. You just have to talk to her a little and see to it that the servants do what they're supposed to. Supervise the household. Take care of your daughters. You have to assume responsibility for them now. Devlin is gone and you don't even want me to try and make him hold up his end. *Maman* has done more than her share all these years. Now it's on your shoulders. You can't

34

leave the children entirely to servants. They need their mother. Once I'm gone, you'll find that you're able to take charge with no trouble at all.'

'Thank you, Julian. It's really decent of you to leave me with that sick old lady and this old house. Well, I can't do it. The way she looks at me with those accusing eyes . . . the only thing left of her that's alive. If you leave me here alone I'll hate you to my dying day. I'll put a curse on you, I swear it!'

'Stop your nonsense! Curses! If you don't get hold of yourself we'll have to put *you* away. For God's sake! Get hold of yourself! Act like a woman and a mother.'

'Get me a divorce!'

'For God's sake, when? This minute? We've got other problems just now. First we have to establish a routine. Get you to run the house, take care of *Maman*. The divorce can wait. Maybe that bastard will come back when he gets good and hungry. Let's wait and see what happens.'

'Damn you, Julian, I don't want him back! I want a divorce! Help me, help me . . .' She began to wail forlornly.

Julian was repelled by the whole situation and desperate to get away. 'I'll help you, Marie. Trust me. I will. You'll get your divorce. Just wait a few months and I promise to help you.'

'I want it *now*, Julian. *Now*. And if you don't help me, I'll leave and there'll be no one to help you take care of *Maman*. You'll have to come and live here or take *Maman* with you to the plantation. Audrey would love that, I'm sure,' she finished with an ugly smile and cold eyes.

They made their bargain. Julian agreed that if Marie took charge of their mother, the children, and the household, he would institute divorce proceedings immediately. He warned her that it would take time – divorce was not easy in Louisiana.

'You can do it, Julian. *Maman* always said you knew

35

where the body was buried.'

Why did all her words suddenly bear such sinister implications? Julian wondered.

'I'll do my best, chérie. And I'll take care of the Church, too.'

She laughed disdainfully. 'Don't be a fool, Julian. I don't give a fig for the Church.'

Before he left for the plantation, he saw the lawyers about instituting the divorce, as he had promised. When finally he was taking his leave, kissing his mother good-bye, Marie stood by the bed and said with a sweet smile and a newfound drawl, 'Be sure you all come back and see us, hear?'

Why did she make him feel so uneasy?

Then, as he sat in the Cord ready to take off, she waved. 'Bring Audrey and the children to see *Maman* too, you hear?'

After the car vanished from sight, Marie went upstairs. Her mother had been lifted into a sitting position in her bed. 'So, *Maman*, you were right about Rory Devlin after all. Smart *Maman*, stupid Marie. Is that what your eyes are saying now, *Maman*? Well, see where being right got you? You're old and sick and crippled. If you were so smart, *Maman*, why did you let me go and be so stupid? And where were your eyes when my own sister was making a shameful fool out of me? Well, I'll tell you one thing, *Maman*. I'm through being stupid. I'm going to get out of this somehow . . . I swear it!'

Marie took up the reins of the household easily. She almost never went into Eugenie du Beaumond's room, never addressed a word to the old woman if she didn't have to. It was hard for her to look at what her mother had become. But she did her duty. She saw to it that the servants fed her, washed her, sat her up in the morning, and laid her back down at night. And she encouraged Absalom to sit and read the Bible to her, as well as the newspaper.

She planned the meals, made up the shopping lists. She never ventured beyond the garden. She didn't want people laughing at her – the foolish abandoned wife. She had one of the servants take the girls to school after she had carefully checked their appearance. They seemed no worse to her than when in their grandmother's charge. In fact, Angel's health improved, as did Kiki's disposition. She seemed to sense that her mother would not put up with her tantrums, as well she would not.

All in all, Marie was pleased with her daughters. They were both lovely to look at, each in her own way. Angel, of course, resembled her father, but Marie did not hold that against her since she did not in any way possess his personality. Kiki perhaps resembled her father in that department, but that too was of no concern. They were her daughters, she loved them, she would do for them, no matter what it entailed.

Kiki and Angel were bewildered by the turn of events, bewildered and bereft, although it was only Angel who permitted her feelings to show. Kiki made a good show of unconcern over the sudden disappearance of her beloved father, and of the state of the grandmother, who had cared for her and who had now, for all practical purposes, assumed the presence of a bedridden ghost.

But Kiki didn't know what to make of her mother; she didn't know how to respond to her, as she had so intuitively known with her father. With him her intuition had been older than her years. Marie was an unknown quantity, and eliciting a show of affection from her did not come easily to Kiki. Certainly not as easily as it did for Angel, who had only to whimper and hang her head. Angel was such a baby and didn't know *anything*. She had to tell Angel everything and help take care of her besides, especially at school where Angel did not make friends easily. She did love her sister, but it wasn't fair . . .

Angel lay awake at night, counting on her fingers.
Before, there had been Daddy, Kiki, *Grand-mère*, and
Maman, in that order. And now there was only Kiki
and *Maman* and she didn't know the order at all. If only
Daddy would come back . . .

7

Julian told Marie with a bit of pride in his voice that an
annulment of her marriage had been effected. He had
done it for her after all, with great difficulty. 'You're a
free woman and still a good-looking one, Marie. In
time you'll find someone else. And this house will
always be a home for you and your girls, and your new
husband too. Even if Audrey and I do come to live
here. But that won't be for a while yet.'

'What *are* you talking about, Julian? I have no
intention of staying in New Orleans . . . much less in
this house. I can't wait to leave. There are two things
in life that are important . . . besides my daughters, of
course. Pride and money. And in this house and in
New Orleans, I can't exist with any pride. Not after
what has happened.'

Julian flushed. 'But we made a bargain, Marie. I
would get you the annulment and you would stay here
and look after *Maman*. After she's gone, you can go
wherever you please.'

She started to cry. 'Julian, I must go now, before I
choke. I can't live here. I'm a prisoner in this house.
Help me to leave now, Julian, while I'm still young
enough to find someone else . . . to have a real life.
Give me my share of the inheritance now. I'll give it
back to you when *Maman* dies.'

'But you have *no* inheritance, Marie. Don't you
know that?'

Her hand lashed out, slapped him across the face. 'What have you done, Julian? Stolen my inheritance? I know you have taken charge of everything, but I warn you – I won't let you get away with cheating me!'

'Stop it, you little fool! I've cheated you of nothing. Go see Louis Partierre. He'll tell you – *Maman* disinherited you when you married Devlin. And now that you're rid of him, thanks to my help, *Maman* isn't physically able to reinstate you in her will. You have nothing except what's on your back. *I've* been keeping you and Devlin's kids. But I'm willing to give you your share of the money, in spite of *Maman's* will. After *Maman's* gone. Mind you, I don't have to do it, but I will. I don't want to see you hurt any more than you've already been. Trust me!' He put his arm around her.

She pushed him away. 'So, my mother disinherited me. That's funny. I *sensed* there was some good reason for me to despise her . . .'

'Don't say that, Marie. God will surely punish you.'

'Not to worry, Julian, I have already been punished.' She looked out the window to see the dark descending, then turned back to face him. 'You say you care what happens to me. If you do, let me go. Keep the whole inheritance. Just let me have enough to get away from here. I have to start over somewhere else.' She fell to her knees, clung to his legs. 'Please, Julian, please! By the time she dies, I'll be too old, too dried up.'

She wants to leave me with the paralyzed old woman!

'Get up, Marie. We made a bargain. I got you your annulment. Now you stay with *Maman* until she goes. She can't last much longer. And then I'll give you your full share of the money. You'll be able to go anywhere in the world you want.'

'You haven't heard a word I've said, Julian. I can't wait!'

'You must! I don't want to seem cruel, but you give me no choice. *Someone* has to stay with *Maman*, and obviously there is no one but you. And I don't have to remind you that if it weren't for you, *Maman* wouldn't be lying there like that.' In his anxiety, he paced back and forth, talking to himself as much as to Marie. 'Maybe I can find Desi! She owes us all too, God knows. I'll tell her that if she wants *her* share of the money when *Maman* dies, she had better come back and look after her. Then you'll be free to go, with my blessings.'

'You're not listening, Julian,' Marie said wearily. 'I can't wait any longer.'

'Just wait until Desi comes back. I'll find her and get her to come back.'

But Marie had left the room and didn't hear his last words.

As soon as Julian was gone, she cleaned out the safe in her mother's room. There was jewelry but little cash. She would have to sell off some of the jewelry immediately. Then she went to the dressing table and took the box of 'small pieces'. She was leaving the room when she looked up to see the woman in the bed watching her with dark sad eyes.

She went over to the bed. 'I've said terrible things about you, *Maman*. But I didn't mean them. It's *adieu* now, and I am truly sorry to have to leave you like this. But it cannot be helped. You raised me to be innocent and dependent, you see, and therefore you should have been stronger yourself and protected me better. You really should have found a way to stop me from marrying Rory, and having failed that, you should have watched out for my marriage better. Poor *Maman*! I know that you tried.' She bent quickly and pressed her lips to her mother's forehead. Then she closed the door quietly after her.

She went through the house collecting all the silver. The smaller pieces she packed into suitcases that she would take along with her, but the larger pieces were too bulky to be transported all the way to New York. She would dispose of them locally. She packed those pieces into boxes and put them in the car. Despite the bad times, there would be no lack of buyers for beautiful old European silver, she was sure.

She packed only a small bag for the girls and another for herself and had everything ready when they came home from school. Without any explanation whatever, she told them to get into the car and she drove to the train station. She parked the car, leaving the keys in the ignition, and got the girls, the bags, and herself aboard the New York train. It was even simpler than she had imagined. She laughed. *They all thought I couldn't cope.*

She hadn't said a word to the servants; she hadn't left a note for Julian. Even if he found out where she had gone, what could he do to her? He couldn't force her to come back and care for their mother. And he wasn't about to send the police after her for stealing the jewelry, the little money, and the silver. Not Julian. He wouldn't expose the family to any more scandal.

Now you can cope, Julian.

She sat the two girls together on the double seat facing hers. Angel sat next to the window and watched New Orleans recede from sight. Tears coursed down her face.

'Why are you crying?' Marie asked her.

'Because we're going away. We're leaving everybody behind. *Grand-mère*. Daddy . . .'

'Come here,' Marie said. 'Sit here beside me.'

Angel sat next to her mother and cuddled against her while Marie wiped away her tears.

'We're not leaving your daddy behind,' Marie said. 'He's already gone. You know that,' she said, putting her arm around the slight body. 'He left a long while ago.'

Then, uncharacteristically, Kiki began to cry loudly. 'Where has he gone to, *Maman*?' she sobbed, getting up and trying to squeeze herself into the tiny space on Marie's free side.

'I don't know,' Marie said, not unkindly. 'Nobody knows. But you'll have to go back to your seat, Kiki. There's not room here for three.'

'But I'm crying too. Just like Angel.'

Marie looked at her with a bemused sadness. 'Very well,' she said. 'You may sit on my lap for a little while. And then you will both go back to your seat and sit together.'

Of course the turn of events was hard on them, Marie thought. Even on Kiki, who was so much tougher than Angel.

'Will we ever see Daddy again?' Kiki asked, trying to snuggle closer. She had stopped crying.

'Perhaps . . .' Marie answered.

Kiki smiled a little twisted smile. 'Are you going to find yourself a new husband, Mother?'

Marie looked at her sharply. She had not called her *Maman* but Mother. Kiki was already adapting, she thought. Then Angel pulled at her sleeve, and she turned to the younger girl again. 'What is it, Angel?'

'I want to sit on your lap, *Maman*. Can't I sit on your lap like Kiki?'

Later that night as the two girls lay together, sharing a berth, Angel cried. This time it was Kiki who wiped away her tears. 'Don't cry, Angel. Some day soon we'll see Daddy again. You'll see.'

'When Kiki?'

'Soon . . .'

PART TWO

New York
1937–1947

'Marie had been in seclusion for years, through circumstance and by her own doing,' Beebie Tyler told her young interviewer. 'There was her pride, you see. She was always very proud, even before she had met Devlin. And now, free from her humiliating marriage and out from under her mother's supervision, she wanted to live her life to its fullest and she savored the idea of independence. Still, she needed security for herself and for her daughters. There was only one way she knew to get that security. So she took her girls to New York, where she had family – her Uncle Paul, her mother's brother, who had left New Orleans before she had been born.

'Paul Manard had met and married a Gertrude Benedict when on a business trip to New York – an impetuous affair – they had married only a few weeks after their first meeting. The Manards did not attend the Protestant wedding, disowned Paul. The Benedicts, however, welcomed him into their family, took him into their insurance firm, allowed him to embrace their Episcopalian faith, and set the couple up in a town-house in the best neighborhood. Paul then gathered a family of five children, all of whom, in turn, made suitable, successful marriages. Marie's mother, Eugenie, had heard from him two or three times over the years, and Marie guessed that he might be pleased to hear from her now.

'She had calculated how long her money, silver, and jewelry would maintain her, had determined that she

45

could manage for two years or so, assuming the jewelry brought an optimum return. Hopefully, she would be established in a good marriage by that time. If not, she would be forced to look elsewhere for support. With that in mind, upon her arrival in New York she rented a suite in a small, proper hotel on the Upper East Side and then called her Uncle Paul.'

Marie had guessed correctly. When Paul Manard heard her voice over the telephone, he was deeply moved. He insisted she come right over with her daughters, and alerted his own children to come welcome their cousins from New Orleans.

With a sense of attractive tragedy about her, Marie related her tale to all the Manards – uncle, aunt, female and male cousins and mates – and by the time she concluded, no one was unmoved or not in love with her. Paul Manard was compelled to think again of the young man who had fallen in love with an outsider and the price he had been forced to pay – severance of family ties and disinheritance. In fact, so engulfed was he in the injustices he himself had suffered, and those visited upon his unfortunate niece, he could hardly muster a sympathetic thought for his sick and paralyzed sister, left with but one of her three children.

He determined right then and there to be a surrogate father to the poor child who had been so grievously abused by fate and whose punishment for falling in love had been a bastard of a husband, a faithless sister, and a selfish brother. Too much – too much! And Lord, what a stunner she was! Old as he was, he could still respond to a beautiful woman.

Before Marie had made her appearance she had done what she had not done in all the years she had been married to Rory Devlin. The hair that had always been so pale now gleamed with the silvery platinum sheen popularized by Jean Harlow. The long blond lashes were swept with mascara, enhancing eyes one cousin swore were green as the ocean, another blue as the sky. She wore an elegant little black 'New York' dress, which despite its length still managed to display legs that were slim and shapely. With the cultivation of a charming New Orleans accent which had not previously tinged her speech, the overall effect was quite devastating. She seduced the whole family, which had been her intention. All the cousins – Paul junior, Hector, Catherine, Helena, and Betsy – were as enchanted with Marie as their father was. And Aunt Gertrude immediately summed up the family's collective reaction to their poor cousin's dilemma: 'We will have to find a husband for her at once, and it appears we will have no difficulties. They'll be breaking down the doors!'

The girl cousins were delighted to be involved in a husband-hunting expedition.

'This is going to be such fun!'

'We'll start entertaining for you at once!'

'And those two little darlings will be no problem at all!'

Everyone looked at Angel and Kiki, who sat like two French dolls, prim and proper in matching velvet dresses, black Mary Janes, flowered ribbons in their long hair. They sat with legs properly crossed at the ankles, hands folded in their laps just as their mother had instructed them.

'Delightful!' Betsy cried.

'Just perfect!' Helena said.

'Yes, adorable!' Catherine agreed.

Uncle Paul and Aunt Gertrude insisted that Marie and the girls move into their Fifth Avenue townhouse immediately, and the girl cousins enthusiastically seconded the motion. 'It's not quite proper for you to stay at a hotel with two little girls, no matter how respectable,' Helena said.

'And it's foolish to go to all the trouble of renting and furnishing an apartment. We don't expect you to stay there very long,' Catherine observed.

'Before you know it, you'll have a house of your own,' Helena said.

'Yes, on Park!' piped Betsy, who lived on Park Avenue with Harold, her rich, paunchy husband.

'No, I think she should buy on Beekman Place,' said

Catherine, who lived on Beekman with her bespectacled, balding, rich Donald.

'I think Marie would love Gramercy Park,' cried Helena who hated the area herself, but whose attractive, strong-willed husband, Stephen, insisted on living there.

'I think we'd better decide whom she's going to marry before we decide where she'll live, don't you think?' This from Hector's small, energetic wife, whose real name was Nancy but who had answered to NaNa since she was two years old.

The female cousins helped Marie and her children settle into the Manard house the very next day. When the three sisters saw how little clothing Marie had brought with her, they grew ecstatic. 'We will have to go shopping first thing tomorrow morning!'

Marie cast her eyes down and said simply, 'I don't know how much shopping I can do. I had to leave home with very little money.'

'Don't you worry your little heart,' Catherine said. 'Mummy and Daddy will be happy to supply you with a wardrobe. After all, you can't go hunting without ammunition.' Her sisters agreed wholeheartedly.

'But I don't know if I can allow them to do that,' Marie offered demurely. 'But maybe you can help me sell these things so I can raise some money myself.' She opened one of her silver-laden suitcases.

When the cousins saw the heirloom silver they moaned in ecstasy. 'We can't let you sell the family silver.'

'No, you must hold on to it. I just know Mummy and Daddy will foot the bill for the clothes. But you *could* give Daddy a little something – as a present. It would make him so happy to own a little piece of his past, a piece of the Manard silver.' Catherine's tone was reverent.

'Do you think so? I'd be delighted to give him something. Something really grand. Dear Uncle Paul! And you girls are such darlings. Choose something for yourselves too! I insist! After all, it's part of your heritage too!'

They all hugged and embraced Marie and, with the tiniest expression of greed, fell upon the silver.

2

It took eight months plus one week for Marie to make a suitable alliance. When Marie's engagement to Edward Taylor Whittier, president of one of the city's foremost brokerage houses (with branches everywhere) and board member of a dozen other prestigious firms, was announced, the cousins were beside themselves with joy and a sense of accomplishment. They had done extremely well by their destitute Southern cousin. Edward Taylor Whittier was 'really, really rich, and none of this *new* money, mind you.' The distinction was an important concern in the society in which they lived.

'And he's handsome, too,' insisted Betsy.

'Yes, you might say so – in a kind of understated fashion,' Helena added, as if not quite sure of her position.

'And distinguished too – all that beautiful white hair,' Catherine observed.

'Yes, white hair *is* distinguished,' Betsy agreed, 'although Edward's *is* receding just a bit at the temples. But that reflects stability, don't you think?'

'You're quite right,' Catherine said. 'You can never totally trust a man with a full head of wavy, dark hair.'

'How did you know Rory Devlin had a head of wavy black hair?' Marie demanded, then blushed, furious with herself for bringing up her former husband's name.

'But I had no idea,' Catherine protested. 'I didn't mean to—'

Betsy cut her off. 'Oh, Marie, tell us about Rory

Devlin. He sounds fascinating.'

'No, I can't . . . I can't talk about him,' Marie said stiffly.

'Of course you can't,' Helena said, chastising her sister with a look. 'Edward is a bit stuffy, Marie. You will have to loosen him up a bit,' she offered, changing the subject.

Marie laughed to herself. How surprised the cousins would be to know that for years her own sister, Desi, had called *her* stuffy, that her Southern charm and vivaciousness were almost as new as the six-carat ring she wore on her left hand.

'The best thing about Edward is that his identical twin daughters, Mickey and Flickey, are grown, married and out of your hair,' Catherine observed.

'Good! I was hoping Edward would be a real father to *my* girls, I am planning to send them to a first-rate boarding school. We'll be shuttling back and forth between the city and the house in Tarrytown, so I won't be able to put them in a day school.'

'Oh, you are the lucky one, Marie! The house in Tarrytown . . . Stoningham . . . is one of the biggest showplaces in the whole state, sitting up there high on the Hudson,' Betsy said with a touch of envy.

'It is a beautiful place, isn't it? And you will all come up for weekends and we'll have lovely parties, but I don't think I'll want to stay there all the time. That would be like being back home, where people have to stay on the plantations when they're dying to live in New Orleans – like my sister-in-law, Audrey . . .' Her voice trailed away. 'Anyhow, I don't intend to be stuck away like some country mouse while my three darling cousins are having all the fun down here in the big city.'

The cousins decided that they would have the ceremony and reception at their parents' home, with the Manards footing the bill, of course. That was proper. 'But there is just one teeny little problem,' Catherine posed. 'Who will perform the ceremony? With you being Catholic and Edward Episcopalian . . .'

'No problem at all,' Marie said briskly. 'I've decided to join Edward's church.'

'Did Edward ask you to?' Betsy wanted to know.

'No. I decided myself that it would be best for the marriage and for Kiki and Angel.'

'I think that's very wise of you.' Catherine said. 'Being Protestant is really much more' – she groped for a word – 'elite. Personally, darling, I think it's just a bit tacky to be Catholic. Oh, it's all right if you're the Pope or if you live in New Orleans. But in New York?'

'And as for Kiki and Angel, being Edward Taylor Whittier's Protestant stepdaughters will secure their place in society so much more,' Helena added.

'Oh, didn't I tell you? Edward is going to adopt the girls.'

'You *are* the clever one,' Betsy giggled. 'Once Kiki and Angel are legal Whittiers, Mickey and Flickey had better just watch out!'

The cousins decided among themselves that there should be a prenuptial agreement about financial matters. When Marie protested that she would be too embarrassed to discuss such a thing with Edward, the cousins declared that where money was involved there was no such thing as embarrassment. 'Only people without money are reluctant to talk about money,' Catherine observed in a shrewd tone. 'One must do for oneself,' Helena hastened to add. 'Mickey and Flickey have their mother's money, but that doesn't mean they're not going to try to get Daddy's too. When a widower with children reweds, there is a problem.'

It was decided that Uncle Paul was the proper person to negotiate an agreement (and the possible settlement) with Edward on Marie's behalf. The cousins agreed that Edward's townhouse should be put in Marie's name, since Stoningham Manor could never accrue to her, as a second wife. Nor would it hurt to see what could be done about the Southampton house. Perhaps that could be a wedding present from Edward to Marie. 'Property is the name of the game,' they told Marie.

Uncle Paul negotiated an advantageous prenuptial agreement, and the wedding went off without a hitch. There was a two-column notice in the *New York Times*, and the honeymooners left for their European holiday while Angel and Kiki stayed with cousins Helena and Stephen.

When they returned from the honeymoon the newlyweds found two surprising wedding gifts. One was Eugenie du Beaumond's Sèvres tea service, accompanied by Julian and Audrey's best wishes. Julian's letter revealed that, in light of recent events, he had forgiven Marie's purloining of the ancestral silver and family jewels.

'Perhaps the fellow means well after all,' Edward said. 'Maybe he'll give you your share of the inheritance without a struggle. Does he say anything of your mother's condition?'

Even Edward wants more. He, too, is waiting for Mother to die.

'Yes. He says Mother is the same. No better, no worse.'

Maman is a tough one. She'll probably live to a hundred and ten and see Julian in his grave.

The thought made her giggle. Now that she no longer needed her mother's money, Marie wished her a long life. What a splendid joke on Julian!

The other present came from California – from, damn him, Rory Devlin! The temerity of the man! A small bronze horse. He had always had a penchant for horses. His note also wished her well and hoped that in her new happiness she could forgive him his weak character. It wasn't that he hadn't loved her – he still thought of her often with regard and affection. He mentioned that he wasn't doing too badly and that his only desire was to see his daughters again, if she could find it in her heart to permit this. He enclosed a check for five hundred dollars, which he hoped she would use for the pleasure of Kiki and Angel.

Marie ripped up the letter and the check as Edward's thin lips worked in disapproval.

'That was rather foolish. It was the girls' money, after all. From their father.'

'*You're* their father now!'

Edward was somewhat taken aback by the cold, aquamarine eyes burning into his. *How can cold eyes burn so?*

'That bastard's not going to worm his way back into their lives with a lousy five hundred dollars!'

It was a tone and vocabulary Edward hadn't heard from his soft-spoken, charming bride before, and he stared at her in disbelief as she continued, 'A week from now, after he's visited the racetrack or one of his tarts, he'll be very grateful to learn he still has that five hundred dollars in his account.' Then, observing his expression, Marie assumed that her husband was still in a state of shock over her tearing up the check, and said, 'I'm really being very kind to him. He's not nearly as prosperous as he'd have us think. I really don't think that his movie career is going very well.'

It was the first time Marie admitted to anyone that she was even aware of Rory Devlin's film career.

Marie had gone alone and in secret to watch her beautiful ex-lover and former husband give second-rate performances in B movies. She had expected to see Rory's good looks and incredible charm trans-muted onto the screen. It was a shock to see that somehow his dark attractiveness emerged on the screen as something unwholesome. His sex appeal, so magnificently extraordinary in the live Rory, was so blatantly obvious on the screen that he looked cheap, tawdry – made her feel tawdry for having wanted him . . . *for still wanting him* . . .

54

No, she could not deny it – she experienced the old familiar flutter in her loins, she felt her heart quicken and her nipples grow taut. And she was ashamed. She thought of the cousins, the new friends and acquaintances, who, like her, would slip curiously into dark theaters to view the screen image of the ex-husband of the beautiful and elegant Marie du Beaumond Whittier, to find this sleazy presence up on the silver screen. Would they desire him, as she still did, or would they snicker? They, who had never trembled at his touch?

Drawn, she went back time and again to see him play villain, gangster, riverboat gambler, Mexican bandit, occasionally she spotted Desi as an extra, once in a nightclub scene, sitting at a table in evening dress, looking every inch the aristocrat, despite the rumors that circulated. Oh yes, she heard them, though she never acknowledged them. In New York one heard *everything* if one circulated in the right circles. The rumors went that Devlin had treated Desi badly, selling her body for immediate cash when he first arrived in Hollywood, and subsequently for whatever movie parts he could barter her for, as well as to pay off the gambling debts he accumulated. A horrid, ugly story. Poor Desi! She could pity her sister now. After all, they shared the same betrayal of their bodies and their hearts.

Edward wasn't one to expend energy on grudges. Energy was intended for practical purposes only. 'When the girls are older,' he said, 'I'm sure they'll want to see their father. That would only be natural.'

Oh, Edward! If it weren't for the green he seemed to worship so, his blood would be pure white for the milk that ran in his veins! Was it her own Latin blood that made for the difference in how they felt? she wondered.

'I'll see him in hell before he calls either of them daughter to her face!' she spat.

Edward found these new facets of his wife's personality disconcerting, to put it mildly. True, Marie had already surprised him on their honeymoon. He knew, of course, that she was French – still, he was unprepared for her attitudes. That night, as he moved to mount her in the conventional missionary position (he secretly yearned to enter her rear but did not dare broach this), Marie reached for his hardness, stroked it with oil-wet hands, caressed his testicles, and finally, after unendurable minutes, placed his agonizingly pulsating phallus in her mouth and massaged it with her tongue and inner cheeks until she had extracted all his gushing excitement.

It was shocking, yet gratifying beyond belief. It was too bad that he could not boast of his wife's accomplishments at his club. It would make him the envy of all New York.

It never occurred to Edward that it wasn't Latin passion that motivated his beautiful wife, but simple experience. He had forgotten another aspect of the French character – pragmatism. Marie had no intention of becoming immediately pregnant, spending another nine months immobile. Nor did she welcome the intimacy of Edward's flaccid, white, blue-veined body pressing against hers; his clammy kisses; his clumsy caresses. The digital-oral technique provided her a certain detachment. It wasn't sex – it was mechanics. And, not incidentally, she could bring him to climax this way in a matter of moments.

For the time being, she was forced to endure his oral love in return. She could scarcely refuse him this lest he discover she had no taste for any part of him, physical or otherwise.

Unfortunately, her tactics served the very opposite of her intentions. They so whetted Edward's sexual appetite that, delicately and hesitatingly, he began demanding his due two and three times daily. She hoped this would soon regulate itself, and also his enchantment with her sexual organ. He seemed inordinately fascinated with her vagina – murmured incessantly about the pale blond hair that seemed to him a strange and exotic covering for the wondrous receptacle.

Marie was determined to wean him away – to make herself unavailable to him. But for the present, she moaned and groaned and writhed in as good an imitation of passion as she could muster. Only rarely did she allow herself to forget where she was and half dream a hazy memory of a black, wavy-haired head poised over her, of perfect white teeth gleaming in a sardonic smile.

3

Kiki and Angel were packed off to school in Massachusetts with their name, Devlin, still intact. When at first Edward sat down with them, man-to-child, and told them of his plan to adopt them and give them his name, Angel burst into tears and Kiki threw a tantrum. Then Marie took Kiki aside, fully recognizing the older girl's sophisticated wisdom which exceeded her actual years, and explained to her that if she wanted to get all the good things in life she had best learn to obey her mother and to know which side her bread was buttered on. Since her own father had deserted her and Edward Whittier was prepared to bring her up like his own daughter, it was better to be a Whittier than a Devlin.

'Do you understand what I'm saying to you, Kiki?' Marie asked.

'Yes,' she answered. She understood that while she desperately wanted to hold on to her father's name – all that she had left of him now – it was better to do what her mother wanted her to. Her father was gone and her mother was here and all she had.

'Then you must help Angel understand that too.'

So Kiki took Angel aside and told her, 'In our hearts we'll still be Devlins. In our hearts we'll still be Daddy's girls. But Edward has all the money and I don't think Daddy has any. How are we going to get any place if we don't have any money?'

'But I want my daddy! I don't care about stupid money. Why do we need money anyway?'

'Because you can't have any fun without money! If you want to have fun and do whatever you want, you must have money. Lots and lots of it. Don't you see? You can say to Edward with your mouth, "Yes, sir! Yes sir!" but in your heart you can say, "Go to hell!" That's how we can get along.'

But Angel could not see the logic in her sister's words. She continued to scream and cry that she wanted to be a Devlin. She didn't want Edward to be her father. She wanted her own father. Marie was prepared to ignore Angel's cries. What did a little girl know of what was good for her? But Edward was adamant that both girls remain Devlins for the time being. He felt that it would be unwise to make Angel resentful of him so early in their relationship. They would see later on.

Kiki was pleased. She would keep her father's name, and at the same time, for a change, it was Angel and not she who had displeased their mother. But then Marie went to soothe the still hysterical Angel, and Kiki bit her lips. Somehow, Angel always won, she thought.

Again, when Marie told the girls they would be attending Protestant services at school, Angel fled to her room, screaming she wouldn't ever, ever give up being a Catholic. But Kiki needed no urging. Her mother was a Protestant; she would be one too. After all, what was she giving up? She didn't like going to church anyway.

'I'm going to be a Protestant no matter what Angel

is,' Kiki told her mother. 'I may *have to* stay a Devlin because of her, but I'm not going to stay a Catholic.'

But her mother wasn't paying any attention to her.

'Sometimes that Angel surprises me,' Marie said to Edward. 'That stubborn streak . . .'

She sighed. *I suppose it's her way of clinging to the past. Clinging to her Catholicism is her way of holding on to Rory . . .*

Kiki sighed. *All she gives a damn about is that baby Angel. She doesn't care what I do.*

'What does it matter?' Edward said. 'Let her be a Catholic. Let Kiki be a Protestant if she wants to, I'm acquainted with quite a few families where the different members are different denominations. As long as they're Christians I don't think it matters too much.'

Marie thought about that and turned to Kiki. 'Why don't you run along and see how your sister's doing? See if she's still crying.'

Kiki stomped up the stairs.

For a few minutes she watched with resentment as Angel knelt in crying, passionate prayer, clutching her rosary. Then she wiped away a couple of tears of her own and went over to her sister's kneeling figure. She shook her head. 'You know, for eight years old you're pretty dumb. Don't you know it's easier to be a Protestant than a Catholic? When you're a Protestant you hardly have to do anything, only go to church for a little while on Sundays, and you never have to go to confession.'

As Angel continued to sniffle, Kiki put her arms around her, sighing once again. It wasn't Angel's fault that their mother liked her better. It was just that she was such a baby. 'Don't cry, Angel. Everything will be all right. You'll see.'

At Chalmer's, the nine-year-old Kiki was a class ahead of her younger sister, but at Marie's insistence they shared a room. She thought the two fatherless girls needed each other for comfort, for the present. Kiki easily adapted to the new environment, but Angel still cried herself to sleep every night. In the mornings she would tell Kiki how she had dreamed of her father.

'Dreams won't bring him back. But if you promise not to tell mother, I'll tell you a secret.'

Angel considered. She didn't like to keep secrets from her mother, because if she did and her mother found out, she would be angry. But finally she promised.

'Okay. The secret is that Daddy's a movie star!'

'Oh, Kiki! Really?'

'Cross my heart and hope to die. After we're here awhile we get to have movie privileges. That means we can go into town and see movies on Saturday afternoons. And then we can see him *in the movies!*'

'Oh, Kiki, I can't believe it!'

'And you know what else? I've been thinking. When we grow up we can go to Hollywood and maybe live with Daddy and be movie stars too!'

'Tonight when I say my prayers that's what I'm going to pray for, then. That we grow up fast and go to Hollywood and live with Daddy and are movie stars, just like him!'

4

With the girls safely tucked away at school Marie was able to concentrate on important matters. She had the house in town to do over entirely, after which she would go to work on Stoningham Manor, and then there was the house in Southampton. She also had to replenish her wardrobe; she still had only the one fur coat Uncle Paul had bought her, while her cousins had at least four or five each. The cousins had also advised her to begin building a jewelry collection. She already had a good foundation. She had never been forced to sell the jewelry she had taken from her mother and she had the diamond engagement ring Edward had given her plus a few pieces from the Whittier family vault. Edward, the cousins assured her, would doubtless give her additions on birthdays and anniversaries, but she would do well to buy herself some really good pieces at discreet intervals.

'After all, if it comes to a divorce, what's yours is already yours and can't be considered part of the settlement,' one of the cousins counseled.

'And you might as well start right away, while hubby is still in heat and won't kick up a fuss over the money you spend. Later on, they all change,' another of the cousins observed.

Another piece of advice was to have a baby quickly before the marriage cooled, which was, after all, a possibility.

Marie bridled. 'What do I need with another baby? I'm not a Catholic anymore, for God's sake!' But they overruled her. 'You need a Whittier heir, especially now that Edward isn't adopting the girls just yet. This will secure your position. Nobody will be able to usurp your rights should it come to a divorce or if Edward should die prematurely. Mickey and Flickey would try to push you out. But if there is a little Whittier, especially a boy – well, then . . .'

Much as she dreaded another pregnancy, Marie had to agree with their logic. 'But I had to stay in bed the whole time I was carrying the girls. And those postnatal blues lingered for ten years!'

It was the time spent at Stoningham Manor that finally persuaded Marie to produce a Whittier heir. The New York city life she had assumed would be so fascinating following her seclusion in New Orleans had palled swiftly. The shopping, dinners, parties, balls, restaurants did not fulfill her fierce yearning for a home of her own. A New York townhouse didn't represent roots. For this you needed land, rolling lawns, stands of trees, gardens; something that had been there for a century before you, and would remain unchanged a century hence. It symbolized dignity, a sense of identity, of belonging. She had never felt that way about the house in the Vieux Carré; that was only *Maman*'s. And the Rose Plantation, that was only Julian's even though it had been in her father's family for decades and decades.

But at Stoningham Manor she felt as if she had come home. Grander than Rose Plantation could ever be; it was more a castle than a house. Vaulted ceilings, leaded windows, a neo-Gothic extravaganza. A house that made its mistress a queen. More and more Marie allowed Edward to return to the city by himself after the weekends. She spent her days walking through the house, touching paneled walls, running her hand over the table in the billiards room, sitting in the conservatory lush with plants and the stunning view of the Hudson, strolling down its art gallery filled with the Dutch Master interiors.

There was an Aubusson rug ordered originally for the ill-fated Empress Carlotta of Mexico and never delivered, Imperial porcelain, tureens from the factory in Sèvres, murals of hunting scenes executed in 1775, a marble mantel decorated with ormolu and transported from some French château. She didn't tire of examining each figurine, every tapestry. She sat in every chair, from the Louis XVI commissioned by another Marie – a foolish, reckless Marie, who lost her head – to the Queen Anne armchairs in the library.

Marie spent hours circling the formal French gardens, daydreaming in the Japanese gardens that formed another level, watching the miniature waterfall descend into the miniature lake, inspecting the horses in the stables and riding down the sun-dappled bridle paths. She even played alone on the three-hole golf course, softly chanting an almost-forgotten French lullaby.

Marie Whittier was in love. Any lust for the social

life of New York City had faded. She resented the time
away from her land, her house. She had to stamp upon
it her own identity – make it indisputably hers. She
realized that the cousins had been right. If Stoningham was to be truly, uncontestedly hers, she would
have to bring forth a son – Edward Taylor Whittier IV.

5

After two miscarriages and another incredibly tedious
bedridden confinement, Marie produced what she had
willed herself to do – a son. America was at war,
millions of people throughout the world were doomed
to death, Edward's daughters, Mickey and Flickey,
would inherit half their father's fortune, but no one,
no one, was going to take Stoningham Manor away
from her.

Edward was not wholly surprised that his wife would
no longer be sexually available. The doctor had
decreed that there be no more children, and Marie
began to grow more and more withdrawn. It seemed
to him as if there had never been any intimacy
between them. Had he imagined it all? She was as
beautiful as ever – but had that locked-away look in
her eyes always been there? He wasn't sure. He could
scarcely believe this was the woman who had taken his
thing in her mouth on the very first night of their
wedded life.

He shrugged philosophically. She was the mother of
his son, the ideal hostess, the elegant beauty, the
faultless mistress of his estate. It was unproductive to
bewail one's fate; sophomoric to expect a perfect
existence.

The birth of Marie's son brought a congratulatory
letter from New Orleans. Obviously Julian managed

to keep up with her news, one way or another, Marie thought as she quickly scanned his message. Then, with an unexpected pang, she read that after years of struggle, her bother had been forced to let Rose Plantation go. Plaintively he revealed how valiantly he had fought to save the place on behalf of the whole family. Marie translated this as meaning that as custodian of his mother's affairs, he had channeled her funds as well as his own into the futile attempts to keep the plantation. No matter – it was gone. He and Audrey and the children had moved into the house in Vieux Carré. If nothing else, Julian was happy to be with their *Maman* at a time when she sorely needed him.

Ah, Julian! How nice for you! Out of the bad had come some good. You can be with your Maman. *You hypocrite!*

But there was more startling news. It seemed Desi had come home from Hollywood to restore her health. Marie laughed aloud. The delicate way Julian phrased it made it sound as if Desi had simply been away on a short vacation in the course of which she had been taken ill.

Marie had previously heard from a 'friend' that 'someone' had seen Desi in California and alleged that she was a ninety-pound alcoholic with a damaged liver, a cocaine habit, sunken eyes, and a social disease. *Poor Desiree!* Of course, that story had been exaggerated by malicious tongues. Still, Marie recalled Desi in her silver-and-white dress the night she had been crowned Queen of Carnival. She had been so heartbreakingly beautiful!

Maman was unchanged, Julian went on. It would be wonderful if Marie could return for a visit, along with her husband, her new baby, and the girls. The doctors couldn't say how long *Maman* would hang on, and with poor Desi home, what better time for a reconciliation, a healing of old wounds? He, Julian, begged her to do it now, before it was too late.

But Marie had forgiven Desi a long time ago. Desi

had betrayed her, but a weakness, stronger than Desi, had betrayed Desi herself. And the sisters had shared this weakness. Still, she had no desire to see her. It would hurt too much. And she could not bear the thought of seeing her mother, seeing what had become of her, considering what part she herself had played in the tragedy. And as for Julian, there was no question of forgiveness. He was less than nothing to her – a man miserly of spirit.

There actually was just one person she could never forgive, because she could never forgive herself *him*, having wanted him, not being able to forget him.

A few days after Julian's letter, *he* emerged again from the spiritual grave to which she tried repeatedly to consign him. Rory Devlin sent little Edward one of those huge teddy bears guaranteed to frighten a baby to death. For his daughters there were tiny gold charm bracelets and tiny lockets with birthstones, jewelry that would fit an eight-year-old throat or a nine-year-old wrist.

Is he becoming senile? All he has to do is look in the mirror to realize that his daughters are in their teens. Or is he living in a kinder past himself?

His note informed her with sardonic humor that he had enlisted in his country's armed forces and was prepared to defend to the death, if necessary, the American way of life. He enclosed a studio publicity shot showing him taking the oath among a number of recruits easily ten and fifteen years younger. And still there was that reaction within her! Would it never end? Would it follow her to the end and exist even there where life ended?

Oh, God, if only he would die a hero's death somewhere so that she could be at peace. And how much better a legacy this would be for his daughters than any he could otherwise orchestrate.

So this was why Desi had come home at last! Not because she's sick or tired, weary of her life with him, but only because he had left her behind.

She read on. He didn't know when he would be leaving for the front. (*The front!* The entire acculturation came from the cheap movies in which he acted.) He did know, however, that he would be going to the European theater of operations and would be passing through New York on his way overseas. He hoped she would let him see his little girls, perhaps for what could be the last time.

Oh no, Rory Devlin! Your cheap theatrics won't work with me!

She threw away the little bracelets and lockets, rejecting them, as she had rejected Rory's requests to see the girls through the years. She would not allow him the opportunity to betray them as he had her. She would not let him intrude.

She would not let any of them intrude – not *Maman*, not Julian, not Desi. They were all only phantoms. Edward had physical form but no substance. For her only Stoningham Manor was real, and baby Edward and Kiki and Angel.

So go, Rory Devlin, into war and die your hero's death. It's the best possible thing you can do for your daughters . . . and for me!

6

Marie read Beebie Tyler's syndicated column.

Hollywood, March 1943

Rory Devlin, one of our very favorites of the silver screen and one of the many brave citizens of Filmland to volunteer for service immediately following the attack on Pearl Harbor, has returned home after several months of hospitalization. Devilishly handsome Rory was wounded in the invasion of North Africa in November of last year. Among the first of our American boys to reach that foreign soil, Rory was injured when a grenade exploded several feet from where he was supervising a Special Service unit filming the action. Gorgeous Rory, who is well known for his many portrayals of film tough guys, is now back in Hollywood, ready for action in front of the cameras, although he is still recuperating from the injuries to his right leg. Rory was awarded the Purple Heart at special ceremonies conducted on his old studio lot at RKO.

We know that all our readers join in wishing Rory a speedy recovery and a hearty thank-you. In the meantime, if you would like to send Rory a get-well greeting, please send them to Rory's friend, Beebie Tyler, yours truly, and I will happily pass them along to Rory Devlin, one of Screenland's finest.

Marie sobbed, not knowing exactly why. *Damn him! He couldn't even manage to be a proper war hero . . . the bastard!*

Rory sent the Purple Heart to his daughters. Marie had no choice but to give it to them. Angel cried bitterly for her father, who had been hurt fighting for his country, while Kiki put the medal carefully away in her underwear drawer. She was, after all, Daddy's older daughter. It was up to her to save it for both of them.

Presently other reports filtered through from Hollywood. Devlin was washed up. There were no parts for him. For one thing, he had been left with a slight limp in his right leg. He was dubbed 'old-fashioned-looking' – something like the little man who stood on top of wedding cakes. Gangster movies were out and war pictures were in, and even with his war-earned disability he did not qualify. Obviously he didn't look like the boy next door who went off to make the world safe for Mom's apple pie. Nor could he play a nasty Jap or a German SS man. Devlin *looked* more World War I than II.

The last Marie heard was that he had moved in with an ancient star who spent her time screening old films of herself while munching bonbons and patting her fat white-blond curls with fat bejeweled fingers. The story went that when a finger became too fat for a ring, she had someone come to the house to saw the ring off.

The saddest part of the story was that Rory Devlin was only one third of a *ménage à trois*, a lesser third. Number one was a black chauffeur, who among his other chores drove the lady's Rolls on her rare forays out of the house.

Sic transit gloria.

Marie went to bed for four days, during which time the household staff and Edward had orders not to disturb her.

PART THREE

New York
1947–1948

The girl from Omaha wriggled in her chair impatiently. Beebie Tyler smiled. 'I know you're dying to hear more about the Devlin girls themselves. But I wanted you to have the background, my dear, to see what they were all about.

'Well, the war was over in '45. Kiki graduated from Chalmer's in '46 and started college in the fall – Vassar in Poughkeepsie, which didn't thrill her at all. She just went there to try to please her mother, but she complained that Poughkeepsie and college were dull. She was determined to be an actress, no matter what her mother said. Marie, snooty as ever, looked down on actresses of all sorts.

'Marie's plan was for Angel to follow Kiki to Vassar the following year, when *she* graduated from Chalmer's. In the meantime, Marie decided that Kiki would not come out until Angel did, in the summer of '47, when they would have one big party for both girls. They were both knockouts, in the bloom of their youth. Kiki, so fair, with her hair as pale gold as her mother's, and those violet-blue eyes . . . or were they greenish-blue? Blue eyes do change colors so . . .

'Angel looked like her father, with a cloud of dark hair and greenish yellow eyes, cat eyes we used to call them. Of course, Rory's were darker, the darkest eyes I've ever seen. Everyone was always comparing the two girls, trying to decide which was the greater beauty. I always leaned toward Angel myself; she had a certain radiance. But who could resist Kiki? She was glamour personified. Even at nineteen she looked like a star!

71

1

Angel looked out the train window, brooding. No one had attended her graduation exercises. As Poet Laureate, she had read her own 'Ode to the Future'. All the other parents had congratulated her and her father, her real father, had sent her a telegram, but even that didn't make up for the fact that her own mother and Kiki had not been present.

She couldn't bring herself to tell anyone the reason that no one from her family was present – that Kiki had just been booted out of Vassar and the disgrace was so deep that even Edward's influence couldn't get her reinstated, and Marie was so angry and humiliated she had gone into seclusion at Stoningham and wouldn't let Edward attend Angel's graduation either, lest curious acquaintances ask questions.

Kiki would have come gladly, even in the face of her disgrace. She had told Angel on the phone that she couldn't bear that her poor little Angel was all alone on a day that meant so much to her, even though it was all a 'crock of shit'. 'But Mother says I must stay in town under lock and key because I'm so naughty. I'm out of favor with old Marie for good. Well, she's always favored you anyway. So who cares?'

'That's not true, Kiki,' Angel protested, even though she did think it was so and even ashamedly took satisfaction in the thought.

'It is, but I told you, I don't care. There's no pleasing that woman. Anyway, I'm not allowed to go to Stoningham because she doesn't want to look at me, and I can't go to the Hamptons because *everyone's* there already and they know I've disgraced the family and they'll say I take after my father, who, of course, is a well-known bounder. Even so, Mother's admonition would not have kept me here and not with you,

Heavenly Angel, except that she says if I break parole, neither of us will have our coming-out party. So forgive me. And try not to care. Who gives a bloody fuck about a silly graduation anyway?'

Angel had asked why Kiki had been expelled.

'You mean Mother didn't tell you?'

'No. She only said you were a disgrace to the Whittiers *and* the Manards. I'm surprised she didn't drag in the du Beaumonds too. When I asked her what happened she said it was better I didn't know for the time being because I'm such a terrible liar, a four-year-old could drag the truth out of me. What did you do, for heaven's sake? Were you caught in bed with the president or did you merely murder the dean?'

'It's no use trying to explain on the phone. I'll tell you when I see you. Just hurry up and graduate, Heavenly Angel, and then come here to New York. Do not go to Stoningham! Come directly here! Then we'll at least have a couple of days together before Marie jumps on my ass. Okay? So I'll see you in two days. Hurry, Angel, your sister is dying of boredom. Hurry! Hurry! . . . Her voice trailed off to a whisper as she hung up.

Angel knew it was childish of her to feel bad about the family's not being there. It really didn't matter. She and Kiki would have their coming-out party, and then she would go off to college in the fall. It wouldn't be Vassar anymore. Kiki had ruined Vassar for her. And she guessed that she wouldn't be allowed to go to Radcliffe. It was more intellectual than social, and her mother would think that that was the wrong emphasis. And she didn't want to go against her mother's wishes. Kiki was the rebel, not she. Of course, Kiki *loved* being the rebel.

Maybe she and Kiki would go off to college together, now that Kiki had probably lost all her first-year credits. But who could tell what Kiki would do now. A dramatic school was all she had ever been interested in. Maybe now that's where she would go.

Kiki had had all the leads in all the plays at Chalmer's,

had been named Class Actress. And she, Angel, had always been given tiny parts, token parts, but it didn't matter. She didn't enjoy being on the stage. Actually, it was agony. She had done it in the first place only because Kiki was doing it, and where Kiki was were all the good times. This year without Kiki had been hard on her.

It was Kiki who had generated all the fun and excitement, and had dragged her along, insisting she *had* to have friends and dates. Of course, when she had gone on a date with Kiki, Kiki had the great guy, while she was stuck with his friend, usually a wimp. It really wasn't Kiki's fault – she was always one of the most popular girls at Chalmer's, had been friends with the other most popular girls, like Sara Gold, Chrissy Marlowe, and beautiful Maeve O'Connor, while Angel had been known as the bookworm.

In one respect, Kiki was like their mother: she never liked to think, much less speak of, the old days, not even about their father much. At first she used to say how they would grow up and go live with him and be actresses in the same movies as he. But then later on she talked differently. 'He's gone, Angel, and that's that. You and I have to get on with our lives, just like Mother did. Someday we may see him again. For now we just have to grow up and see to our futures.'

But still and all it had been Kiki who had found out what pictures their father was in and somehow managed it that they got permission to go into town when one of his pictures was playing. If you kept up your lessons and accumulated no demerits you were allowed to go to the movies every other Saturday. It was amazing that they got to go, as Kiki always had *some* demerits.

But it was Angel, not Kiki, who was disappointed by Rory Devlin's image on the screen. She couldn't understand why he didn't get roles like Errol Flynn's or Tyrone Power's. That was the way she had always pictured him – brave and gallant, brandishing his fist or his sword in defense of some beautiful girl who melted in his arms from love and rapture. Instead, he was always being shot, clubbed or electrocuted.

Kike thought their father was simply great. 'I love those parts he plays! Those gangsters don't give a shit about anything. I think he's smashing!'

'Doesn't seeing him on the screen make you feel like crying – that he's gone and we can't see him?'

'I think it's simply super that if we can't see him in the flesh, we can at least see him up there on the screen. As for him leaving, he did what he had to do. Don't get me wrong. I admire Mother. I think she's beautiful, and she's plenty tough. But can you actually see Daddy with Mother? He had to go! He was that kind of guy . . .'

Then Kiki had an idea. She wrote to their father's studio, and before long they had wonderful letters from him. Marie Whittier had never thought to alert the school to possible correspondence between them and their father. He even sent money orders in small amounts – ten dollars, twenty-five – which they were able to cash at the post office in town.

'Nobody would believe that we would be so happy over such tiny crumbs. I must say, Edward and Mother are the *stingiest*! We must get the smallest allowances in the whole school,' Kiki complained. 'But I'm warning you, Angel – don't get all goody-goody on me and confess to Mother about the letters and the money. She'd have a shit hemorrhage and put a stop to it mighty fast. I think I'd better swear you to silence.'

'That's really not necessary, Kiki Devlin. I said I wouldn't tell. That's enough.'

'Oh, I don't know. I think you love to tattle on me to Mother just so she'll like you best.'

'That's the biggest lie I ever heard,' Angel said, hurt. She almost *never* told on Kiki, and only when it was in Kiki's best interest, when she was getting herself into trouble.

'All right, I'll let you go this time,' Kiki laughed. 'Besides, just remember, it's you, too, who's getting letters and money from Daddy – not just me.'

In his letters their father repeatedly told them how much he loved them and how he longed to see them, and that any day he'd be popping up to see them. In the meantime he sent them photographs along with the letters – stills from some of his movies.

Those were the happiest times for Angel – seeing her father on the screen and receiving letters full of love. But after a while there didn't seem to be many movies in which he appeared. Then he wrote that he was up for a really terrific role so he had given up all the other pictures. And then he was in the army and he wrote them from different places and then from the hospital as well. And then the letters stopped coming. For a while she and Kiki asked each other the reason, speculated. Was it Marie, or what?

Angel had secretly hoped he would turn up for her graduation. It was her secret dream. She would be up on the platform reciting her ode and suddenly she would see him in the audience – so tall, so dark, so handsome, his beautiful white teeth flashing beneath his debonair mustache, and afterward she would fly into his arms and he would shower her with kisses and she would take him around so proudly and show him off to all the girls and all of them would be so jealous of her beautiful father . . .

Part of the dream had been that Kiki was not there, so that she wouldn't have to share him with her. That part of the dream she was ashamed of – to deny Kiki even in a dream when it was Kiki who had looked after her all these years at Chalmer's.

But it was a silly dream. How would her father have even known she was graduating? Neither she nor Kiki knew where to reach him now. But then somehow he had found out after all, because there had been the telegram from him congratulating her. Had Kiki found out where he was and not told her? Had her mother gotten in touch with him and told him?

As graduation had drawn near someone had asked her if her father was coming, and Mimi Truewell, who was a terrible bitch and who knew all the latest movie-star gossip, had answered for Angel. 'How can he? I just read he's in the South of France. Has been there ever since that old fat slob, Marta Gretchen, threw him out of her house. Guess he got too mangy for even her to sleep with anymore.'

Stunned, Angel wondered if it were true. Was that why they hadn't heard from him in so long? Had Kiki known and not told her? Angel wanted to die. If only Kiki had been there to tell Mimi Truewell off. She would really fix Mimi, make her wish she had never been born. She had to tell Mimi off herself, even though she was terrible at that sort of thing.

'Vicious slander, Mimi Truewell! You should know better than to repeat gossip – especially gossip that's false. And who are you to call someone else fat when you yourself are a tub of grits!'

'Oh, go climb a tree, Devlin. Everyone knows your old man was Gretchen's lover, along with her chauffeur. I guess the chauffeur won out and your father had to hightail it to the Riviera to find himself some other old cunt willing to pay for her screwing!'

Angel was struck dumb, completely overwhelmed. She *knew* she should think of something terrible to say back to Mimi, but she couldn't. It was all she could do to fight back her tears until she got out of sight. So she just walked away, a nice girl in her Bermuda shorts and knee-high socks, her head lifted out of her shoulders as she had been taught. She didn't break into a run and tears until she was yards away.

Coming out of Grand Central, Angel hailed a cab and sat on the edge of the seat for the twenty minutes or so it took to get to the house. The driver offered to carry the bags into the house for her.

'No,' she told him. 'Just leave them on the stairs,

77

thank you. I want to surprise someone.' She gave him a big tip and one of the ingratiating smiles she had been practicing in the loneliness of her room.

She opened the door quietly with her key. She hoped there weren't any servants around. Since the war, the staff had been reduced. The house was quiet, seemed deserted. She tiptoed across the marble entrance hall decorated in black and white diamond shapes, going around the huge circular table in the middle of the hall. She noticed that even though her mother was away at Stoningham the table still displayed an arrangement of all white flowers. Marie disliked bouquets of many colors.

She peeked into the drawing room. The draperies were drawn, so that despite the bright sunshine outside, the rose-and-white room was dim and cool. The sudden darkness after the brightness outside blinded her temporarily. But there was no one in the drawing room, either.

The double doors to the library were closed. Angel turned one knob, hesitantly, but it was locked. Now she *knew* that Kiki must be in there, maintaining her privacy even though the rest of the house was empty. She didn't knock – she was determined to surprise her sister. Instead, she went into the dining room. Both the dining room and library, adjacent rooms, were lined by French doors that opened to a small enclosed terrace on one side of the house. By exiting out the French door of the dining room, she would be able to reenter the house by way of the library's French doors.

She tiptoed across the terrace and slowly opened the draped library door. She peeped around to see if Kiki was really holed up in there. Here too it was very dark in contrast to the sun-drenched terrace. She blinked and waited for her eyes to adjust. The dark crimson of the draperies and the dark paneling of the walls made it no easier to see. The furniture stood out in shadowy silhouette. Was that Edward sitting there by the fireplace in the brown leather wing chair?

He must be stealing a catnap. And he's locked the door so as not to be disturbed or observed. Yes – now she could make out his head thrown back against the high rise of the chair. His eyes were closed and his mouth hung slightly open. Angel stifled a giggle. He must be snoring, too. But she heard no snores, only heavy breathing. Little moans escaped his lips. He must be having a bad dream poor man, thought Angel, who had had so many.

She was ready to back out of the room and leave Edward to his secret nap when she realized with stunning awareness that there was a third person in the room. It was Kiki, kneeling before Edward, her hair silvery in the semidarkness!

Oh, God, Jesus help me!

The chair prevented a precise view, but there was no mistaking Kiki's face bent to its task, head revolving in a circular motion, mouth open, working, eyes fixed intently on Edward's face.

Mary, Mother of God, help us all!

Angel watched Edward's body jerk and quiver as the soft moans grew louder. *I must get out of here!*

She closed the door and backed out onto the terrace. She put both hands to her face. *What shall I do?*

She ran quickly back into the dining room, out into the hall, then up the stairs to her room. She sat down at the dressing table and started to brush her hair furiously, harder and harder.

Then, like a storm, Kiki burst into the room.

'Sweet Angel you're home at last! I'm so glad to see you, Baby. Mmm . . . Mmm . . .' She rained kisses all over her sister's face.

Angel drew back. 'Kiki, I just saw you,' she said, striving for control.

Kiki looked at her evenly; only her eyelids fluttered. 'I know you did. I caught you out of the corner of my eye.'

'Kilkee Devlin, how *could* you?'

'For God's sake, Angel, it was only a little blow job. No big shucks.'

'*Only?*'

'Yes. Only. It's not like having sex. It's just an accommodation, a little favor to repay Edward for some little favors he's done us – like giving us a good home and a good education.'

'You're not funny, Kiki. In fact, you're positively disgustingly revolting! And how can you say it's *not* having sex? And with your own stepfather?'

'Because it's *really* not like having sex. He doesn't do anything to me. I mean, he's fondled me once in a while, a little feel here and there, but he's never put it *in* me!'

'Oh, God, but you're vulgar! How could you do this to Mother?'

'The way I look at it, I'm helping her out. Every time *I* do it to him, she doesn't have to. And believe me, it probably *kills* her to do it, and I don't mind at all. It's kind of fun watching the old bastard's poker face contort.'

'I don't believe Mother ever did *that*'

'Oh, for God's sake, don't be such an innocent! I saw her doing it to him, for God's sake, with my own two eyes. I walked in on them once. Of course, it was quite a while ago.'

'Suppose Mother walks in on the two of you just as I did today?'

'She has.'

'Oh, my God! What did she do?'

'Closed the door and walked away.'

'And never even mentioned it? I find that hard to believe.'

'Oh, you know how Marie hates scenes. Or maybe she thought if she acknowledged it she'd have to throw us both out and she didn't want to. Or maybe she was just relieved Edward was getting it somewhere else and not bothering her. And besides, it was only me. Now if it were *you* instead of rotten little me, then surely she have made a fuss,' Kiki said with a heavy dose of sarcasm.

'Kiki Devlin, you're lying. Mother never walked in on you.'

'Okay, so I'm lying.'

'Oh, Kiki, why?'

'Because it was a fun story to tell about old Marie. Can you just picture the look on her face if it really happened?'

'I'd rather not, if you don't mind. Kiki, how could you do it? To Edward, I mean. How?'

'I told you. It's fun turning the old coot on. And besides, there was money. Marie and Edward were so damn stingy. I couldn't bear it that we had the least spending money of anyone at school. And hardly a thing to wear besides those damn uniforms! I mean, look at the clothes Sara Gold had! Four fur coats! And Marie was always saying how unfitting it was for schoolchildren to have too much money! Jesus, Angel, we would have hardly had change for the movies if Marie had had her way. You could hardly count the few dollars we used to get from Daddy. And I always shared the money I got from Edward with you, even if you didn't know it. When we went shopping for clothes, didn't I always urge you to get the most expensive? And when I got a sheared beaver last Christmas from dear old Edward, who else got one? You. Who insisted on it? Me. And this summer, guess which two sisters are finally going to get their own cars? I'm sick and tired of taking whatever's hanging around the driveway at Hampton, as if we were servants running errands. "If you must, Jeffrey, take the Buick into the village, but be sure you're back by two."'

The perfect imitation of their mother forced a laugh out of Angel despite her anger. Then: 'So you did it for money, just like a . . .'

'Well, don't stop. Say it. *Just like a whore*,' Kiki drawled, drawing the word out and thrusting her face into Angel's. 'And no, it wasn't *just* the money. I told you – it was fun. Arousing Edward. Putting one over on Marie.'

'But why would you want to do that? Put one over on Mother?'

'I've got plenty of reasons. For one thing, I suspect it's Marie who's keeping Daddy away from us. And the reason that I like the most is that I'm getting even with Marie for always favoring you. First comes baby brother, Eddie, and then comes you, and then comes *me*. Last. Shit!'

'Oh, Kiki, it's simply not true.'

'Oh yes it is. *You're* the good little girl. Miss Innocent. Don't tell me you're not always shining up to her. Ever since Daddy walked out of the house that day you've been doing your best to be Miss Number One.'

'Oh, Kiki, no!'

'Let's drop it, okay? The real reason I sucked my stepfather off was because it was an erotic experience and I never had an erotic experience before.' She laughed harshly.

Angel was anxious to drop the whole subject too. It was all too much to think about, too disagreeable, too disgusting. 'I'll never be able to look Edward in the face again,' she said. 'That filthy old pig!'

'Oh, come off it. He's really harmless. Let's talk about something else. I'm bored with Edward.'

Angel gazed at her sister in amazement. The whole thing had really meant nothing to her. And Kiki even managed to make *her* feel ridiculous.

'All right. Let's talk about why you were kicked out of Vassar instead.'

'Those hicks. Who wants to hang around in that fucking Poughkeepsie anyway?'

'Me, that's who. You know I was dying to go there, and now I won't be able to.'

'I really did you a big favor. Bor-ing!'

'You still haven't told me why they kicked you out.'

'Okay. It was midnight and I had run out of ciggies. There's a cigarette machine in the lobby. So I picked myself up and went downstairs and somebody saw me and then somebody else reported me. And *voilà* – out!'

'They expelled you just for going downstairs at midnight?'

'Well, I was a teensy bit nude at the time, you see. And the porter saw me, and then that dyke of a dreary

82

dean saw that poor Negro man gawking at me . . . I bet they kicked me out just because *he* was looking. I bet if he had been white they wouldn't have cared less!'

'Why *did* you go downstairs nude?'

'I was in bed reading this really raunchy book. I forget the name but it was very explicit. You know – hot! And the room was hot too! So I had my clothes off because it was so stifling and it would be easier to diddle myself if I weren't wearing anything—'

'Will you stop teasing?'

'—and there I was just dying for a fag and the pack was empty. So I trundled down to the lobby. How could I know that old man would be there sweeping up? Well, he got so excited he dropped his broom and dustpan and made this terrible racket and Old Pruneface Plimpton came running out and threw a fucking fit! I thought they'd have to take her to the booby hatch. Well, the dean said I was a disgrace to the Whittiers – did you know that dear Edward's Flickey and Mickey were Vassar girls? And then she said as for the Devlins, she could see how my father had earned his reputation. That was a bit much even for me, and I cracked the old bag across the noggin with her very own nameplate. After that they packed my bags for me and told me to be out of there in an hour, which was just fine with me.' She grinned. 'It's rather like something Daddy would have done, you know? A real Devlin escapade!'

Then Angel wondered whether it had all been deliberate. Had Kiki wanted – intended – to be thrown out? Had she just wanted to emulate their father, live up to his reputation? Or just infuriate their mother?

'What exactly did Mother say?'

'Oh, she was really raving until I told her about the crack the dean made about Daddy. Then she said she *knew* it had been a mistake not to have our name changed and that it was all *your* fault. About our name not being changed. So she's mad at you too, which I must say makes for a pleasant change.' Angel made a face, and she went on, 'So then she left for Stoningham in her usual state of seclusion when she's upset, after forbidding me to leave the house. I dare say the whole thing will blow over in a couple of weeks and then we'll all head out for the Island.'

'Well, I don't know what you were thinking of, going downstairs naked, but I'm glad you smacked that old witch for the crack about Daddy. If I'd been there, I would have done it myself!'

'Oh, no you wouldn't. You would have drawn yourself up, tossed your hair, and, with a tiny proud smile to hide the quiver of your lips, walked out silently. That's *your* way.'

How right you are, Angel thought.

'Oh, the hell with it! Let's not get all serious and drippy. Let's get ravishingly done up and go out for a drink. How about "21"?'

'How about the Copa Lounge?' Angel retorted, knowing exactly what Kiki would say.

'Heavenly Angel, will you *never* learn? The Copa is for the fucking tourists!'

2

Kiki stood surveying herself in front of the full-length mirror and liked what she saw. The silvery-gold mane, the blue-green eyes glinting with self-approval. She stroked the string of pearls she wore, fingers playing with the diamond clasp. Angel joined her at the mirror. 'Whose idea were the pearls as our coming-out present?' she asked. 'Mother's or Edward's?'

Kiki laughed delightedly. 'Whose do you think?'

'Yours?'

'But of course, precious. Now, tell me true, am I not the most absolutely gorgeous deb anybody has seen this year or any other fucking year?'

Angel touched the cloud of dark hair, gazed more intently into the mirror, widened her yellowish-green eyes. 'You are . . . until they see *me*.' She stuck her tongue out at Kiki.

They both giggled, and Kiki bumped her with her hips. 'Just remember the pecking order here. I'm number one and you're only number two, sister. And remember whose charms got us the pearl necklaces, if you please. And, Angel, do not forget to thank dear stepdaddy for your gift . . .'

'Should I kiss him on the forehead, do you think, or on the cheek?'

'Careful, precious, or I *will* tell you exactly where.'

The coming-out party was covered by *Life*, and they took pictures of everything – the flowered canopy; the centerpieces of yellow and white daisies on daisy-strewn tablecloths; the platters of cold turkey, glazed duck, and chef-carved rare pink beef; the sculpted ice swans. There were far more pictures taken of Kiki than of Angel, the photographers naturally gravitating to her effervescence. They snapped her revealing a red garter on a shapely if very slender leg; holding a slice of the duck to the lips of California congressman Dick Power, orange sauce dripping down Power's chin; pushing society wag Randy Haskell into the pool; leading the conga line encircling the dance floor. All in all, the party was a huge success – largely because it lasted until six in the morning, when a breakfast of scrambled eggs and caviar was served, and also because the final tally of persons pushed into the pool came to nineteen, a record for the season.

A week after the party there was a picture of Angel in a tabloid called *Whisper*. It caught her out in the gardens looking forlorn and was captioned: 'Debutante Runs from Her Own Party.' The accompanying story, subtitled 'Why Deb Is Sad,' revealed all the juicy details of Rory Devlin's life, starting with New Orleans and continuing through his career in Hollywood and his sordid tale of descent into gray obscurity.

Kiki left the magazine open to the story at Marie's place at the breakfast table. Marie read it quickly. She looked at Kiki. 'Who wrote this trash?' she demanded crossly, incensed, almost as if it were all Kiki's responsibility.

'There's no byline, Marie. There never is in these kind of stories.' She was familiar with the publication.

'But who took the picture?' Angel wondered. 'I don't even remember being out in the garden by myself. And we didn't invite a photographer from *Whisper* . . .'

'Of course we didn't,' Marie snapped. 'He must have sneaked in with the *Life* people. I'd like to wring the necks of everyone responsible for this intrusion. Well, at least the people we know don't read this trash.'

Kiki was swift to disabuse her. 'Everyone and his third cousin reads this trash, Marie. *I* always do. It's loads of fun. Though this story is—'

'Would you please refrain from calling me Marie, Kiki? I find it very rude—'

'Wait a moment!' Angel broke in. 'I think I do know who took that picture of me. Remember that tall, dark fellow who followed me around practically every second? I thought he was from *Life*. *Very* nice looking. Remember, Kiki? I told you he reminded me of someone.'

'Oh, for heaven's sake, Angel, you know perfectly well who – he looked a lot like Daddy.'

Marie looked at Kiki sharply, intending to silence her, but Kiki went on:

'Don't deny it, Angel. You thought he looked like Daddy and you were prancing about trying to get his attention. Didn't you notice him, Marie? He was the picture of Daddy. And didn't you notice Angel knocking herself out, trying to get his attention?'

'That's not true—'

'Oh yes it is. He practically had to fall over you – he couldn't help it, what with you dodging his footsteps, as it were.'

'Stop it, Kiki! You're jealous because he took *my*

picture instead of yours.'

'That crummy picture?'

'Stop this bickering at once! I don't want to hear another word about this man or the picture!' Marie snapped.

But Angel was too aroused to listen. 'It's *not* a crummy picture,' she said. 'It's a perfectly beautiful picture. And he was a perfectly beautiful looking man. And I didn't have to *try* to get his attention. The minute he walked in he started taking pictures of me. He must have taken oodles . . .'

'Well, the *Life* people took oodles and oodles of pictures of me.'

'Why wouldn't they? You were dancing around like a circus pony.'

Suddenly, Kiki broke out in laughter. 'I was kind of cute, wasn't I? And we do have to look on the bright side of things. The story in *Whisper* plus the article in *Life* does make us appear most fascinating. Not just your usual debs. We're sure to be picked as twin debs of the year, like Sara Gold and Maeve O'Connor were last year. Then, when I go on the stage, why, I'll already be well known . . .'

At this last remark, Marie threw her daughter an indignant look and left the room in a huff, and Angel laughed slyly. 'I don't think we're going to make debs of the year. Everyone says Cholly Knickerbocker will pick Jackie Bouvier. Everyone says he's simply crazy about her.'

Then Kiki walked out of the room in a huff and left Angel to study her picture. Of course she had noticed the photographer immediately. How could she not? He was tall, slim, dark-haired, and olive-skinned – he even had a mustache. Practically the only thing missing was the flashing smile.

Almost immediately after the issue of *Life* that had covered the coming-out party of the Devlin sisters appeared, Marie heard from her brother, Julian. He wrote how gratified he, Audrey, and Desi were to see how beautiful the girls had turned out and how beautiful, she, Marie, had remained. They were equally delighted to see how everything had turned out so well for them all, that Marie had done such a splendid job of raising her daughters, that she had managed to provide for them so nicely.

With no thanks to you, Julian.

They had even shown the spread in the magazine to *Maman*, Julian wrote, who, of course, could not comment, but still, he felt that he had seen extreme joy in her eyes, which were as sharp as ever, *Dieu merci.* Then he twisted the knife a little. He, Desi, Audrey, and his children were disappointed Marie had not seen fit to invite them to the girls' party. They would have liked to have shared in Marie's pride on such an occasion, and it was regrettable that despite her good fortune she could not find it in her heart to forgive and forget, and love them as they did her.

Marie smiled to herself but soon experienced a sickish feeling as Julian went on to say that the old house in the Vieux Carré was gone. He had sold it to the Restoration Society and they all had moved into a large, lovely house in the Garden District. It had become impossible to stay on in the old house . . . the neighborhood had become so run-down . . . warehouses and all kinds of undesirables.

So it has finally come to pass. The house where the Duc d'Orléans had dined – gone. The blue-and-white bedroom. The salon with the huge crystal chandelier where she had been married . . .

Well, perhaps it was for the best, Marie thought. The house and its history all belonged to the past. They would guide strangers through the house and relate its ancient history. It was *all* ancient history.

It was a summer of parties, tennis, sailing, swimming, lazy hot days. Evenings of club-hopping, dancing, drinking, flirting under the stars. Then it was fall, and Angel went away to Smith and Kiki eloped.

One night Kiki, Randy Haskell, and Tracy Mansfield, of Southampton, Palm Beach, and the usual assorted places, were making the rounds of the local watering holes, and for want of something better to do, Randy proposed that they fly to Reno and he and Kiki tie the knot.

Kiki laughed. 'You've proposed to half the Hamptons this summer. If they all turned you down, why shouldn't I? And you're too old anyway. You must be pushing – what is it, thirty-five? Everyone says you've been around for years doing the debutante scene, dropping proposals like cigarette ashes.'

'That's a fucking lie,' Randy protested hotly. 'Well, all right, if not me how about you and Tracy doing the big thing and I'll stand up for you?'

Tracy was far drunker than either of them. 'Why not? I've never been married before . . . and I've never been to Reno.'

After a weekend of marriage, drinking, and playing the tables, the couple returned to New York to break the news to their respective parents.

Marie was aghast. 'Why Tracy Mansfield, of all people? He hasn't a penny of his own, he has never held a job, and his mother keeps him on a tight leash. And you didn't even have a proper wedding.'

But Kiki was unconcerned. 'I thought you'd give us a small reception – no more than two hundred or so – and a nice wedding present. Under the circumstances, I'm sure the Mansfields will match your present. We'll buy a nice apartment with the money, furnish it with the wedding gifts, and the Mansfields will find something for Sonny Boy to do. Nothing too intense, mind you. Tracy *is* a bit of a boob, you know.'

'That still doesn't answer my question,' Marie said. 'Why did you marry him?' Then, like her own mother before her: 'Are you pregnant?'

'For God's sake, Mother, don't you know *anything?* Tracy's a *fruit*, for Christ's sake!'

'I don't understand.'

'A pansy, Mother! A fairy! For Christ's sake, we all shared a room at the hotel – me, Tracy, *and* Randy. Twin beds, and *they* slept in one bed while I, all alone, slept in the other.' She burst into howls of laughter. 'Isn't that an absolute scream?'

Marie stared at her daughter for a long time. 'Are you insane, or what?'

Kiki shrugged. 'I was drunk, they were drunk, and we had nothing better to do. It just seemed like a fun thing at the time.'

'I see,' Marie said drily. 'Fun! As soon as Tracy gets here, you're to tell him we're filing for an annulment and sending him back to his mother.'

'Just one fucking minute—'

'Don't use your foul language in my presence, if you please. You all acted under the influence of alcohol and the marriage was never consummated. It's all clear-cut. The longer we wait, the more people will gossip. It's already bad enough. You've already been very stupid and you've damaged your reputation, such as it is. It won't help your future prospects any, either.'

'Just hold your damned horses, Marie! Leave this to me! I fully intend to give my future a healthy boost in the ass.'

Just as Kiki had predicted, the Mansfields came up with something for Tracy. He was assigned to a branch of the investment company that bore the family name and was given a large office in which to shuffle papers. His parents were not displeased to have Edward Whittier's stepdaughter for a daughter-in-law, and were extremely pleased to have their son respectably married and off their hands. He had been drinking rather heavily and his 'problem' had begun to become a source of embarrassment. They were so delighted that they bought Tracy and Kiki a brownstone on East Sixty-fifth Street, and promised her a large trust fund if she produced an heir, and the quicker the better. During the year Kiki and Tracy stayed married, she did give some thought to becoming pregnant, one way or another, and collecting her reward. Finally she decided that this was too hard a way to earn a dollar and instead informed the Mansfields that she was filing for a divorce.

She offered her in-laws a choice. For a settlement of the brownstone and three hundred thousand dollars in cash, she would obtain a quiet divorce in Nevada. Otherwise, it would be a noisy one in New York, where, of course, the only grounds were adultery, in which case she would be forced to produce explicit pictures of Tracy with Randy Haskell and assorted male lovers, some of them truly socially unacceptable. She was reluctant to do this, since Tracy was one of her very best friends in the whole world and she had only taken the pictures at his request. Of course, she might be forced to raise the money for her legal fees by selling some of these very same photos to *Whisper*, or to one of its sister publications, much as she hated to part with them, as they were part of her very private collection.

Kiki got the quiet divorce in Reno, spending the required six weeks playing horsie with a musclebound rodeo performer. Then she resumed residence in her brownstone on East Sixty-fifth Street, right off Fifth Avenue. She had Edward invest the quarter of a million she had settled for in blue-chip stocks, and announced that she was going on the stage. Her friend from Chalmer's, Sara Gold, was studying drama at the New School with Stella Adler and was having ever so much fun meeting wonderfully fascinating people, especially men! And she, Kiki, had been the one elected Class Actress, *not* Sara. Besides, no one could deny it was in her blood.

Marie was furious. 'I absolutely forbid it!'

But in the end Kiki, as always, did exactly as she pleased. She enrolled in an acting class and started going on casting calls. She told Angel that anytime she tired of playing schoolgirl at Smith, she could move in with her. They'd have loads of fun. 'God knows,' Kiki said, 'life can be terribly boring if we don't try to spice it up.' Then she added, 'But of course having money helps, Angel. That's why you have to get some of your own, as I have, one way or another.'

She had even made up a little poem to celebrate the settlement she had received from the Mansfields. 'Do you want to hear it? It's not as poetic as *your* poetry, but it's apt.

She recited:

> 'If you're rich,
> You may be a bitch.
> But if you're poor,
> Darling, you're a boor!'

PART FOUR

New York
1949

'Kiki did quite well on the stage,' Beebie Tyler went on. 'Nothing serious or heavy, as they say these days, but she was very good in the drawing-room comedy sort of thing. You know, like dear Connie Bennett, God rest her soul. She certainly was attractive, and she was always the clotheshorse, and sophistication was her cup of tea. I know she received offers to go to Hollywood, but she loved New York – and she *was* successful. She was also quite infamous for her alliances, onstage and off. They said she went to bed with practically every one of her leading men. Now, I'm sure that must have been an exaggeration, but Kiki Devlin did have a huge appetite for life – and love.

'And after attending Smith College for two years, Angel decided to leave and come to New York, move in with her sister. She would do something in the arts, she thought. She had always painted a little and written little poems. The truth was, she was lonely at Smith. Always shy, she didn't make friends easily, had always relied on her sister for companionship.

'Marie, of course, was against it. She had other ideas as to what Angel should do. She thought Angel's place was with her, doing the sort of thing postdebutantes did until they found the proper person to marry. But sometimes even Angel could be very stubborn and willful, and move in with Kiki she did, despite her mother's objections. But going on the stage was the last thing she planned on. It was an accident – a surprise to everyone concerned.'

1

'Aren't you a bit dressy for a rehearsal? Angel asked, eyeing Kiki's latest Dior, a garnet-red taffeta with full skirt and plunging neckline, and her four-inch platform sandals.

'I'm dressed for the cocktail party we're doing at the Stork at five. Remember? Allison Coolidge's soirée.'

'Oh yes, of course . . .' Angel said vaguely.

'What am I going to do with you, Angel? I won't have you sitting at home when there are places to go and people to see. Now hurry and get dressed. I'll wait for you. You'll come to rehearsal with me and then we'll go on to Allison's party together. Besides, I want you to see how I'm putting that English Bitch, Elena Barstow, in her place. They started out giving her all the good lines.'

'Well, her part is supposed to be the bigger one, isn't it?'

'You're still hopelessly naïve. Do you think just giving a performance is what acting is all about? Do you think that's how one gets to be a star? Simply reciting lines? It's managing, always managing.'

When they arrived at the theater they found an air of calamity, a demoralized group of people. It seemed that Elena Barstow had left the play in a huff, declaring that she was going back to England, where people were more civilized, where actors were gentlemen, and where – particularly – actresses were ladies.

Judson Smith, the producer, confronted Kiki.

'It's *you* with all your little tricks who made Elena quit,' he spat through pouty, dewy lips. 'I warned you to stop your shenanigans. I hope you're satisfied. Two weeks before we open in Boston—'

'Why, you twit! You blame *me* for *her* unprofessional behavior? I apologized for spilling that glass of water down her tits, didn't I? Scared shitless, that's what she was. Afraid that the American critics would tear her to pieces, which they would have. Anyhow, what's the fuss about? She can be replaced. *Anybody* could replace Elena – a fourteen-year-old girl could. Why, my sister here, Angel, could do better than that English tart – and *she* wouldn't forget her lines, either. *She's* a quick study!'

Judson Smith stared at Angel. Physically she was exactly right. She had the beauty, the delicacy, that vulnerable quality. And the personality seemed just right – a foil for the abrasive Kiki.

'*Are* you a quick study, my dear?' he lisped.

'Yes . . . I think so . . . but . . .' Angel answered in bewilderment, turning to Kiki.

'I was just making a point,' Kiki said. 'I wasn't suggesting that—'

Judson Smith huddled with Ken Siegel, the playwright, and Myles Porter, the director, and the three whispered excitedly. Then the director approached Angel.

'Have you any theatrical experience at all?'

'Just little things at school. I—'

'Good. Then we'll start almost fresh. No bad habits to break. Would you run through a scene with Kiki, please? All you have to do is read.'

'But I'm no actress. I couldn't possibly . . .' She turned to Kiki in appeal.

In the end, and albeit reluctantly, Kiki talked Angel into running through the lines. She was personally convinced her sister would be wooden, not good at all, but she could hardly act less than enthusiastic, considering that Jason, Ken, and Myles blamed her for Barstow's flight back to England.

Before the afternoon was over, Angel was experiencing a certain new, exhilarating headiness. Admittedly terrified; still, there was that excitement coursing through her body, rushing to her head. And it helped that the director seemed quite taken with her, was being quietly, excessively courteous, gallantly and warmly supportive.

Kiki was beside herself. The situation had gotten out of hand and she had no one to blame but herself. Goddamn it! Not only was Angel going to be in *her* play, but that fucking Myles Porter was acting like she was the most exciting thing he had seen in ages. Clearly it was going to be Angel who was going to get all the favored attention onstage.

'Really, Angel, first all that charming, shy reticence and then making goo-goo eyes at Myles,' Kiki said later, after the part had definitely been given to Angel.

Angel protested in vain. 'But it was you who suggested me for the role. I didn't do anything at all—'

'Sure,' Kiki said. 'Well, just don't make me sorry by trying to upstage me.' She wasn't joking.

'I won't. I wouldn't even know how. But you promise me one thing. Promise you won't spill a glass of anything down *my* dress.'

They both laughed, but Angel was surprised, even shocked and hurt, when Kiki announced that under no circumstances could Angel be Angel Devlin on the marquee.

'But it's my name,' she protested.

'One Devlin is quite sufficient. Two Devlins are confusing.'

'How about the Lane sisters? They all had the same name.' She had always adored Rosemary Lane, had gone to see all her movies.

'True. But only one – Rosemary – was really a star. Correct me if I'm wrong.'

Angel couldn't, but still she was close to tears. She couldn't bear it that she couldn't use her father's name. 'What name shall I use then?'

'You could use Edward's name. Angelique Whittier. Now that has a nice refined ring to it,' she said maliciously. What fun, she thought, to give Edward and her mother a jolt by spreading the Whittier name across Broadway's sordid lights.

'Oh, Kiki, you *are* mean . . . making me use Edward's

name.'

'Well, how about Mother's name, du Beaumond? You couldn't ask for a more beautiful, aristocratic name than that, could you? Angela du Beaumond! My God, it's so beautiful it sounds made up.'

Angela du Beaumond. It did sound kind of lovely. Still, it wasn't Daddy's name. And somehow, that made all the difference.

2

The reviews, though not ecstatic , were good. The play was amusing, the presentation attractive. Kiki Devlin was irrepressible, charming, and certainly a treat for the eyes. The brightest spot on the scene, however, was a newcomer, a shiny new star in the galaxy, the critics agreed – Angela du Beaumond, who looked like an angel and whose interpretation of the role of Vita was sensitive and illuminating. They predicted a sparkling future for the young woman.

Kiki read the reviews with mixed feelings. On one hand, a much lesser hand, she was proud of her ingenue sister. On the other, she was furious. Once again Angel had managed to upstage her – if not on the stage, in life. She swore to herself she would never appear in a play with Angel again.

Angel gazed again and again at the photo in *Look*. The picture showed her taking a curtain call, with a brief paragraph extolling the virtues of the new angel of the Broadway stage. The credit line mentioned Nick Dominguez as the photographer, and it was truly a lovely picture. Angel hoped that her father, wherever he was, saw it and was pleased.

Marie congratulated both her daughters on their performances. Rather than taking pleasure in her mother's complimentary words, Kiki was full of anger. How like her mother! When it was only she, Kiki, who had been acting, her mother disapproved. But now that Angel had joined her in the profession, Marie had suddenly decided that it wasn't so terrible to be an actress, it wasn't so déclassé, after all. Well, that figured, didn't it? After all, Angel couldn't do *anything* wrong.

During the next evening's performance, there was a small incident onstage. While drinking a glass of ginger ale, supposedly champagne, Kiki Devlin spilled the drink down Angela du Beaumond's bosom. Then, during curtain calls, Angela du Beaumond repeatedly stood in front of Kiki Devlin, blocking her from view.

That night they had a good fight about their evening 'performances', and then they had a good laugh, and then Angel confessed to Kiki that she had been seeing a man secretively for the last couple of years – all the time she had been in college.

'You sly little fox,' Kiki said. 'Who is he?'

'Dick Power.'

'Dick Power? I can hardly believe it. You *are* the sly one – carrying on behind my back.'

She had developed a crush on Richard Power when she had first met him at a club dance in Southampton when she had been just sixteen. The circumstances had been very romantic. It had been her first formal dance, it had been wartime, and Major Richard Power, ten years her senior, had been a very attractive glamorous figure in his pilot's uniform.

They first spoke over the buffet. There were only two portions of the Oysters Rockefeller left on the silver platter, and when both Angel and the major reached for them at the same time, he solemnly handed her one and took the last for himself. 'Good,' he said as he wolfed his down. 'Do you know why they're called Oysters Rockefeller?' he asked her gravely.

'Yes, I think I do,' she said earnestly. 'To convey the richness of the dish, oysters prepared in a very special,

100

opulent manner.'

'Wrong!' he said. 'They were first served this way in New Orleans. It seems that old John D. was coming to dine at a very famous restaurant there and the chef wanted to prepare a very special dish in the old pirate's honor. He racked his brain until he came up with a new recipe using a bed of spinach – most likely because spinach was green like Mr Rockefeller's money – and thus, Oysters Rockefeller.'

She gave him a sweet smile, looking up at him from under thick eyelashes. 'I'm sure you're right. But do you know that they're serving them incorrectly?'

He inclined his head toward her. 'How so?'

'Oysters Rockefeller are always served on a bed of rock salt, and these are not.'

He smiled in acquiescence of her knowledge and led her to the dance floor.

The second time they danced together was two years later – at the sisters' coming out party. Though Richard Power and the Devlin girls were scarcely acquainted, his name was on the list of eligible bachelors used by the social secretaries doing the invitations to the deb parties that year. (Although he was now the newly elected congressman from California, his family still had an estate in East Hampton.)

He asked Angel to dance after making a great to-do about putting out his cigar.

'You see how much I value you? A woman is only a woman, but a good cigar is a smoke.'

'Rudyard Kipling,' she said. '"The Betrothed."'

He laughed uproariously. 'Excellent! I'm glad to see you've been properly educated. I'm very much in favor of a good education for young women.'

'It produces great praise to a lady to spell well,' Angel said with a demure smile.

'Thomas Jefferson.'

'Very good, sir. I am pleased that a man who would be a political force in his country and a benefactor to mankind is well educated too.'

Again he was forced to laugh in appreciation of her quick wit.

She enjoyed the exchange, although she was not as smitten with him on that occasion as she had been when she was only sixteen. Actually, she had been preoccupied with the good-looking photographer who seemed to be wherever she was all evening. And comparing the physical attributes of the two men, she had to acknowledge that the photographer's dark looks appealed to her far more than Power's blond hair and blue eyes.

A year later, Angel and Dick Power met again.

He had just come off the grass courts of the Meadow Club and was on his way to the locker room. She had been watching him play and deliberating whether to call attention to herself. He *was* attractive with his height, his tanned body, the amazingly white teeth gleaming because he had won the match. And then, although she hadn't made any move to attract his notice, he stopped in front of her and said, 'You're lucky you're not in the city this minute.'

She took off her sunglasses and looked directly into the startlingly blue eyes. 'Why?'

He pointed to her cigarette. 'In 1908 a Sullivan Ordinance was passed forbidding women to smoke in New York City's public places under a penalty of fine, imprisonment, or both.'

'That's why I'm smoking *here* instead of there. In the 1923 Lady's Etiquette Guide it says: "One may smoke and chew gum while walking on a country lane, but never on a city thoroughfare."'

'If you promise not to chew gum, or tobacco for that matter, I may be persuaded to buy you a drink, provided you're old enough to drink legally.'

'I promise . . . and I am. Once you come out you're old enough to drink, you know.'

'In that case, I'll meet you in the bar.'

'And we've been seeing each other ever since,' Angel admitted to her sister. 'I've visited him in Washington, too, while I was at school. *Nobody* knew. Of course, I did stay at the Mayflower, and he never came up to my room. But now that I'm staying here with you I don't want to keep on sneaking around, keeping the whole thing a secret. And it's silly. After all, I'm an actress now, and there's no reason to.'

Kiki immediately advised her not to go to bed with him.

Agitated, Angel said, 'You of all people to say a thing like that? *You* go to bed with everyone. But anyhow, I haven't . . . because he hasn't even tried. I wonder why. Do you suppose I lack sex appeal? You know darn well I've never been to bed with anybody.'

'Well, it's high time you have, but never screw a man you might take seriously in the future. Suppose you decided to marry him. The fact that you haven't fucked yet gives an edge to the whole thing. And men like Dick Power screw every girl who passes their path that's willing, but then never marry the girls they screw. Generally speaking, if you go to bed with people who *matter*, then you've given away something. *If* you want to fuck, go to bed with people that don't matter, men you hardly know exist except for their bodies. A bellhop, a bartender, a cabbie. And afterward, forget they ever existed. If you jazz around with nobodies, then you're always fresh and tantalizing to the guys you run with socially.'

'So you *did* fool around with those townies when we were at Miss Chalmer's?'

'Of course I did, you little fool. How else was I supposed to get any practice? So remember that if you really like Dick Power, don't let him lay a glove on you. Everyone says he's practically a satyr. And if you do it with a satyr, you'll never be taken seriously. A satyr doesn't care who or what he screws, as long as he's screwing.'

Angel made a grimace of disgust. 'How do you know he's a satyr? Have you . . .'

First Kiki smiled knowingly, but then she said, 'Of course not.'

'Oh, I forgot,' Angel said with irritation. 'You couldn't have done it with him because he's a *somebody*.'

'Oh, that rule doesn't apply to me anymore. I'm a divorcée. Divorcées can do it with anybody. But, of course, if I were thinking of marrying somebody maybe I wouldn't. It all depends—'

'Oh, you make up your rules as you go along,' Angel said with disgust. 'Who can follow you? But those stories about Dick. What nonsense! People just like to gossip about him because he's rich and from a prominent family. And everybody likes to tell stories about his father, because he's a powerful man, a head of a movie studio. People are just jealous.'

'Listen to me. I can't personally swear whether the stories are true or not, but I've heard them in different places. When I was in *Love Lost* with Rita Glover . . . now there's a hot number for you . . . he showed up at her dressing-room door a couple of times. Not that that really means anything. Rita eats guys for breakfast and spits them out for lunch.' Then she smiled a bit maliciously. 'But if you're really serious about him I wouldn't say a thing to Marie. She'd have a fucking fit. She'd be very, very angry with her little Angel, and you don't want that now, do you?'

'Really, Kiki! I'm just dating him, you know. I'm not really serious about him. I really don't like blond men.'

'I know. You've always liked boys that looked like Daddy. I remember how even when you were a little girl you were always pulling tricks to push me out of the way so that you could be first with Daddy.'

Angel didn't answer her. She wouldn't give Kiki the satisfaction. Kiki was always saying things like that, that she first tried to curry favor with her father, and then, after he had gone out of their lives, with their mother.

Maybe Kiki was right. Maybe that was why, after over two years, she was still thinking about that silly photographer, just because . . . Well, if it were true she should have her head examined. Any other girl would be thrilled to have Dick Power as a suitor. She was being a fool, to keep thinking about a man she had seen only once, when she had Dick Power.

'Look, Kiki, it *isn't* serious,' she reiterated, 'but *if* it were, why would mother object? Dick *is* eligible – socially, financially.'

'Really, Angel. You *know* how Mother feels about Catholics, especially *Irish* Catholics.'

'But that's ridiculous. I'm still a Catholic myself, even if you and Mother aren't. She knows I've always intended to marry within the Church.'

'I guess she was always hoping that in the end you'd switch and come over with the rest of us. And you must know that although she hardly knows the Power family, she despises them all completely. She thinks old man Power is particularly common. And he's in the *movie business*, my dear. It's bad enough her daughters are in the theater, but the *movie business?* I repeat: go with him – just don't tell Marie!'

But Angel stopped seeing Dick. She hadn't realized that her mother would be so opposed to her dating him. But Kiki must be right. Her mother would probably be very much against it. Maybe she herself had realized that from the beginning – that was why she had dated him in secret all this time. She wouldn't risk incurring her mother's anger, her disfavor . . . she just couldn't.

3

Just about the same time as their play was due to close, Kiki got an offer from Hollywood. She had been offered a contract at Columbia and she decided to take it.

Hollywood had always been her goal, even though Marie would have conniptions. And while she would miss Angel – it had been fun living together – she was just as glad not to be in the same theater of operations, not after Angel had walked away with the glowing reviews.

Angel was disconsolate.

'How will I get along without you?' she asked plaintively.

Kiki laughed. 'Just terrifically, I think. Myles Porter wants you for his next play. He's crazy about you. And you can go on living here in my house. What more do you need?'

'You.'

Kiki was touched. 'Listen, if you want to come to Hollywood too, you're welcome. But only if you promise not to do films,' she joked.

Angel smiled. 'All right. If the time comes that I can't get along without you, I'll come out to Hollywood and I won't do films. I promise.'

'That's a good girl,' Kiki said, and kissed her.

'But I *will* miss you,' Angel said forlornly.

'Of course you will. You're supposed to. I *am* your best friend, and don't you forget it! We'll always be best friends, no matter where I am or where you are.'

Shortly before Kiki left for Hollywood, Angel found her making a list.

'What's that?' she asked.

Kiki looked up and winked.

'What's *that* supposed to mean?' Angel demanded.

'Remember when we were at Chalmer's and we made lists of the movie stars we'd most like to date?'

'Yes. Is that what you're doing now?'

'Don't be ridiculous. I was a teenager then. I'm in my twenties now, and this is a list of the movie stars I most want to *fuck!*'

Angel giggled. 'Kiki! How awful of you! Let me see.' She made a grab for the list, but Kiki held it out of reach.

'No! First you make *your* list, and then, and only then, we'll compare.'

'All right.' Angel sat down, and for an hour she pondered, scribbled, and scratched out. Finally she said, 'I have mine ready.'

'Okay, let's have it.' She began to read aloud from Angel's. 'Oh, my God! Bing Crosby? Gary Cooper! Ugh! I've always hated him. William Holden? Well, he's not terrible, but he's certainly no virgin's dream.'

'Listen, if you're going to scoff at every one of my selections . . .'

'Well, can I help it if you've picked the marshmallows of all time? Alan Ladd. For Christ's sake. He's pretty tough, but my God, he's positively *tiny!* Paul Henreid . . . Van Heflin . . . I must say, you've got the weirdest tastes.'

Angel snatched her list back from Kiki's hands. 'That's all. I'm not letting you read another name. Now give me yours.'

'Uh-uh. I only read . . . let's see . . . six of yours, so you only get to hear six of mine.'

'How many are on your list altogether? Sixty?'

'Very funny. Are you ready?'

'Panting.'

'Clark Gable . . .'

'I might have known.'

'What does *that* mean?'

'Everybody always said that Daddy was the image of Gable.'

Kiki was nettled. 'Is that so? Do you want to hear the rest or not?'

'Please. Do go on.'

'Errol Flynn, Gilbert Roland, Charles Boyer, Laurence Olivier, Ronald Colman, Louis Jourdan . . . there, that makes seven. I gave you an extra one. Why are you staring at me like that?'

'With the exception of Louis Jourdan, and maybe Olivier, every one of those men has a mustache, and all of them are dark-haired and swarthy. Kiki, you say I want men who look like Daddy but that's what you've picked!'

'So what of it?' Kiki snapped.

'Kiki,' Angel said sadly, 'you *can't* make love to your own father.'

'You bitch!' Kiki snarled. 'And what kind of men did you pick? Every one the *opposite* of Daddy, which means just one thing to me.'

'Yes? Don't stop now,' Angel said through clenched lips.

'You're *afraid* of what you feel. You're afraid of committing incest!'

'What a hateful thing to say! God, but you're insufferable. And so utterly tasteless. I'm glad you're going to Hollywood. That's where you belong, with all the other phonies and bleached blonds.'

'Bleached!' Kiki practically shrieked. 'You've known me all my life and my hair's always been the same shade. You're really reaching.'

'Oh, am I? *Mother* thinks you're touching it up, too, so there!'

'So you've done it again, have you? Turned Mother against me one more time.'

'That's a lie, I've *never* tried to turn Mother against you.'

Kiki was quiet now. 'Oh, Angel, you have – over and over again. Consciously and subconsciously. And I think that's the saddest thing of all. We're practically fatherless, you and I . . . and Marie's all we have, you and I . . .'

There were tears in both sister's eyes, and they fell into each other's arms, ashamed of all the mean, ugly things they had said to each other.

'We have to stick together, Angel. Even when I'm far away in Hollywood.'

But, even in Kiki's arms, Angel couldn't stop thinking of what Kiki had said, that she was afraid of committing incest. It was a terrible thing to say, and she wasn't sure that she could ever forgive her. Even if Kiki

108

were right, and God knows, maybe she was . . . hadn't she gone with Dick Power all that time, and he certainly was different from their father . . . in all possible ways. And then, even though she had felt content in their relationship, she had given him up, just because Kiki had said her mother would not approve. Was Kiki right about that too? That she was always trying to curry favor with their mother? What kind of person was she? Did she do everything just because of what other people said? Why couldn't she think for herself?

She decided then and there that from that time on, she, herself, would make her own decisions, no matter what her mother and Kiki thought. If she wanted to date Dick Power, she would! How could anyone know better than she what was good for her? And Kiki was going to Hollywood, no matter what her mother said. Kiki always did what she wanted, and in the end, Kiki always had more fun.

Tearfully, she kissed Kiki good-bye and watched her board the train. Oh, she would miss her! Lucky Kiki! She was going to have such a good time in Hollywood. Already she had a million people calling her, anticipating her arrival there. And she would be spending the evenings alone in Kiki's house, missing her, being lonely and frightened at being alone. But she didn't have to be alone and frightened – she could call Dick Power in Washington. If anyone made her feel secure, it was Dick Power. He was a reassuring kind of person . . . he knew so definitely what he was about.

PART FIVE

New York
1950–1951

'After *City Girl*, the play that the girls were in together, they went their separate ways. Kiki went to Hollywood and Angel stayed in New York. I don't know which one was more successful. Hollywood and Broadway are so different, you know. Kiki went to work for Harry Cohn at Columbia and did romantic comedy. I always thought of Kiki as a Connie Bennett type, or a Carole Lombard – elegant romantic comedy. Anyhow, that's the way she was received. As a successor to poor Carole, who went down in that plane during the war. Rumor had it that she succeeded Carole in another department, too, with Gable.

'She *was* a terror. The stories that circulated about her. I didn't print half the ones that went around. Why, if they were all to be believed, one would have to credit Kiki with bedding half the leading men in this town. I befriended her and tried to caution her that she was burning her candle at both ends. And that she would do better to get her beauty sleep instead of staying up all night at Ciro's or doing the cha-cha at the Grove.

'But she certainly knew how to get her name in print. She was always a self-promoter, as they say these days. She and I were the best of friends, and she always called me first before she did anything newsworthy.

'Angel, on the other hand, was more secretive about her romances, whom she was seeing. For a while she went with the director, Myles Porter, but most quietly. It wasn't all over the columns. Then she started seeing Richard Power, the congressman from our own California, *publicly*. Only she and the congressman knew they had been seeing each other for some time in secret, even before she went on the stage.'

113

1

Kiki arrived in Hollywood in style. She had a house waiting for her – a rental on Benedict above Sunset – and a host of people lined up to entertain her, friends from the East. She was wined and feted, photographed and interviewed, and taken out on publicity dates to all the right restaurants and clubs. All she needed to be a real star was that first picture.

She went to see Harry Cohn, the head of Columbia. Conscious of her star image, she wore white silk and fox for the appointment. Harry, she had been told, liked to see his stars dress like stars, and she was eager to impress him so that he would give her a really great picture and an important male co-star to launch her career properly.

But Harry only tossed a pillow to her.

'What's that for?' she asked.

'I don't want you to get housemaid's knee.'

It took Kiki a full minute to comprehend what it was he wanted; then she threw the pillow back, hitting him in the face. 'Mr Cohn, I've heard about you, but this time you've made a mistake.'

'Miss Devlin, I've heard about *you* and your old man, and Harry Cohn doesn't make mistakes.'

'Mr Cohn, you'd better get something straight. I already have a contract with your studio; I'm not one of your little beauty-contest winners from East Texas, and Kiki Devlin always chooses the pricks she sucks.'

'Miss Devlin, you get one thing straight. Rita Hayworth you're not.' But he did not further pursue the matter.

She began work on a picture with Bill Holden, who was a very nice man, an attractive one, and a pleasure to work with. Unfortunately, he was not on her list but on Angel's.

When a friend, Susan Davis, asked her if she would like to go to a private party on Mulholland, Kiki asked who would be there.

'Brando. He's not a big star yet, but he is very handsome.'

'I already know Bud from New York, and I pass.'

'Well, the party is at Errol Flynn's and they say Gable is going to be there too.'

'Really? In that case you can count on me.'

After all, both Flynn and Gable *were* on her list.

After everybody else went home, Susan ended up with Gable and Kiki with their host. But while Errol's bedroom ceiling was covered with mirrors, which was very sexy, Errol himself was so filled with booze that his performance suffered and he had to take a sniff of something before he could continue. And then, just before he passed out cold, he muttered, 'Next time we'll do better, old dear.'

Old dear indeed! Where, oh where, was that smoldering steamy passion she had envisioned? Next time it would be Gable for sure, she promised herself. And she always got what she wanted.

Gable was something else again. He *was* the dream come true. Why, he really did cock that eyebrow, his eyes really did crinkle up when he smiled, and oh, that rakish, devil-may-care grin. His gaze was really sardonic, and the whole effect was as dashing as anything she could remember. He *was* the King, and he *had* headed her list.

Kiki fell a little bit in love with Clark, and she swore to herself that she would never ever reveal to anyone that the King was not absolutely regal in bed.

After Beebie Tyler wrote in her column that a newcomer to the silver screen, Kiki Devlin of the New York stage, reminded her of Lombard, duplicating her special brand of comedic elegance, Harry Cohn cleverly cast Kiki in a remake of one of Lombard's pictures and tried to borrow Gable from MGM to play opposite her.

'Who would get top billing?' Kiki asked Harry.

'Jesus, *you're* screwing the guy. You tell me – who comes first?'

Harry was so vulgar, she reflected, but he *was* funny.

Still, it was just as well they weren't able to get Clark. She could never feel close to a man who insisted on having his name above hers. And if the picture bombed she would never be able to forgive him.

Soon they were spending much of their free time together, and while Clark called her Ma, Kiki realized that part of her attraction for him was her society background. And while she secretly yearned to be at LaRue's or Ciro's, she really tried to seem gung-ho about riding, fishing, and hunting out at Clark's spread in Encino. And when he proposed that they officially become Ma and Pa, she took a long time before finally turning him down. She was more in love with him than she had ever been with anybody, and it would have been *such* a coup to marry the legendary Gable. She wanted to say yes very much, but something held her back. She told herself that it was that she couldn't take a back seat to anybody, and with Clark it would always be that she reminded him so much of Carole.

But they parted friends, which was lovely. She couldn't have borne it if they had not. It was all so bittersweet. They kissed good-bye, and it was a real movie kiss. First he cocked his eyebrow, then he crinkled up his eyes, and then he fixed her with a sardonic amused look. The kiss lasted for at least two minutes, and Kiki wiped away a tear or two.

She went back to her list. Olivier was out of the country, and Colman, while attractive, was really out of the question. She thought about Boyer, and then, laughing uproariously, she thought about Bill Holden. What a funny joke on Angel! And after Holden, why not Cooper?

116

2

Kiki was in town doing a publicity tour for *Homeward Bound* when Angel broke the news to both her mother and sister that she was becoming formally engaged to Dick Power and that she was retiring from the stage, temporarily anyway.

Kiki thought she was crazy to give up her career for a man – any man.

'But you *always* wanted to be an actress and I only wanted to be one because you did. I really don't care that much. Honestly. I'm going to devote myself to being a helpmeet to Dick . . . and to being a mother, I hope.'

Marie was furious, not about Angel's temporary retirement from the stage, but certainly about the engagement. 'I should have nipped this thing in the bud but I surely thought you would have more sense than to take Dick Power seriously. Don't you see that he is nothing more than an ambitious upstart? You only have to look at that family of his. I knew them when they still lived here – before that awful, coarse, common father of his became one of those awful movie moguls. His reputation was always dubious, a completely unethical man. And the apple probably doesn't fall far from the tree. That man! Do you think he would permit his son to marry you if you weren't Edward's stepdaughter, for one thing, and one of the few socially impeccable Catholic girls around, for another? And besides, you have just the right amount of public visibility as a stage actress. Politicians need that visibility. But of course you have to retire from the stage and assume the image of the perfect wife. Can't you see beyond the nose on your face? It's not *you* they want – it's your image!'

'It's no wonder Kiki talks the way she does, Mother. You and she say the same things, only you use different words. But you have the wrong conception of Dick. When you get to know him better, you'll see. He's really warm. And he knows everything. He's steady and strong, and I feel safe with him. I know he'll take care of me.'

Marie made a gesture of impatience. 'I only hope it's not that professional Irish politician's grin and that blond wavy hair and those blue eyes that have duped you into thinking you're getting something you're not. You gaze into those eyes like some lovesick dove and see warmth and security. I see ambition, greed, and design.'

'Greed? Design? What nonsense, Mother! I don't have a penny! Nor do I have any power. What can I possibly provide except my love?'

'I've told you – your stepfather's good name and standing. Your religion. And your other assets – your good looks, your breeding, taste, and your publicity value as a former stage actress.'

'If those qualities will make me a better wife then I'm glad I have them. Besides, Mother, you are always talking about suitability in choosing mates. Why do you object to Dick seeking that very same suitability?'

'Because I know *you*. And I want you to be happy.' Marie softened her tone. 'If you're to be happy, it's essential for you to have someone who loves you very, very much. Maybe it is not terribly necessary for Kiki, but it is vital for you. Oh, my dear, you need a *poet*, not a politician.'

Then Marie threw reserve to the winds. '*My* mother warned me against marrying your father, and I lived to regret not listening to her.'

'Oh, Mother! But don't you see? I'm not marrying somebody like Daddy at all!'

Exactly. Marie was afraid that she saw all too well.

To a certain extent, Kiki agreed with her mother. It was

obvious to everyone but her sister, who was still the naïve schoolgirl, why Dick Power was after her. But if he was what Angel wanted at the moment, she should have him. Kiki believed in instant gratification and the devil take the hindmost, and there was always divorce. And while she thought Angel was a fool to give up the stage for marriage, it was with a certain relief that she viewed Angel's retirement. She loved Angel but she couldn't say she was really crazy about Angel's success on the stage. It wouldn't have been too long before Angel decided to go to the Coast to try her luck in the movies, and now that it looked like Columbia was not going to pick up her option . . .

'You can always get a divorce, so it's really no big deal. I mean, this is not the Dark Ages.'

'Divorce?' Angel shrieked. 'You know my views on that.'

'Darling Angel, every Catholic says that before the fact. When you really want or need a divorce, you'll feel differently. All your high-minded principles won't mean a heap of *merde*.'

3

When it came to the planning of the wedding, everyone involved wanted different things. Dick Power wanted to please his father, and his father wanted the wedding in California, where it made political sense for a congressman with his eye on the governor's mansion to take a wife with all the local publicity and exposure this would generate. A big church wedding in California for six or seven hundred guests was what he had in mind. As quickly as that plan was expressed, Marie vetoed it. A bride was married near her parents' home. Anyone familiar with the proper way of doing things knew *that*.

Liam Power gave in gracefully enough on that point, then very politely suggested that if the wedding were

119

to be held in the East, why not St Patrick's Cathedral, with a reception at one of the hotels on the park? Or if Marie didn't like the idea of a New York City hotel, why not the Hamptons, where both families had homes?

Marie vetoed both these ideas. She and Edward would not consider any other place but Stoningham Manor for both the ceremony and the reception. She loved the idea of a garden ceremony, where they would be surrounded by all the beauty of Stoningham's oppulent grounds and nature's own fragrance. She did so dislike the musty odors of churches.

Liam Power was outraged. A Catholic wedding not in a church? He had never heard of such a thing.

Marie made him one concession: she would allow him his choice of the bishop or cardinal or whoever to perform the ceremony.

All Angel really cared about at this point was the notion that had become something of an obsession with her, that her father – her real father, and not Edward – walk down the aisle with her and give her away.

'Oh, please, Mother, please!' she begged. 'I'll never ask anything else of you the rest of my life.'

'Even if I could contemplate such a thing, I wouldn't have the slightest idea where to reach your father. I really don't know how you can even ask such a thing of me. I think it's very selfish of you, Angel, to open old, painful wounds. Your father betrayed me and abandoned all three of us, you and Kiki as well as me. It was I who fought for a place in society for you both. Besides, Edward has earned the right to give you away. He has taken the place of your father, he has given you a home all these years, he has educated you, and he *is* paying the bills for this wedding.'

Angel was so distraught by her mother's adamant refusal she was almost tempted to scream, 'Oh, yes, Edward brought us up . . . paid our bills . . . and let my sister suck his cock!' But of course she didn't.

But Angel did have an idea. Liam Power! Perhaps he would help her locate her father, would welcome the opportunity to strike back at her mother for refusing to hold the wedding first in California, and then at St Patrick's. Then, once Rory Devlin was there already, her mother would not be able to keep him from performing his fatherly duty.

She called Liam Power in California, and he practically gnashed his teeth in frustration. He would have loved to humiliate Marie. But he couldn't do it. It would only boomerang. Rory Devlin was bad news, could hurt Dick politically. So he explained to Angel that while he sympathized with her in her desire to have her father present, he could not be instrumental in distressing her mother, who was a fine woman, and it behooved them all to consider her feelings. And he hoped that Angel herself would consider the kind of publicity her father's presence could generate. She had to think of them all.

Still, Angel would not give up. She knew she couldn't go to Dick for help, his father's refusal precluded Dick's assistance. But Kiki was staying in New York now that her contract with Columbia had not been renewed, while her new agent was trying to negotiate a contract with another studio, and Angel just knew Kiki would want her father there as much as she herself did.

Kiki's eyes filled at the suggestion. Oh, yes, she wanted her father to come to the wedding, and she would put detectives on his trail at once. 'Don't worry,' she told Angel, 'we'll find him. And what fun to see the look on everyone's face when he shows up! And hell! I'll just bet seeing Daddy again will light a fire in old Marie's vj! Believe me, Marie's old vj could *use* a bit of warming up after all these years with Edward. Just picture Edward, the old cocksucker. And Liam Power! Guaranteed stroke time! Oh, we'll fix them all. I'm going to get Rory here if it's the last fucking thing I do!'

Ten days later, Kiki triumphantly informed Angel that she had located their father. She had actually talked to him on the phone, and what was more, he had promised to be present at the nuptials to give his younger daughter away. 'And, Angel, he cried! Our daddy cried!'

They fell into each other's arms, weeping.

'Thank you, Kiki. I knew that you wouldn't let me down,' Angel whispered.

Kiki decided not to tell Angel that she had done it as much for herself as for her baby sister – maybe more so.

4

. As the wedding was to take place early in August, the month of July was devoted to the preparations as well as to assembling the trousseau. Kiki turned down an offer to do summer stock, she claimed, to be available to help Angel shop, thereby freeing Marie to concentrate on the wedding itself.

'I really want to be in on the shopping without Marie along so I can compensate for the deficiencies in the budget she and Edward have allotted you.'

'But I can't let you help pay for my trousseau!'

'Are you mad! I don't intend paying for anything myself. I'm going along to see that you *charge* more than the puny amount they've allowed you.'

'Mother says the budget is more than adequate.'

'Pooh! I just knew Edward would become parsimonious once the blow jobs stopped.'

'Please, Kiki! Don't remind me of that. Besides, I don't think it's Edward. I think it's Mother's sense of propriety.'

'You mean Marie's acquired Puritan ethic? It's really too bad she stopped counting the beads. She was less of a pain in the ass when she was a Catholic, don't you think?'

Early in July the Ula Gallery on Madison announced an exhibition of photographs by a virtually unknown photographer, one Nicholas Dominguez. The exhibition was entitled 'The Debutante as Actress.'

News of the show reached Kiki's ears quickly, and she raced over to see it before she mentioned it to Angel. After she had carefully reviewed it, she told Angel about it. 'Don't go into shock, sweetie, but *you* are the whole exhibit!'

'Me? But I don't understand. How can it be an exhibition of pictures of me? I never posed for any pictures.' Then, although she knew it was impossible, she asked, 'There aren't any . . . nudes . . . or anything, are there?'

Kiki looked at her strangely. 'How can you ask a question like that if you never posed for any pictures? Are you sure you don't know anything about this?'

'Of course I'm sure. I don't know why I asked that question. I just thought that if I didn't know about any of the other pictures, well, maybe . . . I don't know.' She was close to tears.

'Well, I'm sorry to say that there aren't any nudes. But there *is* one sort of half naked. You're wearing the bottom of a bathing suit, your back is nude, and you're holding a towel to your front. Now, you tell me, Angel du Beaumond Devlin, where did *that* picture come from?'

'I don't know. I just don't know,' Angel agonized. 'Who is Nicholas Dominguez? Wait . . . That was the photographer's name on that lovely picture of me in *Look*. You remember, the one of me taking the curtain call in *City Girl*. Oh my goodness!' Her hand flew to her mouth. 'I have a feeling – I just bet he's the same photographer who was at our debut. The one that took the picture of me that was in *Whisper*.

'How do you know that?'

'I told you, it's just a guess.'

'I think maybe you *know* him and you're just feigning all this innocence.'

'No!'

She went with Kiki to see the show. Kiki had made it

sound as if all New York was atwitter over the show, but that afternoon the gallery was almost deserted. A hot summer day wasn't exactly the busiest time, specially for a not very exciting collection of photographs of a very young actress. There was a photograph of her riding a horse, another on a tennis court, another in evening dress. Many showed her onstage, endowed with a presence she was sure she did not possess. One photograph showed her at the ballet, smiling at the performance, but managed to make her appear the star performer. The one picture that Kiki had mentioned – the one with her bare back exposed, a towel shielding her front – was perhaps the most artistic. It must have been taken when she was sunbathing in Southampton, when she had assumed she had privacy.

She was bewildered. Why had this Dominguez chosen her as the subject of a whole show? And why had the gallery chosen to exhibit it? She couldn't believe that the general public would find it of much interest.

'Look, Kiki, there's one of us walking in Central Park. Did you ever notice a man with a camera following us?'

'No. If I had, I would have turned around and posed. What wonderful publicity this is,' Kiki said with a touch of envy. *Lucky Angel*. Why *had* Dominguez chosen Angel instead of her as the subject of his show? For that matter, why had Dominguez chosen Angel rather than herself at their coming-out party? Angel *did* have her air of vulnerability, of innocence. She looked at Angel speculatively. What *was* that particular quality Angel possessed that engaged people so?

The more Angel looked at the pictures, the more she was entranced. The pictures *were* lovely, and somehow she felt that they had been taken with some kind of affection, with care to make her look better even than her best – to make her look like some kind of princess.

Then Kiki said irritably, 'You really ought to sue

him. Only that would give him more publicity than he deserves. And I suppose you do sort of qualify as a celebrity – *technically* you were on the stage – so he does have a legal right.'

'What do you mean, *technically*?' Angel asked, dumbfounded. Sometimes Kiki was so irritating.

'Well, you were on the stage for so short a time, and you *are* retiring . . .'

'It's all academic, Kiki, I haven't the faintest desire to sue him. I *love* the pictures.'

'Really?' Kiki asked. 'I would think the whole thing would make you feel creepy, to have that weird man following you around.'

'No, I can't say that it does. And what makes you use the word *weird*? I think he's a very fine photographer.'

'Angel Devlin, I swear, I think this whole perverted thing is giving you a kick! I think you're pleased by this whole vulgar display! As if he were a secret admirer who has made a public declaration of an infatuation!'

'Oh, come on, Kiki! Don't tell me you wouldn't be pleased to have a whole exhibition devoted to a display of you!'

'No, I wouldn't. I think the whole thing is cheap and vulgar.'

But Angel didn't quite believe her.

'I think I'd like to meet Nick Dominguez. I think I'll leave a message for him with the gallery.'

A picture of Dominguez, as he appeared at their coming-out party, dark, handsome, smoldering, flashed through Kiki's mind. 'Don't you dare do such a thing. It would be so . . .' She searched for a word. Finally she said, 'I'm sure Marie would think it disgustingly indiscreet of you to acknowledge this man's existence.'

Torn between her desire to meet Nick Dominguez and Kiki's admonitions, Angel decided to let the whole matter drop. Later, years later, she would think how different her life might have been if she had not listened to Kiki.

Still, she returned to the gallery alone, many times, as if she were seeking some clue to the pictures themselves – the reason why Nick Dominguez had assembled the collection in the first place.

5

Together, the sisters covered every store on Fifth Avenue and Fifty-seventh Street. Gucci, Bendel, Saks, Bergdorf's, Cartier's as well as Tiffany's. Angel's engagement ring had come from Tiffany's and Kiki would have liked to trade it in for another. She found its diamond too small and its fishtail setting gauche. The least Dick could have done, she felt, was to have had *her* accompany him so that Angel wouldn't have ended up with a too-small, too-tacky ring. But as her mother said, what could you expect of parvenus?

They concluded each shopping trip at some fashionable bar, and that afternoon they decided on the Oak Room at the Plaza. Running up the steps, they were startled to see a tall, dark-haired man with a camera poised in front of them. There was a flash of white teeth as he smiled. Dominguez! Why, he looks exactly as he did that night at the coming-out party, Angel thought. Why did she expect him to look different?

'Get lost!' Kiki hissed angrily, and his smile quickly faded. He didn't look at Kiki but at Angel, who stood frozen in place. His expression was so strange, she thought, almost entreating. She wanted to go up to him, thank him for the lovely exhibition, but she couldn't move, and Kiki pulled her along, shoved her through the revolving door.

They were being seated at a table in the bar when Kiki spied a silver blonde sitting with Earl Wilson. 'It's L. C. Potter. Let's go over and sit with them and dish the latest dirt. Wilson isn't all that spicy, but L. C. Potter knows the raunchiest stories in town!'

'No.' Angel shook her head.

'For God's sake, will you stop acting so shook by that schnook? He isn't *anybody*, I tell you. He's one lousy photographer in a world full of photographers. Only he's a sick one. And if you pay any attention to him you're even sicker. Don't get some crazy notion in your head about him just because he looks like your father. God knows, he could be our half brother, what with Daddy's reputation as a lover. And where would you be then?'

'Kiki, if you don't stop this nonsense this instant I'm walking out of here and I'm never speaking to you again!'

'Relax, will you? I'm just trying to save you from yourself. Besides he can't possibly be our half brother. I've had him checked out. He was born in the Bronx in 1927, and I doubt if Daddy ever heard of the Bronx.'

'You had him checked out?' Angel's voice was incredulous. 'Why did you do that?'

'Oh, just in case you were interested in him.'

'Kiki, I'm engaged—'

'Engagements have been known to be broken. I told you, I don't want you getting ideas about this creep just because you think he's a reincarnation of your father.'

'Kiki, will you stop? I am not getting ideas about this man, although he *is* a very attractive man. As for him looking like our father, you and I really don't have any idea what Daddy looks like these days, do we?'

Was Kiki really worried that she, Angel, would have an affair or something with Nick Dominguez? And if so, was it concern or jealousy? She never knew with Kiki. Maybe Kiki herself didn't know what motivated her.

They ordered their drinks, and Kiki said, 'If we can stop talking about that nerd for a while, I have a bit of news for you.'

'Daddy's not coming to the wedding!' Angel cried. 'Is that it?'

'No, calm down. My news has nothing to do with Daddy. And it's not bad news, either. You see, I want a sable coat, and I don't want to have to buy it myself!'

Angel stared at her. Kiki always said if one wanted a new fur coat, one should get oneself a new husband. The waiter brought the drinks, and she drank hers almost completely down in one swallow. 'You're telling me that you're getting married? Is that it?'

Kiki sucked her olive and nodded her head.

'Oh my goodness. Who is it this time? Why haven't you said anything before?'

'I didn't want to upstage you.'

'Oh, you! Who is it?'

'The reason I haven't said anything was because I didn't make up my mind until yesterday.'

'Who is it?'

'Guess. First clue – tall.'

'Kiki!'

'All right. Second clue – blond, blue-eyed.'

'Oh great. Only half the male population of America.'

'Half the male population isn't stunningly gorgeous.'

'Is that a clue too?'

'Bet your ass.'

'All right. You can stop playing games. I don't want to know and we won't talk about it. Did you really like that black satin dress with the pegged skirt? Do you think the pegged style is going to last?'

'It better had. I bought one almost exactly like it for my wedding dress. In champagne satin. Mary, Mother of Jesus! It's my second time around and I'm still not getting married in a proper wedding dress.'

'I believe I said I don't want to know who he is. That means I don't care to discuss your wedding, or your wedding dress, either.'

'All right.' Kiki laughed. 'He's an actor and he lives in Hollywood.'

'Is he what you'd call a movie star kind of actor?'

'If we were playing Twenty Questions I'd say yes and no.'

'Kiki, I'm going to kill you, and then you'll never get married at all.'

'Do you care to ask another question?'

'Is he a big movie star?'

'You're getting hot. I'd say he's the *biggest!*'

Angel thought a few moments. 'Brad Cranford?'

'Right with Eversharp! How did you guess?'

'My goodness. Brad Cranford!'

'We're shooting down to Mexico to get hitched day after tomorrow. And you, Angel du Beaumond, are going to be my maid of honor.'

'You want me to go to Mexico with you?'

'Why not? I'm going to stand up for you, so you have to repay the favor.'

'Can Dick come too?'

'If he won't act stuffy.'

'Dick's not stuffy,' Angel said, hurt.

'Oh, isn't he? Just a little bit?'

'No!'

'Okay then. He can come if he wants to.'

'But why are you going to Mexico? Why can't you have a wedding here? A real wedding like me. Oh, I know! Why don't we have a double wedding? If we really hurry we can—'

'Oh no! I'm not sharing the limelight with you again. Look what happened the last time I appeared with you. You got all the rave notices. Besides, who could bear to go through a wedding with Marie? Wait till she hears I'm marrying Brad Cranford. She'll have a stroke. No credentials at all, other than being America's big glamour puss. Anyhow, if I wait until August I might change my mind. And I don't really want to. I've been single for years, or so it seems. This is going to be Hollywood's dream marriage. We should get oodles of publicity. We both have the same agent and we're both going to be working for the same studio. Maybe we'll even make pictures together – Hollywood's dream couple co-stars. Of course, I'll have top billing. Brad's a gentleman.'

'You never told me you signed a new contract with a new studio.'

'Our agent just finished negotiating the contract. And wait till you hear this bit of "small world, isn't it?" The studio's none other than PIF!'

'Power International Films?'

'Yes. Isn't that a fucking riot?'

'But nobody said anything. Dick didn't.'

'I just signed the contract a couple of days ago.'

'You met with Dick's father?'

'No. I signed the contract here in New York. But I'm sure Dick's father knows that his studio signed me up. I doubt if anything happens at that studio that Daddy Power doesn't have his finger in the middle of.'

'I'm sure of that.' Angel sighed. Then she brightened. 'Now that it's definite you're going back to Hollywood it means that we will be together lots of the time. When I'm not in Washington, I'll be in California too.'

'Oh, goody! I'm so thrilled!' Kiki said, sounding anything but.

Angel was hurt. 'Don't you want us to be together?'

'I was only teasing, for God's sake. Of course I do. But just make me one promise. Don't decide to give up your career again and become a movie star too.'

'Kiki!'

'Well, can you blame me? It's enough that everyone is always saying "Angel is the sweet one" or "Angel is the smart one" or "Angel is the lady." And everyone knows that Marie prefers you to me.'

'And how about Daddy? *You* were always Daddy's girl. Isn't that what everyone in New Orleans used to say?'

Kiki smiled a little smile. 'Maybe. I guess.' Then she felt generous. 'But Daddy adored you. Remember how he called you his littlest angel.'

'Oh yes, I remember. Oh, Kiki, if only I could hear

him say it once more.'

'But you will, Angel baby. He's coming to your wedding. Haven't I arranged that for you?' *For both of us.*

'Oh, yes, darling, you have. I don't know what I would do without you.'

'You just remember you said that.'

'Oh, I will. So tell me your plans. Where will you be living?'

'Brad has a house on Rodeo Drive, right across the street from Beebie Tyler. Isn't that a riot? She'll be able to keep tabs on all our comings and goings – she'll have all the scoops on us. But the house is terribly decorated now – plastic roses, of all things. The first thing I'll have to do is redecorate. You can help me. The minute you arrive in Hollywood we'll redo my house, and then I'll help you do yours. And we'll entertain. Hollywood *is* parties, you know. Far more than here. Brad told me there are three social sets in town. There are the A's, the B's, and the C's. Well, I don't have to tell you who the C's are – you can imagine! The A's are the kind Marie might invite if she lived there. Gigi Anders's lived on the Coast and she says the A's are not the fun crowd. They're the stuffies. So I suppose the B's must be the fun people. We can't ask Brad, because between you and me, he's a bit of a stuffo himself. Do you know what his real name is? Alan Hopeberry. Isn't that a howl?'

'Have you gone to bed with him?'

'Of course, you silly baby. I told you, once you're a divorcée you can do *anything*. Besides, I had to make sure I wasn't going to end up with another queen, didn't I? Once it's a lark, but twice?'

'Are you madly in love with him, Kiki?'

'What kind of a dumb question is that? Of course I love him madly. What do they say? The first time you marry for money, the second time for love?'

Angel giggled. 'It's the other way around. The first time for love, the second for money.'

'Well, whatever. Anyhow, you can say I'm madly in

131

love with his money, and that covers all the territory.'

'Is he that rich?'

'Stinking. You can't be *numero uno* at the box office and not be rich. Still,' she added thoughtfully, 'I won't be as rich as you. You're marrying into one of the really boffo families.'

'But you have your own money. That's very important, I think.'

'My settlement from Tracy? Peanuts. And as for the money I've made myself, that's nothing to write home about.'

'But now you're going to be a big movie star!'

'And you're going to be the wife of the future Governor of California!'

'*Future* is the key word there. And it's still not the same thing as being somebody in your own right,' Angel said wistfully. 'You've always been somebody in your own right, Kiki.'

Kiki put her hand over hers. 'You'll be somebody in your own right, too. You'll see. *If* you don't let the Power boys overpower you.' She laughed at her pun.

But Angel didn't laugh. 'That *will* be a struggle, won't it?'

'You'll have to be strong. Like I will have to be in dealing with old man Power myself. After all, I will be working for him, and the word is that he's the biggest son of a bitch in a business that features them.'

'So far he's been very sweet to me.'

'Sure. So far you haven't challenged him.'

'God, I don't think I want to be there when you tell Mother.'

'*You're* going to tell Marie all about it when you get back from Mexico. Brad and I are taking a week in Acapulco, then Brad takes off for Italy. He's doing a picture there. But I'll join him. I don't have to report to the studio for a while yet.'

'You mean I have to come back here and face Mother all by myself while you're in Acapulco loving it up with Brad?'

'Well, you do have your way with Mother, don't you? Besides, Edward already knows. He'll help you break the news.'

'You told Edward?'

'Yes. I wanted him to do something about my money before the wedding. Put it in trust or in someone else's name or whatever. Edward knows what to do.'

'I don't understand.'

'One has to be practical, no matter how much one is in love. How do I know how long I'll be married to Brad? California does have this community-property thing. *Comprendez-vous?* When we do get divorced I'll get half of his, and if I don't have anything in my name I can't very well give him half of mine, now can I? I'm not about to marry in haste and go broke in leisure. And just in case I'm not around when you're ready to divorce Dickie boy, let me—'

'I won't even contemplate such a thing!'

'Oh, okay, but if you do decide to contemplate, see me first. Anyhow, the first thing we must do when I get back from Mexico is haul you off to Maggie Sanger's.'

'But I'm a . . . you can't get one of those things if you haven't . . . can you?'

'You mean old Dickey still hasn't even dipped a finger?'

'Kiki, if you're going to talk dirty, I'm leaving!'

'Oh, hush. In that case, before we hit Sanger's we'll take you to a doctor to be cut and stretched.

'Are you crazy?'

'Many young women who haven't enjoyed the advantage of the back seat of a jalopy resort to the skillful fingers of the gynecologist. A poor substitute, I must admit, but if the doctor breaks your cherry it will facilitate matters on your wedding night, and I have the feeling you'll need all the facilities you can get. Seriously, Angel, it's a good idea – it'll make the first time easier and more fun. And then you can get your diaphragm right off, which is important before the fact, not after. I'm not letting you get pregnant the minute you're violated and start dropping babies like a brood cow.'

'Dick is counting on a large family.'

'For political reasons? In that case, you'd better let him give birth for you. Otherwise, your tits will dangle to your knees and they'll use your stretch marks for road maps.'

Angel shook her head. 'You get more impossible by the minute. But I'm not getting a diaphragm. We're going to use the rhythm method.'

'May the saints preserve us! All I can say is that I hope you and Dick always sing in key.'

After another round of drinks, Angel began to giggle.

'What's so funny?' Kiki demanded.

'You are.'

'Oh, really. How so?'

'Remember how you said *I* picked men that were totally unlike Daddy because I was afraid of committing mental incest?'

'So?'

'Look who *you're* marrying, after having actually refused the great Gable. Brad Cranford! We're both marrying men with blond hair and blue eyes!'

Kiki was annoyed. She couldn't have Angel having the last word, at her expense.

'I was wondering about that myself. If it were really true. Because there you are, with this absolutely manic attraction for that dark devilish presence, Nick Dominguez. I almost think you'd be ready to break your engagement to Dick just to throw youself into his arms . . .'

Angel immediately stopped laughing. 'Kiki, you're so mean. Besides, I think you're drunk.'

When they had entered the hotel it had been late afternoon but the sun had still been shining. Now, as they came out on Central Park South and waited for the doorman to get them a cab, twilight was upon them. Angel's eyes darted about, searching for a sign of Nick Dominguez. She didn't want his camera to catch her off guard, she told herself. But there was no sight of him.

Her eyes met Kiki's. Did Kiki know what she was thinking? Kiki always seemed to. But did Kiki know that she was experiencing, so ridiculously, a letdown because there was no sight of Dominguez anywhere?

6

The papers were full of the elopement – it was superstar Brad Cranford's first marriage. Beebie Tyler had the story first. Kiki had been sure to call her immediately after the ceremony. Beebie would never have forgiven either Brad or her if she didn't have the scoop, and Beebie, Kiki knew, could be an enemy if her fur wasn't properly stroked. Beebie could make or break a career.

Marie Whittier did not read Tyler, but it was difficult to ignore all the newspapers that carried the story after Tyler's syndicated column featured it. When the evening news on television announced it as well, Marie switched the set off in disgust. The news broadcasts were the only thing on television she watched, she often boasted, and now even the news had betrayed her. Then the phones started ringing with congratulatory calls, and Marie turned to Angel with heavy irony. 'With your wedding only a week or so away, it seems Kiki has managed to steal the spotlight from you.'

Angel only looked at her mother, but when the full comprehension of the implication hit her, she gasped. 'You make it sound as if Kiki did it just for that reason!'

'Didn't she? She marries "the most popular movie

star in America" – I believe that's the expression used in the tabloids – just a few days before your own marriage to a mere congressman.'

'But Kiki's being going with Brad Cranford for almost a year. That's what she said.'

'Well, your wedding will be rather anticlimactic after all this fuss wouldn't you say? It makes one wonder why Kiki has chosen to legitimize her tawdry little affair at this precise moment. And how clever of her to elope – she's gotten so much more publicity this way.'

Marie left Southampton for Stoningham Manor for the final week's preparations for the wedding, and Angel went back to New York City to await her father's arrival and Kiki's return from Acapulco.

Angel found it hard to believe that her mother was right about Kiki's reasons for marrying Brad Cranford now, but she didn't have time to think about it. She already had enough anxieties to cope with. Getting married wasn't a completely uplifting occasion – too much preparation, too many details; the war going on between her mother and Liam Power as they dickered daily over the phone over guests that Power wanted to include. There was even the anxiety she felt when she contemplated her wedding night. Would Dick, with all his experience, find her adequate? The only aspect of it all that soothed her was her father's imminent arrival.

She wouldn't allow anyone to dispel her good feelings about that, not even Dick, who had refused to accompany her to Mexico for Kiki's elopement and was now carrying on about her father coming to the wedding. She was sorry she had told him about it. It would have been better to let him be surprised too, along with her mother and his parents. He was angry because she had proceeded in the face of his father's disapproval and because he himself had been coerced into promising to keep the secret, and finally he was angry at both her and Kiki for being 'selfish and disregarding the feelings of others', and for foisting an old scandal that had nothing to do with him on his carefully guarded reputation. 'And this whole reconciliation will bring you nothing but disappointment. A romantic exercise in futility if you're lucky, a disaster if you're not. Can't you get it through your head that he's no longer the dashing, handsome god on a white horse that you dream about? Most probably he's a dissolute wreck.

'I don't blame you as much as I do Kiki. She's wiser in the ways of the world than you are, and she should have known better. You've romanticized the situation so long you can't evaluate it. And Kiki has taken advantage of that romanticism to be manipulative and malicious . . . wanting to see me and my parents embarrassed and your stepfather and your mother ridiculed.'

Angel had been stunned to hear Dick speak so bitterly about her father and Kiki. She had sensed that he wasn't overly fond of Kiki – perhaps he found her too aggressive and challenging. But her father? It was all gossip and rumor. Once he saw Rory Devlin, he would see how wonderful he was.

The argument proved academic. Two days before the wedding, Kiki returned from Acapulco only minutes before the delivery of a small package, accompanied by a short note: '. . . as much as he wanted to be with his two little girls on Angel's wedding day . . . an occasion he had dreamed of . . . walking proudly down the aisle with his littlest angel . . . his health would not permit him to travel at this time . . .' The little box contained his gift – a gold pin in the shape of a horse, its face set with two diamond chips and a tiny ruby.

Kiki, pinning the little gold horse on Angel's black faille suit, smiled and bit her lips simultaneously. She felt an overwhelming urge to scream, 'So that's how the son of a bitch spent the money I sent him for the fare!' Instead she said, 'There. Mr Horse looks very elegant on black,' and gently wiped the tears that coursed down Angel's face. 'I guess Daddy just didn't want to embarrass Mother. That was really decent of him, I think. What a charming pin. Daddy does have such good taste.'

She excused herself to go to her room. No sooner had she closed the door than she collapsed on the bed, muffling her screams with her pillow. Oh, it had never been for Angel alone . . .

An hour later, Kiki had a brilliant idea. Why didn't Angel and Dick scrap their plans for their honeymoon and fly with her to Rome after the wedding? 'We'll really have ourselves a time. *La dolce vita* and all that jazz. And you won't have to worry about enough privacy, either. Brad and I will want to be alone too, so you'll have plenty of time to fuck your brains out.'

The idea appealed to Angel enormously, but she told Kiki that it was impossible. Dick would never consider abandoning their plan to honeymoon on the island off the Southern Californian coastline that Liam Power had recently bought, intending to sell his place in the Hamptons. To intimates he had confessed that he had had enough of stuck-up shits there. And after all, he and his family were Californians. They were making their living in the golden state and his boy was going to be its governor someday. You could count on it!

Liam Power was planning on naming his island Power's International Retreat, after his studio, and subjecting it to a complete renovation. It was said that Valentino had often used the island as a hideaway for the purposes of amour. There was presently a swimming pool there and a tennis court, as well as the house that had been built in the nineteenth century. Eventually there would be a new swimming pool, new tennis courts, a new dock, and houses enough for the whole family. But in the meantime the existing house would serve as a 'real honeymoon cottage'. What better place for a honeymoon? Solitary, peaceful . . . the Pacific at its most magnificent. Maybe they could even arrange for a photographer from *Life* or one of those other magazines to come down and take a few pictures of the congressman and the actress. Great publicity! And there was a couple there, a caretaker and his wife, who would take care of all their needs. Besides, Dick really shouldn't stay away from his congressional duties for too long. A man in Dick's position had to keep his nose to the grindstone, not be gadding about Europe with decadent foreigners. 'Right?' Liam Power demanded, and nobody dared contradict him.

'Why can't you choose the place?' Kiki demanded. 'Why does it have to be Dick's choice? No – not even Dick's but that old bastard's. I hope I haven't made a mistake signing with his studio, but I really do think I have.'

While Kiki pondered that possible mistake, Angel fretted. Kiki was right. Dick's father did have tremendous gall to tell them where to honeymoon. And she was disappointed in Dick that he so blindly obeyed. Was Dick a real Daddy's boy? Why hadn't Dick at least consulted with her? Asked *her* if she wanted to go on the island? Maybe her mother had been right – that she really didn't know Dick all that well.

Well, perhaps being isolated on Power's International Retreat would help them forge a really close relationship. Actually, she reasoned, the crux of the matter was not *where* they would spend this honeymoon time, but *what* they would say to each other between sailing and making love. What *did* newlyweds discuss over their breakfast coffee? No one put that in books.

They had hardly ever been alone; almost always they were in the company of other people, at movies or the theater, restaurants, clubs and parties, museums and exhibitions, or at official functions – dinners, dedications, that sort of thing. Even at casual play like tennis, sailing, or swimming, they were usually with others.

Doubts were filling her mind. Did Dick really love her? Was she, as both Kiki and her mother had suggested, climbing a tree not to marry a man like her father? Was she making a mistake? Or was she beginning to doubt her own judgment because of her mother and Kiki? She couldn't do that. Both her mother and her sister were cynical women. If she didn't have faith in her own judgment she had nothing.

7

Mr and Mrs Liam Power gave the dinner for the bridal party at the hotel at which they were staying in Tarrytown, upon which occasion they presented Angel with an antique diamond pendant. Angel thought it quite lovely but Kiki pronounced it 'quaint'. And Marie, back at Stoningham later that evening, drily observed, 'The Power family obviously considers large diamonds ostentatious,' and she looked pointedly from Angel's engagement ring to the pendant.

On her dressing table stood a jewelry chest inlaid with mother-of-pearl – Eugenie's chest, which Marie had carried off to New York when she made her escape from New Orleans. She planned now to divide its contents between the two women as their wedding presents. She was still severely vexed with Kiki, and she had toyed with the thought of giving all the jewelry to Angel in reproof, but she had second thoughts about it. She knew that Kiki would not only never forgive her, but would hold it against Angel as well. Kiki was like that. She could never bear for others to have what she coveted. Marie had no wish to cause a bitterness between the sisters, one that could be perpetuated even after she herself was gone.

It was her intention now to distribute the jewelry,

more or less equally, piece by piece. Angel protested, 'You can't give it all away to us, Mother. You must keep some of it for yourself.'

Marie smiled her ironic little smile. 'No. I no longer have need of the du Beaumond heritage. I am a Whittier now. I feel like a Whittier. And it is you, after all, who is . . . was . . . known as Angela du Beaumond, so it must be you who has the du Beaumond jewelry. And Kiki, of course,' she added in a low polite murmur.

Kiki acknowledged the patronizing remark with a toss of her blond mane. Just more proof that her mother always favored Angel. But then Marie offered her first choice, to make up for any slight.

Each choice was debated, with Kiki's eyes narrowing and sharpening repeatedly, so that Angel kept offering to exchange with her any piece that she indicated by look or word that she wanted. To Angel it hardly mattered at all, and Kiki cared about such things.

Finally the chest was empty, and Marie said, 'I *will* keep the chest for myself. May you both find happiness in these jewels and in your future lives.'

Being of a sentimental bent, Angel cried. Kiki said, 'I hope there isn't a curse on any of this stuff. It comes from New Orleans, and you never can tell.'

Marie smiled sadly. 'Things aren't cursed. Only people are.'

Angélique du Beaumond Devlin was married in her mother's bridal gown, although Marie refused to even acknowledge aquaintance with the dress, insisted on referring to it as 'that gown from Bergdorf's,' which the girls thought very funny. When she had done this at least twenty times, even Kiki grew weary of correcting her and started calling it 'that Bergdorf dress' herself. It was she who had gotten the dress from New Orleans to New York. She had sent a plaintive letter to Uncle Julian begging the dress for her sister – it was sort of a wedding present from her to Angel, who was a sentimental little fool. She had written that the gown her mother had worn, which Eugenie had worn before her, and Eugenie's mother before *her*, would mean so much to Angel, who still recalled the days in Louisiana with Uncle Julian and his family with such fondness. And Julian had obliged, probably hoping that Marie would respond with an invitation for him and his family. Of course, Marie did nothing of the sort.

The ceremony took place in the gardens of Stoningham Manor. Kilkee Devlin Cranford was matron of honor, while the groom's brother, Sean Power, was best man. The stepfather, Edward Whittier, gave the bride away, and Edward Taylor IV, the bride's young brother, was ringbearer. Julia Loud, the round-as-a-butterball daughter of the groom's sister Colleen, was flower girl. Unfortunately, plump little Julia had a perpetually running nose, and Marie, with a shudder of revulsion, later claimed the child positively ruined the pageantry of the affair.

The reception that followed was held on the sprawling Stoningham grounds, and the extensive menu was French with a New Orleans influence, perhaps to emphasize the bride's aristocratic background. Much to Liam Power's annoyance, Marie told at least a hundred of his guests how Angel had been born in the very house where the Duc d'Orléans was entertained long before the Louisiana Purchase, and certainly before any Power set foot on American soil.

The next day the society columns provided full coverage of the nuptials. There was some small mention of the actress bride's father, who had been both movie player and war hero, detailed information on the bride's stepfather, and much space devoted to the groom and his family. To Kiki's chagrin, there was scarcely a mention of her accomplishments, except that she had most recently married Brad Cranford of silver screen fame. There was the traditional picture of the bride in her heirloom wedding gown.

On the other hand, *Whisper* had a front-page shot of the bride entering the Sherry Netherland on her wedding night, looking particularly wistful. The groom had been cropped out the picture, and the caption read: 'Is the Angel sad because Daddy Devlin didn't make it from the south of France for the nuptials?' The article focused on Devlin's career – his origins, his reputation as a lover, his ultimate fall from grace. Also described in full detail was actress Kiki Devlin's first marriage and divorce, before the article launched into her second marriage. Then Congressman Power's alleged alliances of the past were thoroughly hashed and rehashed.

Angel herself never saw the article, so she could not wonder if the credit for the photo belonged to Nicholas Dominguez or not. A friend gave Kiki a copy as she boarded the plane for Rome, and an anonymous donor sent a copy to Marie to enjoy.

After spending the night at the Sherry Netherland in New York, the newlyweds flew to their own little honeymoon island off Newport Beach, California. The Power island lay close to the mainland, but it exuded a sense of isolation not unlike that of a deserted isle. The existing two-and-a-half-story building had been built by a transplanted New England master mariner and had gone through many alterations. It was now a Maine salt box with a widow's walk and touches of Spanish Mission.

Dick, a history buff, was very excited about the house. He took Angel on a tour straight off, pointing out various items of interest. The staircase leading up from the front hall had balusters of six different patterns, all allegedly carved by sailors at sea and sold to different builders once their ships reached port. 'And see here.' Dick pointed out the top of a newel post. 'That's a peace button – it was put there after the whole building was completed by the builder, a New England custom. It signified that his bill had been paid and that the owner of the house was satisfied with the work.'

He talked about the wallpaper in the front hall. 'The pattern is known as "Sailor's Farewell."' And then about a collection of boxes: 'These were all brought back by seafaring men from the Orient. Just look at the intricate work on this one,' he urged, indicating an ivory spice box from Ceylon. 'And look at these – they're models of ships built in neighboring towns on the mainland.'

Angel loved his enthusiasm, but he had a habit of abruptly, unexpectedly turning it off, like a valve. This meant, she had learned, that he was bored and ready to go on to something else. It was a characteristic that made her anxious. Did he tire of everything so rapidly?

He took her hand and suddenly drew her into the room called the Bride's Room; it seemed the original owner had brought his new wife there on their wedding day. She and Dick made love on the four-poster, heavily draped in rose toile, a most romantic setting – but the lovemaking was as it had been on their wedding night, athletic and economical. Not a motion wasted. She had experienced some pain and had assumed, when she inadvertently cried out, that he would stop and comfort her before going on. But he hadn't. Poised above her, blue eyes gazing steadfastly into hers, he had pumped relentlessly until his organ had penetrated her, then plunged in and out, ignoring her gasps until he had spent himself. He then dismounted and asked in a conversational tone, 'Did you have an orgasm?'

All she could do was shake her head no, and he seemed less disappointed than annoyed. He patted her bare rump briskly. 'I guess it takes time. You will,' he said confidently.

Now, in the canopied bed, he kissed her twice, sucked her breasts one after the other, and mounted her. Again he thrust in and out, in and out, staring into her eyes until she closed them.

Again he asked: 'Did you have an orgasm?'

Again she was forced to respond in the negative. He pondered this a moment, then said, 'You're not relaxed enough. *Force* yourself to let go.' He used two of his broad fingers to manipulate her clitoris. He kept looking deep into her eyes until he felt her body twitch again and again, then asked, 'Is that better?'

Embarrassed, she murmured, 'Yes.'

He grinned. 'Good!' He sprang out of bed, tanned and muscular, his thighs big and taut. 'Come on, let's go for a swim.'

They ate, swam, played tennis on the rather primitive court, sailed peacefully in the yawl, and raced through the water in the speedboat, yet she could feel the restlessness growing within him. She was no match for him at tennis; she had played for years but wasn't particularly good at it. They had played together before, but only doubles. Now he quickly grew bored beating her, and soon they stopped playing altogether.

She wasn't all that mad for sailing, either, but she tried to hide this from him. What she would have preferred to do was lie by the antiquated pool, talk at great length, take brief dips in the cool water, and discuss with him books she had read. She would have liked to sit on the beach and paint his portrait. She had brought some painting things with her, and it would have been wonderful if he posed for her while they chatted about this, that and the other. But the most he would do would be to sit stiffly for charcoal sketches that took no more than a few minutes. Even then, she wouldn't put down four or five strokes before he would leap up and say, 'Let's jump in the ocean!'

She herself preferred the pool to the ocean. The ocean was rough, and the rocks jutting into the sea seemed mysteriously ominous. Still, she went in with him whenever he suggested it.

She tried reading poetry to him as they basked in

145

the sun, but as soon as she had read a few lines he would begin to squirm and flex his body. Soon he would be up on his feet and say, 'Let's go in the house and screw!'

Never before had he used such words in speaking to her. Before he had even appeared uncomfortable when Kiki said something slightly off color. Now he surprised her. He dropped his trunks on the beach and tried to pull off her suit. She was horrified lest Roberto and Maria see them from the house, but as always, she did as he wanted.

On the fourth day she remembered the present she had brought along to give him. She had come across the book in an antiquarian bookstore and, recalling fondly that he had once quoted to her from Proust, she had bought the illustrated, leather-bound copy of *Remembrance of Things Past* and put it away to present to him on their honeymoon.

He was doing something to the sailboat, and she brought the book down to the water's edge. He flipped through the pages, sitting crosslegged on the wooden dock. 'It's a very handsome book. Thank you.'

'You don't like it,' she said quickly.

'I do. Very much. I've read it, you know. Years ago.'

'Yes. I thought you might have. But this copy isn't just to read. It's to look at, treasure . . .' Her voice trailed away. She felt awkward, deceived.

'I told you, I like it very much.'

But she was embarrassed. She had given him a foolish, inappropriate gift. The book would suit a poet, not a man of action, a mover of men. Then she remembered what her mother had said – that she should have a poet instead of a politician.

He sensed her disappointment and was resentful. He didn't like to be found wanting. 'What did you expect – rapture? Like one of Kiki's fag friends? What do you want of me?'

She looked down, incapable of putting her feelings into words. If she tried to talk now, she would cry.

146

'But I do like the book,' he said. 'I like the fact you went to the trouble of finding it for me. I appreciate the thought behind it.'

A pause. She still didn't speak, and he felt he should add something warm, tender. 'I'll treasure it always.'

She said quietly, 'I thought perhaps we might read it together. Discuss it . . .'

He grinned. 'Right now I'd rather screw than discuss Proust. Didn't Freud say a woman's nature is strongly determined by sexual function?'

She smiled thinly. 'There's more to that particular quote, I believe. Something about remembering that an individual woman may be a human being apart from this.'

'His stress was on the word *individual*, I think.'

Was Dick implying that she wasn't *that* individual woman? she wondered.

'What did Freud know about women anyway?' Dick asked her. 'His question was "What do women really want?" Obviously, even he didn't know. You tell me. What do *you* want?'

She didn't answer him, couldn't answer him, since she really didn't know.

'Come here,' Dick said, and held out his hand. He helped her over the gunwale and made love to her there on the boat deck. It was cramped and not very comfortable, but at least it was spontaneous and even romantic to be made love to on a boat, Angel decided. And this time at least he didn't ask her if she had achieved orgasm and she didn't have to answer that she hadn't.

On the seventh day of the honeymoon, Colleen, Dick's sister, and her husband, Keith showed up, along with Hugh and Paula Godfrey. Keith managed the family's finances and Hugh was Dick's first assistant, as well as his good friend from college. They came unannounced on a launch, just in time for lunch. Angel was devastated. She couldn't believe it. How dare they? she seethed, until the realization dawned upon her that Dick, incredibly, must have been expecting them, had invited them.

'Did you need competitors for tennis so badly you couldn't get through another week?'

Dick protested, declared his innocence, but Angel did not believe him.

The island's solitude was shattered. The guests sat around the pool wolfing down the steaks Dick barbecued on the grill, drinking, gossiping, and passionately arguing the merits of Ed Lopat versus Warren Spahn.

Directly after lunch, Angel retired to her bedroom. 'I'm sure you won't miss my presence, since your reinforcements have arrived,' she told Dick with a glacial quality in her voice.

'Will you cut that injured-child act? I didn't know they were coming. They just sort of dropped—'

'You mean they were sort of in the neighborhood?' she asked with a sarcasm that sounded more like Kiki than she.

'—and then I had to ask them to stay,' he went on, ignoring her remark completely. 'Look, there's plenty of room here. And they'll leave us alone as much as we want them to. Suppose we had gone to Rome, as Kiki suggested. We would have had Brad and Kiki . . .'

'But we *didn't* go to Rome. We came here, so we could be alone, or so I thought.'

Keith and Hugh, watching her go upstairs, made the inevitable, 'just married' jokes about the bride needing her rest. Colleen and Paula laughed heartily, aligning themselves with their men.

From her upstairs window Angel watched them choose partners for the tennis doubles she knew would take up the rest of the afternoon, with one person serving as dummy alternately. She took a Miltown from a small white bottle that Kiki had thoughtfully provided and stretched out on the silken comforter. She took a perverse pleasure in lying on it.

148

It was an antique, to be folded back ever so carefully when the bed was in use. There was a story to the comforter. A young Mexican girl had quilted it for her trousseau but her intended had been killed fighting for Juárez and the poor girl had never married, had never used the comforter. But who knows? Maybe the little Mexican girl had been lucky, Angel thought with bitterness.

She wasn't used to the tranquilizer and fell asleep almost immediately, to dream that she was a little girl back in New Orleans. Her father was there, and Kiki. She and Kiki were both tugging at his arms, each trying to pull him in her direction. Then he pulled away from both of them and disappeared and Marie took his place, and she and Kiki started to tug away at her.

The two couples stayed three more days, during which time Angel kept mostly to herself. At one time she would have worried about what Colleen and Paula would make of her seclusion, but now she couldn't have cared less. She sunned herself on the beach, read, fooled around with her paints. In the mornings she wouldn't even drag herself out of bed to join the others for breakfast on the terrace. The boisterous talk and raucous laughter were particularly grating so early in the morning.

But finally they left, and Angel thought perhaps the honeymoon could still be salvaged – if she worked hard at it. But then Dick told her they had to cut their stay short – something had come up. They would have to leave early the next morning. That was all he said – an emergency situation had arisen that she wouldn't understand. He made no further effort to explain.

A chauffeured limousine met them at the dock and they rode back to Los Angeles in near silence. First stop was Dick's old apartment in West Hollywood, where he deposited her along with the luggage, then proceeded in the limousine to his office.

Angel wandered aimlessly through the rooms. *Letdown. End of honeymoon. Life begins.*

The apartment in a supposedly luxury building, she decided, was nice enough for a bachelor but not nearly big enough for a couple. And not big enough to entertain in, either. But of course they wouldn't really be living here. Mostly they would be in Washington, where they would be going in just a couple of weeks. And she supposed that in time they would buy a home of their own in Los Angeles.

She trailed her fingers along the dining-room table, and they came up dusty. It appeared Dick hadn't kept much of a staff. The place needed a thorough cleaning, but she was in no mood now to contend with employment agencies. Perhaps the management could send up a maid . . . tomorrow. Actually there were things for her to do. All her clothes, books, and personal possessions, as well as all the wedding presents, had been delivered in her absence and were waiting to be unpacked. But then she would only have to repack everything for the move to Washington, she reasoned.

Listlessly she put some things aside for the cleaners, made a pile of other things for which she would have to find a hand laundress. The apartment was overly warm, stuffy, and she turned on the air conditioning, but it didn't seem to help. She would have to report it to the manager of the building.

She looked out the window. The light was pure yellow, the sun blinding. Everything was so pretty, so clean; flowers were everywhere. She saw a group entering her building, two girls and two men laughing under the striped canopy of the entrance. She had never fully understood the expression *quiet desperation*. Now she did. She ran to the telephone and put in a call to Rome. And wonders of wonders, she actually found Kiki in.

'Oh, Kiki!' she cried, grateful to have reached her.

'When are you coming back?'

'Angel! Back from the honeymoon so soon?'

'Yes, Dick had to come back. Some kind of crisis.'

'Well, how did it go, the old honeymoon? Did you do it in the water?'

'Oh, Kiki!' Angel cried. 'It's so good to hear your voice! Of course we did it in the water! When are you coming back?'

'Brad won't be through here for at least two weeks and then we're going to Paris for a few days. I know what – if Dick is busy working, why don't you fly here by yourself? Rome is divine. I've met the most divine people.'

Kiki always met the most divine people.

'Oh, I can't leave. We'll be going to Washington soon. Besides, I have to do something about this apartment. It's rather depressing.'

'Well, cheer up. We'll see each other soon. You sound awful!'

Oh, poor Angel! It sounds like things are already falling apart. She wondered what had happened so soon.

'It's just that I miss you.'

'Well, I'll be back in California before you know it. And I'll call you from Paris.'

Angel put down the receiver and stared at the phone with an overwhelming surge of envy. Things were so easy for Kiki. When she came back from Europe she would have everything waiting for her – ready-made friends, a house on Rodeo Drive, a career. She would be a movie star with millions of adoring fans. With an adoring husband to boot.

And what did she have? A few acquaintances, Dick's family, and a husband who, so far, hadn't lasted a complete honeymoon. And she had agreed to give up her career. A mistake? She bit her lip. What was the matter with her? Married a few more days than a week and singing the blues already? She was acting like a spoiled child.

She would get busy, do what she had to. Should she

call the employment service or go out and look at furniture? Then she thought of dinner. That was what she would do – cook her first dinner for Dick. He would be surprised and delighted to find that she could really cook. Actually, she could do all kinds of things that would surprise him. During the war, when domestic help was almost impossible to find or keep, she and Kiki had learned to do all sorts of things around the house and grounds. They had even done some of the topiary at Stoningham.

Cooking dinner for two would be simple. She would start with Oysters Rockefeller, since she and Dick had met over them, in a manner of speaking. She would follow with an authentic New Orleans dinner. Somewhere among her books she had a Louisiana cookbook. She had come upon it in a secondhand-book store some years ago. She had been delighted to find it, recalling most of the dishes from her childhood.

She heaped books from the cartons all over the floor until she found it. There it was – *Recipes of Old Louisiana*. She pored over the pages, searching for a recipe that was not too difficult or too time-consuming. *Poulet Marengo*. She even liked the sound of it rolling across her tongue. She wrote down the ingredients she would need for the whole meal: oysters, spinach – she would forgo the rock salt this time, even though Dick was sure to note its absence and make mention of it – chicken parts, olive oil, green pepper, green onions, garlic, parsley, white wine, tomatoes, small white onions. There was nothing in the kitchen at all, not even salt and pepper. She added spices to the list.

She would have to prepare a vegetable too – a true Creole meal required at least one vegetable. She would have liked to make stewed okra and tomatoes, but where on earth would she find fresh okra in West Hollywood? She would make tomatoes stuffed with mushrooms instead.

For dessert she needed something really special. She leafed through the pages of the cookbook rapidly.

Chocolate rum soufflé? Yummy! No, that had to be refrigerated over night. French chocolate silk pie? Simply scrumptious! And impressive! The recipe called for vanilla wafers. That was easy enough. She would make the pie. She added more ingredients to her shopping list – wafers, eggs, whipping cream, almonds, sugar, unsweetened chocolate, butter.

Heavens, she would be busy buying groceries all afternoon. She still had to find a market.

Finally the dinner was ready. The pie was in the refrigerator, the chicken and vegetables were keeping warm in the oven, the Oysters Rockefeller were waiting in the silver chafing dish that had been one of her wedding presents, and it was nearly seven o'clock. Her table resembled something out of *Town and Country*, set with a Porthault tablecloth, silver candlesticks, the flatware her mother had given her with the heavily engraved *Du B*. The crowning touch was the red roses she had picked up from a vendor on Hollywood Boulevard.

She whisked through a quick shower and put on the pink satin hostess gown Kiki had chosen. Plunging neckline, the wide skirt perfect for lounging on the floor in front of a fireplace, Kiki had said. A perfect shot for one of the movie fan magazines. Unfortunately, there was no fireplace here . . . no photographer from the fan magazines.

She was all ready, but where was Dick? She checked the clock again. Seven thirty!

At ten past eight he called. 'Sorry not to be home on our first evening but I'm all jammed up.'

God! Talk about your clichés!

'Where are you?'

'I'm having dinner with Mike Gross and Phil McKinley at the Ambassador. There was so much to catch up on. Sorry. I was going to take you to the Coconut Grove for dinner. Would you mind calling and cancelling? I guess you have a lot to do there at the apartment, unpacking and everything. I'll try not to be late.'

She called the restaurant and cancelled. She turned off the oven and threw away the food. She didn't want to see it again. She took two Miltowns to be sure not to be awake when Dick returned.

But she was. When she heard Dick's key in the door, she glanced at the clock on the night table. It showed ten minutes past two. She closed her eyes, and when he called to her in a loud whisper as he entered the bedroom, she didn't answer. He got into the bed and put his arms around her. *Does he know I'm only feigning sleep?* He kissed her, but she murmured sleepily, turned away.

'Cut the act, will you? It couldn't be helped.'

She made little half-sleep noises.

He flipped her onto her back and mounted her. She made no move as he pumped away and then discharged into her. Soon after that he was asleep and she awake, gripping the pillow with fingers that ached.

He was up and gone before she awoke, leaving a note indicating that he had to fly to Washington. He would be gone for three or four days, and suggested that she run out to his folks' Malibu house for a few days. 'Mom and Dad and the girls will be glad to see you,' he had scrawled. She assumed the girls he referred to were his sisters, Colleen and Lily, whom she was not particularly eager to see.

'I don't even have a car,' she said piteously to herself, feeling ridiculous to find herself some kind of fifth wheel only a few days after her wedding.

She went to the window, stared out at the street. It was still early in the day but the sun was already producing a white-hot glare. Yesterday everything had seemed so fresh – the flowers, the palms. Today everything seemed dry, arid, charred. Of course, Malibu wouldn't be like this, but she was not in the mood for Dick's mother and sisters. After all, they were really but strangers. What would Kiki do? she asked herself.

She ordered a limousine to take her to the airport.

When Angel arrived at the beachfront house in Southampton, she found her mother playing croquet with her little brother.

'Go on!' Marie urged her son. 'Peg it out!'

Then she spotted Angel. Kissing her on the cheek, she asked, 'Where did you spring from? I didn't hear a car.'

'You were too engrossed in your game.' Angel smiled.

'I *am* surprised to see you. Aren't you supposed to be on that quaint little island off California?'

'We had to come back early. Some sort of official business. Dick flew to Washington.'

'And you flew here instead of remaining in Los Angeles or going with Dick to Washington?' Her eyes looked directly into Angel's.

'Obviously, Mother. I'm here!'

'It's not necessary to raise your voice.'

'Sorry.' She *was* being testy, and it was not her mother's fault that she had been stranded in Los Angeles without a husband. 'What's new around here? Did you win your bridge tournament?'

Marie looked at her, not answering for a moment, then said, 'Your Uncle Julian called. Your grandmother has passed away.' She had tried for a matter-of-fact tone, but her voice betrayed her.

Angel sat down on the grass. She wanted to cry but the tears wouldn't come. Her mother seemed cool enough, but Angel guessed that she was holding herself together with effort. 'When is the funeral? I'll go with you. Oh, if only Kiki were here. She could go with us too.'

'Could she? I'm not going. I think it's rather pointless after all these years. The time for me to go back has passed. But you can go if you like . . . if you think it will make you feel any better.'

'Feel better?'

'Yes. Sometimes it helps if you're able to say good-bye to a person . . . or a place . . . or just a time in your life.'

What was her mother trying to tell her? She wasn't sure and she didn't want to ask.

'Well, you think about it. If you decide not to go to New Orleans you can go with Edward and me to Lolly Reed's party at the Maidstone tomorrow night. It's supposed to be the most important party of the season. If you think it won't look too strange that you're partying without your husband so soon after your wedding.'

'Is that what you think, Mother? That it's strange I'm here without my husband?'

Marie looked down and did not answer, and Eddie tugged at her arm. 'I'm tired of playing croquet. Can't we go swimming now?'

To whom would it make a difference if I did go to the funeral? My grandmother's dead.

And she was *not* ready to say good-bye to that time in her life, nor to the one person from that time who mattered.

'Come on, Eddie,' she said to her little brother. 'We'll go to the club for a swim.'

'Why can't we go in the ocean? I like it better than that old beachclub pool.'

'Maybe tomorrow, Eddie. Tomorrow we'll go swimming in the ocean.'

But she was no longer really sure about tomorrows. Could one ever be sure? Could you really rely on someone else for your tomorrows? No, she rather thought not. You had to make your own. As Kiki did. Fathers, husbands – Kiki didn't rely on them. Without them, she had become a star. With them or without them, she would remain a star. Lucky Kiki.

PART SIX

Washington, Hollywood
1951–1952

'You might say that first year in California was a better year for Angel than for Kiki. When Kiki returned from Europe with that darling Brad Cranford and moved into that grand house right across the street from me she barely turned around before they put her into an awful little stinker of a vehicle called *Child Wife*, which bombed most dreadfully. Then they wanted her to do a picture called *Rio*, which really called for an actress along the lines of little Janie Powell, or maybe Joanie Caulfield, not for a sophisticated type like Kiki. Well, Kiki turned it down, simply refused to do it, and as a result the studio put her on suspension. That's how they punished actors those days. Suspension. And Liam Power, the head of PIF, was death on actresses who refused to do as they were told. He was worse than Jack Warner, and could I tell you stories about *him*! Kiki was right to turn down *Rio* – it laid the egg of the year. But still, her refusal to do it put her career on ice for months.

'On the other hand, Angel became an overnight celebrity in Washington. She was only in the capital a few months when she was named to its Ten Best-Dressed list. Now, most of the women who appeared on the list had hired publicists to achieve this honor, and don't let anyone tell you differently. But all Angel did was lead the life of a congressman's wife. Not your ordinary congressman's wife, of course. They were rather a special couple, all things considered. Most Washington couples lacked their glamour, their attractiveness, their background, not to mention their money. How many of those ordinary congressmen's wives had been on the stage or had had a debut covered by *Life*? How many of those congressmen's wives could look the way Angel Power did when she danced the night through in a Balenciaga gown? She was a picture, let me tell you! And there *were* pictures of her, everywhere – shots of her helping to welcome the shah, gowned in a pink satin sheath and long white kid gloves, or attending a luncheon at the Mayflower in a white wool Dior. And she was a *wonderful* hostess. Everyone vied to be invited to her exquisite dinner parties. She served the best food in town and her tables were an absolute picture and she had the most eligible guests, not to mention Kiki and Kiki's darling hubby, that handsome Brad Cranford, whenever they were in town. Of course, when I was in town Angel always included me in her guest list. She said of all the newspeople in either Washington or California, I was the only one she could trust.

'And I was there at the White House the night Angel was invited by Harry Truman to join him at the piano. I had gone to Washington to interview Angel – I was doing a piece on the two sister actresses, a really cute piece that compared their different lifestyles. *Life* did one too later that year, but I did it first!'

1

The Powers leased a small but elegant house in Georgetown with a charming garden in the rear. There were azaleas, rhododendrons, even a Japanese cherry tree with the most exquisite pink blossoms. Everyone said it was probably the most beautifully decorated house in Washington, although Kiki thought it was too understated, which was always the trouble with Angel's taste. Very good but definitely understated, which was also true of Marie's. Her own ran more to flamboyance with dash. Probably because she had a touch more flair, she told herself.

Angel had wanted a house of their own, preferably in the Virginia countryside, where she could keep a horse. Riding was one of the few athletic activities in which she excelled. She had been riding since she was a little girl. But Dick wouldn't hear of buying a house. It was bad enough, he said, that they had to maintain two residences. Anyway, it would be foolish to buy when he had his eye on the governor's mansion in Sacramento.

Each day with Dick was a revelation to Angel. There was nothing like marriage to really get to know a man – that he slept in his shorts, went through piles of handkerchiefs in a day, made funny noises when he slept, and sometimes even neglected to close the door when he used the john. Angel wondered how she had ended up marrying a man about whom she knew almost nothing except that he was a fair dancer, a very good tennis player, ambitious and clever, given to quotes, and blessed with large, healthy teeth. She hadn't even known if he bathed daily. But one thing she knew now. Dick Power was tricky.

One minute he'd be quoting Oliver Wendell Holmes. Quoting was his favorite parlor stunt, the little boy showing off. But she had known about *that* parlor trick.

What she hadn't known was that he could add a forty-item column of five-digit figures in thirty seconds. A trick, but she couldn't figure out exactly how he managed it. And he was an absolute fiend about accounts. He not only expected her to keep lists of expenditures but expected her to go over them with him and check them out, item by item, often defending them. A heading of 'Household Expenditures' wasn't enough by far. It had to be subdivided into: '*Food:* Canned. Fresh. Meat. Etc. *Cleaning Supplies:* Soap. Paper Towels. Furniture Polish . . .'

She had to sit by his side while he added up the columns, went back over each listing ad infinitum . . . ad nauseam. He actually *enjoyed* the whole procedure. It invariably led to squabbles. But Angel consoled herself that the squabbles weren't all that bad – they *were* a form of communication, and a psych professor at Smith had maintained that any form of communication was positive, be it anger, the infliction of pain, whatever.

Dick was particularly disturbed by the outlays for furniture. To be more accurate, he went slightly berserk over them. There was the secretary, a desk she had bought at auction. She gave Dick the nomenclature and pedigree of the piece with a great deal of pride, since she was something of an expert on antiques, a subject with which *he* was less than familiar. She pronounced it a 'steal' at eighteen hundred dollars. It was the word *steal* that set him off, his ruddy face flushing even a deeper pink.

The bill from the house painter proved irritating too, particularly since the house had already been freshly painted and papered when they moved in, with the floors newly scraped and stained. 'Those floors were in perfect condition!' he shouted. 'Why did they have to be redone?'

'But those awful yellow-varnished floors, Dick. Such a vulgar color! The Aubusson would have simply refused to rest its lovely head on that floor.'

Her answer seemed only to feed his rage. 'Did we need, did we *really* need, an Aubusson for a *rented* house? And did it matter what color the floor was *under* the Aubusson?'

'The borders showed.'

Were those handsome white teeth really meant for snarling?

And the telephone bills!

Oh, she knew that married people always bickered over money. She might have been sheltered but she wasn't a fool. But a Power carrying on about something as mundane as a telephone bill?

'You may not call Kiki every day. You *will not* call Kiki every day,' he lectured her in a pedantic tone. 'You may call her once a week. Or better still, let her alternate calls with you. We *cannot* tolerate daily calls to California. We do not receive special rates, even if your stepfather owns half the Bell Company, as rumor has it.'

'Is that what rumor says? I wonder if Mother knows.'

'You are not at all funny. I don't think two hundred and fifty dollars' worth of calls to Hollywood is amusing.'

He was even more petty on the subject of food bills. She couldn't believe that a man of means could stoop so low as to whine about the price of a cheese. It was true that he had the tastes of a peasant when it came to food, so how could he be expected to savor the joys of delicate stalks of fresh asparagus out of season at out-of-season prices, or lobsters flown in from Maine? Still . . .

'And while I appreciate the great job you're doing in the entertainment department and cannot say that I'm displeased, have you noticed that when we go to other people's houses for dinner we don't get Beluga caviar or French champagne? We get domestic wines, which in our case is exactly what we should serve, since I am from California and we do have a wine industry there, remember?'

He was absolutely right about serving California wines. She could offer no objection to that.

'And one more thing, before you get warmed up about the different kind of wines – I don't give a damn about your notions of a proper *library of wines*. My God! You and your pretensions!'

She wanted to protest, to say that she was only trying to enhance his reputation, to make him proud of his home and her expertise as a hostess, but before she could speak, he continued:

'And while we're on the subject of your pretensions, why can't we shop at the local supermarket like other families? Joan Diedrich buys at the supermarket, and her credentials are *almost* as good as yours. Of course, *her* father wasn't a notorious bounder, but she does the best she can.'

Now that was snide. It was more than snide, it was hitting her below the belt. It was filthy, it reduced her to tears, it made a rejoinder impossible.

'I think you have a misconception of just who you are, or what we're doing here, and of how much money is at our disposal. First of all, any kind of ostentation is out in politics. We're not here, you know, to impress people like your sister Kiki's smart-ass friends.'

He *had* to interject Kiki's name. No argument was complete, it seemed, without Dick bringing in Kiki's name.

'But to be fair,' he went on and on, 'the problem of your extravagance is partially my fault. I haven't really acquainted you with the details of our financial situation. The cold facts are that we have an income from a trust fund that is not the largest in the world. Which means that if you keep spending money at the rate you have – thirty-five-hundred-dollar sofas and three-hundred-dollar monthly telephone bills – well, I just don't know where the money's going to come from. And all this conspicuous consumption stinks! Think of my image! For God's sake, look, just look at

164

the staff you've hired. Six lousy rooms and you've hired a couple plus a gardener *plus* a cleaning lady. And you're buying clothes again. No one would guess that you had a complete trousseau just weeks old!'

At first Angel had assumed that he would calm down about the money, but as time went by he became worse. If they had strawberries Romanoff for dessert, he would demand to know how much strawberries cost out of season.

'You're being positively horrid! I absolutely refuse to discuss the price of strawberries,' and she stalked from the room as if the subject were beneath discussion. The truth was, she had no idea how much the strawberries cost – she simply ordered them over the telephone without asking, and she wasn't going to admit *that* to Dick.

Oh, yes, she was constantly discovering new facets of her new husband's personality. Such as his habit of working through the evenings and neglecting to call. It would be hers to assume that if he didn't call it was because he didn't have the time to do so.

She learned. She adjusted. She ceased demanding explanations. It wasn't all that unpleasant to be alone. It was peaceful, for one thing. The evenings spent with Dick at home were always filled with a kind of tension. Unable to relax, he always wanted people around, lots of people. Gradually she grew inured to the lack of a 'normal' married life – those precious hours of togetherness people talked about, doing nothing special with the person you loved.

But she needed something. More and more she thought about the career she had given up, the poor little career that had hardly had time to take off. Maybe she had been foolish to give it up so easily, to forsake it so willingly in the name of her new marriage.

Maybe what she needed was something to bolster her marriage . . . that something in which she could place new dreams . . . a who . . . a small thing she could hold in her arms and to whom she could croon a lullaby.

2

Kiki half reclined on dozens of small white satin pillows in the white-satin-upholstered bed, break-fasted off a white wicker bed tray while she read the morning paper. Brad lounged on the white satin chaise, drinking black coffee, eating one lone piece of toast. Kiki wolfed sausages, pancakes and eggs, read, and conversed all at the same time. 'I wish you'd eat something, Brad. You make me feel like an over-stuffed pig.'

'Sorry, sweetheart,' he said apologetically. 'But you know I have to watch my weight when I'm working.'

'Don't rub it in.'

He immediately regretted his words. He knew how nervous she was, more so every day, as her suspension lengthened.

'You'll be working before you know it. It's only been a few weeks. You'll see how quick Liam Power will lift the suspension as soon as he finds a picture he wants you for. You know the story about Harry Cohn. If he gets mad at someone he says, "That bastard will never work for me again! . . . Until I need him." They're all like that. Mayer, Selznick, all of them.'

'I bet they're all not as vindictive as Power. I'd swear on that. How about Hughes? I'm sure he's not such a son of a bitch. I was a fool to sign with PIF. Why did you let me? He's got it in for my whole family, especially Mother. He resents us you know, because he knows we're better than he is. The minute Angel said she was going to marry Dick I should have known to stay away from the old fart instead of placing myself in a position where he could control me.

166

Control is what that bastard's all about. He wants to control his son's political career, he wants to tell Angel how to live. Before you know it, *you'll* be on suspension!'

'Take it easy, sweetheart.'

Kiki was so high-strung. He supposed it was because of her superior breeding.

'Nobody's going to control you,' he tried to reassure her. 'Except for me, of course,' he joked. He more than anybody knew what a joke that was. 'Seriously, Liam Power's studio is too important to him to allow his personal feelings for your family to come between him and what's best for the business. You're a big star – he's not going to allow you to go to waste.'

'Oh, I don't know about that. He threw me into that bomb, *Child Wife*. I wasn't only wasted, I was crucified. Whatever possessed me to agree to wear pigtails all through that fucking picture?' She ran her fingers through her hair. 'He probably thinks he can use me to keep Angel in line.'

Brad shook his head. Kiki's thinking was too complicated for him. She was always attributing crazy motives to people. 'Use you to control Angel?'

'Never mind, Brad. You have a sweet, uncomplicated mind. Mine is not as sweet or artless. That's why *I* understand Liam Power. At least better than you do. Besides,' she said peevishly, 'you've never crossed him. That's why you get along so well with him. You do every goddamn thing he says.'

'But I've done very well at PIF,' Brad said uncomprehendingly. 'All my pictures have done terrifically at the box office. I—'

'Oh? Now you're throwing *Child Wife* up at me too?'

'No, of course not, sweetheart. I didn't mean to—'

'There is such a thing, you know, as shaping your own career, picking your pictures, trying to develop yourself into something more than a pretty face—' She gave out a yelp. 'Look at this. In Beebie Tyler's column: ". . . what a lucky girl little Lane Hayman is.

167

Little Miss Mississippi has just been signed by Howard Hughes to a seven-year contract. Howard says little Miss Mississippi's first starring role will be opposite Kirk Douglas in *The Woman in White*." That's the role I was dying for. That role could have been written for me. If Power wasn't such a bastard, he could have lent me to RKO for that picture!'

'Hughes signs girls to contracts every day and ninety-nine percent of them never make a picture, never even see a set. He parks them in apartments and houses all over Hollywood while he's supposedly grooming them for stardom, and all that ever happens is that he sleeps with them.'

Kiki sniffed. '*You* should know better than to believe everything you hear in this town. Look at what he did for Jane Russell.'

Brad was going to say that Hughes had kept Russell off the screen for years while the only pictures the public saw of her were publicity stills, but he decided to drop it. He knew from experience that he couldn't convince Kiki of anything.

'Why don't you just relax and enjoy your leisure, sweetheart? As soon as I finish *Her Secret Past* we'll go down to Palm Springs, play a little golf, okay? In the meantime, why don't we give a big party, and be sure to invite Beebie Tyler. The studios are always owing her favors, for suppressing certain stories as well as for printing others. Maybe Power owes her one. And she does like to be courted . . .'

'I know she does.' Kiki sighed. 'Okay. We'll give a party, invite old Beebie. Maybe Angel will come too, if she can tear herself away from Washinton. She's so busy playing the toast of the town there that she can't think of anything else. I don't know who she thinks she is – maybe Perle Mesta,' she grunted.

3

Brad had already gone to the studio, having had a six-o'clock call that morning, and Kiki sat alone on the terrace overlooking the heart-shaped pool, eating her breakfast. She ate three slices of toast, each slice thickly coated with marmalade. She knew she was eating too much. She had gained five pounds since her suspension had gone into effect, but sometimes only food, liquor, or chocolates made up for the depression, the boredom. Eating, drinking, shopping, planning silly parties – that was what her life had become. And all she wanted, all she had ever wanted, was to be onstage, before the cameras, before the lights, to be a star. Shit, shit, shit. She had to figure out some way to get out of her contract with PIF, to get out from under the old bastard. Now, if some studio wanted her so much they would offer to buy out her contract . . . Some studio like RKO. Howard did seem to like her. The other night at Ciro's she could have sworn it was his leg pressing against hers. Everybody said he was crazy about blondes. Maybe, just maybe, that was where her path lay . . .

She turned the pages of the morning paper, read Beebie's column first off. This morning, Beebie's column carried a Washington dateline. Oh, my God! she thought, as she read of her own little baby sister playing piano with the President – a duet with old Harry! The two of them had given a jazzy rendition of 'St Louis Woman.' Kiki studied the accompanying picture. Angel looked – well, radiant. And no wonder. What she herself wouldn't do for such a picture. What wonderful publicity! Then Kiki noticed her hand holding the newspaper. It was trembling, and shame flooded her for the terrible envy she felt for her sister.

Oh, God, I have to do something! Maybe I'll just swallow shit and beg the old fucker to let me work. No! Dammit, I won't! I'll sit him out if it takes a year – years. No . . . better still, I'll call Hughes. It can't hurt. I'll make a date for lunch or a drink or something . . .

After all, she reasoned, it would be a business date. Oh, it was all well and fine for Brad to talk about the way Howard functioned – how he only wanted to fuck the women he signed. It was easy for Brad to talk. *He* was working and getting about a million fan letters a day . . .

Suddenly a wave of nausea hit her. She pushed herself away from the table and ran for the powder room. My God! This was the fifth day in a row she had thrown up, and the tenth day she was late.

As she knelt on the floor, emptying her stomach into the toilet bowl, she thought of how Howard Hughes would have to wait a few months. Then, as she washed her face, she thought of Liam Power. What a joke on him!

She went back to the terrace and lay back on the chaise, thought of whom she should tell first – her mother or Angel or Brad, or . . . of course, Beebie Tyler! If she gave another exclusive to Beebie, wouldn't Beebie just owe her!

'Yes, darling, I'm very, very happy for you.' Kiki hung up the phone and turned to Brad, who was sprawled on the white sofa, reading a script. 'Guess who's going to have a baby too?'

'Who?'

'Angel, that's who.'

'That's super, Kiki. Now little Kiki will have a cousin to play with – about the same age.'

'Are you so sure it's going to be a girl?'

'Yep. One as beautiful as her mother. Hey! Wouldn't it be great if Angel had a girl too?'

'Oh sure. Angel and Kiki all over again.'

Brad looked at her, unsure whether her words were tinged with sarcasm.

'Leave it to Angel to get pregnant just because I did. All her life she's been trying to do exactly what I do.'

'But I thought she's been trying to get pregnant for a while.'

Ignoring Brad's words, Kiki shook her head. 'She's always tried to follow in my footsteps. When I went on the stage she had to too.'

'But she went to college first, while you went on the stage,' he pointed out.

Kiki whirled around. 'But it didn't take long for her to follow, did it?'

'But now she's retired from acting,' he said, trying to mollify her.

'You wouldn't know it from all the publicity she gets.'

'If somebody didn't know better, Kiki, they'd think you resented Angel.'

'Me? Resent Angel? That's ridiculous. I adore Angel. I always have. Ever since she was a baby. I've always looked out for her. But you know, I wouldn't put it past her to have twins – just to top me.'

4

Life did a follow-up spread on the debutantes of their 1947 issue – the Devlin girls turned congressman's wife and movie star. The article disclosed that both ladies were ladies-in-waiting, with Kiki Devlin Cranford in her fourth month and Angel Devlin Power in her third. Angel Devlin Power was the former actress Angela du Beaumond.

At first Angel didn't want to do the piece. Not many months before, she had submitted to another article about the sisters Devlin – Beebie Tyler's, featured in the magazine *Screen Stars*, although Angel had never been seen on the screen. She hadn't wanted to cooperate on that article, but Kiki had insisted. Then when *Life* said they wanted to do one, Kiki had insisted again – she could use the publicity. She told Angel not to be so selfish. Then Dick insisted. He wanted the exposure. So Angel had to give in, unable to withstand the pressure from both of them, even though the presence of the photographers and writers would be an intrusion during this critical period of her life. She was already preparing for her baby's arrival – shopping for a layette, fixing up a guest room in the Georgetown house as a yellow-and-white nursery, going through the usual lists of names. She had great hopes for this baby – that he would bring a new intimacy to her marriage.

The article focused on the contrast in the sisters' lives. There was Angel in her Georgetown home; kneeling in the garden; smiling at a huge soufflé in her kitchen – Mrs Power was a gourmet cook; attending a party for the Indian ambassador, white satin sheath, elbow-length kid gloves; at the ballet, black satin sheath. And a reprint of the by now famous picture – Angel and Mr Truman hamming it up on the White House piano.

Kiki was shown at the Racquet Club in Palm Springs and poolside at her home there; on the terrace of her Beverly Hills mansion; attending a premiere with her film-star husband at Grauman's; laughing it up with Rosalind Russell at Chasen's; dancing so spiritedly at a party at the home of movie exec Charlie Gospan, that her dress ballooned high over her stocking tops; and the topper – gorgeous Brad Cranford serving his wife breakfast in their all-white bedroom.

There wasn't a smart household in all Washington without that issue on its coffee table. Comparatively few people saw that week's issue of *Peek*, a fairly new tabloid, which showed, of all things, an old, fuzzy picture of two little girls sitting on a horse with veteran actor Rory Devlin standing beside them. The accompanying article observed that Devlin was currently down at his heels in Europe, and speculated on which of his rich and famous daughters would take Daddy in.

The minute the article was called to Angel's attention, she called Kiki in Palm Springs.

'Have you seen *Peek*?'

'Yes. Forget it.'

'Where do you think they got that picture?'

'I haven't the foggiest. Forget it. It's not important.'
Kiki herself was trying to dismiss the picture from
her mind; her father's hand holding Angel steady,
not touching *her* at all . . . 'The spread in *Life* is
scrumptious, isn't it? Didn't you just love the shot of
my legs? You can't tell either one of us is pregnant.'

Angel studied the pages objectively. No, even
though Kiki was a month further along, you couldn't
detect her pregnant condition, even in the swimsuit
pictures, while she herself displayed merely an
obligatory smile. Angel smiled now, musing how
women all over the country were looking at the
pictures in *Life* with envy, trying to envision
themselves in the sisters' glorious, carefree, sunny-
bright world.

Then she went back to *Peek* to look at the old picture
again. She looked for a photographer's credit, then
realized how foolish that was. It was a very old
picture. It certainly didn't matter anyhow. Now that
her comings and goings were so regularly reported in
the press, she had gotten used to all kinds of coverage.
But she found herself looking for the photographer's
credit constantly, and when she found Nick Dominguez's
name she was pleased, knowing that it was ridiculous
of her. But ridiculous or not, she was content that he
was still in her life . . . taking her picture, although she
was never aware of it at the time. And ridiculous or
not, she found herself wishing that they would
meet . . . talk.

And while it seemed amazing that she never saw
him, at the same time it was surprising how often he
managed to catch her alone. But while she might
appear wistful or unsmiling in some of the pictures,
there was not one that was unflattering. In
Dominguez's pictures of her there was no such thing
as anger, displeasure, tears, or even a frown. It was as

if she were really an angel in Nick Dominguez's
pictures.

5

In Key West for the winter months following the
holidays, Marie longed to be near her daughters, to
discuss the different aspects of their pregnancies, to
speculate on the gender of the awaited babies, even to
talk about maternity clothes. She didn't enjoy Key
West – perhaps it reminded her too much of New
Orleans. For the hundredth time she wondered what
she was doing in the godforsaken house Edward had
owned long before they were married. It was Edward
who insisted they come here every year. He had
friends who wintered here, and he found the local
social scene subdued, more to his taste than the
flashiness of Palm Beach, where even the Jews had
managed to make inroads into the Old Guard society.
But then, of course, Edward didn't stay – *he* commuted
to New York, and it was she who had to endure the
entire season.

She sat in the living room now, with the large, old-
fashioned ceiling fan turning lazily, the shutters closed
as usual against the strong sun, and opened the letter
Edward had forwarded from New York. It was from
her brother, Julian, but this time it had been addressed
to Edward instead of her. She read the letter quickly.
Julian wrote that he was appealing directly to Edward
because he never received a response from the sister
he held so dear. Things were not going well with the
family in New Orleans. It seemed that after all had
been settled and done, there wasn't very much money
left over from his mother's estate. Her money had not
been invested wisely. The lawyers had mismanaged
the estate, and then, of course, much of his mother's
resources had been used in the vain effort to save the

family plantation.

Marie laughed bitterly. *He's blaming it on the lawyers when it was he who had had the dim sense to sink good money after bad into the plantation.*

She read on: He had planned, as everyone knew, to give Marie a full third of the estate, even though *Maman* had disinherited her in the will. Unfortunately, there was not very much left to divide, so it was pointless to pursue that idea any further, what with Marie's own secure financial position. Needless to say, he was still assuming all financial responsibility for their sister, Desiree. He appealed to Edward to have Marie send back two thirds of the family jewelry and silver she had seen fit to take with her when she left New Orleans. Certainly Edward could see that it would be the only fair thing for her to do, considering the circumstances. He fervently hoped that Edward would prevail upon Marie to comply.

Marie noted the absence of any personal comment on the letter from her husband. He had simply forwarded it. *Edward knows damn well that would be the last thing I would do.* Of course the jewelry was all gone – she had given all of it to her daughters. But there still was some silver left, silver from the Manards and the du Beaumonds. But she was not going to send any of that back either.

The letter concluded with a plea: now that he was no longer a plantation owner, he was selling securities and would appreciate any business Edward could throw his way.

She walked over to the huge fireplace. So much time had elapsed and now everything was coming full circle. *Maman* dead. Both the old house and the plantation gone. Julian peddling securities . . . Desi at the mercy of Julian's largesse . . . Rory Devlin fallen on hard times.

She looked into the mirror above the fireplace. She was not that much changed. Her hair was still silvery blond, still almost the shade of Kiki's. Her eyes were

still large and her skin still flawless. She tore up
Julian's letter and threw it into the fireplace.

Well, one thing was sure. This would be her last
season in Key West. Life was too fleeting to be wasted
in places she really didn't want to be. She had learned
that many, many years ago. She would look into Palm
Springs, California.

6

Dick was running for reelection to his congressional
seat and Angel had been busy, in spite of her
pregnancy, making personal appearances, but she was
tired. And it was not yet spring. The weather was
getting her down. She wanted to get out of
Washington. She considered going to Florida and
staying with her mother, but she decided she wasn't in
the mood for that either. She thought she would like
to stay in California for a while, but not in the West
Hollywood apartment, which she disliked. She would
stay with Kiki, she told Dick.

Dick agreed that she needed a respite, that she
should go to Los Angeles for a little vacation, and
while she was there she could make a few local
appearances for the campaign – teas, luncheons, and
that sort of thing – but why didn't she stay with his
folks in Bel Air? They had the guest house and would
really make her comfortable. Or maybe she wanted to
go out to their place in Malibu? He was sure his
mother would be delighted to stay out there with her,
or maybe one of his sisters would. Obviously Dick
didn't want her with Kiki because of the bad feelings
between his dad and her sister. But that was movie
business and didn't have anything to do with their
personal lives. Or did it? Anyhow, it was *her* little
vacation, and this time she prevailed.

*

It was such fun visiting with Kiki and Brad. No tension in the air, no arguments, no bickering over budgets and dress allowances. There was only lazy lounging by the pool and breakfasts in bed with Kiki while Brad, if he was home, stretched out on the chaise and gossiped with them. There was shopping on Rodeo, luncheons at the Derby with friends stopping by to say hello, cocktails at the Pecks' or the Stewarts' or wherever, dinner at Ciro's or Chasen's, wherever Kiki thought it would be the most fun. It was going to parties or giving them. It seemed to Angel that Kiki entertained so effortlessly – no brooding over menus or wine lists to determine which vintage would be the cheapest without appearing so. Kiki might decide upon stuffed squab with Madeira sauce and would simply call one of her favorite restaurants to say, 'Giorgio?' – Kiki's people were always called Giorgio or Emilio or something like that – 'Giorgio, I want stuffed squab for twenty-four tomorrow. No, darling, don't tell me you can't do it, or you know what I'll do – I'll announce to everybody that we *are* having it and *you're* sending it over, and then when we have nothing everyone will think *you* let them down. It will ruin you. Yes, Cary is coming, and the Duke, and you don't want to let them down, do you? Yes, darling, eight thirty will be fine. And those little Viennese apple tortes that you do so beautifully. Yes, yes, yes.' And everything would go off smooth as glass.

Or Kiki might decide to have a barbecue by the pool that very night. She would make her calls, and only after she had as many people as she wanted would she tell the cook, 'We'll make it one of those South American buffets.' And there would be Italian sausage, both sweet and hot; chorizos; lamb chops; ribs of beef and grilled sweetbreads; all kinds of salads – everything produced as if by miracle in a matter of hours. And later, after everyone had gone home, the three of them, Kiki, Brad, and Angel, would stay up late, talking about everybody and laughing until Angel thought her sides would actually split. Oh, how she envied Kiki her Brad, so easygoing and good-natured, so attentive and adoring, until she realized she was being envious and then felt guilty.

Kiki took one look at Angel in her maternity smocks and declared her dreary. 'I can't believe *you* made Washington's Best-Dressed list. Those icky little smocks – *yecch!* What are you thinking of? That sort of thing might be fine for PTA teas or hitting the campaign trail in San Jose or Fresno, but Hollywood? You look like a knocked-up Rebecca of Sunnybrook Farm.'

So Angel acquired a whole new maternity wardrobe. Caftans, saris, velvet robes that disclosed not a hint of belly, whirls of floating colored chiffon, taffeta tops in a jeweler's array of colors worn over miraculously stick-straight white trousers. She knew that Dick would hit the ceiling when he saw the bills, but she was having such a good time, she couldn't have cared less. Especially when she saw in the newspapers that he had come to California from Washington to campaign and hadn't, unbelievably, even called her.

But the items in the newspapers that made mention of Dick's attendance at an affair in Washington with some attractive woman whose husband was tending to business in Asia or Africa, or simply campaigning back in his home state, did not disturb her at all; at least, not until Kiki made an issue of it. It was *normal* in Washington for a husband or wife to attend functions with someone who needed an escort for the evening. And she knew the same sort of thing went on in Hollywood. But Kiki wasn't so sure it didn't mean *something*.

'It *can* mean something, or it cannot,' Kiki said with authority. 'For instance, it's perfectly innocent for Dick to take Liz Udelli to a dinner dance at the French embassy. You're here and her husband is attending that World Conference on Arms, and you're all such good friends. But it would all be marvelously convenient – you here and hubby there – if something between Liz and Dick *was* brewing. It doesn't mean he *is* creeping into her sack, but it doesn't mean he ain't either. And if he ain't now, he might yet.'

'Kiki, Liz is a *friend*.'

'I wish I could say that makes a difference, but I can't. All I'm saying, precious, is that when they print the names together, it could be innocent, or it could not. It's the blind items you really have to watch for. Like this one from Hopper's column: "What tall, blue-eyed congressman was seen tête-à-tête at a small, dark restaurant in Chevy Chase with the most fetching, recently divorced sexpot of the silver screen who's in town for a benefit? And where is the congressman's slightly *enceinte* wife?" Do you see what I mean?'

Angel's eyes filled with tears. 'I know I'm going to be sorry I asked you, but can you guess who the sexpot is?'

'It must be Gena Grant. I can't imagine who else they could be talking about.'

'He met her at *your* house the last time we were here!' Angel sounded almost accusatory.

'Well, I like that – as if it were my fault your husband is fooling around.'

When Angel flinched, Kiki was instantly remorseful. 'Oh, look, what does a blind item mean? It could just be a release Gena's publicity people gave out. It's probably all rot. Maybe they were together, maybe not.'

'You're a big help, I must say,' Angel said bitterly. 'It *may* be true. It *may not* be true.'

'I'm only trying to help. Do I blame *you* that I'm on suspension? It *is* your son of a bitch father-in-law that's keeping me from working. I could have had that wonderful part in *The Bad and the Beautiful* if it weren't for him. He could have loaned me out for it if he weren't such a bastard.'

'But Lana Turner's doing that.'

'Don't I know it! I had my eye on that role after I didn't get *Detective Story*. I would have been perfect for it, but Eleanor Parker got that.'

'I'm sorry that you didn't get those roles but I don't see how . . . You know, Kiki, you should count your blessings. You have Brad, after all, and he's simply crazy about you.'

'Oh, Brad's all right but he's square. He's sweet, but a square. I thought when I came out to Hollywood my life would be a series of wild parties and orgies, to which I was eagerly looking forward. Instead, I'm married to Mr Goody Two Shoes. All he wants is to be clean and correct and keep a flat belly. He doesn't smoke, only drinks wine, and always washes his hands after he goes to the bathroom.'

Angel giggled. 'Kiki, you're terrible. He's the sweetest man.'

'He might be the sweetest man, but he married me for ulterior motives all the same, not just love sweet love.'

'Ulterior motives? You're crazy.'

'He married me for my aristocratic background, if you can believe it. I've come to the conclusion he *doesn't* want me to work. If he had insisted I play opposite him, maybe I— No, he's secretly thrilled I'm not working and that I'm having a baby.'

'But—' Angel started to protest.

'Let me explain. Most little boys want to grow up and marry the beautiful movie star, right? Not Brad. His father was a migrant fruit picker. They went from crop to crop. And Brad grew up to be the beautiful movie star himself. So he didn't have to marry one. He has a different scenario to fulfill his success story. Okie boy grows up, becomes rich, handsome movie star, then marries one of America's fairest *with* a social background.

'Why, the first thing Brad wanted after the wedding was not to screw me, but for me to redecorate the house. Now that has to say something. And after the baby comes, he wants to sell this house and buy a bigger one in Bel Air. With more grounds. With a Roman pool with statuary, English gardens, a tennis court. And imagine, Brad hadn't even heard the stories about Daddy before he married me. If he did, maybe he wouldn't have.'

'Oh, come on, Kiki, you always ascribe the worst motives to everybody. Here's this sweet man who adores you – I mean, anyone can see he's simply mad about you.'

'Of course he is. I'm the answer to all his dreams, and a terrific fuck in the bargain.'

Angel laughed. 'How do you know you're so great?'

'How? Everybody says so!'

Angel laughed again. 'I don't think I am.'

'That's because you don't get enough practice.'

'And I don't intend to either, so cut it out, you troublemaker!'

'You might as well, you know. If Dickie boy is fucking around, why shouldn't you?'

'Then you do believe those stories? Ten minutes ago you said there wasn't necessarily any truth to rumors.'

'Listen Angel. Dick Power was always a chaser. I did warn you. Remember? He must have had half the women under forty in Southampton.'

'That was before we were married. He is ten years older than I. But he wouldn't dare risk the scandal now – his reputation!'

'That's what he's probably counting on to carry him through his escapades – people saying he wouldn't do anything to risk his political reputation.'

'Please, Kiki,' Angel said as she readjusted her position to relieve the pressure on her back. 'Let's talk about something else. Names for babies. If we have a boy, we're calling it Dick junior. I can't make up my mind what to call it if it's a girl. What do you think of Pamela? I sort of like it.

'Pam is nice. Pammy . . . cute. If I have a boy, guess

what I'm going to call him.'

'Brad?'

'Rory.'

'Oh!' Angel was dumbstruck. 'You can't! Mother will have an absolute fit!'

'Mother will? Or you will? It's my baby, and I'll name it after my father if I like. I think I'll name it Rory even if the baby's a girl. I love boy's names for girls, don't you? Yes, that's what I'll do, name the baby Rory whether it's a boy or a girl,' Kiki said, pleased that it was her own option and hers alone. 'But Richard is a perfectly nice name,' she said generously. 'And I *love* Pammy.'

'I'm not so sure about Pammy,' Angel said, 'now that I think about it. I think that if my baby is a girl, I'll call it Marie.'

7

Dick's campaign staff were eager to have Angel back in Washington for some publicity shots in her pregnant condition. So she packed up all her new maternity clothes and prepared to leave, and Kiki proposed a farewell lunch at the Polo Lounge.

Kiki and Angel sat side by side on one of the Polo Lounge's green banquettes where they could watch all the comings and goings, which Kiki said was half the fun of being there. 'The Polo Lounge is absolutely my favorite place for lunch,' she told Angel as she ordered a crab salad. 'It's not the food, of course – it's the ambience.'

Angel ordered apple pancakes. 'By *ambience* do you mean the plastic greenery?'

'Don't be snide, Angel. It doesn't become you.'

'But the greenery *is* plastic.'

'But the Lounge is known for that greenery. Here

it's chic. It's part and parcel of the Beverly Hills Hotel's twenties-thirties mystique. It's . . . Hollywood!'

'I see,' Angel said. 'And you really love it all, don't you? All of it. The movie business, Hollywood, all the razzle-dazzle . . .'

'Oh, I do! I can't imagine living any place else anymore. This is where I belong.'

'You're lucky to know where you belong,' Angel said softly.

When the waiter brought their food, Angel saw Kiki looking at her pancakes with a hard eye. 'What is it?'

'Those pancakes. They look delicious. I wish I had ordered them instead of the crab salad.'

'Do you want to trade?'

'Oh, never mind,' Kiki said, as if Angel had somehow taken advantage of her. 'Look . . . over there. It's Grace Kelly with Oleg Cassini. She's making *High Noon* with Cooper.' Her mood changed again. 'I would have been perfect for that.'

'Oh, Kiki, don't dwell on it. You're pregnant, so you couldn't have made it anyway.'

'But I didn't *have* to be pregnant. I could have done something about it.'

'Kiki!'

But Kiki's attention was elsewhere. 'Look – it's that photographer, the one that's so taken with you, or you with him. He just came in.'

Slowly Angel raised her eyes, as her pulse quickened. She felt her face grow hot as their eyes met and he smiled at her. She wanted to greet him. Would he approach her? No . . . he would think that presumptuous of himself. She lowered her eyes, wondering what she should do. She could send the waiter over to his table, ask him to join them for a drink. That would be permissible . . . discreet. But what would Kiki say to that?

'I forgot to tell you,' Kiki said as she speared a piece of Angel's pancake. 'While you've been busy being the star of Washington our photographer friend has set

183

up shop here and is doing very well for himself. He's fast becoming the Avedon of the Wicked West. He's even done Marlene. I guess he doesn't have to work for the exploitation sheets anymore.'

'He hasn't done that for a long time. He—'

'Are you defending him after he's exploited you?'

'But I don't think he's done that. In fact, of all the pictures he's taken of me, not one has been uncomplimentary.'

'Oh! So you *do* like him taking your picture? You *are* flattered?'

'I didn't say that. I—' No, she wouldn't be able to ask him over to their table. It was too late to even smile at him, or even to wave. *Oh, Kiki! Damn it!*

'Well, I think he has a hell of a nerve to follow us in here and intrude on our privacy!'

Angel nervously darted a look in Nick Dominguez's direction, but now his gaze was averted. 'I'm not sure he did follow us in. He doesn't even have a—'

'No. Of course not *us*. You!' Kiki's voice had become shrill. People were starting to look in their direction.

The situation was becoming impossible, Angel thought. 'I think I'd like to leave, Kiki.'

'Because of him? We haven't finished our lunch. If anybody's leaving, *he* is!' She beckoned to the maître d'.

'No, Kiki, please!' Angel stood up and in her confusion dropped her bag.

The maître d' rushed over, stooped to pick up Angel's bag, and turned to Kiki. 'Yes, Mrs Cranford? What may I do for you?'

Mrs Cranford? This jackass doesn't even know he's talking to Kiki Devlin!

Furious, she pointed with a scarlet-tipped finger. 'I want that man out of here!'

The maître d' raised an eyebrow. 'I beg your pardon?'

'He is being rude. He's making my sister uncomfortable.'

'I don't think I understand . . .'

'What is there to understand? My sister is Mrs Richard Power, the Congressman's wife, and that man is embarrassing her.'

'What is he doing, Mrs Cranford, that is embarrassing?'

'He's taking her picture!'

'But I see no camera.'

Everyone was looking at them now. Out of the corner of her eye Angel could see that Nick Dominguez was embarrassed, red-faced, as he stared impassively ahead. And of course, there was no camera in sight.

'Kiki, I'm leaving!'

'No!' Kiki was riding on a crest of fury now. 'We are not! He is!'

Angel opened her bag, pulled out some money, put it on the table, and started to stride toward the entrance, her pregnant belly preceding her. She had to pass his table but averted her eyes. Kiki ran after her, and as she passed Dominguez's table she swung at him with her handbag, catching him full on the left cheek. But he sat there, not looking up from the menu, not looking at Kiki.

Angel ran through the lobby as fast as she could manage, Kiki, in high heels, running after her.

'How could you? How dare you make such a scene?' Angel demanded, going through the door, leaving Kiki to scurry through.

They stood in the porte-cochere waiting for their car as the attendants raced back and forth, bringing up cars, taking them away.

'You were the one who wanted to leave because of him. I did it for you.'

'Me? I wanted to leave because you started a scene. You were acting like a fishwife!'

Kiki's Rolls appeared, and she walked around to the driver's side.

'Fishwife! I like that! That's what I get for trying to help you.'

The attendant helped Angel into the car.

'Help me? How? I didn't want him thrown out. You did.'

'Now what do you mean?' Kiki sped down the driveway to Sunset Boulevard. 'What are you implying?'

'You acted hatefully toward that man. I think you're mad because he's always taking my picture and not yours. That's what I think.' Then she sat up straight, astonished. 'Kiki Devlin, are you crazy? You just went through a red light!'

The next day, Beebie Tyler took note in her column:

Lunchers at the Polo Lounge were wondering what all the fracas was about when Kiki Devlin Cranford and her sister, Angela du Beaumond Power (yes, *that* Power), stormed out of the pink-and-green room after Kiki hit filmdom's newest and most chic photographer, Nick Dominguez, in the face with her purse, having demanded that maître d' Pepe throw the poor man out. Shame, shame on you, Kiki. Most unbecoming behavior, especially for a lady in your condition. That nice Nicky couldn't have done anything so terrible to warrant such a breach of manners. As for you, Angela, please keep in mind your husband is running for reelection (and we hear rumors that he intends to run for governor of our fair state in '54) and such conduct can only reflect unfavorably upon him.

The next day Beebie Tyler received a package by messenger. Inside was a skunk with the message 'A polecat for a polecat.'

8

As she had promised, Kiki named her daughter Rory. Marie offered no objection – not verbally, at least. She was in Palm Springs at the time, buying a house and trying to choose between a Spanish villa and a style that could only be described as desert ranch. As she was a traditionalist at heart, the Spanish villa won out.

A month after Rory Cranford was born, Richard Power, Jr, came into the world and was promptly registered at Stanford. Dick Power had gone to Yale, but he felt it behooved the future governor of California to send his son to a California school. UCLA might have been even a better political choice, but as far as the Powers knew, it didn't accept premature registrations.

Angel, although temporarily ensconced in the guest house of her in-laws' Bel Air home, was happy to be in Los Angeles so that she and Kiki could get together often to exchange notes on their babies. She had long since forgiven Kiki for the terrible scene at the Polo Lounge.

But she didn't get to see as much of Kiki as she would have liked. It seemed that Kiki was terribly busy, and not with her baby. On one occasion when Kiki *was* visiting with little Rory, Angel wondered aloud how Kiki could bear to leave the infant alone so much while she traipsed all over town.

Kiki sipped a martini. 'Are you implying that you're a better mother than I am? Well, I'm sure you are, Angel. You're also a better daughter, a better wife, have a better disposition, and in general are a better person. But what can I do? I just have to put up with my less-than-perfect self.'

'Oh, Kiki, of course I didn't mean to imply you weren't a good mother. I was only saying—'

'Oh, come on, Angel. I *know* you didn't mean anything. But I'm really not leaving the baby alone. She's hardly alone. She does have a nurse, and if I'm around too much it makes the nurse nervous. Now, we can't have that. Besides, Brad can barely tear himself away to get to work. He hovers over Rory's crib like an old grandma. Mr Perfect Husband is turning out to be Mr Perfect Daddy. Wouldn't you know it? Perfection. Just like you. Boy, what a team you two would have made.' She laughed. Seeing the expression on Angel's face, she added quickly, 'I'm only kidding. God! You've completely lost your sense of humor.'

Angel wasn't sure that Kiki *was* kidding, but she said, 'Tell me, what have you been up to that's keeping you on the run?'

'The usual. Still trying to get out of my contract with your fucking father-in-law. He's out to destroy me. I'm convinced of it. They just offer me turd bombs that they know I can't accept. By the time my contract runs out, I'll be all washed up, whether I accept these roles or keep sitting them out on suspension.'

'Kiki, I'll talk to him—'

'Oh no you won't. If you do, he'll know he's succeeding and it will only encourage him. Can't you see past the nose on your face? He's trying to destroy my career only to show you what he can do if *you* get out of line.'

'But what about Brad? Doesn't he try to intercede for you? He's probably the biggest star the studio has.'

'Brad's just quietly finishing out his contract with PIF. He only has about a year to go on it, then he'll go independent. Sign contracts for one film at a time. That's the future, you know. The studio-star system with long-term contracts is finished. I'll probably be the only player left with a long-term contract. One who doesn't make films. That's why I'm running around like a chicken without a head trying to get Howard Hughes to put pressure on Liam Power to sell him my contract.'

'But you just said that studios aren't making long-term contracts. Why would Hughes buy yours?'

Kiki gave her a long, lingering look. 'Howard isn't like anybody else. He doesn't follow the rules. He's different.'

Whoever billed Howard Hughes as one of the world's great lovers was either its biggest liar or had never gone to bed with him, Kiki mused that afternoon as Howard methodically went about the business of

188

trying to achieve climax. Besides which, she wasn't getting anyplace. The wily Hughes continued to out-fox her.

'Grab it! Quick!' Howard yelled fiercely as he withdrew himself from her, and Kiki obeyed, taking his organ in her white hand and working it with slender fingers, tipped with frosted-white pearl nails. 'Stop! Quick!'

She let go of his penis and held her breath, awaiting the next order, hoping it wouldn't be what she expected. But it was. 'Turn over! Quick!' Howard apparently preferred rumps to vaginas.

As he snaked himself into her, she pressed her face into the pillow and fought back tears. Kiki Devlin didn't cry, dammit!

Each time he had promised he would make an offer Liam Power wouldn't, couldn't possibly resist. He would then feature her in one great vehicle after the other, making her the biggest star Hollywood had ever known, bigger that Pickford, bigger than Dietrich, bigger than Garbo. 'I'll settle for bigger than Turner,' she always said, not quite the gullible fool he apparently considered her.

But it had all come to naught and she was tired of the whole thing. His body was unappetizing and his personality humorless. She wondered how he had gotten his reputation as a fascinating lover, even allowing for the gaggle of would-be stars who accepted promises of a great future and then were left waiting by their telephones.

Then Howard abruptly pulled out again, and she waited for the next order. Goddammit! She wasn't about to take it in her mouth this time. Not after he had been in her goddamn asshole, for God's sake!

'The Vaseline! Quick!'

She knew what that meant, the pervert! She took the jar of Vaseline Hughes had brought with him from the bedstand, dunked in her middlefinger and forefinger, and, grimacing, inserted them in his rear.

189

Nobody could say she wasn't a good sport. She was finished with him and *still* she was being a good sport. When he gave a little scream and collapsed flatly on the bed, she withdrew, smiling grimly as she raked him with long pointed nails.

She went to the bathroom, and when she came back he was wearing his white shirt and sneakers and nothing else. She started to dress, telling him that it was all over. No more afternoons in the house in the Hollywood Hills. No more sex, and no more rotten, unkept promises.

Howard looked at her warily, nervously, apparently anticipating a ploy to corner him one way or another.

'All right, I'll marry you,' he said finally.

'What? Are you crazy? I'm perfectly happily married. What makes you think I want you to marry me?' *You old queer!*

Howard blinked. 'That's what everyone wants.' Then, paying no mind to what she had just said, he pronounced, 'First you have to divorce Brad. But you can't let on why you're divorcing him. I wouldn't want him to think that I was trying to pull something on him. But of course,' he said, thinking hard, 'we can't see each other in the meantime. And you can't stay in the same house as Brad. You'll have to move in here while you're getting the divorce. It's leased, but not in my name. But don't worry. You won't see me, but the rent will be paid every month.'

Kiki knew all about how Howard parked attractive things in houses all over town, paying the rent and sometimes never seeing them again, the only requisite being that the lady in question didn't see anybody else either.

'Howard,' she said firmly, 'I don't want to marry you. I have no intention of moving into this house or of divorcing Brad.'

He still didn't quite believe her.

'Just tell me one thing, Howard. Did you *ever* try to buy my contract from Liam Power?'

'Of course.'

'What did he say?'

'He said you'll never work in this town again.'

Howard was rumored to be a genius, so she asked him, 'Howard, what do you think I should do?'

'The way I see it, you have two choices. Either sit out the remainder of the contract or get yourself a good lawyer, the best lawyer available, to break it.'

Sit out another five years? Her career would be over for good by that time! She would be Mrs Brad Cranford, wife and mother, and Kiki Devlin would be dead.

'Would you suggest a lawyer?'

Howard appeared startled, then suspicious. 'Me? I don't know any lawyers.'

Kiki sighed. What a bum! Howard was involved in more lawsuits than any other person she knew.

But he was thinking hard again. 'If you don't plan on divorcing Brad, then we *can* go on seeing each other. I'm going out of town Wednesday. How about Friday? Two o'clock? Here?'

'No insult intended, Howard, but go fuck yourself!'

'Well, then . . . maybe I can take you and Brad to Ciro's Friday night?'

Louella Parsons wrote in her syndicated column that she, Louella herself, was personally thankful that Howard Hughes's affair with the very pretty wife of one of filmdom's handsomest movie stars was over. As a new mother, the lady in question should *behave* better, Howie Hughes should *know* better, and filmland's nicest movie personality *deserved* better.

Brad brought the item to Kiki's attention. 'Got any idea who Louella has in mind?' he asked gravely.

'Somebody ought to do something about that woman. She's probably jealous because somebody gave Beebie a story instead of her. Or maybe they gave the story to Hopper. Anyone who takes up with Howard Hughes is a pervert. Why, the man is as queer as a three-dollar bill.'

'How do you know that, Kiki?' Brad's eyes bored into hers.

'Don't be ridiculous, Brad. Everybody knows it. Didn't you hear the story about Howard and Errol Flynn?'

He shook his head.

She would have liked to strangle old Lolly. Where did the old bitch get that story? Certainly not from Howard! She probably had spies who followed people around and peered through windows.

Oh, my God! All those fucking kinky things I had to do with Howard!

It was Dick who showed the item to Angel. She read it and looked at him with a question in her eyes. 'You think Louella is talking about Kiki, don't you?'

'I don't *think*. Dad's furious. He'd like to ram the morality clause in Kiki's contract down her throat, only he doesn't want to cause any more scandal that could reflect on me.'

'For God's sake, why doesn't he simply let Kiki go? That's all she wants.'

'He'll never do that.'

'But why? *Why?*' Kiki had said that Liam Power was using her to keep Angel herself in line. Would Dick dare admit that? 'What has Kiki done to him that is so terrible he has to ruin her?'

'For one thing, she has a big mouth. She's badmouthed him all over town. He'll never forget or forgive that.'

'But that was only after he wouldn't let her out of her contract. What about before that?'

But Dick would say no more except that Kiki was a fool, and an indiscreet one at that.

'I don't believe Louella's story. Louella is wrong half the time. Besides, it's a blind item.'

Dick shook his head. 'It won't wash. There's this house in the Hollywood Hills. Kiki's Rolls has been spotted there two, three times a week. Alongside a decrepit old Chevy.'

'A decrepit old Chevy? I don't understand.'

'Hughes has this thing about secrecy. He has a fleet of old Chevies he drives around in. So nobody will know it's he. Only those decrepit Chevies are the worst-kept secret in town.'

'Oh . . .' Angel said, feeling sick, although she had known the truth all along.

Dick gave a short laugh. 'Only I would have thought Kiki was smarter that that. RKO hasn't had a successful film in a long time. Why she was messing around with Hughes is beyond me.'

When Howard Hughes was taken to the hospital so severely beaten that he had to remain there eight days, nobody carried the story. Not Parsons or Hopper or Beebie Tyler. Brad Cranford was everybody's favorite. And Hughes never preferred any charges. He was a man disposed to discretion at any cost.

9

Eisenhower won the election that November, as did Dick Power. There was a huge victory celebration at the Power home in Bel Air. His campaign workers were there, as well as political friends from all over the country, in addition to all of Liam Power's friends in the movie industry. Even Brad and Kiki were invited, although they did not accept the invitation.

And then it was almost Christmas. Marie was taking up winter residence in her new home in Palm Springs and wanted her daughters to come for the housewarming-holiday celebration. But Dick insisted he had to be in Bel Air for the holiday. It was a family tradition. He hadn't missed Christmas with his family ever – not even during the war. It would be bad luck to break that tradition. That was all he had to say to Angel, who was by nature superstitious. They compromised. They would spend Christmas in Bel Air, and New Year's in Palm Springs, when her mother would be holding an open house. Kiki planned on going to Palm Springs and staying from before Christmas through New Year's Day. She and Brad did have their own place there and she knew everybody, and there were loads of holiday parties to choose from. In fact, Hetty Weiss was giving a party on the twenty-sixth, with strippers imported from Vegas, and it was sure to be a gas!

Despite all the boisterous revelry, Angel didn't much enjoy her Christmas. She was uncomfortable with the whole Power family and she could hardly bear to speak with Liam at all. She impatiently waited for the twenty-eighth, when they would leave for Palm Springs.

On the morning of the twenty-eighth, Dick packed Angel, the baby, and the nurse into a limousine but told her he wouldn't be able to leave until that evening. He had a pile of work to catch up with at his office in town, had to clear the decks for his new term. But that evening he called instead. One of his biggest campaign contributors, Harris Gordon, was down from San Francisco and was throwing a party at the Wilshire. Why didn't Angel drive back to LA and bring Brad and Kiki with her? Harris was just crazy about the idea of having Brad Cranford at his party.

Angel didn't care for the idea at all. Dick maligned Kiki at every opportunity but now he was prepared to use her husband to curry favor with the multimillionaire Gordon. But Kiki, already bored with the parties in Palm Springs, said she didn't mind going. 'What the hell. A party is a party. Let's go.'

After they left the Gordon party, Dick suggested they look in on a late party at the Ambassador for his pal Jake McFeeney. Jake had wangled an ambassadorship to some banana republic and was celebrating.

By the time they all awoke the next day in Angel and Dick's apartment, Brad remembered that his agent was throwing a holiday party that afternoon. He felt obligated to put in an appearance. But he assured Dick that it wasn't necessary for him to go. Dick, in true holiday spirit, said that of course they would go – what was fair was fair, and tit for tat. Brad and Kiki had gone along to Dick's parties, now he would go along with Brad. 'Isn't that right, Angel?'

Angel, thrilled to see how well Kiki and Dick were getting along, agreed completely. And after the agent's party, there was Pooh (Patricia) Stanford Greenberg's holiday buffet to attend. Pooh had been Kiki's best friend at Vassar before Kiki was kicked out. Since then, Pooh had married Norm Greenberg, one of filmdom's most esteemed lawyers.

Now, as they walked through the huge iron door of Pooh's Moorish castle, it dawned upon Kiki that the lawyer she needed to fight Liam Power was right here all along, almost on her very doorstep, or more accurately, on Pooh's own doorstep. Why hadn't she thought of it before? She would seek Norman out immediately.

But the first person Kiki spied once inside the huge, beamed drawing room was Gena Grant. Kiki whispered apologetically to Angel, 'I *am* sorry we came, sweetie. If I had had the least little idea old GG was here, I certainly wouldn't have—'

'What are you talking about?'

'Gena Grant, dopey. You know – the other half of that blind item in the gossip column. She's the one – the GG.'

'We never knew for sure it was Dick – or Gena Grant, for that matter, if you remember,' Angel reminded her sharply.

Kiki shrugged, and Angel watched Gena Grant out of the corner of her eyes. It was hard not to look at her, Angel had to admit to herself. Gena Grant was a sizzler. In a strapless red gown with obviously nothing underneath, tossing her golden hair this way and that, she made Angel feel almost dowdy. She did see Dick speaking animatedly to Gena, but only for a moment. And, in all fairness, he spoke to everyone in that glib politician's way of his.

But Kiki was less than sanguine about it. 'That's exactly what makes me suspicious – that he spoke to her so *casually*. I'd really feel better about it if he acted more excited about such a spectacularly attractive broad. As any normal man would.'

'Oh, Kiki,' Angel said wearily, 'with you, no one can ever win, no matter what.'

'Oh, I'm going to win, one way or another,' Kiki said, making a bee-line for the portly but good-looking Norm Greenberg.

The foursome returned to Palm Springs on the thirty-first. Marie's house was decorated and lit, ready for the party that would be starting in a few hours. In the meantime Angel went to check on her baby son while Kiki helped with the flowers. Brad and Dick had a quick drink with Edward, then changed into their whites for an equally quick set of tennis.

Then, just as the guests started to arrive, there was a call from Bel Air. Dick came back looking worried. Mother was sick, he said, and he didn't know how serious it was. Dad had said that her pressure was way up. The doctor had put her to bed but she kept asking for *him*. He was awfully sorry not to be there to welcome in the New Year with her and her family, but he had no choice but to grab a helicopter back to LA.

'It sounds pretty serious,' Angel agreed. 'Maybe I should go with you.'

'No, no, I don't want to spoil your party. I'll try to get back tomorrow. If not, I'll call.'

At five minutes past midnight, Angel picked up the phone and dialed the Bel Air number. At least she could give Dick his New Year's greeting over the phone. And, of course, inquire after her mother-in-law.

There was so much noise in the background – music, screaming, horns blowing – that for an instant Angel didn't realize that it was her mother-in-law herself who answered the phone. She sounded healthy enough. In fact, Angel decided, she sounded not a *little* bit tipsy as she asked, 'How is Dick, Angel? Is something wrong?'

'No, no, it's all right. And I'm glad you're feeling better, Mother Power.'

'Better? Better than what, Angel dear?'

And to think she used to think of Dick as the honorable King Richard, Richard the Lion-hearted! *Oh, King Richard! You have become very faint of heart. You're nothing more than a dirty rat!*

PART SEVEN

*Tarrytown,   Sacramento,   Hollywood,   The
Riviera
1953*

'I believe 1953 was the year Angel went to Sacramento. If memory serves me, the then present governor of California resigned to take a federal post in Washington under Mr Eisenhower and Dick Power was appointed to the governorship until the next election and he resigned his seat in the House. Yes, I think that's right.

'Angel was a very charming First Lady of our fair state. She settled down in the rather shabby California "White House" in Sacramento and did her duty – she was able to utilize many of her considerable talents in the performance of that duty. There was an "Invest in California" promotion, and as part of that Angel narrated the documentary showing all the glories of our proud state. She was a knockout, and although the film was made originally for commercial reasons, it was shown on TV as a travelogue sort of thing, with all the fees going to the state treasury, of course.

'Thinking back, it seems to me the year that Angel went to Sacramento was the very same year of Kiki's terrible scandal, the one that involved one of our town's biggest barristers . . . Norman Greenberg. I was forced to chastize her in print . . . oh, yes.'

1

Marie Whittier returned to Tarrytown from Palm Springs just in time for the spring cleaning. The pantries were being turned inside out and all the crystal and stemware rewashed to a new sparkle. The windows, the floors, all had to be done. The blue sitting room on the second floor needed new draperies. Every bed in the house would be freshly made up with the new flowered Porthaults she had ordered while still in the Springs, her own bed with the pale peach silk sheets of which she was so fond.

She looked out the window at the layer of snow that had fallen during the night, although it was nearly April and time for the daffodils. She thought of Angel in the governor's mansion in Sacramento, trying so desperately not to be lonely as her husband ignored her for his own pursuits, legitimate and otherwise. And Kiki! Much as Marie had disliked the idea of Kiki marrying Brad Cranford, she now admired the man – a kind, strong man of refinement, whether acquired or not. She hoped that Kiki would have the sense to hold on to him, to appreciate him.

Herman brought in the morning mail on a salver. She flipped through it in a distracted way, still thinking of her daughters. She wished that she could have stayed in California to be near them, in case they needed her. But what was she to do? Eddie was in school in Massachusetts and he was just a boy; he needed his mother too. And Stoningham! She loved it so.

She came to an envelope that bore a New Orleans return address. An unfamiliar one, not Julian's. Her heart beat faster. What now? Her hand trembled a bit as she slit the envelope open.

She glanced through the pages quickly to get to the

signature at the end of the long handwritten letter. 'Your loving sister, Desiree.' *Desi!*

She settled herself back in the desk chair.

My dear Marie,

I dare say you're surprised to hear from me. I hope it's not too terrible a shock. In all fairness, I've already given you all the shocks any one person is entitled to give another in one lifetime. I guess the less said about that the better. I could say after all this time that I'm sorry, but that sounds absolutely ridiculous. When I sat down to write this letter the first time, about two weeks ago, I swore to myself I wouldn't say it. 'I'm sorry,' I mean. And I've been working on this letter every day since, so you can get an idea how difficult it has been to get it down and to say certain things, and not say other things.

You must be wondering why I'm writing to you at all, if not to say 'I'm sorry' and ask your forgiveness. I'm *not* asking your forgiveness, not only because I don't think you would give it, but because it doesn't really matter anymore. What's done is done, and nothing is going to change anything that's happened to us both because of what I've done.

So why am I writing to you? Just to keep the record straight, I guess. I have just married and I wanted you to know that. It's a loose thread in the pattern of our lives, and somehow it won't be all neatly tied up until I've told you about it. And I'm tired of loose threads. I'm getting to be a much more tidy person.

I married a few months ago. Without too much rehashing or bringing up of painful subjects, I'd like to tell you a bit about what has happened till now.

I returned from California in '42, as I think you know. When Rory went into the army. We were just about washed up anyhow. I am *not* going to discuss those five years or so I spent with him except to say they weren't as bad as you might have heard. Rory, while no hero, was not the villain that he's been painted. But nor was it as heavenly as I thought it would be. What ever happened to me was more my fault than his. You might have heard that I became a 'dope fiend'. That isn't true. I did fool

203

around with some of the stuff – cocaine mostly – but it was only malnutrition from drinking that did me in, as they say. But my hell on earth really started only when I came home to New Orleans – to Julian and Audrey and *Maman* sitting in that bed and looking at me with those eyes. It's safe to assume that *Maman* died without forgiving me. And she was right not to forgive me. Only a fool would have done that, and *Maman* may have been many things, but she was no fool. She always did have my number.

If you want to hear that I suffered for my crimes (and somehow I don't really believe that after all this time you really do) let me say that the years I spent with Julian and Audrey took care of that.

A couple of years ago I decided it was time to pull myself together and get free of them. I was finally physically able to get a job and I went to work in a drugstore as a cashier. (I still am the cashier.) I took a furnished room and I worked all day and I went home at night to my little room and that was it. It wasn't much of a life, but it was freedom, and that was a joy.

I guess you've guessed by now that I married the boss, Pierre Lazarus. How do you like that for a moniker? Yes, he's half Jewish, and *Maman* is probably still cursing me from her grave, but I'm sure God isn't. Pierre is sweet and kind and very good to me, and I'm lucky to have him, even if he's not the match *Maman* would have deemed appropriate. But Pierre knows my whole story and he doesn't judge me. And he thinks I'm beautiful! It's been a long time since anyone else said that Desiree du Beaumond was beautiful.

Pierre makes up the prescriptions and I take care of the money and keep the books. (We also have clerks, as it's a large store.) We have a lovely apartment right near the store because we keep late hours. As *Maman* would say, I have become part of the petite bourgeoisie. It's not so bad, believe me. I sit by the register in a black dress (I think it's appropriate for the store) and pearls and my hair is worn in a chignon and I wear four rings and have long red nails. (Cashiers always keep nice hands and nails and wear rings. Did you know that?) Also, I wear heavenly French perfume (the best in the house.)

We go to the movies once a week, and quite frequently to Antoine's and all the other wonderful restaurants, just like in the old days. And wonder of wonders, I'm happy! And so is Pierre!

So there you have it. That's the story, Morning Glory, as we used to say when we were little. And now we can close out the books.

I've written a lot of brave words about not asking for your forgiveness. And I won't ask you to wish me well. I know you're not a Catholic anymore, and I don't even know what I am. Not anything, I guess. But still I got a feeling, Little Sister, that Jesus will love you if you don't hate me so much anymore.

Your loving sister,

Desiree

P.S. I've seen pictures of Kiki and Angel all over the place and they're just terrific! I can't help but cry a little when I look at them. Just a little.

Marie reread the letter and brushed at her eyes with her handkerchief. Then she sat down at the desk and took one of her informal note papers. She wrote:

Dear Sister,
I don't hate; I forgive; I wish you well.

Marie

Then she tore the note up. She went down to the pantries, where there was much activity going on – four of the servants washing china and glassware and polishing silver.

'Herman, please get a very large wooden crate. We're going to ship some of this silver and I want it carefully packed so that nothing gets dented.'

She had given some of the du Beaumond and the Manard silver to the cousins, and a few pieces to Uncle Paul before his death. And she had given all the jewelry to her daughters, as well as the flatware and most of the large pieces. Now there were only about ten or twelve pieces left of the antique silver – vases and platters, bowls and ornate candlesticks – and she grouped them together. Yes, it was time to close out the books, as Desiree put it. To fully complete the circle.

She wrote out the address for the shipping label and handed it to the butler. 'These are the pieces to be shipped, Herman.'

'All of it, madam?'

'Yes, all of it. It's a wedding present.'

Marie was glad Edward was not there to witness her *beau geste*. She would have felt ridiculous. But there it was. Her *beau geste* all the same. And she felt wonderful.

2

Kiki intended using Norm Greenberg, trading . . . doing *anything* she had to to gain her ends. But Norm Greenberg had his own ideas about who would use whom. Kiki Devlin was rich, blonde, and beautiful, but he didn't need her money, beautiful bodies were a dime a dozen in Hollywood, and he had a very classy blonde wife at home. And his preoccupation was not sex but his own reputation as a legal genius.

He found Kiki's predicament with Liam Power and the PIF studio interesting, a legal puzzle with fascinating challenges and sidelights. There was Power's son, the appointed governor of the state and Kiki's brother-in-law. There was Kiki's sister, a celebrity in her own right, in the centre of it all, if Kiki was right about old man Power's use of her to show Angel what he was capable of if she ever stepped out of line. And there was the studio itself. Liam Power was chief honcho, the majority stockholder, but there were other stockholders, whose interests were being violated if Kiki Devlin's potential as a big star moneymaker was being suppressed by Power for personal reasons. And there was the true center of the situation: did a studio have the constitutional right to deny an actor the right to work and earn a living by use of the suspension clause in contracts, at the same time restraining her from working elsewhere for the lifetime of the contract?

By God, he was going to test it in the courts and he was going to try it not only before the lower courts but before the Supreme Court itself, before he was done! He could be responsible for a landmark decision in the field of entertainment! He might effect a major change in the way the studio-star system worked for all time to come! And he himself would get headlines all across the country! Everybody was interested in a court case that came out of Hollywood!

'Let him sue *us*?' Kiki asked. 'But I don't understand. I just want to break my contract. My idea was that I sue him.'

'The only way we're going to get a legal decision on the validity of your studio suspension and subsequent inability to work anywhere else is for you to go ahead and make a picture. And then let Power sue you. We defend you, and then, hopefully, the courts decide in our favor – they hand down a decision that what he has done is illegal and you'll be free of him. It's very simple.'

Simple? she thought. *This man is simple. He's a naïve fool.*

'But how do I make a picture? *Who* will put me in a picture? No studio will use me. *They'll* be afraid of being sued. Besides, they all work hand-in-glove to keep us poor actors in line. *If he's the Harvard legal eagle he's supposed to be, why doesn't he know that?*

Norman smiled at her. 'We don't want a studio. We need an independent producer.'

'And where will we find this independent producer

who will star me in a film? Even *I* know I'm not exactly the hottest number around at this point. Why would even an independent producer touch me, with my legal problems?'

Norm smiled again. 'What we're trying to do is *set* Liam Power up. So we *set up* a company to make the picture. Our own company. Your company. Devlin Productions, or better still, Cranford Productions. We find a property. We hire ourselves a director. We get ourselves a big male star and we raise money. There's only one thing – we must do all this in complete secrecy until we're ready to roll, so that Power can't act until we're ready for him.'

'A big male star, you say?'

He nodded.

'Like Brad Cranford?'

He nodded. 'Do you think he'd do it?'

'Yes, I'm sure he would if I asked him to.'

'Good. But don't say a word to Brad just yet. Not until we have a property and a script. We want to keep this sotto voce as much as possible.' He leaned back in his big leather chair and smiled. 'Wouldn't it be a scream if we got us a hit in the bargain?'

'A scream,' she said, but she was still confused. Norm hadn't made any kind of sexual move in her direction. Now he was talking about a movie to be made expressly for her, but starring her husband. 'Why do we need Brad?'

'He's the name we need to raise the money.'

So it had come to this – her own name wasn't enough.

'It's a fucking pity we couldn't get your sister.' He laughed at the thought of getting Angela du Beaumond Power to set up Liam Power. 'Now there's a name for you. We could raise millions. Why with Brad Cranford and Angela du Beaumond Power we could remake *Gone with the Wind!*'

'And what part would I get to play? Mammy or Aunt Pitty Pat?' Kiki asked bitterly, but Norm

Greenberg just laughed and laughed.

'The important thing, Kiki, is absolute secrecy. We won't meet here in my office again. I don't want even my associates to know what's going on. You start reading novels and plays, all the scripts that people send to Brad, and in the meantime I'll get this thing organized, get it off the ground. I'll be in touch. I'll call you when we have to meet again. I'll find someplace entirely private.'

Uh-huh, Kiki thought. *Very private, I'll bet.*

When Norm did call her to arrange a meeting at a small motel in Hollywood, she thought, This is it . . . She wondered what the agenda would be. A little business first, then the tentative hand on the ass – or maybe a kiss on the neck? No – business first, then a drink, *then* the hand on the ass. Norman looked like a scotch-and-ass man.

But she was wrong. She and Norman continued to meet at the motel but there was never anything but business on the agenda. Not even a bottle of gin or a whiff of a joint. Norman was high only on their project. Brad had not yet been brought into the picture. Kiki was discussing with Norman the possibility of raising the money herself, investing her own funds, getting her stepfather to contribute.

Norman walked her to her car. He told her that he wanted outside money, that only a fool invested his own money and he didn't want a fool for a client. He helped her in and kissed her forehead, and then a Porsche pulled into the parking space next to her car, a Porsche that looked like Brad's . . . and then a man who looked like Brad waved a gun, and then Norm Greenberg screamed and collapsed to his knees, the blood from his crotch spurting everywhere, splattering the landscape.

'Oh, my God!' Kiki cried. 'Oh, my God! You've shot away his balls!'

*

Parsons, Hopper, and Tyler would gladly have suppressed the story if they could have. Brad Cranford was the one movie star who was genuinely liked by everyone in the industry, from the heads of studios down to the last grip and gaffer on the lots, including all the columnists who fed off the movie industry. But nobody was able to keep the lid on a story so spectacular.

Norman Greenberg eventually recovered physically, and no one involved ever revealed whether or not he had permanently lost his manhood. He did not wish to proffer charges, but the district attorney would not allow the matter to drop, seeing an opportunity to make a name for himself by riding the Cranford name into notoriety, if not fame. But by pleading guilty, Brad managed to avoid a trial that would have been a glorious field day for the press.

On the day Brad was to be sentenced, everyone begged Kiki not to attend the proceedings. 'I have nothing to hide, I'm innocent,' she bravely contended, and went, resplendent in a white Dior suit, complemented by a white fox stole, looking every inch the movie star, and was hissed and booed by the mob of fans waiting for a sight of Brad Cranford. Her sister, the governor's wife, accompanied her. Brad was given a suspended sentence. Someone said that PIF had paid off the judge.

They went home to a celebratory buffet, to which Kiki had invited a hundred well-wishers.

'Kiki, how could you?' Angel asked, referring to the party.

'Why not? Brad's not going to jail and I'm innocent. Norm Greenberg never laid a finger on me.' Then, thinking about it, she added, 'Nor I on him. Don't you believe me?'

'If you say so, Kiki. But what about Brad? What does he believe?'

'He won't say. All he says is that it's over and we should put it behind us.' Kiki broke into tears. 'But we

210

really can't you know. It's just too much. And what really hurts is that no matter what you and he really think, for once in my lifetime I *was* innocent. And now I'm really washed up in Hollywood. There's nothing left for me here.'

'Don't be ridiculous, Kiki. Of course there're things for you here . . . everything.'

'No,' Kiki sobbed. 'And do you want to know something else? I haven't heard a word, not one word, from my own mother. What do you have to say to that?'

Angel could think of nothing to say.

'You see, no one's on my side.'

'I am, Kiki. Really I am.'

'No, I don't think so. You're on Brad's side. You're on Mother's side.'

Angel shook her head helplessly.

3

Angel was down from Sacramento for a few days and staying at the guest house on the Power estate in Bel Air. Kiki, who was leaving for a European vacation, came to say good-bye. She was not in the best of moods.

'It was sweet of you, Kiki, to come over here. I know how you hate to set foot on this place, and I don't blame you.'

Kiki walked over to a window. 'They're only a stone's throw from you, aren't they.'

Angel joined her at the window, looked up at the large brick edifice squatting higher up the hillside. 'They're at least three or four stone throws away.' Then she drew the draperies, as if the sight of the Power house offended her, too. 'How long will you be gone?'

'I don't know. I'll see. I'll go to Switzerland first. And

then Paris. To buy some clothes.'

'What about Rory?'

'What about Rory? She has her nurse and her father. It's just not working out, Angel. I'm trying. Really I am. But where's the future in it? It's all right for you to talk. Even as the governor's wife you've got more of a career than I have. You're always making those promotional things.'

'Really, Kiki, they're no more than commercials or travelogues.'

'It's something. It's more than I have.'

'Is it? If you'd just work at it, you'd have Brad.'

And I – I have Dick . . . Or do I?

4

Kiki was back from Europe in six weeks and came up to visit her sister in Sacramento.

'I stopped in New York for a few days between planes. Do you know New York isn't what it used to be either? I thought California was boring, but New York? Twice as dull. I really think I prefer Europe.'

'Not to live?' Angel asked, incredulous. She knew how Kiki had loved California.

'I can work there, you know. Italian films are marvelous.'

'You don't speak Italian.'

'I can learn. Besides, I only have to memorize the lines. And I can do all my own dubbing for the American market. That's what counts. The American market.'

'You sound as if you've already given this a lot of thought.'

'Well, I met the most wonderful director when I was in Rome. A genius, really. And he has his own studio.'

'I didn't even know you were in Rome. You said you were going to Switzerland and then Paris and—'

'Switzerland is boring. All those chintzy little chalets. I spent a few days in Paris and then I decided to go to Rome. Rome is where it's happening in Europe these days. A marvelous city! It's open all night. It's more cosmopolitan than New York. It makes Los Angeles look like a one-cow town, for God's sake. And the men! Oh, they're exciting, Angel. They really make you feel like a woman. And this director I met – Count Vittorio Rosa. Vic! Sexy! So sexy. I haven't seen a man so sexy in ages. And a count – royalty. And rich. Apart from his movie studio. Money from way back. Probably from the Medicis,' she said with authority.

Angel laughed, certain that Kiki didn't know what she was talking about.

'He's tall, dark and handsome. And suave. He has a mustache and a certain way of smiling. He lifts one eyebrow just like Clark. And you know how mad I was about Clark . . .'

'Listen to you.' Angel smiled a sad smile. 'You sound like an infatuated schoolgirl.'

'Oh, Angel, I *feel* like an infatuated schoolgirl.'

'And how do you feel about Brad, Kiki? Aren't you acting a little foolishly, considering Brad and Rory?'

'Don't start, Angel!'

'Well, considering you are a married woman and a mother, don't you think you're acting a bit juvenile?'

'It's the same old story with you, Angel. As soon as I say I met a man who has the same physical characteristics as your father and that photographer of yours—'

'Of *mine?*'

'—you go into a tizzy.'

'But you always said—'

'Never mind what I said. We're mature women now. And if I happen to meet a man who just incidentally resembles our father, so what? Daddy was handsome and so is Vic. So what? Are you so jealous you have to spoil for me what was only a very mild flirtation?'

Angel didn't want to fight. She was not in the mood

for a serious confrontation, so she backed off. 'And how was the count in you-know-what?' she asked teasingly.

Kiki didn't want to fight either. 'Naughty, naughty, Angélique! So unlike you. I didn't go to bed with him. Maybe next time. It's a mistake, you know, to let a European screw you the first time out. Especially Italians. They get the wrong idea. They don't respect women as it is. Except their mothers or sisters. Those they worship. Or sometimes they worship their wives. But only if they stay at home, keep out of their way, and remain terribly, terribly pure.'

'Honestly, Kiki, you make my head spin. Didn't he try?'

'Of course he tried. But the fact that I resisted him didn't repress him. Quite *au contraire*, my dear. Italian men take refusal as encouragement. It only makes them try harder, and it makes the game more fun, too. In fact, it's the game that's the important thing – the style, the subtlety, the nuances . . . like an orchestrated piece of music. And if they want you, they never give up. Never. Not even if it takes twenty years.'

Angel laughed, wanting to laugh, wanting to dispel the despair that enveloped her.

'I'd love to see that. You in twenty years with Count Vittorio chasing you, cane in one hand, magnifying glass in the other the better to see your fading attributes.'

'Don't be ridiculous. My attributes will never fade. I simply won't let them. After all, there are face lifts and ass lifts and tit lifts and all those darling shots you get in Switzerland. In fact, when I go back to Europe in a couple of months I might just check into a clinic for a little cellular rejuvenation. And if you're not the fool I'm sure you are, you'll come with me. It's never too early to get a jump on old age.'

'Hold on. You just came back from Europe and you're planning another trip already?'

They stared at each other. It was as if they both were looking into the same crystal ball and both could see the future but neither one was ready to talk about it.

'Come with me,' Kiki said in what she hoped was a blithe tone. 'And you'll get a chance to eyeball my lechy count, and then we can be roomies at the clinic, just like in the old days at school. Doesn't that sound like fun?'

Angel shook her head. 'I still think we're too young. God, Kiki! We're still in our twenties, even if it *feels* like our forties.'

'We won't have anything lifted, ninny. Just a few shots. I told you – a girl is never too young to start fighting off the ravages of age. After all, the day you hit puberty you're on the skids. It's all downhill after that. It's nature's revenge. As soon as you start menstruating, your skin is drying up by the minute. That's why you have to start right in frigging and fucking. Coming helps keep the skin soft and pliable.'

'Imagine! There I was, all washed up at twelve, and I didn't even know it.'

'You think I'm joking? Think of all those eggs inside you getting older by the minute.'

'What *are* you talking about? What eggs?'

'Whan a girl child is born, she has all the eggs capable of becoming babies already inside her,' Kiki said with a certain amount of smugness. 'Every time she gets the dot, she loses an egg, but the rest just lie there, getting older and older, month after month.' Kiki laughed at Angel's expression. 'Not bad for a girl who was kicked out of Vassar at nineteen, eh? You never knew I was so smart, did you? Anyhow, that's why I decided to have Rory when I did.'

'Great reason to have a baby.'

'Listen to me. If, and I stress *if*, you're going to have any more babies, there's no time like the present. Wait! Scratch that! What *am* I saying? I do get carried away with my own superior knowledge. Don't you

215

dare have another baby now. If you start knocking out a brat every year you will really need a tit lift soon. You can't believe how many women need a bazoom lift before they're thirty-five.'

But now Angel wasn't listening to Kiki rattling on with her nonsense. She was thinking about the conversation she had just had with Dick on the subject of her having another baby.

'We're going to have to tighten our belts,' Dick said grimly.

'Oh? Why is that?' Angel picked moodily at her eggs Benedict. Apparently they were going to have one of *those* conversations.

'Several reasons,' he said, wolfing his sausage and eggs. 'One is that you've spent thousands fixing up this state-owned wreck for which there is no allocation of funds in the state budget. We'll have to eat it ourselves.'

Angel started to say that the decaying mansion had been unliveable without the refurbishing, but decided to let it go. She didn't have the energy to pursue it.

'Another reason is that you've been spending inordinate amounts of money on clothes. Your last month's bills alone would support a family of ten in Calcutta for a lifetime.'

She decided to defend herself. 'Families in Calcutta aren't always in the public eye with little people from newspapers taking notes on what they're wearing. Would you like it if they wrote that Mrs Richard Power was seen at the opera wearing last year's' – she groped for a word – 'tutu, the very same tutu she wore to the state orgy for the visiting King of Transylvania?'

'Fun-ny! You know what really is funny? You and your sister thinking you're so goddamned clever. You're both such smart-asses. And for God's sake, do you have to eat eggs Benedict for *breakfast*? It's so goddamn affected. Why can't you eat plain scrambled eggs like everyone else? It makes me sick to look at

216

that mess so early in the morning.'

She looked at him steely-eyed across the table. The nerve of him, telling her what to eat! At that moment she would have gladly stuck her fork into his large, red hand.

As if sensing her rage, he apologized. 'Sorry, I have a lot on my mind.'

'For instance?'

'Us having another baby.'

'In case you haven't had the time to look lately, we have had a baby recently.'

'We could use another.'

'Would you listen to yourself?' she asked incredulously. '*Use* another baby!'

'C'mon. You know what I mean. It's a good time to have another baby.'

She stared down into her plate. The eggs Benedict *did* look particularly unappealing. Dick leaned towards her and spoke in a conspiratorial tone. 'Dad's willing to take responsibility for this one.'

She fought to keep from laughing. 'You mean he's going to climb in the sack with me in place of you?'

He drew back in shock. 'Your sense of humor is growing more warped by the day.'

'Oh, come now. You act as if I insulted the Pope himself.'

'I only meant that Dad'll put a million into trust for us if we have another baby.'

'Really? You mean if I have a baby each year for the next ten years we'll be worth something like ten million dollars? Maybe we could work out an accelerating scale. A mil for this year's baby, one and a half mil for the next, and so on. Sounds exciting. What do we get if I drop twins?'

The maid came in and poured the coffee. After she left the room again, Dick lit his first cigar of the day and leaned back in his chair. 'Just think about it, okay? You know how you're always complaining about not having enough money. Maybe we'd even be able to build a house to your exact specifications.'

'You mean that if I have another baby I may get a house of my own as a reward. No baby, no house?'

'You know you sound more and more like your sister every day . . . like a grating buzz saw.' Then, softly, persuasively: 'Just think about it, Angel, will you?'

He had to relight his cigar, and she noticed now that he was using matches and not the gold lighter from Dunhill's that she had given him the previous Christmas.

'What happened to your lighter?'

'I probably left it at the office.'

She took notice of the surrealistic design of the matchbook cover. Swirls of red, fuchsia, and pink. She picked it up. *The Round-Up. Las Vegas.* 'Where did you get these?'

Dick moistened his lips with his tongue. He shrugged. 'You know how it is. Somebody puts down a book of matches . . . I must have picked them up somewhere. Last week somebody left a book of matches on my desk that came from a saloon in Alaska.'

A long explanation. Much too long.

After Dick left Angel dialed his personal secretary at the offices at the Capitol building. It was just a hunch – a shot in the dark.

'Leila, Governor Power wanted me to ask you to check with the hotel in Las Vegas, just in case it slipped his mind when he saw you. He thinks he left his gold cigarette lighter there.'

'Oh, yes, Mrs Power. He did leave it at the Sands. They just called, as a matter of fact. They put it in the mail.'

'Oh, good,' Angel said, with as much enthusiasm as she could muster.

She hung up the phone. It was true. Dick had been in Las Vegas when she had been told he was in Washington.

*

'What are you thinking about?' Kiki narrowed her eyes. 'You were miles away. You weren't listening to a word I said.'

Angel was not about to get into Dick's being in Las Vegas when he was supposed to be in Washington. 'I was thinking you haven't said a word about Rory or Brad. How did you find them on your return?'

Kiki shrugged. 'Rory's more beautiful than ever. And Brad's Brad. Sweet as sugar, as usual. Only he doesn't smile as much anymore.' She looked down at her long fingernails, which were painted brown. 'I just don't understand it. The one time in my life that I was innocent . . . *You* believe me, don't you?'

Angel ran to her, knelt by her chair. 'Of course I do!'

'Well, then you're the only one. Even my own mother doesn't, you know.'

'Oh, Kiki, I'm sure she does. We've talked about it.'

'When?'

'Oh, don't you know? While you were in Europe Mother was out here. She bought a house! Right next to Cole Porter in Brentwood.'

'Nobody tells me anything. What am I around here? A stepdaughter? Cinderella? Why did she buy a house in Brentwood, anyway? She just bought a house in Palm Springs, not to mention the three homes she already has in New York.'

'Just maybe to be near her daughters.'

'Oh yes? *One* daughter is more like it. It's you she wants to be near.'

'She wants to be close to us both.'

'*Sure.* Well, I'm not sure how long *this* daughter is going to be around.

5

Angel would not have hesitated so long in agreeing to

being part of the feature the *New York Times Magazine* wanted to do on the restored California governor's mansion if she had dreamed that the photographer on the project would be Nick Dominguez.

She had labored long and hard on the restoration and had absolutely loved the dignified layout *Town and Country* had produced, featuring both her and the house. She knew the *Times* would do an entirely different kind of interpretation, and she was wary, especially since she was two months pregnant and not feeling all that well. But Dick had pushed. The whole thing wouldn't take up more than a couple of days, he argued, and it would be nice if they could get some Eastern exposure. God knows, the administration could use a little well-placed publicity. He *was* running for election to the governor's post the following year, and he'd like as many people as possible to see what had been done with the mansion.

In the end, it hadn't been her choice. And that day when she came downstairs to meet the people from the magazine and their photographer, who turned out to be Dominguez, she thought she might pass out. But she couldn't. She was the governor's wife and she had to act with dignity. She had to pretend she didn't even know who he was, this man who had become such a presence in her life. Her heart beat fast. Was she really drawn to this man, she wondered, or was it some kind of fascination only because he seemed fascinated with her? She could hardly tell anymore.

She smiled. His face lit up. She extended her hand, almost in a way that presumed it would be taken reverently, kissed in the most courtly manner. She was queenly.

He shook her hand instead of kissing it, but yes, the reverence was there, the courtliness. He lowered his eyes, almost as if he didn't deserve to look at the queen. Was he thinking about the terrible scene at the Polo Lounge? He murmured something. It sounded like he was honored.

He had come a long way, she thought. From photographer for that cheap rag *Whisper* to an accredited photojournalist, not to mention his standing in Hollywood circles as a photographer-artist. What had Kiki called him – the Avedon of the Wicked West?

Yes, there was a presence about him. She could sense it. So could the others, the editorial people. It was almost as if they stepped back, acknowledging the force of his artistry. *He* chose the format of the pictures; the editorial content would follow his lead. In the end, she knew she would not be at all regretful. She knew the essay would be perfect, would surpass the dignity that *Town and Country* had conveyed, would only compliment her and what she had accomplished.

And it turned out exactly that way. He had posed her like a princess and she had emerged a queen, the restored governor's mansion her palace.

There were congratulatory comments from all over the country. And Dick was pleased. His reflected image had been covered with glory.

Angel felt a contentment she didn't quite understand. It was a contentment that flooded her being for days.

6

The transatlantic call from Kiki in San Remo began early in the morning, and Angel waited for its completion impatiently. It had been three months since Kiki had left for Italy to make the movie for Vittorio Rosa, and she hadn't heard from her in all that time.

She sat by the phone waiting, smoked several cigarettes, drank several cups of coffee, didn't get dressed. She was still in a state of depression, although it was several weeks since she had miscarried. The only time her depression was relieved was when she spent time with her son, but usually her schedule allowed little time even for this.

Finally the operator was back and produced Kiki's voice. 'Let's not waste any more time before we're cut off again.' She talked rapidly. 'We wrapped the picture last week and we're celebrating here on the Riviera and I've just talked to Vic and he *insists* you join us here. There's a crowd of people coming and going and it'll do you good to get your mind off your troubles. A miscarriage isn't the absolute end of the world. Besides, you had no business getting preggy so soon. It's bad for your plumbing. That's probably why you lost it – your insides weren't strong enough yet. That son of a bitch had no business knocking you up so soon.'

Angel didn't even have time to speak up in defense of Dick; Kiki just kept rolling along. 'Just forget it, there's time enough next year. In the meantime, get your ass over here. We'll cheer you up.'

'How much longer will you be in San Remo? If you finished the picture last week shouldn't you be coming home? Isn't Brad upset? Even Mother's said she hoped you'd be home soon. She said Rory needs you.'

'Don't be ridiculous. Rory is very well looked after. We came down here just in time for the Grand Prix. Vic raced, you know.' She giggled. 'He was furious when I teased him about losing. Everybody was here. The weather was stinko, but that didn't seem to keep them away. Half the crowd was so bombed they didn't know who won the race. Too bad you missed it. Nobody slept the whole weekend. It was just back and forth from the bar at the Hôtel de Paris to the villas for more drinking. We had a great bash here Friday night. Guess what the high spot of the evening was? Vic *flashed* in front of everybody!'

'Sounds pretty juvenile to me,' Angel said grumpily.

'You're just in a bad mood, darling. Vic had just finished the picture. He was exhausted, poor darling.

222

He had to let go, let something down. This time it was his pants. Angel, sweetheart, you're just so depressed, you can't find anything amusing. Fly to me, my sweet, on wings of love and Kiki will make you laugh. It's time you got out of Sacramento anyway. It's June already. My God, suppose you dropped dead tomorrow. What would everyone say? "She was found dead in Sacramento in *June*, of all times and places."'

Angel laughed.

'See? What you need is your big sister. Make your arrangements immediately. Let me know when you're arriving. You can land in Nice and we'll pick you up.'

'I'd love to, Kiki, but I just don't know. Dick will have a fit. He'll be worried about adverse publicity . . . about my mingling with the international set. I'm afraid he's looking ahead already to the time when he'll make a bid for the presidency.'

'Oh, for God's sake. Now you have to live your life on the remote possibility of the White House?'

'I know, I know, it's ridiculous. Still, he will worry about me mixing with all those princes, pashas, and dukes. The American public isn't crazy about that sort of thing, you know. And what about those demimondaines on the Riviera?'

'Oh, my dear sweet ass, you *are* impossible! If you mean the high-class hookers, La Bette Otero must have gone out of business around 1900, along with her boyfriend, the Prince of Wales. You can tell Dick Power from me to go fuck himself. That way, at least no one gets knocked up. You just lost a baby, didn't you? You need a little rest and recreation. Get yourself over here, you hear? Immediately! After all, *I* can't stay here forever. I have a husband and baby waiting for me at home, I think. As for Dick, he doesn't worry about the publicity when he's romancing with you know who.'

Dick objected, but just a little. Angel suspected that he was secretly relieved. She supposed she *was* a bore with her eternal depression. Or was he just waiting for an opportunity, her absence, to indulge himself in a little rendezvous or two?

'Just try to keep a low profile, will you?' he asked. 'Stay out of the papers, for God's sake. That's a pretty wild crew Kiki is running with. Vic Rosa might be hailed as a cinematic genius but those Italian films can get pretty raunchy.

'I'll make a deal with you. I'll try to keep out of the headlines if you try to stay out of the gossip columns.'

'What's *that* supposed to mean?'

She didn't answer, merely looked at him knowingly.

He dropped it.

'*Carissima*, let's get started or your sister will be left stranded at the airport.'

'I'm coming, I'm coming. I was just trying to cram in a little nourishment before I start cheering up poor Angel.' Carrying a plate with several rounds of toast heaped with caviar, Kiki got into the low-slung car.

'That is a terrible habit of yours, my darling, eating those little fish eggs for breakfast.'

'Everybody eats eggs for breakfast, don't they?' Kiki flicked away a tiny nodule of grayish matter from her cerise satin pajamas with a silver-colored nail. One of the things she adored about the Riviera was the chance to wear these delicious, decadent clothes.

'Not fishy ones.'

'I've always adored caviar. This is a really good batch. What kind is it?'

'Beluga, *carissima*.'

'Good,' she said, finishing up and licking her fingers. She set the plate down on the floor of the car, and, throwing both arms around his neck, she commenced to lick his face as he drove.

He pushed her away, laughing. 'You smell from fish, my darling.'

'Then we'll have to stop for a drink to kill the aroma.'

'It's too early for drinks, and we are late for your sister.'

'Just a quickie. It will only take a minute. I must have a drink to wash down the fish. Vodka. I must, I must . . .' She pinched him in the crotch.

'Stop that, you wretch! You're getting me full of that smell.'

'You really don't mind, do you, darling?' She rubbed his rising swell with the heel of her palm, fast, faster.

'All right, all right. We'll stop in Monte Carlo.' Keeping his eyes on the road, he reached for her mouth with his and bit her lip hard.

'Mmmm. You hurt!'

'We'll make it a very fast one at the Hôtel de Paris bar.'

He drove the car along the Avenue de Monte Carlo, where the traffic was, as usual, moving slowly.

'Hold it!' Kiki screamed.

'What is it?'

'Stop the car!'

Vic shrugged, pulled over to the sea wall.

Slowly Kiki got out of the car, turned to face the white Rolls parked in front of the Fourreurs Weil fur shop, to take a long and hard look at the man leaning against the car. He was tall, slim, dressed in white flannels and a navy yachting blazer.

'Oh, my God!' Kiki moaned. 'Oh, dear God! It's him. It's really him!'

Vic got out of the car too, came around to stand beside her. 'Who is this him?' he demanded, and then he saw the man too.

Tears rolling down her cheeks, Kiki wasn't even aware of Vic standing next to her.

He looks so beautiful, so beautiful! Everyone's always said he was a wreck, a ruin. But he's not. He's beautiful.

Oh, he looked . . . weathered . . . but in a beautiful, manly way. He was deeply tanned, with very black hair and not a touch of gray. Not the wave of pompadour, not the mustache, not the long sideburns. Such was her entrancement, it didn't occur to her that the hair was probably dyed.

And he wasn't down on his luck like they all said. Why, he looked rich! Prosperous! That beautiful white Rolls! It's providence, she thought. On the very day Angel was arriving! The skies were so blue and the air so golden and she had found her father, *their* father. But then, for a moment, just a moment, her mind clouded with an intense regret that she wouldn't have this one day with her father alone, that she would have to share him with Angel, as she had always had to share him.

She started forward, broke into a run.

But Vic's hand was on her arm, holding back. 'Stop, *cara mia!*'

'Let go of me, you idiot! It's my father! It's my Daddy!'

'Wait! You do not understand! It will be an embarrassment!'

Then Kiki saw the woman who came out of the fur shop with a huge box – an old, terribly old, woman with blue, waved hair and fully covered, or so it seemed, with jewelry flashing garishly in the noonday sun . . . an ugly, really old lady. Her father almost jumped to attention, it seemed, ran, with his slight limp, to take the package from her. And then, sickened, Kiki saw him help her into the car, run his hands over her shriveled behind. She saw him kiss her before he closed the door, and as he limped over to the driver's side she saw the horrible woman smile with yellowish false teeth.

'Come.' Vic led the numbed Kiki gently back to their car.

'But why?' she moaned plaintively. 'Why?'

He revved the engine. 'She's very, very rich. She's the Countess Jeane Claude La Charbonne. A widow. American-born. In France she keeps horses. Here she has a château at Cap Ferrat.' He handed Kiki his handkerchief so that she could wipe her eyes.

226

'Listen,' she told Vic. 'While my sister is here I want to be careful not to run into them. At least I can spare *her* the fucking sight of him.'

'We will be careful. Now we must go pick her up, and then the three of us will have a drink to clear the palate.'

Yes, she had a bitter taste in her mouth. She slipped her hand into Vittorio's waistband, then down.

'Stop! I will have the accident,' he muttered.

But she unzipped his pants and slid down onto the floor of the car.

'We will have the accident, I warn you!' he reiterated, his breath coming in gasps.

'Oh shit!' Kiki said, while trying to keep him from slipping out of her mouth. 'What are you bitching about? It's me whose getting fucked up the ass by your goddamned stick shift!'

Fresh tears rolled down her cheeks.

Oh, fuck you, Daddy! Fuck you in hell!

7

The very first thing Vittorio said to Angel was how fortunate it was that he preferred blondes – otherwise he would have been forced to drop Kiki for her.

Kiki giggled. 'Don't pay attention to a word he says. All Italians talk that way, and especially Italian moviemakers. It doesn't mean a thing.'

'I hope not!' Angel tried to joke, but she was resentful of the filmmaker's proprietary air toward Kiki. *Poor Brad!*

When they arrived at the pink villa in San Remo, Angel – still resentful – waited until Vittorio was out of hearing, then attacked. 'Why on earth does he keep a villa here? The French Riviera is much more chic.'

'Because his family had this villa before anyone even knew there was a French Riviera. Besides, who told you the Italian Riviera isn't chic? The shops here are much better, and some of the best hotels are here. If you came here to be bitchy, you can turn right around and go home. At least wait until you've seen the place before you knock it.'

Grudgingly, Angel had to concede that the villa was indeed very grand. Savonnerie rugs, marble floors, gilt-framed mirrors, statuary worked in vermeil, chandeliers with crystals large as a child's fist, seventeenth-century paintings, and small pieces of Fabergé everywhere.

'And that's just the house. Vic has a yacht, too.'

'Where is it?'

'Right now it's moored in Monte Carlo. We left it there the other night and came back by car. Actually, nobody goes very far in their yachts. Either they use them as hotels or as transportation to somebody *else's* yacht to party.

'It sounds very wasteful to me. Very decadent.'

'Decadent my ass. You're just in a very foul mood. *Bitchy* is the word, I think.'

'I *am* sorry for being bitchy, Kiki. I just don't like that man acting as if he owns you. After all, you are still married to Brad.

'*That* man, as you have referred to him, is going to make me the hottest star in Europe.'

'Oh, Kiki, you don't need him for that,' Angel said sadly. 'You *are* a star! You've always been a star!'

'Says who? I haven't seen any evidence of it lately. Besides, nothing's going on between me and that man. Nothing serious, anyway. So you can stop with the Miss Outraged Virtue routine before I sock you one in the puss.'

They both laughed in a kind of bittersweet way. Kiki hadn't said that to her since they were children.

'Look at you.' Kiki surveyed Angel from head to toe, her tone purposefully, consciously upbeat. 'You're all dressed up like a schoolmarm from Des Moines. That dress and that hat! Who wears cartwheel hats with flowers beside Beebie Tyler these days?'

'I might remind you that when I was in Washington I was considered one of the best-dressed women in America. And look at you! Running around like a trashy starlet in hot-pink satin pajamas! Mother would faint!'

'They are gorgeously trashy, aren't they? And I love them! And we're going to get you some fancy duds too, just like them – to get you out of your doldrums.'

'Dick warned me before I left that I wasn't to buy a thing.'

'Warned, were you? Then that's just the time to go on a spree. After every birth and every miscarriage a girl needs a new wardrobe. And shops here are just marvelous. There's even a Cartier's.'

'Just what I need. All I have to do is buy some diamonds and a divorce is certain.'

'Goody! Shall we find out?'

Angel laughed but said, 'Seriously, Kiki, when *are* you coming home?'

'Soon. When Vic goes back to Rome. But I told you. I'll have to be going back and forth from now on. I plan to star in *all* of Vic's movies. I am not going to rot in Hollywood.'

'But what about Brad, Kiki? What about your daughter? What about your marriage?'

'Will you stop worrying about my marriage? What about your own? It's not all that hot, as far as I can see.'

Angel didn't answer, only looked hurt, and Kiki sighed. 'Now, I suppose, I've hurt your feelings.'

'Yes, you have. If you really want to know, Kiki, I think *you're* pretty jittery, on edge. And that's not like you.'

'Oh, shit! Let's cut out all this dreary talk. You'd better take a nap after the flight and all. We're going to a cocktail party at Villefranche later this afternoon. The duke and duchess are going to be there. And the hippo herself – Elsa. After that, it will be go, go, go till six in the morning. So I'll run along and let you get some rest.' She started out of the gold-velvet draped bedroom. 'Nap well, baby.'

'Wait, Kiki! I haven't told you the marvelous plan I thought up on the plane. I thought that while we're both here on the Riviera we would look for Daddy. It's not a big place, after all. All these villages are on top of each other. Oh, please, Kiki, say yes! It's a wonderful idea, isn't it?'

Kiki didn't look at Angel but straight ahead at the door. 'It would be, only I've already thought of it . . . and I've already looked. He's nowhere to be found. He must have picked up and left . . . who knows when or where.' She was silent for a few seconds. Then: 'Look, Angel, let's forget him, huh? That's the way he must want it; otherwise in all these years he would have done something about it. About us, I mean. I guess he needs his obscurity. For *his* own reasons. I guess we should allow him that. Just let it go.'

She started for the door. At least she had spared Angel the truth. The truth was something she alone would have to live with. *There, Mother, I am not the selfish bitch you think I am. I've taken care of my little sister, just like you always told me to.*

Then she turned around. 'If you must know, he's a shit! And I'm sick to death of talking about him or thinking of him. He's out of my life for good. If I saw him crawling on the ground, I wouldn't help him up. And don't you dare mention him to me again. Ever!' She slammed the door behind her.

Angel took off her dress and lay down on the bed in her slip. But she felt cold. She got up and took a robe out of one of her suitcases and slipped it on. She turned back the heavy quilted spread on the bed, climbed in underneath, and pulled the spread back over her shoulders. This was supposed to be the finest climate in the world, so why the hell was it so cold? And she was so tired. She was a young woman and she

230

was so damn tired.

Angel couldn't really blame Dick for being furious about the pictures of Kiki and her sunbathing in the nude on the deck of the *Fontana*, Vic Rosa's yacht, pictures that showed up in the American scandal sheets after first appearing in similar rags in Italy. But how anybody managed to get them was beyond her. They had been out at sea at the time.

Kiki took it all in stride. 'You can't imagine the ingenuity of the *paparazzi* here. You could be fucking in a dark closet in a room barricaded from inside, in a castle with a moat around it, and they'll get their pictures.'

'Did you hear from Brad? Is he angry?'

'No, Brad is hardly ever angry. With two notable exceptions. But he knows how these things are. After all, what were we doing? Only sunbathing in what was supposed to be privacy. It's different if we had been docked in the harbor, but we were at sea. Besides, Brad was too busy talking about Rory. You'd think the sun never set on anything as lovely.'

'He never even mentioned the nude pictures?'

'Barely. Big deal! We were only nude on top – nobody saw our cunts.'

'Kiki!'

'Oh, Kiki yourself! So what did the big man say?'

Angel laughed, but ruefully. 'He was furious! And he said he was very disappointed in me. He said he thought I was a lady, even if *you* weren't.'

Kiki snickered at that. 'You know, it pisses me off. That holier-than-thou routine, and in the meantime he's screwing Gena Grant's ass off.'

'Don't say that!' Angel cried. 'You have no proof.'

'Proof?' Kiki sneered. 'I didn't want to say anything to upset you when you were pregnant, but I might as well tell you. This little gal in Beverly Hills who does my pedicures told me that one of her customers told her that she was at a party in Palm Springs a few months ago and who was there but Gena Grant and you-know-who showed up and both of them disappeared for an hour or so. I'm willing to grant you that one quickie at a party does not an affair make, but these stories have been making the rounds for some time now. I'm not one to call the kettle black and I know *everybody* fools around, but *you* don't! And then he has the gall to preach to you into the bargain! It's too much.'

'He wants me to come home,' Angel said.

'Because of those ridiculous pictures? Well, you're not going! For God's sake, you just got here. And besides, Zev Mizrachi is coming. He's going to be our house guest. He and his Swedish girlfriend.'

'Zev Mizrachi? Who's he?'

Kiki looked pityingly at her. 'Don't you live in the real world? He's many things. He's one of the biggest industrialists in the world, for God's sake. But more importantly, he's also the Israeli movie producer who's grabbing all the prizes at the film festivals. Besides which, he's richer than God!'

Angel laughed, grateful that Kiki was off on a subject other than Dick. 'Is he a greater moviemaker than your Vittorio? Is he richer?' If Kiki wanted to make a point, it was always 'the biggest', 'the greatest', 'the richest'.

'Well, I don't know if he's a greater moviemaker than Vic. He doesn't direct, he only produces. But he certainly is richer. Although Vic is a lot prettier and much sexier. But Zev Mizrachi *is* a fascinating man. You'll see what I mean when you meet him. He's an Israeli but he sprang out of nowhere. Some people say he's really German-born, but nobody knows for sure. He's a producer, but he's supposed to own half the oil in the Arab countries. I think he was raised in England, but he *was* one of the Stern gang in Palestine – ran guns and stuff against the English blockade. And now that Germany is on its feet again, they say he's the man behind the scenes there. Car plants, shipping, steel, everything.'

'You sound fascinated with him, Kiki. Do you have your eye on him too?' Angel chided.

'Oh, I'm not interested in him *that* way. He's strange, weird. First of all, he's a giant of a man, and fairly old. And absolutely hairless. He has that disease – I can't remember the name of it – where you lose all your hair . . .'

'Alopecia,' Angel supplied.

'Whatever. Anyhow, the most fascinating thing about Zev is not his money, but his reputation as a producer and as a power. I don't pretend not to love money, but it's not the most important thing in my life. And I have enough money to do me, after all. It's the two *s*'s that really turn me on.'

'The two *s*'s?'

'Sex and stardom, sweet sister.'

'I can only think of one thing that would be of utmost importance to me.'

'Yes?'

'Can't you guess?'

'You're talking about love, aren't you?'

'I guess I am.'

They sat silent again. Then Kiki said, getting up, 'Enough of this small talk. Let's go shopping.'

'I don't know if I dare spend any money after Dick said—'

'Oh yes, you dare! It's really very easy. You *do* it, then you simply say, "Fuck off!" It's as simple as that. Try it and see.'

She would. Someday.

8

Angel wore the new flowered chiffon lounging pajamas Kiki had bullied her into buying. They cost $550 and the shop had been delighted to charge them, since hardly anyone of their select clientele carried cash or even a checkbook.

'Those pajamas give you a devastating gypsy look that's . . . well, devastating! And I love your hair wild like that. All you need now is a pair of gold hoop earrings to complete the look.'

'Yes, I think so too,' Angel surprisingly agreed. 'Let's go right now and get them.'

Kiki laughed. 'I knew all it would take to get you started was just a wee bit of encouragement. But we still have to pick up the gowns for tomorrow's ball. We can get the earrings when we get the dresses.'

'I think I did go a little overboard on that ball gown. Twelve hundred and fifty dollars! I had no idea I would need such a lavish gown or I would have brought something with me. I thought all one needed in San Remo was a swimsuit and a pair of jeans. If I brought a gown with me, I could have saved all that money,' she groaned in mock anguish.

'Well, it *is* a Balmain. And you can't very well go to a charity ball at the Sporting Club in a swimsuit. But we'll have to save the shopping for later in the day. We're expecting Zev Mizrachi any minute now. Mizrachi and his girl friend, Liza Olmsburg, the Swedish actress, if one chooses to use the term. And Zev's bringing some other people. The Baroness von Lowenhaus. Wait till you get a load of her. And she'll have her little friend with her – I think his name is Guido, or something like that. And Johnny Dunham is coming with them too. He's the publisher. The baroness is English, not German. Her name is Violet. Her old man, the baron, kicked the bucket and left her really stinking. He was the munitions king. As for little Guido, he lives with her. He's little only in height, I hear. They say his wang is a good foot long.'

Kiki stopped and waited for Angel to remonstrate with her over her language. Angel gasped dutifully, and Kiki went on joyously. 'Guido was a footman in the employ of Horty Sturgis, of the Philadelphia

Sturgises, and when the baroness was a house guest of Horty's she fell in love with Guido's dick.'

Angel had to laugh in spite of herself, then said thoughtfully, 'You know, I've met Johnny Dunham before. In New York. He's really very nice. I wonder what he's doing with this crowd.'

'Having a ball. What do you think? You're very nice too, aren't you? Now you're going to be part of the very same crowd for the next few days, and somebody's bound to say, "I wonder what that nice Angel Power is doing with *that* crowd."'

'I'm wondering myself.'

Lisa Olmsburg was a surprise to Angel. She was expecting a beauty, and Lisa Olmsburg was *fat* – that was the only word one could accurately use. She had enormous breasts, broad hips, and big, weighty legs. Her one and only exceptional feature was her flaxen-colored hair, which reached to her waist. She had a raucous laugh and spoke a loud, broken English. But if the Swedish actress was a surprise, Zev Mizrachi was overwhelming. Kiki had described him, had told her about his alopecia; still, no one could be prepared for the man. He was bigger than any person she had ever seen, and his hairlessness on top of his size was rather frightening. He looked like a Nubian warrior but one with very white skin, and his pale blue, lashless gaze was disconcerting. However, his demeanor was refined, and he spoke English with no trace of accent.

It was immediately obvious that Vic was courting Mizrachi, even to the exclusion of Kiki. Obviously Mizrachi's money and stature and power were taking precedence over romance, for whatever reason. Studying the man, Angel found him not unpleasant, grotesque as he was physically. There *was* something fascinating about him, and he was a most intesting conversationalist.

Kiki told Angel that Mizrachi had left his yacht in the harbor at Monte Carlo in order to join them in San

Remo, and described the yacht. Red-velvet salons, gold-encrusted furniture, an Olympian swimming pool, paintings rumored to have disappeared from France during the war.

'Then why did he come here with his guests? With such a splendid yacht, one would think that he would have invited us aboard this floating palace.'

'He came *here* because Vic invited him and he graciously accepted. But if we're both extra nice to him, he'll probably invite us on his yacht next. And I've heard that he frequently entertains the duke and duchess on his yacht.'

'Imagine that!' Angel drawled, amused.

'You're not impressed? I heard that Mrs Robert Young of the railroad Youngs built a house in Palm Beach just to entertain the Windsors. So there! Now Brad wouldn't be impressed with the Windsors. If he had a choice, he'd probably rather have Hepburn and Tracy to dinner. You've entertained some of the biggest political names in the country. If you had your ultimate choice, whom would you rather play with? High society, the biggest movie stars, or the most powerful political figures in the world?' Kiki asked, playing the game of choices again.

'I don't know. I've never thought about it. Which would you choose?'

'I want it all. Just like men. One at a time, and then all of them together. In one big round bed, each doing something else to me at the same time.'

Angel laughed so hard she thought she would choke. Finally she said, 'You're greedy.'

'Why not? If you don't covet, you don't get.'

Angel's mood changed with Kiki's words.

'You have so much self-confidence, Kiki. Why don't I?' she asked plaintively.

'I don't know, baby. Where *did* you go wrong? Maybe you should practice. Every day when you wake up, say over and over! "I'm the best! I'm the most beautiful! I deserve everything!" Believe me, it's better than saying your prayers every night.'

'Prayers. That reminds me. Is there a church nearby? I have to go to Mass.'

'A church nearby, she asks. In *this* country? Sure, there's a church nearby, if that's all you have to do with yourself. I told you – practice my religion instead. Recite after me: "I'm the best! I'm the most beautiful! I deserve everything!"'

'Do you really recite that every morning?'

'Of course I do! It comes naturally. I stretch my arms out, throw back my head, and yell, "I'm wonderful, God. Do Your best for me, and the best is none too good. You hear me, God? *Nothing* is too good for me!"'

'Aren't you worried you'll be punished for such sacrilege? For your vanity and arrogance?'

'Don't be silly! I *know* only good things will happen to me. And when they don't, I just help them along, to the best of my ability. It's all *very* religious. I just take the blessings God bestowed upon me and I try to run with them. Obviously I was meant to be rich and beautiful and a star, and I simply go on from there.'

'It doesn't always work, though, does it?'

'No, but I try.'

'And suppose you weren't rich or beautiful?'

'I'd take advantage of my other qualities. I'd be smart, I'd be witty, I'd be charming, I'd be strong . . .'

Kiki *was* blessed, Angel thought. Kiki knew who she was. And she herself was less sure now than she was at seventeen. She was mother, wife . . . but it wasn't enough.

'If I weren't married to Dick I wonder what I would be doing with myself. I probably wouldn't even be acting anymore. I'd probably be a nothing, a nobody. Who would know I'm alive, outside of you and Mother?'

'What about Nick Dominguez?' Kiki teased.

'Nick Dominguez! Why do you bring him up?'

'I saw that spread in the *New York Times Magazine*. The article was supposed to be about the restored

237

governor's mansion. But with those pictures it ended up being about you. Glorifying you!' she said.

Angel knew it was true, but she said, 'That's silly. It was quite lovely, but it wasn't—'

'The man's obsessed with you, clearly. *L'obsession magnifique.*' Kiki pursed her mouth. 'It would really be terribly romantic if it weren't so sordid.'

'Sordid! What kind of a word is that to use?'

Kiki raised her eyebrows and sucked in her cheeks. 'Well, just think about it. The man is of lowly origins, obviously. He starts out with that awful little rag, *Whisper*. Nothing more than a peeping Tom with a camera. I don't care what he is now. I mean – suddenly he's a big deal, an *artiste*, for God's sake. And respectable. Does one really become a silk purse from a sow's ear? Never. Not if he lived to be a hundred! And this alley cat is enamored of you, fixated on you. It's more than sordid – it's creepy, disgusting . . . and you, you're flattered!'

Suddenly, Angel's hand lashed out, of its own volition, and slapped her sister across the face. 'You're just jealous!' Angel raged. 'You can't bear it that anyone is taken with anyone but you!'

Then her hand went to her mouth and she was devastated. She had never done anything like that before. She had never struck anyone before, and now she had struck of all the people in the world, her own darling Kiki.

'Oh, Kiki, forgive me. I don't know how I could have done such a thing! It was just what you said. It was—'

Kiki smiled coldly, her face flaming red where Angel had struck her. 'It's all right. I forgive you. You're not yourself. And in a way, I even understand. You do need something, don't you? Somebody? What with Dick . . .'

She left the room, and it was a good thing. Angel had the urge to slap her again.

Angry with Kiki, Angel nevertheless felt guilty and

ashamed. She had been dreaming of Nick Dominguez of late – dreaming of his making love to her. And he was not the only one. Since she had come to the Riviera she had dreamed of Kiki's Vic, too, even though on a conscious level she disapproved of Kiki's involvement with the man. Oh, but it *was* easy to see why Kiki was smitten with him. Vic Rosa was amusing, charming, as well as handsome, with the same dark looks Nick possessed. And of course there was his blatant sexuality, too obvious to be denied.

9

Angel discovered that having guests on the Côte d'Azur meant dining with them, partying with them, gambling with them in the evenings, but for the most part leaving them to their own devices. For the Baroness von Lowenhaus and her friend, Guido, this meant spending most of their days in their bedroom. The baroness never showed herself until cocktail hour approached, while Guido came out occasionally only to sun his body, but he never spoke to anyone but the baroness, and then only in Italian.

As for Zev Mizrachi and his girlfriend, they had hardly arrived at the villa before the quarreling began. The din from their room was incredible. It came roaring down from the second floor and even out the French doors on to the terrace – yelling and cursing in a blend of German, English, and Hebrew, accompanied by the sounds of furniture crashing and china shattering.

Kiki expressed some concern for the objects of destruction, but Vic was cavalier. 'It is nothing,' he said. 'I understand that they frequently do battle. Simply expressing their passion.' He smiled. 'They are both people of intense emotion.'

'You can say that again. Everyone says she fucked

239

her late husband to death. Literally.'

'Kiki . . .' Vic remonstrated, but he was amused.

Angel was fascinated. 'Tell me about it.'

'It's true.' Kiki happily bobbed her head up and down in affirmation. 'She was married to this Swede who it seemed was not as sexually driven as our Lisa, who demanded to be screwed six times a day. And if there wasn't anyone around to help to take the pressure off poor Carl, she beat him until he complied. When he was utterly spent, poor soul, and couldn't keep up the pace, she dragged him to Vevey to the clinic where they inject you with live cells from animals. I told you about that, Angel. I heard those needles are as big as your arm and you can see all those pink worms wriggling around inside . . .'

'Kiki, stop! That's revolting!'

'Excuse me! Do you want to hear the rest of the story or not?'

Vic knew the story well, but he still enjoyed hearing Kiki tell it. 'Of course, my love, we are dying to hear the story. Aren't we, Angel?'

'Yes, I am, but, Kiki, do you have to be so graphic?'

'Well, the doctor kept shooting those pink little squiggles into Carl's ass. I *think* it's the ass. Isn't it the ass, Vic?'

'Most probably, *carissima*.'

'Only the shots didn't seem to do a thing for his pr – excuse me, Angel, for his performance, although he didn't have a wrinkle on his face by this time.'

Angel had to laugh despite herself as the footman brought out a silver tea service, along with tiny crustless sandwiches.

'Angélique, my sweet, will you pour and let me get on with my story?'

'Yes, Kiki, do,' Vittorio urged.

'Very well. So Lisa drags him to another clinic. At Lausanne, wasn't it, Vic?'

'I think so, yes. I haven't been there myself yet, thank God.'

'At this clinic, they're supposed to give you vitamin shots with a very special ingredient which makes you so feisty you'll climb mountains and take on bears barehanded. You can screw for hours after one of those injections. Lisa was sending him there so often, they finally took a house there. Carl kept getting the shots and kept screwing away, until one day while he was fucking his ass off – her ass off, I guess you might say – he dropped dead. The mystery remains: was it the shots or the fucking that killed him? The general conclusion is that he just burst his heart from sticking it to her so frequently and in so many different ways. Anyhow, *finis* Carl.'

'What a terrible story!' Angel said, revolted but fascinated. 'When did poor Carl die?'

'Oh, a couple of years ago.'

'And do you think Zev and Lisa will marry?'

'I doubt it,' Vic said with a wise and knowing smile. 'Men like Mizrachi don't marry women like Lisa Olmsburg. Do not let that fighting and noise fool you. Zev Mizrachi is a man very much in control. He may enjoy a little, how do you say, roll in the dirt, but he will not marry it.'

'Probably he's afraid she'll send *him* for those shots,' Kiki drawled.

'I really fail to see her attractions.' Angel shook her head.

Kiki giggled. 'Those hips!'

Vittorio laughed. 'But European men like those voluptuous hips, the big—' He gestured with his hands. 'They consider that very sexy. And she is a very passionate woman, and that does possess its own attraction.'

'But does she give the best head in all Europe?' Kiki challenged, while Angel practically wriggled in embarrassment.

Vic ignored the question. 'You left out the most amusing part of the story, Kiki. You have not told Angel that now he, Mizrachi, himself, has bought a

241

beautiful house right near Vevey, in the hills, just above Noel's villa, I believe and very near those clinics.'

'To take which shots?' Angel asked. 'The live, pink squirming things or the vitamin ones?'

'I doubt Zev needs either,' Vic said. 'It makes for an amusing story, but it is probably only the taxes, after all. There are many reasons, you know, to take up residence in Switzerland – to be near one's money in Zurich, to be near one's doctor, to be near one's favorite skiing trails, or most urgently, to escape the taxes of one's native land. And I do not believe Mizrachi skiis,' he sneered.

'But I'm sure that if he did, he would do it most marvelously,' Kiki said, looking at Vic and not at Angel. 'Zev does seem to do everything better than most other people, don't you think, Vic dear?' It seemed to Angel that Kiki was needling Vic, and it must have seemed so to him too, because he rose from his chair and said:

'Yes, I do. Mizrachi also knows how to deal very well with women, too, and probably especially well with American women with sharp tongues. A sharp tongue is a most unattractive attribute, much more so than too-large hips. And now I will excuse myself. I must see to the comfort of my esteemed guest.'

He stalked off, and Angel turned to Kiki. 'I get the impression that Vic really doesn't like Zev Mizrachi.'

'It doesn't take a mind reader to deduce that.'

'So why did he invite him here?'

'God! Angel, the eternal innocent! For money! Why did you think? And for distribution of my film. Mizrachi just about controls the film industry in Europe, the theaters, everything. And people say he secretly controls half the studios in Hollywood.'

'I see,' Angel said, but wondered exactly how much she really did.

'I think I'll go find Vic and put him in a better mood, as only I can.' Kiki winked and left the room.

So, Angel thought, Vic is after Zev Mizrachi and

Kiki is after Vic, and this was not just a pleasant little sojourn on the Riviera. But then, she had never thought that it was – not really.

Much as the interplay of personalities at the villa made Angel edgy, especially watching Kiki stalking her Italian moviemaker, she found the days glorious – the intense colors of the flowers, the sky, and the sea excited the dormant artist in her. Although she hadn't done any painting or drawing since her school days, she picked up a set of pastels, some paper, and a small portable easel in Nice and went down to the sea.

She had already executed three quick studies when John Dunham joined her on the beach. 'Don't let me interrupt you,' he said. 'I'll just sit here quietly and watch you, if you don't mind. There's something so lovely about a solitary beach. No wonder people buy these big places just for the little piece of private shoreline that comes with them.'

'Yes, but I did have some company.' She showed him the sketch she had done of a little girl playing in the sand while her two older brothers splashed in the water. She offered the picture shyly but still expectantly.

'Say, that's super! You really caught the little girl's concentration – as if digging in sand wasn't play but very serious business.'

Angel was delighted. 'That's exactly what I was after! Her solemnity about building sand castles.' She moved to the side so that he could see the sketch that was on her easel. 'But I'm not doing so well with this one. I thought the Mediterranean was placid, but somehow the water keeps changing all the time. Each time I look up it's different. This is my first experience with pastel. It's not as easy as I thought.'

'No. Pastel will fool you.'

She looked at him inquiringly.

'I was a painter once,' he explained. 'Not a very good one.'

When did you give it up? Why?'

'I gave it up the day I discovered I wasn't very good. I was in Paris studying. I hung around the cafés and all the rest of it, but I never accomplished much. After five years of that I took a good long look at myself and my work and decided that it wasn't for me. I came home and went into the family business and found that I loved it.'

She looked at him quickly to determine if he meant it: that he really loved the publishing business and wasn't mourning a career lost. She had never really looked at John Dunham before. She decided that the most suitable word to describe him would be *pleasant-looking*. Sandy hair worn a bit long; a long, narrow, craggy face; soft brown eyes. A man a woman would like for a friend.

'No regrets?' she asked.

'About giving up art?'

'Yes.'

'None. I told you – I wasn't a very good painter. I had nothing to show for those five years except some good memories. Good days, good nights, good friends. But nothing in the way of decent art. And I'm good at publishing. What about you? Have you ever studied art?'

'Not really. Just the usual courses that everybody takes somewhere along the line during their school days.' She laughed deprecatingly. 'I never really studied anything seriously. Not even the dramatic arts, although, I suppose, I would have to call that my profession . . . my ex-profession. Not that I had much of a career.'

'Please don't make so little of it. I saw you in *Sunday Afternoon* and I thought you were superb. You looked lovely, of course, but your characterization of Jenny was so beautifully interpreted that it transcended the physical.'

Angel was speechless. What a perfectly lovely thing to say.

'I always thought it was a shame that you left the theater.'

Angel's hands fluttered helplessly, more eloquent than words.

He looked at her paintings again. 'But you're a lady of many talents. I think you could have made a fine painter, too. These studies show enormous feeling. Even though I never made it as a painter myself, I think I can recognize talent in others.'

'I think you're just trying to be nice.'

'That would be patronizing, and I wouldn't patronize you.'

She believed him.

'Tell me then what I'm doing wrong here, with the water.' She indicated the sketch with which she'd been having a problem.

'It's the color. Color behaves the same whether you're working in oil, watercolor, or pastel. Your blues and greens tend to recede, your reds and yellows tend to advance and shout, while the violets tend to be shy little things. The sea is a vital force and you've used only your shy, receding colors. This is the first time you've used pastels – you have to do a lot more experimenting to discover how the colors work for you.'

He went to her easel, picked up a stick of color, and executed a series of strokes on the paper. 'There are different methods of applying pastel. It can be stroked on, dotted, laid in thickly, or scumbled – rubbed in with your fingers or with rags and stumps. You can even paint into it with a brush, or dip your stick into fixative and lay it on wet. Degas, who was the master pastelist, let steam drift over his paintings, then worked into the wet mass.

'If you're really interested in learning about color in pastel, I would be pleased to send you some books when I get back to New York. We've published works on Seurat and Signac. Pointillism is a particularly useful approach. Even Vermeer used it in his interiors.'

'I'd love to have the books. Thank you.'

He picked up the rendering of the two boys playing with a beachball in the water. 'I do like this one.'

'Would you like to have it?' she asked impulsively, wanting to thank him in some way for all the lovely things he had said to her. Then she felt foolish, offering a gift of an amateur's endeavor. For all she knew, he might have Degas or Seurat hanging on his walls. She laughed in embarrassment. 'How silly. Why would . . . ?' She shook her head.

'I'd love to have it,' he said. 'I would consider it a most favored possession by one of my most favorite actresses. You'll have to sign it for me, though – I insist on that.'

She signed it with a flourish: *Angela du Beaumond*. That *was* her professional name, after all.

Hours later they climbed the hill to the villa. Kiki was waiting on the terrace.

'I was going to send for the police. Where did you disappear to? The only thing that stopped me from calling the *flics* was that I didn't want to create an international scandal. What *were* you two doing all this time?'

'Discussing art,' John said. When Kiki smirked, he added, 'I'm afraid that's all there was to it.'

Kiki leered, looked as if she were about to pursue the subject further, then thought better of it. 'You'll both have to hurry and change. Mimi Dudley's having cocktails, then it's dinner at that cute place in Antibes that's decorated like a pirate's den.'

'Sounds excruciating,' John said, smiling. 'I'll be ready in a flash.' He went inside.

Kiki grinned at Angel. 'Now you tell me the truth. What *were* the two of you doing all afternoon? Something delicious, I hope?'

'Sort of delicious. A delicious conversation about art and life. I'm so sorry to disappoint you but everytime a

246

man and a woman are together they aren't necessarily having an orgy, Mrs Cranford.'

'Yes. Well. He does wear his pants really tight. I've noticed that before. I wonder what that means.'

'Really! Don't you have anything better to do than to look at men's crotches, for heaven's sake?' Angel said, trying to keep Kiki from spoiling what had been a wonderful day for her.

'Whatever. Crotches or not, he is an attractive man.'

Yes, he is, Angel thought. He's a poet.

10

They were a group of five lunching at the little waterfront café, all that was left of their house party: Vic, Kiki, Angel, John Dunham, and Zev Mizrachi. The baroness and Guido with their ten pieces of Vuitton luggage, had left for the Costa del Sol that morning, and Lisa Olmsburg had departed the villa the day before with *her* five pieces of Vuitton, in an apparent rage since she had called a taxi to take her to Nice without even so much as a good-bye to her host or the sisters, leaving only a trail of invectives behind. They assumed she was gone for good, but no one dared ask Zev Mizrachi why she had left, and he volunteered no information, nor did he seem in any way upset. In fact, it was he who had insisted they all go to the Summer Casino in Monte Carlo the same evening.

He had been most attentive to Angel, explaining the tables to her, giving her chips to play with. She had quickly lost them all and grown depressed. Couldn't she win at anything? She had played a secret game with herself. If she could win just one chip, it would be a good omen. But no, she had lost consistently.

Mizrachi, it seemed, was lucky. He said to Angel, 'I *always* win.' Angel believed him and envied him. It was

247

a gift to be lucky, and she herself had never been. As for saying 'Lucky at cards, unlucky at love,' that was sheer nonsense. From her observations, he who was lucky at cards was lucky at everything else.

Earlier that morning, as they strolled the streets of Cannes, stopping here, darting in there, Mizrachi insisted on buying both Kiki and Angel a gift with the proceeds of his winnings of the night before. When the little gift turned out to be a gold slave bracelet embedded with small rubies, Angel protested. But Mizrachi said, 'If you do not share my good fortune with me you will turn fate's evil eye upon me.'

'Oh, for Christ's sake,' Kiki whispered loudly as she admired her own bracelet, already on her wrist, 'take the fucking bracelet and stop acting like a nun.'

'May the evil eye be thwarted,' Angel said, extending her narrow wrist for the bracelet, and Zev clasped it on with a grunt of satisfaction.

Now, as they sat at the café table, Angel looked at the bracelet with misgivings. What would Dick say. What would *she* say in the way of explanation? That Kiki had received the same present? That its presentation obviously didn't mean a thing? That would hardly satisfy Dick. It would only end with Dick making some derogatory remark about Kiki and her way with men and presents.

She worked the bracelet around her wrist like so many worry beads. She looked up to see John Dunham gazing at her with a deeply compassionate look, as if he were reading her thoughts, aware of the predicament in which she found herself. Or was he thinking that ladies didn't accept presents from men like Zev Mizrachi? Well, if that's what he's thinking, for God's sake, then maybe he should grow up too, she thought irritably. The age of Victoria was long past.

Mizrachi ordered for everyone. He insisted they all

248

have the crayfish soufflé. 'It is as good here as at the Hôtel de Paris.' The café didn't give the impression that a light, airy soufflé would be its specialty, but no one disputed Mizrachi's authority. Then he asked the waiter for the wine list, but the waiter said they had none and recited the wines that were available, all Italian wines. Still, Zev demanded a 1948 Château Lafite Rothschild. When the waiter spread his hands as if to say, 'I cannot serve what we do not have,' Zev berated the man loudly. Angel stared down at her bracelet, mortified. She could not believe Zev's arrogant vulgar behavior.

As Kiki commiserated with Zev, Angel's eyes met John's. He seemed as embarrassed as she. Finally the scene came to an end with the waiter bringing them an Italian regional wine, and Mizrachi sneered as if to say, 'I've done my best, but this dolt—' Then he invited them all to join him for a short cruise on his yacht, the *Venus*, for a few days.

John said, 'Count me out. I'm due back in New York as of yesterday.' And no one sought to dissuade him. But then Angel said that she couldn't possibly stay more than another day or two herself, and Vic, Kiki, and Mizrachi sent up a storm of protest. Vic, in fact, was the most vehement, and Angel wondered at the reason. Could it possibly be that what he had in mind was a cozy little foursome?

Angel glanced sharply at Kiki, who studied her fingernails with an intense concentration. Yes, it was so, and Kiki was in on it, she realized, feeling sick.

'I absolutely must go home. I've been away from my little boy far too long already,' Angel said, crushed by her sister's deviousness.

'But after a few days on the yacht, I will fly you home in my private plane. It's almost as well outfitted as the *Venus*. You'll love it, I assure you.' Mizrachi put his hand on hers.

'No, I couldn't possibly. I've already overstayed my leave. And you, Kiki,' she said pointedly. 'You must get home to Brad and Rory, too. Rory must be dying to see her mommy. And Brad . . . Brad is so devoted,' she said to the others.

Kiki was unconcerned. 'I'm sure Rory doesn't even know I'm gone,' she drawled. 'And you don't have to rush home either. Everything will still be there when you get back. Everything will be as usual.'

Zev's hand pressed hers. 'You will spoil the cruise for us all if you don't come. I insist you join us.'

He had a quiet but imperative way of mesmerizing whomever he was addressing. Angel felt almost hypnotically compelled to obey him. She wanted to remove his hand from hers but felt powerless to do so.

She just managed to control her voice sufficiently to say, 'I think you'll all have a perfectly lovely time without me. I've never been accused of being the most entertaining person – there are loads of people who would be more fun on a cruise than I, and these same people would probably sell their souls for an invitation from you, Mr Mizrachi.'

'You *are* wicked, Angela. You promised to call me Zev. At least ten times you have promised and you keep slipping back to this Mr Mizrachi.'

'I am sorry, Zev. But I still don't feel free to go on the cruise. My husband has been urging me to come home for days now.'

And then they were lingering over dessert – rum cheesecake, which Zev Mizrachi ordered for everyone, declaring that they had never eaten such cheesecake. Angel was anxious to be gone from the restaurant now, to be gone from the Riviera, to be away from the unsavory threesome, but especially from Kiki. Vic and Mizrachi were nothing to her, but Kiki! To try to set her up in such a manner – to use her to gain favor with someone like Mizrachi . . .

Now Zev took her hand again and said, 'Ah! If you were not the governor's wife, what a luminous star you could be! I would make you the brightest star of the continent, of all the continents!'

Angel smiled smugly, looking not at Mizrachi but directly at Kiki, hoping that her sister would be irritated with his words . . . *knowing* she would be. Kiki didn't mind if her sister's star shone as long as it did not shine quite as brightly as her own.

But then a crowd of people entered the restaurant, obviously Americans, and Angel and Kiki both spotted Nick Dominguez at the exact same time he saw them.

Angel's eyes widened in surprised pleasure as Kiki fumed, 'The nerve of that man, following you here!'

'That's ridiculous,' Angel remonstrated, discomfited that Kiki would discuss such a personal thing in front of the others. 'I'm sure he hasn't followed me. He wouldn't do that. We're friends now. I told you. He must be on an assignment here . . . and just came in for lunch with those other people,' she whispered to Kiki, not wanting Mizrachi, sitting on her other side, to hear. Then, worried that Nick Dominguez would come over to their table to greet her and be exposed to Kiki's venom and to Mizrachi's all-enveloping scrutiny, she rose and started across the room.

'What do you think you're doing?' Kiki called after her. She watched as Dominguez and Angel shook hands and, smiling as if they were truly old friends, exchanged a few words. Then she turned to Mizrachi and Vic, related how Dominguez had dogged Angel for years, had absolutely driven her to distraction, and now Angel was forced to befriend him in order to protect herself from him.

Angel returned to the table, her color high. 'I was right,' she blurted out, eager to forestall further comment from Kiki. 'He is here on an assignment. He's covering the gala at the—'

'Please spare us the stories, Angel. We all know what he's up to. He's probably been spying on you.' Kiki looked at the others as if to say, 'See how she explains. She has to protect him in order to protect herself.'

Spying on her? Was it true? Angel wondered. Had

he seen her on the beach at San Remo? Had he observed her last night gambling at the casino with Zev Mizrachi? Had he seen her this morning going into the jewelry shop with Mizrachi at her elbow? Had he taken a picture of Zev clasping the damned bracelet around her wrist?

She looked at him again as Kiki prattled on and *knew* it wasn't true. After she and he had finally met, and after that beautiful layout he had done on her and the mansion, and especially after she had looked into his eyes, she just knew that he was her friend and would not betray her, regardless of what Kiki said. How at home he looked here by the sea in his white ducks and fisherman's shirt, the top buttons undone, revealing the dark, curling chest hair. He might have been a fisherman of the Mediterranean himself – dark, saturnine, brooding. She looked up to see John watching her now. Oh, dear! Was he reading her thoughts? How complicated everything was.

And then the waiter was at their table with a squat, fat bottle of some dark liquor. 'Compliments of Mr Dominguez.' He was careful to present its label to Angel and not to Mizrachi.

She smiled widely at Nick across the room, acknowledging her acceptance, thanking him, displaying her pleasure, as Mizrachi said to the others, 'Why is it her husband has tolerated this man's behavior?' as his elbow hit the bottle and sent it spinning to the floor, shattering in all directions.

'Oh no!' Angel cried.

'My apologies,' Mizrachi said dispassionately, beckoning a busboy to clean up the mess.

Kiki seemed to exult, Vic to smile in admiration, while John Dunham only looked horrified. Angel felt sick, quickly glanced across the room again, but Nick was gazing down, his face impassive. What *was* he thinking?

Once again there had been interference in their relationship. Once again it had been Kiki who was at the center of that interference. Only this time Kiki had had an ally.

It was indeed time to go home.

PART EIGHT

Hollywood, Sacramento, Milan, Vevey,
Monte Carlo
1954–1957

'The next few years were tumultuous ones in the lives of the girls,' Beebie told the young journalist. 'Ups and downs . . . Kiki, who hadn't done well in Hollywood, was a sensation in the Italian films she made with Vittorio Rosa. He was a gifted filmmaker and they were a team. And Angel got pregnant again, very soon after her miscarriage. God gives and God takes away, I always say.

'Dick Power was especially pleased when she became pregnant again. You know how politicians feel about a pregnant wife. A great asset. But I always thought that there was trouble in the marriage by that time, despite the pregnancy. There were always rumors about Power and other women, especially about a certain blonde movie star, but naturally I didn't print anything about that. I never liked to print that sort of thing, because I think that a marriage that's in trouble doesn't need gossip to further complicate things, if you know what I mean.

'As for Kiki, what with her getting involved professionally with Rosa, an excitingly handsome man, after the Greenberg scandal . . . well, *that* was an explosive situation as far as her marriage to darling Brad Cranford was concerned.

'And then there were always those stories about the girls' father cropping up . . . but I said, "Show me some proof and I'll print it." I never would print anything that I didn't absolutely know was the God's honest truth.'

1

Angel's plane from Sacramento landed on time at the Los Angeles airport, but Kiki was late. She didn't show up to pick her up until a half hour later.

'Kiki, how could you keep me standing around after I dropped everything and fought with Dick about it, just to come down the minute you called me?'

'Kiki is sorry, precious. I couldn't help it. I was on the phone with Vic making last-minute plans and I completely lost track of the time. It's been hectic. Don't be mad, baby. I'll make it up to you the minute I get you home. I'll give you a nice warm bubble bath to relax you and put you to bed and let you rest up your poor little pregnant self.'

'Dick was positively furious. He says that if I lose this baby he's going to kill us both. You and me, that is, not him and me.' She giggled.

'Oh, Dick's always furious about something or other. And there's no reason a little plane trip would cause a miscarriage, for God's sake. The doctor didn't say you couldn't take a plane trip, did he?'

'No, but he advised me to take it easy. And, really, if you hadn't said you absolutely needed me, I wouldn't have chanced it. I'm dying to see Rory. I haven't seen her in months. Has she grown much?'

'Oh, she's the usual two-year-old size, I suppose. But she is gorgeous. She's not home now.'

'Where is she?'

'Brad took her to Palm Springs. He never lets her out of his sight.'

'When will they be back? I want to see them.'

'Oh, I guess they'll be back in a couple of days,' Kiki said vaguely.

'Well, what is it? You wouldn't say on the phone. Is

it really an emergency?'

'We'll talk about it when I get you home and into bed for your restie. Hold on to your panties! Here we go!' Abruptly, Kiki darted out from the far left lane and moved across three lanes of traffic to the right to make her exit, only narrowly missing being hit. That seemed to cheer her a bit, and she said, 'We'll be home in a sec. Just don't get any labor pains on me, will you? I don't think I could cope just now.'

Ten minutes later they pulled into the driveway of the Cranford home.

'Let's get you right upstairs.'

They went inside, where the housekeeper stood waiting. 'Is the bed turned down for Mrs Power, Hannah?'

'No, ma'am. I didn't know Mrs Power would be going to bed. I'll go right up and do it.'

'Never mind. I'll do it. Just get the bags, will you? Do you want something to eat, Angel? Tea? Coffee? Alcohol?'

'Tea.'

'Bring tea, Hannah, and a bourbon on the rocks.'

She took Angel upstairs, into what she called the Blue Room. 'I'll run a bath for you with some lovely bubbles while you get undressed.'

'I don't want a bath. I'll just lie down while you tell me what this is all about.'

'How about a shower? A nice hot shower?'

'Kiki, what's gotten into you?'

'Well, first a big dick, then a tiny seed.'

Angel looked bewildered for a second, then said, 'You're pregnant?'

'Yes. Little Kiki has gotten herself just a wee bit knocked up.'

'That's wonderful! We're both pregnant at the same time again!' Then, realizing that Kiki was barely back from Rome, having just finished another film, she asked, 'Who's the father?'

'Obviously you've already figured that one out.

That's why I need you to go down to Mexico with me. I'm getting a divorce and married all at the same time.'

'So,' Angel said, 'it's really all over with you and Brad. Oh, Kiki . . .'

'Don't start. Okay? Just don't start. It's as much Brad's fault as mine. I never screwed Norman and Brad didn't believe it and that really was the end.'

'How about when Brad beat up Howard Hughes? Were you innocent then?'

Kiki sat down on the bed next to Angel. 'Listen to me and listen hard. I'm your sister. And you're either for me or agin me. There *is* nothing else. And if you're not with me you can leave now and I don't want to ever see you again! If you're for me, you accept everything about me and you shut up about what I've done or may have done wrong. And you root for me. Always!'

The tears welled up in Angel's eyes. 'Oh, Kiki, I love you. Of course I'm on your side. But does that mean I have to be mad at Brad?'

'No, you silly. *I'm* not mad at Brad. Brad's a brick. In fact, *he's* going down to Mexico with us to help get the quickie divorce.' She smoothed Angel's hair. 'It's just over, Angel. It's been over for quite a while.' The tears rolled down Kiki's cheeks. 'When something's over you just have to face it and call it quits and go on and make the best of it. Like with Father. It was over with him and us a long time ago and eventually we had to face up to it, didn't we?'

When Angel didn't answer, she repeated: 'Well, didn't we?'

Angel nodded, unable to speak.

'So now I'm divorcing Brad and marrying Vic, who is the father of the child inside me. He loves me, I think, and will do everything to make me happy, including giving me the opportunity to be the movie star I want to be. Now that's making the best of it, is it not?'

Angel put her arms around Kiki. 'But Vic is a Catholic, isn't he? And you're a Protestant and twice

260

divorced . . .'

Hannah knocked and then brought in the tea tray and Kiki's drink and put them on the table near the bed. 'Shall I pour?'

'No, I'll do it. Thank you.' Kiki dismissed her.

Kiki poured Angel's tea, then picked up her drink and took a swallow. 'I'm rejoining the Church. I *was* a Catholic, after all, wasn't I? So since the Church doesn't recognize any marriage not performed under its auspices, it can't very well recognize my divorces, can it? As far as it's concerned, I'm a virgin going to the well for the first time. And I'll be married by a priest this time. A Mexican priest in some quaint little Mexican church.'

'And that's all there is to it?'

'What the hell did you expect, cannons and fireworks?'

Kiki rose, went out into the hall, leaned over the balcony, and bellowed down: 'Hannah! Hannah! Bring me another drink! A double!' She remained out in the hall, waited for the housekeeper to bring her drink, then came back into the room and closed the door. 'I don't want *that one* listening in. She never liked me. She's always favored Brad.'

'Does she know you're leaving?'

'I don't issue printed announcements to the help, if that's what you mean. She saw my bags packed. Four trunks and twelve suitcases. New. But I didn't charge them to Brad. I didn't think that would be nice.'

Then, suddenly, she seemed to deflate. 'I *had* to do it, Angel. The way things were going, if I didn't get myself pregnant, it would have taken me years to get Vittorio to the altar, and God knows if he would still want me by then. Now that this baby is a fact of life, he's hot to get his brand on me. I knew he wouldn't be able to resist a kid of his own. When a man gets to be a certain age, he starts having regrets about not leaving an heir. It all has to do with male ego and immortality. Anyhow, Vic's absolutely insane about the idea of

261

being a daddy. And Angel, I'm really in love!'

'You were in love with Brad, too,' Angel pointed out.

'No. I *loved* Brad. And I still do. Who wouldn't? But I'm madly *in* love with Vic. He's the only man that excites me – who makes me feel like I'm going to jump out of my skin if I don't have him right there and then. Just looking at him gets me wet all over – I want to get down and give him head, I want to spread and have his tongue all over me. I wake up at night thinking about him and I have to stick a pillow between my legs.'

Angel listened and felt her own loins stirring.

'I've got the right to have the man I want, just like anybody else, don't I? Don't I? I married . . . what was his name? . . .'

'Tracy?'

'Tracy. And he was only a very casual friend. And a fag besides. And Brad – a *very* good friend. The best. But now I want to marry just for love, like any normal American girl. For love and for sucking and fucking my brains out.'

Angel smiled the smile she had acquired in the past year – a little bitter, derisive smile. 'You're marrying for love and ending up with a man who's richer.'

Kiki laughed. 'Well, you know my motto. If you're rich, you may be a bitch, but if you're poor, darling, you're a boor!' She was clearly delighted with her own wit.

'You weren't exactly poor with Brad.'

'No, of course not. And Vic's not *that* much richer. Besides, this really has nothing to do with money. It's got to do with . . . well, other things. My marriage to Brad was great while it lasted, and Brad's a wonderful guy – a real sport. But I'm being a real sport about it too. I'm not asking Brad for a thing – not a fucking thing. Not this house and not the one in the Springs. Not a cent of cash, either. The only thing I'm taking out of this marriage are my clothes and my jewels.'

How like Kiki to remember to mention her clothes and her jewelry but not her daughter, Angel marveled.

'And your daughter? Remember her?'

'No,' Kiki said expressionlessly. 'Not my daughter. She stays here. With her father.'

'Kiki!'

'What can I do? That's the way Brad wants it. Insists upon it. That's the only condition he's making.'

Angel shook her head from side to side. 'Kiki! Kiki!' she mourned.

'Will you stop saying that like a parrot? "Kiki! Kiki!" I had no choice. Don't you see that? Well, fuck you if you don't. Jesus! It's not like I won't ever see her again, you know. Every time I come to the States I'll see her. And Brad'll let her come visit me. You know Brad. Not a mean bone in his whole body.'

Angel wept and didn't know for whom. For Kiki? For Rory? For herself?

'Oh, for God's sake, I'm sorry I ever asked you to come. Damn! Why did I ask you? I don't need this. And I don't need you! Don't you see I had to do it? Why can't you see that?'

'I see . . . I see,' Angel cried. 'But, Kiki, what will Mother say when she hears about this?'

Kiki looked at her stonily. 'Why don't you tell her about it and find out?'

The plane trip was rough. They hadn't missed a single air pocket in the whole sky. In the space of fifteen minutes she had been to the tiny rest room twice, and there was no room there to even throw up in comfort.

Only five days had passed since she had flown down to Los Angeles and taken this trip back. Five days, and the whole mess was done with – the divorce, the marriage, Brad back in Palm Springs with his daughter, Vic and Kiki bound for Italy. Five days only, in which she, Angel, had descended deeper and deeper into depression. Regardless of the reason, Kiki was giving up her daughter, and that had to be a mistake.

She had tried. God knows she had tried. She had pleaded with Kiki over and over during the two days they waited for Vic to show up.

'Don't give up your child so easily, so thoughtlessly, so selfishly,' she had begged Kiki.

'I'm not being selfish,' Kiki had said so reasonably, so totally sure of herself. 'It would be different if I were abandoning Rory to the fates. All I'm doing is leaving a kid in her father's care for the time being. A father who adores her, who spends all his free waking time with her, who supplies her with every material thing. Is that abandonment? And besides, I didn't make my mind up as quickly or recklessly as you may think. I added up all the things I had, all the things I wanted, and all the things I would be getting. Then I subtracted one from the other, and the pluses outweighed the minuses.

'You're sticking it out, Angel, and what good is it? What do *you* have that you're so afraid to give up? You wanted a man of your own who would love you desperately, and you ended up with a cold, selfish son of a bitch who doesn't mind screwing around on you if he can only do it discreetly – the discretion being out of consideration for his own name and position, not for you. A son of a bitch whose passion is his career, and *you* don't run a close second, or even a third. What does that leave you? An obligatory fuck once a month? You're worse off than if you had no man at all.

'I don't doubt that you did love Dick, but I believe that that spent itself a long, long time ago. So you don't have that. No love received, no love given. You wanted a house and land to call your own, and you have neither. You wanted money to spend without having to account for every cent, and even that dignity is denied you. So what do you have? Little Dickie? Fine. What else?

'You add it up, sister of mine. What do you have that you can sit in judgement of me like you were Jesus Christ himself? No man, no love, no house, no money of your own. It looks to me like you've got a great big fat zero. You can't even have your acting career. Oh,

264

no! No life of your own for you, Angelique! Even Mother has what she wants. *She* wasn't looking for another great love, as you well know. *She* got exactly what she went after. And *I'm* going to have what I want. And instead of crying over me, you'd do better to think about yourself. And if you start crying again, I swear I'm going to bust you one. Grow up! Grow up, will you, please?'

Kiki's words seared, and Angel had nothing to say in refutation. She did as she was asked. As soon as Vic arrived, Kiki called Brad in Palm Springs, and presently they all went down across the border. Brad was as nice to Angel as usual, and almost as friendly. He just managed not to be alone with Kiki, or even with her. She had wanted to offer him some words of comfort, to demonstrate the honest affection she felt for him, her concern, her grief at what was happening. But, politely, he never gave her the chance.

He was graciousness itself to Vittorio, who, to his credit, displayed deep embarrassment over the situation. It was a toss-up which man put on a better display of gentlemanly demeanor. Angel was proud of Brad, but she was afraid her own heart was going to burst with the pain of it all.

And now Kiki would be an ocean plus a continent away from her and from Rory, and she was left with only Kiki's accurate estimation of her existence, her big fat zero of a life.

Upon landing, Angel was met by a staff underling. As usual, Dick couldn't get away. When he came home late that evening, she was waiting up in bed to tell him the latest in the way of family news, as any wife would, although she suspected that he would denounce Kiki as a cold, unfeeling bitch, or express sympathy for Brad, whom he liked. But he surprised her. He listened to the whole story, shook his head, and said only, 'Great! Now we'll have *daily* trans-atlantic calls on our bill instead of just occasional ones.'

265

But he was wrong. For the present, Angel had had sufficient conversation with her sister to last her for quite a while.

2

Timothy Francis Xavier Power was born on October 12, and Kiki gave birth to her second daughter in November – Nicole, already known as Nikki. Only hours after the birth, Kiki called and told Angel that Nikki was born as ugly as Rory had been beautiful. 'She's this tiny, scrawny, ratty-looking thing with a mop of black curls. Would you believe it? A full head of hair! The nurses say she'll probably lose most of it. I hope not, because it looks like that's all she's going to have in the way of beauty, poor baby. The nurses have already sort of trained it into one big curl that sits on top of her head. She looks so funny!

'But Vic, of course, thinks she's gorgeous. He says she looks just like his mother, God rest her soul. The "God rest her soul" are Vic's words, not mine.

'Will you fly out here and take a look at the little wretch? Please, Angel. I miss you!'

'I can't now, Kiki, I'm still pooped from giving birth. I'm so tired. I'm spending half my days in bed. But Mother's flying over. I just spoke to her on the phone.'

'Poor Marie. When she sees this one, she'll probably faint in horror. She will think it very inelegant of me to have given birth to a chimpanzee . . . But she certainly raved to me about *your* son.'

Only a few weeks later, Kiki called Angel from Idlewild in New York.

'What are you doing in the States? I had no idea—'

'I'm in between flights. I'm staying at the motel . . . hotel . . . whatever the hell it is. I'm catching the plane out to the Coast in a couple of hours.

Mother's on her way here from Tarrytown to see me between planes. It was just an impulse. I just *had* to see Rory. But I have to see you too, of course. When I get to LA I'll call you again. You'll come down from Sacramento?'

'Of course. Does Brad know you're coming?'

'No. I told you, it was all an impulse. I'm just going to surprise them. I can only stay a few days. I have to be back in Rome for Christmas. So I'll see you soon. Wait for my call . . .'

The call from Kiki didn't come until a week later. In the meantime Angel had repeatedly called the Cranford house without learning anything – the housekeeper managed to give her no information. Finally, when Kiki did call, it was from the airport in Sacramento.

How different Kiki appeared. She had always been a clotheshorse, but not so formal, so dignified. Why, she *looked* like a foreign movie star! Her silver-blonde hair was piled into a meticulously curled and sprayed upsweep. She wore an ankle-length sable coat, a tailored black suit, a black silk crepe shirt. However, she flew at Angel in her old way, smothered her with kisses, and acted – or tried to act – as impetuously gay as ever. This time she did not quite carry it off.

'Lord, I'm tired, Angel.'

This – Kiki admitting fatigue, depression – was a first.

'How did you find Rory? Was she bigger? Was she thrilled to see you? How did Brad act? Was he glad to see you? Was he . . . warm?'

'Hold on.' Kiki laughed, but in a weary way. 'Yes, to everything. Rory was definitely taller. And more beautiful than ever. And talk? A blue streak, like her mother. Brad was nice and warm and sweet.'

'So what was the problem?'

Kiki leaned back in the car and closed her eyes. 'We'll

talk about it later. Right now I just want to go home with you, have an icy martini, and see your two boys. Don't forget, I haven't even seen the baby yet. I've got a load of toys for them.'

'Timmy's only a couple of months old.'

'I know, but it's almost Christmas.'

'Dick's not here. He's at a conference in Hawaii.'

Kiki smiled. 'There are always things to be grateful for, aren't there? No matter what else.'

Kiki rallied herself beautifully to play with little Dickie and fuss over baby Timmy, and it wasn't until Angel and she were upstairs in Angel's bedroom, both lying down on the big oversized bed in dressing gowns and sipping martinis, that she broke down and confessed that her visit had been a disaster.

'But you did see Rory? She was glad to see you?'

'How could she be glad? She didn't even know who I was? She was terribly sweet – she has such a sweet nature – she sat in my lap and said I was a pretty lady. Then, when this actress came in, this Diane Lane, Rory ran to her and called her a pretty lady too. That was in Texas.'

'Texas?'

'Must you repeat everything I say as a question? You always do that, and it's very irritating. If you'd just wait a minute you'd hear everything.'

'I'm sorry. But I didn't know you were going to Texas. How did *you* end up in Texas?'

'There, you're doing it again. Can't you hold on a sec? I went straight to the house when I landed in LA. Hannah acted as if she had never seen me before. Like I was a vacuum-cleaner salesman. She wouldn't even let me in the house. Into *my* house! She said, "Yes, ma'am, what can I do for you?"

'Well, let me tell you I pushed my way in and demanded to see Rory. But she said Rory wasn't there. Nor was Brad. At first I didn't believe her. But I finally browbeat her into telling me where they were, that bitch! And after *I* was the one who hired her in the first place!'

Kiki lay there a moment silently fuming about the housekeeper. She refilled her glass from the pitcher on the night table. Impatiently, Angel prodded: 'So she told you Brad and Rory were in Texas?'

'No. She told me they were in Sun Valley.'

'Sun Valley? I thought you said Texas.'

'There you go again. With that question mark at the end. I'm going to kill you if you don't quit that nasty habit. That dyke bitch said Brad had gone to Sun Valley for a few days' skiing and had taken Rory and the nurse along.'

'What did you do then?'

'You know, you'd make a great straight man in a comedy routine.'

Ignoring the remark, Angel prompted, 'So you went to Sun Valley?'

'Oh, God! Yes, I went to Sun Valley. And it's hell to get to Sun Valley. Do you remember that? I had to go in this flimsy little two-engine thing, and it was a miserable trip. I was absolutely puking by the time we landed at Hailey airport. Then I still had to find transportation to the lodge. I finally made it, but I was toting around fifty pounds of Christmas presents for Rory. Well, I get to the lodge and learn that Brad had been there and was gone. I was absolutely devastated. There I am in Sun Valley with the fifty pounds of presents and my own things and the sun is shining like it's summertime and if you happened to be on the south side of the lodge, which I was, it's ninety degrees. I'm dripping perspiration in my fur coat while all those dodos are hitting the old Baldy slopes. And I had no idea where Brad had picked up and gone. I could have cried. I never felt like bawling so much in my whole damn life.'

Angel murmured commiseration, and Kiki went on: 'Then I ran into one of the Mellons. I can't remember which one. Florence? I don't know. Anyhow, she thought Brad had gone north on one of those dumb float trips on some dumb river with a bunch of other people and a guide. Someone said Papa Hemingway was with them. I didn't know *what* to do. Those trips last a week! So I decided to hang around for a couple of days and see what developed. I bought some ski clothes and rented a pair of skis and I hit the slopes too. Actually, the skiing there is marvelous – easily as good as Switzerland. You can go up and down those Baldy mountains and there are always new trails to try.'

'I don't understand you, Kiki. How could you spend your time skiing when you were trying to find Brad and Rory?'

'I was *just* skiing. I went swimming in the pool, too, and I sat for hours in the Duchin Room. Do you know Hap Miller's Orchestra is still there? Playing all the old songs.' She started singing the refrain to 'The Way You Look Tonight.'

Angel cut in. 'Why didn't you call Brad's agent in Hollywood? Or his manager? They would have known where he was.'

'I finally did. But it didn't occur to me to do that until later,' Kiki said indignantly. 'It just happened that in the meantime I met some old friends. The Pierreponts were there, and Jimmy and Gloria and Gary and Rocky. And then I ran into Bill Holden! Well, what can I say? You know that Bill and I had a thing going way back . . .' She ignored the dark look Angel threw her. 'And *then* it occurred to me to call Marv Friedman. So he told me Brad had been called back to reshoot some scenes in this flick they had just made near Houston. So there I was on the road again. I can't tell you how hard it was to get out of Ketchum in Idaho. I had to take this rinky-dink plane held together with rubber bands, fly to Salt Lake City, then get a connection to Houston, and then a cab for another hundred miles or so to find them – Brad, Rory, and Hazel – that's the nurse – all in a trailer out on location. They were spending the nights in some fleabag motel. And then, the topper! Rory doesn't even remember I'm her mama!'

Kiki suddenly stopped rattling along and broke into dry sobs. Angel put her arms around her. 'She's only a baby. Each time she sees you from now on, she'll remember you better.'

'How many times do you think I can go through this? Walk in on them and she touches my hair and says, "pretty lady." Then she said it to Brad's co-star too. So I spent a day – no, a day and a half altogether – there with her. Gave her the presents, played with her, fed her. But it got to be too much. It hurt like hell, every minute of it. So I just beat it.' She pounded her pillow.

Angel almost said, 'Well, what did you expect?' but she didn't. Instead she asked, 'And how was Brad?'

'True blue. I have to hand it to him, the guy's got class. Really. He kissed me on the cheek, gave me a big fat hug, told me to stay as long as I wanted, even paid for my crummy motel room.'

'Is he . . . seeing anybody?'

Kiki shrugged. 'That Diane Lane acted like she owned him. I'm surprised Rory wasn't calling her "Mommy,"' she said bitterly.

'Well' – Angel proceeded slowly and carefully – 'eventually Brad will find somebody else . . . And Rory is so young . . .'

'Come on, spit it out,' Kiki said, drinking steadily from her glass. 'What you're trying to say is that Rory is young enough to think of *anyone* Brad marries as her mother. Don't you think I've thought of that?'

'But Brad will allow her to visit you in Italy as she gets older, and you and she and Nikki will all get to really know each other.'

'Do you really think so?'

'Of course,' Angel forced herself to say.

'Anyway, how are things between you and Dick?'

'Pretty much the same.'

'Pretty lousy?'

'Please, Kiki, don't start.'

'Well, life is supposed to be wonderful, they tell me.

271

Not just pretty much the same.'

'Dick says that soon we can build our own house so we can get away from Sacramento once in a while without having to stay at his parents' house.'

'That old refrain. He's been singing that tune for too long already. Are you still falling for it?'

Angel shrugged. 'I think we're both getting maudlin. Have we had too much to drink, do you think?'

'No, we haven't had enough by a long shot. Call down and tell them to shoot up another pitcherful.'

'Oh, I don't know, Kiki. What will they think down there?'

'Oh, for God's sake, Angel! Are you still worrying about what people will think? You're in charge here. Hand me that phone!'

'I'll do it! I'll do it! Do you think I'm really afraid of my own staff?'

'Frankly, yes.'

Angel picked up the phone and ordered another pitcher of martinis. 'There. Didn't I do fine?'

'Great! And tell me – what do you hear from Nick Dominguez?'

Angel stiffened. 'I haven't heard from him. There's no reason why I should.'

'No pictures of you recently?'

'None that I've seen.'

'Disappointed?'

'Kiki!'

'Okay. I'll drop it. When are you coming to Rome to visit me? You haven't seen my Nikki yet, poor ugly little thing! Boy, Brad and I sure hit the jackpot when we made Rory. His genes and my genes really hit it off like gangbusters, you know?' She burst into tears.

3

It was the first week in July. Angel and Dick were in

272

Los Angeles to fulfill their duties as honorary chairmen of the West Los Angeles Women's Mardi Gras to raise money for handicapped children, and staying at the Bel-Air guest house on the Power estate. In a couple of days Angel would leave for Southampton with her sons, to visit with her mother.

Her mother had her schedule to keep her going, Angel reflected. Summers in the Hamptons, the fall at her beloved Stoningham Manor, winters in Palm Springs, and spring in Los Angeles in her Brentwood home. And in between she would take a quick dash to Italy to see Kiki and Nikki. (It always seemed that when she, Angel, needed her, that was where she was.) At least her mother didn't have a chance to get bored, did exactly as she pleased, even if she wasn't especially happy. She and Edward had an 'understanding,' were hardly ever, it seemed, in the same place at the same time. Marie had chosen security instead of love her second time around, and Angel often wondered if she ever regretted her choice.

She herself had chosen love, which was really ironic considering the state of her marriage. It wasn't only that her marriage had deteriorated into nothingness, into a complete stalemate. What was so disturbing was the overwhelming feeling she had that there was something else out there waiting for her, something wonderful, alive and exciting, that would give her life meaning, if *only* she had the courage to go out and look for it. But she knew that, unlike Kiki, she was a coward, without the courage to do what was necessary . . . *demand a divorce.* In recent months, unbidden, those words repeated themselves in her head over and over.

But how could she divorce? There was the Church. There were the boys. There was the fact that their father was the governor. How could the governor's wife divorce the governor? How could a Catholic woman divorce the Catholic father of her Catholic children? Kiki always said Catholics were against

273

divorce and abortion until they needed one. Maybe Kiki was right again.

Look at Kiki now. The toast of Rome! The stardom she had dreamed of! Those sexy, funny pictures that the Italians did so well. Even Marie said the pictures were entertaining and that Kiki looked adorable in them. *That* was a shock to her. And now Kiki was better known to American filmgoers from the imported films than she had ever been before. And besides all that, Kiki had Vic, the man who looked like Daddy and who, in Kiki's own words, 'makes me feel like I'm going to jump out of my skin if I don't have him inside my little pussy.' God! How many women could make a statement like that?

Often she would be ashamed of her secret, bitter thoughts. She did have more than most people. She had her sons. She lived in comfort with a large staff to take care of almost all her needs. She was treated with reverence as the governor's wife. She was frequently honored. She had to count her blessings. But then that little voice whispered in her head: *You're not yet thirty. What are you going to do for warmth the rest of your life?* Oh, how she wanted to be warm!

She had to do some last-minute shopping in Beverly Hills that morning before she left for the East. Dick caught her just before she left. 'As long as you have the limousine today and you're going to be in the vicinity of Wilshire, would you drop some papers off at the office? I'd rather they didn't go with a messenger.' She knew he referred to the Power family's personal office, which took charge of the family's fiscal matters.

'Certainly,' she said as she drew on her white string gloves. She stowed the papers he handed her inside the straw bag. 'Anything else I can do for you while I'm out?' she asked brightly, making a conscious effort to be cheery and pleasant.

'Yes. Try not to buy out the stores. You know you'll only start shopping again the minute you hit

Southampton.'

'I'll do my best,' she said evenly. 'Anything else?'

'Yes. The Bankers' Association dinner tonight.'

'Yes? What about it?' Attendance at the dinner was her last official obligation for several weeks.

'I'd like you to wear something conservative . . . something that covers you completely, so we don't get a lot of negative publicity. That dress you wore last night reminded me of something Kiki might wear – that one-shouldered thing with all the spangles.'

'Yes, sir. I'll be as plainly dressed as a mother superior. Is there anything else? Any more requests?' Well, she had tried.

'Yes. You can try being less sarcastic and more agreeable. It's beyond me what gets into you.'

'Not very much these days, if we're being candid.'

He looked at her for a few seconds as if he wanted to say something monumental, but shook his head finally and muttered, 'Her sister's voice . . .'

She considered sending the chauffeur up to the office with the papers but decided to go up herself and say hello to some of the people there. She gave the papers to Julie Anderson, who said, 'Oh, gee, Mrs Power, Mr Richmond just sent out this bill for approval. It seems the governor never approved this one for payment, along with the other bills. Somehow it slipped through without being checked. Do you think it would be all right if I asked you to do it now?'

'Why not?' Angel smiled.

'Well, I don't know if it's all right to bother you with it.'

'It's absolutely all right, Julie. Let me take a look at it and I'll initial it.'

The bill was from Tiffany's.

'I don't think I bought anything at Tiffany's lately,' she said, looking it over quickly.

'Oh, my goodness,' Julie said. 'Maybe it's a surprise for you and I spoiled it . . .'

The bill was from the New York store, not the Beverly Hills branch, and it was for a diamond bracelet costing $2,200. Then she saw clipped to the underside a delivery receipt signed in a perfect textbook longhand: Gena Grant.

No wonder there had been some kind of a mix-up regarding the bill. Dick probably never intended for it to go through the office, had intended some other means of payment.

She looked up at Julie, who was watching her. 'It's all right, Julie. It wasn't a surprise for me. I just remembered . . . I did make this purchase – it just slipped my mind. I'll initial it. Just make me a copy of it, will you, so I'll remember to put it in my records. I like to keep a list of what I give whom, you know?'

'Oh, yes, certainly, Mrs Power. I'll copy it for you right away,' and she dashed for the copier, relieved that she hadn't caused any trouble.

Well, there it was, in black-and-white. No more suspicions, Angel thought. Only certainty. No surprise, no anger. Imagine! Only $2,200 for a diamond bracelet from Tiffany's! Either it was a great bargain or it didn't have too many diamonds. Even Gena Grant hadn't made a big sport out of Dick Power.

She tucked the copy into her bag very carefully. It just might be her passport to freedom.

As the chauffeur started the motor, a cab pulled up at the curb and she saw Nick Dominguez get out. She wanted to shout to the chauffeur to stop the car, to wait while she dashed out, while she spoke to him, looked into his eyes, made small talk . . . But the moment was gone. Her car sped away, and Nick Dominguez disappeared into a building.

Angel wore the prescribed long dinner gown for the bankers' fête – black, long sleeves, high mandarin neck. She turned to Dick, who was adjusting his tie, and smiled prettily. 'Don't you think a touch of diamonds

276

would set this dress on fire?'

'Wear something with it if you think it needs it. What do I know of these things? You, on the other hand, are known for your impeccable taste, and we have the bills to prove it,' he said, obviously pleased with his wit.

She smiled like a Cheshire cat. 'I think a diamond bracelet would do the trick.'

'Why don't you wear that little trinket you picked up while you were killing time on the Riviera last year? Gold, wasn't it? With rubies?' he taunted.

She almost hit him, loathing that smug, sarcastic tanned face. Still, she smiled. 'No, I think a *little* diamond bracelet. Something slender, not too many diamonds, not *too* much flash.'

He watched her carefully now, alert. He knew she was making points, leading up to something. 'Wear whatever you please,' he said without inflection.

'Well, where is it?' she held out her hand.

'Where is what?'

'The diamond bracelet I'm going to wear tonight,' she said patiently. 'The one I just described.'

He was wary and didn't respond.

'Or are you saving it for a surprise for another occasion? Oh, goodness, did Julie Anderson spoil your little surprise?'

She held out the bill. He took the paper and looked at it. A muscle twitched in his cheek. He put the bill down and resumed dressing. 'It's not what you think.' He seemed in total command of himself.

She picked up the bill and extended it again. 'You missed the receipt affixed to the bill. Here, underneath.' She flicked the smaller piece of paper with her fingernail.

'I saw it. I wasn't trying to hide anything. It was a token present to Gena for performing at a fund raiser.'

'Which fund raiser?'

'Chicago – I don't remember the date . . .'

'And you – you personally were paying for a token

gift for the performer at a fund raiser in Chicago? A national fund raiser, then? Would you like another shot at something a bit more plausible? We still have a little time.'

He looked at her again, rubbing his mouth with the back of his hand and considering whether to try for another explanation.

'All right. I gave it to her,' he confessed. 'Not that there was really anything between us. But she *thought* there was, and the bracelet was sort of a . . . farewell gift, so that she would stop annoying me. I just couldn't get rid of her.'

'I see. A farewell present to Gena. But what do *I* get as my farewell present? I think I should have something grander than a twenty-two-hundred-dollar bracelet under the circumstances, don't you think?'

But he was still cool, still assuming he had the situation well in hand, not really believing that she would leave him. He grinned. 'Okay. You get a present. A make-up present. Whatever you want. To say I'm sorry. How about a sable coat just like Kiki's? You've always wanted a sable.'

'No, I don't think so. Maybe later. Maybe later on I'll buy myself a sable from my settlement money. *After* the divorce.'

But something was wrong. He was still grinning. He wasn't taking her seriously. 'You want to punish me? Go ahead. I don't blame you. You've got that coming. I was stupid and I admit it. It's just that she kept showing up wherever I was, whenever you weren't around.'

The *whenever you weren't around* was stressed slightly. Spreading the guilt around, Angel thought. Running true to form.

'She kept throwing herself at me. The first time I had had too much to drink and it just went on from there. But it never amounted to anything. She couldn't mean anything to me. And the bracelet really was a good-bye present. I swear it! She was just a . . . a

278

lay.' He looked down at the floor, then up again at her. 'And you were always . . . *so* cold. You never seemed to enjoy making love,' he went on, warming to his subject. 'It's always been you I wanted, only you.' He came over and tried to put his arms around her. She disengaged herself.

'That won't wash,' she said icily. And then, mournfully: 'I was so in love with you in the beginning . . . But not anymore. Nothing is left. Nothing!'

He pushed her down on the bed and she struggled to get out from under him, but his body was a dead weight on hers. His hands were free, and with one he held her face in place as he kissed her roughly; with the other he unzipped his pants. Then, with the same hand, he pulled up her gown and inserted himself into her violently, as if firm penetration were the solution to all their problems. He whispered vulgar words into her mouth and spent himself hotly, deep inside her.

He dismounted and went into the bathroom. When he came out again, he was smiling his charming, boyish grin. He acted as if the air had been cleared and everything between them was right again. She came up close and spat full into his face, watching the smile disappear. She said, 'If you've gotten me pregnant I'll kill it and then you!'

'Let me know when you're through with your heroics. We're late.' he said, wiping his face.

'I am through. We're through. Get that through your head. I'm going to Southampton tomorrow and I'm not coming back. Not to you. Is that through enough?'

Still he was calm. Didn't he believe her?

'I'm leaving you, I'm really leaving you. I'm going to get a divorce. And that bracelet is going to be my evidence. I'm going to divorce you on the grounds of adultery.'

'What about the Church? And what about our sons? Are you going to do this to your own sons? You want them to grow up under a cloud of a scandal, as you yourself did? Destroy me and you'll destroy them too. I can't believe that you would do that to Timmy and Dickie over one lousy bracelet.' He spoke so softly.

'There doesn't have to be a scandal. If you'll just let me go, I won't have to use adultery as grounds,' she said, less forcibly now.

'Don't be ridiculous. I can't let you divorce me,' he said dispassionately. 'It would ruin me. So I'll have to fight you if you decide on that course. It's your choice. Your choice and your sons.'

He had managed to turn the tables on her. She was so weak, so easily defeated. She had held all the aces and somehow, still, he had won the game. Self-loathing flooded her. Kiki would never have allowed him to do that to her. Kiki always called the shots, and Kiki was never the victim.

She needed more training. She had to grow stronger . . . and more callous. She would have to practice caring only about what she wanted, what she needed. She would have to bide her time.

4

The captain's voice came over the loudspeaker informing his passengers that they would be landing in twenty minutes. He announced the weather in Milan and wished them a pleasant stay. Angel tried counting back. How many times had she flown to see Kiki? How many times had she picked Kiki up at an airport herself?

They fell into each other's arms. It was over a year since they had seen each other last.

'Kiki, let me look at you!'

'What are you looking for? Crow's-feet? You won't find any. The only advantage in living in Milan is its proximity to Switzerland.' Then, as Angel inspected her face: 'No, I haven't really done anything . . . yet. I was only kidding.'

'It's your hair I'm looking at. How could you cut off all your beautiful hair?'

Kiki sported a boyish bob, the pale blonde hair nestled into a point at the nape of her neck, a front bang running diagonally across her forehead into one eye.

'Don't you love it? I look like a little faggot, don't I? *Très chic, non?* Every peasant wears long hair these days. So boring. Maybe you'll get yours cut while you're here. Aren't you tired of wearing your hair the same old way? Of course, we'll have to go to Rome to have it done. As far as I'm concerned, you have to go to Rome even for a decent manicure.'

A chauffeur helped them into the white Rolls. It was from the thirties, outfitted with a bar, a telephone, and bud vases. Each vase held a barely opened red rose.

'You, Kiki, being driven by a chauffeur? But you love to drive yourself. You always drove yourself when you were in Los Angeles.'

'Oh, I brought this car along just to impress you.'

'I'm impressed, but it's not you. I always picture you hurtling along in a little sports car with racing stripes. But you *are* a contradiction these days. You're not even wearing your sable.'

Kiki opened her poplin raincoat to reveal its sable lining. 'Better?' she asked.

'Better. I hate to think of you changing.'

'But I see my little sister is wearing sable too. What happened? How did you manage to pry that out of Mr Tight-ass? Did the sable become available at the same time as that diamond-bracelet thing?'

'I see that you haven't really changed. You're as relentless as ever.'

'Of course. What made you think I would change?'

'Well, you *have* – just a tiny bit.'

281

'How?' Kiki asked defensively.

'You're not as bubbly as usual. You're *trying* but you're really not. Somehow, there's something very serious about you . . . underneath.'

'It must be the Milan influence. Really, I had no idea life here was going to be such a drag. If it weren't for the weekends in St Moritz or for the few days in Rome, I don't know how I would bear up. Jesus, what I wouldn't do to be having dinner at Chasen's or going to a real hot party in Hollywood again! I remember one when Marilyn Monroe and Jayne Mansfield were trying to out-tit each other. God, it was a scream! And there was the time we went to the beach and a lot of the crowd got to running around balls naked. Not Brad, of course. And not old Bogie, although he was there too – in a tux, of all things. And then these other jokers pretended they were the cops and everyone ran for cover . . .' She sighed deeply.

'But, Kiki, you used to complain that Hollywood was dull.'

'I know. But that was before I lived in Milan. What did I know of Europe then? The Riviera. Paris. Skiing in Switzerland. Rome. Great places. But Milan? My own dinner parties are such a bore I can hardly stay awake. A roomful of men talking about machinery, factories, strikes, and export taxes.' She looked out the window of the car. 'Well, here we are – home. If that's what you choose to call it.'

Angel looked up. High in the hills, a house rose from the landscape like a soaring bird, all concrete, glass, and steel, with a cantilevered terrace seemingly carved out of the mountainside.

'My goodness. I was expecting an Italian villa, Renaissance maybe. Not *this*.'

Kiki sighed deeply again. 'I know. If Milan is nothing else, it is a forerunner in modern architecture. They say the best architects in Europe are here. We did live in a villa in Rome, you know, Vic's ancestral home. And I loved it! All that rococo opulence . . .'

'Baroque opulence. The French developed the rococo. A more refined style,' Angel corrected her.

'As I was saying before I was so rudely interrupted, I adored that house. I adore Rome!'

They walked toward the house.

'So what happened? Why did you leave Rome and come here? You never told me. Is there a movie industry in Milan?'

'Of course not. Not anybody else's movie industry, that is. Only the Mizrachi-Rosa Film Company's movie industry,' Kiki said irritably.

'What *are* you talking about?'

'Later. Now you might as well come in and see the rest of this Milanese monstrosity. And your niece, of course.'

'Mother said she's exceedingly bright.'

'People always say a child's bright when they can't say she's pretty, and Nikki's not about to win any beauty prizes.'

'What do looks really matter?'

'Looks matter. How do you think Nikki's going to feel when she grows up and finds out she's the ugly duckling halfsister of Miss Universe?'

They entered the house and were inside a two-story-high courtyard topped with a stained-glass skylight. 'This is the atrium,' Kiki said. The enclosure resembled a jungle and exuded the moist air of the tropics. 'The house is built around it,' she explained. 'See, every room in the house looks out onto it, including the bedrooms upstairs.'

'Why, this is lovely, Kiki.'

They walked through polished steel doors into the living room.

'Oh, Kiki, it *is* very elegant!' The furniture was art deco, all curves and rectangles, dark green satin upholstered pieces and marble floors. The dining room was steel and glass and polished chrome. The library was black leather sofas and Breuer suede lounge chairs, steel bookcases and pewter accessories.

'Would you care for a dip in the pool?' Kiki asked, her fur-lined raincoat still on but opened, hands thrust into the pockets of her black trousers. She looked more like a sleek young boy than ever. 'It's indoors, of course, and heated. You enter it from the living room.'

'Not right now, Kiki, for goodness sake. Right now I want to see Nikki!'

They went up the open staircase, its steel trusses exposed. Inside the nursery, an older woman and a young girl hovered about. Nikki was in a playpen, also of a spectacular design. Kikki spoke to the women in Italian and the younger one took the little girl from the playpen and placed her on the floor, where she stood for a moment before tottering over to Kiki.

Kiki scooped her up and planted kisses all over her face. The little girl had a headful of black curls, black-currant eyes, and a nose already much too large for the gamin face. Her bottom lip hung slightly open. Kiki thrust her into Angel's waiting arms. 'It's a good thing her daddy's rich, 'cause she sure ain't good-lookin'.'

'Will you stop that? She's darling. Cute as a button. What curls! They're gorgeous.'

'Yes,' Kiki drawled. 'Whenever anyone's at a loss what to say about her, they talk about her curls.'

Angel spoke to the little girl encouragingly in low murmurs, but she didn't respond. 'She won't talk,' Kiki said. 'I guess she hasn't anything to say yet. She does say *Papa* to Vic, but to me, nothing!'

The old woman whispered something to Kiki.

'Give the poor monkey back to her keepers. It's time for her lunch.'

'Why don't we give her her lunch? I've hardly become acquainted.'

'The good Lord forbid! They'd faint if the contessa fed baby herself. We'll see Nikki later. Come on, I'll show you your room.'

The guest room was mostly black and glittering chrome, with suede Barcelona chairs, black carpeting, and a bed covered in gray suede. Kiki laughed at the expression on Angel's face. 'Not very cozy. Let's go to my room.'

Kiki's room *was* more inviting. The floor was covered in deep pink velvety carpeting, the walls swathed in pink silk, the ceiling lined with pink smoked mirrors. 'What do you think?' Kiki asked.

Angel laughed. 'It makes me think of a warm, pink womb.'

'It *is* supposed to be a room to fuck in. That is, if the man of the house were here often enough to fuck.'

'Where *is* Vic?'

'One minute.' Kike went to the bathroom; its door stood open. She spoke to the maid who was wiping the pink marble. The girl left, and Kiki complained, 'I swear, you can't take a leak in this place without someone skulking about. We must have a staff of at least twenty. Maybe more. I try not to keep track. Mother likes having a huge staff but it gives me a royal pain in the ass. Everything here is so fucking formal. In BH I had Hannah and Carlotta. If the windows needed washing, Hannah didn't ask me – she got somebody in to do them. If the floors needed waxing, she called someone else, and I hardly knew anyone was there. If we had twenty for dinner, Carlotta managed fine. If we had fifty, we called a caterer. No sweat. By the time we went to bed they were gone. Here, even the chauffeur has a helper to wash the cars.'

She threw herself on the bed, then quickly jumped up and went to a huge armoire. She flipped a button, and the doors opened to reveal a bar lined with pink Carrara marble.

'Bourbon?' she asked Angel. 'Martoonis?'

'Can we have champagne?'

'And why not indeed?' She flicked a switch and a refrigerator door opened. She took out a bottle, picked up two champagne glasses, and went back to the bed. She threw the glasses down on the pink velvet coverlet and wrestled with the bottle. It popped softly, and she poured.

Angel looked at the label and sighed deeply. 'Heavenly. I haven't had French champagne in ages. We drink only California.'

'Worse things can happen,' Kiki observed gloomily. 'As long as it's alcohol.'

'So where is Vic?'

'In Israel.'

'What is he doing there?'

'Making a movie. I'm sure I told you. With this Israeli actress. Dorit Avnir is her name.'

'But why? What's going on, Kiki? Why *are* you living here in Milan when you'd rather be in Rome? Why has Vic moved the studio here, and why is he making a movie in Israel instead of making one here with you?'

'I have a one-word answer for you – Mizrachi. The sorriest day of our lives was when Vic went into a partnership with him. It was supposed to be a one-time thing, but gradually Mizrachi started taking over everything. It was he who insisted we move the studio here. He said it was because the labor situation was better here and the money thing was better and I, as Vic's star, was safer here, away from the possibility of a kidnapping.'

'Is that true?'

'The possibility of a kidnapping? There's always that danger in Rome. But who pays attention? I think Mizrachi just didn't want us to have a life of our own. You see, it was *our* kind of life in Rome. We had our friends there and we were with other film people. It was fun. It isn't fun here. It's a different kind of people here, a different climate. And Vic doesn't seem able to get the right people he needs here. He finds it hard to function here. Then Mizrachi decided Vic should make a couple of pictures for him at his Mizrachi studios. In Haifa.'

'But why does Vic feel obliged to listen?'

'Because Mizrachi has his screws into him, that's

why. If he pulled the money rug out from under Vic, we'd probably lose everything. He's the shrewdest bastard that ever lived. Too smart for Vic, let me tell you. You know, Mizrachi also owns a car plant in Israel. If General Motors ever started doing business with Zev Mizrachi there wouldn't be any more General Motors. There'd just be Mizrachi Motors sitting there in Detroit.'

'How much money would it take to be free of him?'

'I don't know anymore. Millions and millions. It isn't just money. It's legal mumbo-jumbo too. Even if Vic got out by the skin of his teeth, Mizrachi would still own everything Vic might produce in the next twenty years.'

'Well, if Vic has to be in Israel, why don't you pick yourself and your baby up and go there to be with him? At least you'd be together. What's the use of you staying here, alone and miserable?'

'I did go for a while, but what the hell am I supposed to do there? I don't have any friends there. You see the hospitals and the schools the American Jews' money built; you see the kibbutzim. Then what's left? The goddamn Wailing Wall. Believe me, you feel like wailing. The high spot of the day is shopping. If you like going to the Arab marketplaces and haggling over sheepskin coats which stink to high heaven. And oh yes, you can buy silver jewelry if that's your kick. The cities are jammed – you can hardly walk the streets; the rest of the country is rock and sand. They don't even have TV. And the restaurants serve *Turkish* food. In a Jewish country! I swear! In New York and Beverly Hills you can get a decent corned-beef sandwich, but not in Israel.'

'You do have the gift for making everything sound charming. But what's your real reason for not going there, Kiki?'

'Well, how much fun do you think it is for me to sit on the sidelines watching my husband do a picture with this sabra princess while I, who should be the biggest star in Europe, vegetate in the field like day-old manure?'

Angel had no answer. Then she asked, 'What about Vic's studio here? Aren't they producing any films that you could play in?'

'They're producing pictures all right. Mizrachi has a bunch of momos working here making spaghetti westerns. But if I took a part in one of those, that would be the surest road to perdition. You really don't understand the movie business, Angel. Taking one wrong role, or a crappy one that demotes you in stature, can finish you off for good.'

'So how long do you think this will go on? What is it Mizrachi wants?'

'God knows. Either of two things. I mean, I think Mizrachi is after one of two things. One is to put Vic entirely out of the running, take everything he has. The other is *you!*'

Angel spilled her champagne. 'I don't think I heard you correctly.'

'Yes you did. I think Zev Mizrachi's got the hots for you.'

'I think you must be mad!'

'I tell you, I've got this gut feeling! He talks about you all the time. He's absolutely fascinated with you. Almost as much as that photographer.' Kiki looked at Angel with grudging admiration. 'How do you do it? What *is* it you've got?'

Angel's eyes became big with rage. 'What is it I have?' she screamed. 'I'll tell you what I have – *nothing!* Nothing! Remember? It was you who told me my life was one big fat zero! And you were right! And you now stand there and have the nerve – no, the stupidity – to say—'

'Calm down, will you? I apologize. The whole house will hear you – Will you please calm down?'

'Yes, by all means. I will calm down so you can go on with your preposterous supposition.'

'But it's *not* supposition, Angel.'

'Well, all right then, tell me. What did Zev Mizrachi say about me?' She was curious and repelled at the same time.

'Nothing in particular. He just talks about you, asks about you constantly. Whenever I see him. He asks all kinds of questions. He wants to know if you're happy. What your husband is like. How the two of you get along. And I don't think he only wants to get into your pants – I have this feeling he wants to *marry* you.'

Angel laughed hollowly. 'Nobody wants to get into my pants. Not even my husband. Not even—'

'Not even who?'

'Nobody.'

'You *were* going to say someone.'

'No, I wasn't. Just stop it, Kiki! And let's drop this whole conversation. You've made me ill!'

'Right. Let's drop it. I know what – let's shoot down to Rome.'

'But I didn't come here to go gallivanting, Kiki,' Angel said, close to tears with frustration. 'I came to see you and Nikki.'

'I know you did. So now you've seen Nikki and we'll be together no matter where we go. If we stay here we'll go nuts. No. We're going to Rome. I'm going to call Gino this very minute.'

'And who is Gino?'

'A friend. A friend and a moviemaker. He's really a prince, a real one, and a prince of a fellow.'

'What kind of a friend, Kiki? No. Don't tell me. I don't think I want to know.'

'Well, what did you expect me to do? Sit around here by myself chewing my aristocratic fingernails with no one to keep me company? I get bored. And lonely!'

'But you didn't *have* to stay here all this time by yourself. You haven't been to the States in over a year. Nearly a year and a half, to be exact. Why didn't you come?'

'It's just too hard to be in the United States. I'd go see Rory and then I'd have to leave her again. It's just too hard.'

'I just knew this was going to happen.'

'Well, bully for you.' Kiki sucked her thumb. They were both silent. Then Kiki jumped up. 'Well, no sense in sitting around feeling sorry. I'm going to phone Gino in Rome right now. I'm going to tell him we're coming. He knows *everybody* in Rome. He'll take us to some parties. And, I know – a circus!'

'I've always hated the circus.'

'Not this one you won't. Not this kind of circus.'

As they were about to leave for Rome, Kiki was called to the phone. She came back confused and disturbed. 'That was Vic. Actually, it was good that we haven't left yet. His Majesty Mizrachi knows you're here. Don't ask me how. Now we all have to go to Vevey for the weekend. He's flying Vic there from Israel and he's sending a little plane for us too. But don't feel bad, darling. We'll go to Rome when we come back. And don't look so scared, for God's sake.'

'Why shouldn't I look scared after what you've told me?'

'Well, what do you think he can do to you, for God's sake? Without your compliance and assistance? Besides, I won't leave you alone with him for a minute, I promise.'

'But why should I go flying to Vevey because he beckons? Kiki, I don't like it.'

'It's only for the weekend. You'll love Zev's villa. You know how you love art. He has a marvelous collection. Rothko. Picasso. Chagall. He even has a Reubens. And the dinners – you'd think you were dining with Louis XIV. Solid-gold service plates. Everything monogrammed like it was the House of Rothschild. Last time I was there, Charlie and Oona were there. I don't know why everyone makes such a fuss over that man – I think he's rather dull myself. Of course, Charlie and Zev don't discuss politics. When they served the fish, the little lemon wedges were covered with gauze. Angel, are you listening to me?'

Angel was staring off into space. 'Yes, I heard you. Gauze-covered lemon wedges. To keep them from drying out and to keep the pits from popping when you squeeze.'

'Darling Angel, you *do* know everything, don't you? And Zev really knows how to serve a fine martooni. You get your own little crystal carafe sitting in a silver bowl of ice, and your glass is iced too, of course. Angel, are you listening? Say something, for God's sake.'

'Dick once asked for a glass of milk at "21" and they gave him a little bottle of milk in a silver bowl of ice. We were just dating then.'

'Please, Angel, will you stop acting like you're in a trance? Look, when we get back, would you like to go to London? Tell you what – we'll stop at the Savoy and buy Fortnum and Mason chocolates and eat them in bed. Do you remember how we used to gobble up whole boxes of chocolates at a time lying in bed? And we'll shop for some of those delicious Swan and Edgar cashmeres and we'll have lunch at— Angel, are you listening to me? It's only for a weekend, for God's sake.'

Before she had asked Kiki what it was that Mizrachi wanted, and Kiki had replied that Mizrachi wanted everything Vic owned . . . or Angel herself. And now they were going to visit Zev Mizrachi on his home ground. And besides, Kiki was acting conciliatory toward her, something she never did. Angel couldn't help but remember one of Kiki's sayings: 'Everybody's a sellout, and it all depends on the price.' How high was Kiki's price?

But the weekend was almost anticlimactic. Angel was wary and watchful, but Mizrachi did nothing more than prove himself a most charming host. And she could not deny that the accommodations were regal and the villa itself, a polished jewel.

The most threatening thing Mizrachi said was the

remark he made at the dinner table on Saturday night, with a splendorous array of European and American theatrical stars present, and if the remark threatened anybody at all, it was not Angel herself.

Sweeping Angel with his intense gaze, taking note of her lovely dark hair piled on top of her head, staring deeply into her large green eyes, not missing the soft high swell of her bosom out of the strapless emerald-green gown, Zev Mizrachi observed, 'If I had my way, you, Angel du Beaumond, would be the biggest, most beautiful star the world has ever known.'

Angel lowered her eyes in modest, silent acknowledgement of his tribute. Raising them again, she saw Kiki staring at her.

As Christmas '56 approached, Angel thought surely Kiki would come to see Rory, but as the time grew near Kiki reaffirmed that she wasn't coming – she just couldn't bear to see her daughter. It was just too painful to see her for a few days, then have to leave her again.

But still, it was *more* of a surprise to Angel when Marie, instead of spending the holidays with her and the boys, decided almost at the last minute to fly to Italy instead.

'But, Mother,' she protested. 'I was counting on being with you in Palm Springs at Christmas.'

'And I was counting on being with you, Angel, but don't you think that Kiki needs me more? Just think how hard it must be for her at this time of year not to be with Rory.'

And how about me, Mother? At least Kiki has Vic. What do I have?

When Humphrey Bogart died the following January, and Kiki, who had been so fond of Bogey and always told funny affectionate stories about him, only called Betty to express her sorrow and did not fly in for the funeral, both Angel and Marie realized that Kiki was

292

quite serious about not coming to the United States
for years to come. And Angel wondered about the
situation that existed there in Italy – about the drama
that was being played out between Kiki, Vic, and Zev
Mizrachi.

5

Angel took Kiki's call from San Remo on the private
line in her bedroom, which adjoined Dick's. The
intervening door was rarely used – only to conduct
conversations of an impersonal nature. The only
reason the bedrooms adjoined at all was to squelch any
possible speculation by the mansion's staff as to the
Powers' marital arrangements. When Angel heard
Kiki's latest request, she was glad to be alone so that
no one could possibly overhear her sister's preposterous suggestion.

'I couldn't possibly go to the Riviera for Grace
Kelly's wedding. You don't understand. If the
Governor of California and his wife didn't get an
official invitation, which we didn't, it would be in poor
taste for me to attend. It's a matter of protocol. What
would Dick say? And what about my other obligations
here?'

'Will you shut up a minute and listen? Vic and I literally
busted our humps to wangle this invitation for you.
Vic *is* an old friend of the Prince's, but still and all, it
wasn't easy. There are six hundred people attending
the religious ceremony in the cathedral alone, not
even counting the receptions. I mean, these invitations
aren't being handed out to just anyone! You can't
imagine what's going on here – royalty from all over
Europe pouring in like mad. All the hotels, the Hôtel
de Paris, the Hermitage, all of them, are completely
booked already. I hear everyone on the Coast was
trying to squeeze an invitation out of poor Grace

before she left California. And *we* even have invitations to the Opera Gala. That'll be on the night between the civil and the religious ceremonies. And a lot of the people who have invitations to the wedding don't have invitations to *that!* The Lanvin people came down from Paris to do Grace's dress. And now you tell me you can't come because of some silly obligations or some nonsense about protocol and bad taste. What the hell do you care what Dick says, you fool? I mean, seeing how things are between the two of you and all that, what the fuck does it matter? What do you owe him? And in the final analysis, what can he do about it if you don't listen to him? Divorce you? That's a laugh! Actually,' she said, moving in for the kill, 'this is a perfect opportunity for you to establish once and for all that while he's *forcing* you to stay married to him and you're going along with him for the sake of the children, you're still not taking orders from him and that you intend to have a life of your own. Believe me, you're entitled!'

Angel started to waver, as she usually did on receipt of one of Kiki's onslaughts. 'How long would I have to be away?'

'Good girl! Now you're talking! I'm proud of you! Look, the first *official* party isn't until the fourteenth. That's the party Grace's ma and pa are throwing. I think it's going to be at the Hôtel de Paris. So why don't you try to get here by the thirteenth? The wedding is on the nineteenth – you can be home by the twentieth. One week, that's all.'

It *would* be fun, Angel thought. She needed a break, and she was tired of worrying about what was correct.

'All right, I'll do it. But if Monaco is crowded, how will I get a plane out of here on the nineteenth or twentieth? Everything must be booked up already.'

'Just get your ass over here. Fly to New York. You can always manage to get a plane out of New York, and we'll take care of the flight back. Vittorio has a

few connections, you know. I'll see you. Hurry, hurry!
Kiss, kiss!'

Kiki had been right about one thing, anyway. The
Riviera *was* a madhouse. When Kiki and Vic picked her
up in Nice, they could hardly make their way through
the crowds.

'Do you know how long it took us to get here? Traffic
is virtually at a standstill. There have never, never been
so many people on the Riviera at one time before. Thank
God we don't have to make it all the way back to San
Remo,' Kiki shouted over the noise of the traffic.

They got into the open car, and Angel wondered if
she had heard correctly. 'Aren't we staying at the villa
in San Remo?'

'No, darling, it's just too much trouble shuttling
back and forth in the traffic between there and
Monaco. Every fleabag along the coast starting from
the Italian Riviera is full up. We're lucky to be staying
in the Monte Carlo harbor, right across from the
Hôtel de Paris and the Casino.'

'Your yacht is in the Harbor? That *is* lucky.'

'No, precious. I'm afraid we couldn't get mooring
space in the harbor. Our boat is in San Remo.'

'But I don't understand. How are we staying in the
harbour in Monte Carlo if your yacht is in San Remo?'
Then realization dawned. 'Oh, no – I don't believe it!'

'Don't believe what?' Kiki shouted above the noise
of the traffic.

'Are we staying on Zev Mizrachi's yacht? Well,
answer me!'

Kiki flushed. 'Yes, we are. But let's not talk about it
now. I can't keep yelling like this, and I really can't
hear you too well.'

Angel wondered what she should do. She felt like
turning her back on the two of them, her conniving
sister and her equally conniving brother-in-law,
turning her back and going straight home. But what
about a plane reservation? How would she ever

explain to Dick and everybody else why she had returned immediately? And all the hotels here were filled. *Oh, Kiki, how could you? How could you betray me this way?*

They drove through the avenues of festively decorated shops in silence, Angel's face averted from Kiki's in frosty disdain. When they finally reached the Monte Carlo Harbor and got out of the car, Angel said, 'I will never forgive you for this.'

Kiki's nose elevated several inches. 'Forgive me for what?'

'For compromising me in this matter.'

'What are you talking about? Vic?' She turned to her husband. 'What is she talking about?'

Vittorio merely shrugged and turned to get Angel's bags from the trunk of the car. Kiki looked at Angel's luggage. 'I do hope you brought along several ball gowns. We are going to be *très, très* formal.'

'Don't talk to me about ball gowns.'

'I don't know what you are talking about. Will you stop being such a bore? I really don't know why I trouble myself to include you in anything! I simply didn't want you to miss all the fun. And I wanted you with me because we hardly see each other anymore. Now what is so terrible about that?'

They boarded the yacht, and Vic quickly disappeared after dispatching a steward to bring the luggage on board.

'What about the terrible publicity I'm going to get at home? What about when Hedda Hopper, who's always carrying on about these terrible foreigners in the movie business, hears about this? Or Beebie Tyler? Or any of the others? Mizrachi is a man of notoriety. I don't have to tell *you* that. It places me in a terribly compromising situation to be his guest when my husband is at home, tending to the business of the state.'

Kiki sneered. 'Pardon me, but aren't you magnifying your importance just a teensy bit? There's a total of

296

one thousand eight hundred and twenty-five reporters and photographers here to cover a royal wedding involving a *real*, famous, American movie star, *not* to record *your* activities. Between you and me, they don't give a bloody shit where a mere governor's wife parks her butt. The place is mobbed with real royalty. Or is that what's upsetting you? What's the matter, Angel baby? Worried no one's going to take your picture?'

Angel's hand lashed out, and for the second time in her life she slapped her sister.

Kiki's hand went up to her cheek, and she burst out crying.

'Why are you crying, Kiki?' Angel asked quietly. 'It's *not* because I slapped you.'

'It's because I'm standing here on a dock in pain,' Kiki sobbed. 'It hurts that my only sister thinks so badly of me. It breaks my heart.'

'What about my heart? *My* heart is breaking that *my* sister not only betrays me but is malicious into the bargain.'

Abruptly, Kiki stopped sobbing. 'Oh, Lord, I'm so sick and tired of you making such a goddamn fuss over everything. I think you're just sorry to be here because one American Catholic beauty, who was a *real* star, got herself a *real* prince, not some crummy bastard politician.'

'That does it! I *am* going home! And I'm never going to speak to you again! Tell that steward to bring back my bags!'

'Tell him yourself!' But the starch had gone out of Kiki. She held her cheek, which was beginning to swell. 'I need some ice,' she whimpered. 'And all you care about are your bags. You're selfish Angel. I never would have believed how incredibly selfish you could be. I kill myself to get you here so you can have a good time, and now I must ask myself, "Why? Why?"'

'Wasn't it to get me here to sleep with Zev Mizrachi so that you and Vic could get off the hook with him?'

Now it was Kiki who reached out and cracked Angel

across the face.

'They were both horrified. Then Kiki laughed with a touch of hysteria. 'Now we're even.'

'Yes,' Angel said. 'Even.'

'Even-steven?' Kiki asked, tentatively smiling. They had said 'even-steven' when they were children, when they had fought and made up.

Angel thought about it, wavered, finally smiled ruefully. 'Even-steven,' she said, and they shook hands, as they used to do.

'We really are staying on the *Venus* because it's so convenient, Angel, and for no other reason. And after all, it *is* Mizrachi who's getting you into the wedding and all the parties. We couldn't very well refuse to stay on his boat.'

Angel stopped laughing. 'But you said Vic and you arranged the invitations for me.'

'Did I? Well, we tried. But Zev already had his invitations. For himself and his guest. And he insisted he'd be honored to escort you. What could we possibly say? And what's the difference anyway who got what invitations?'

'Oh, Kiki, Kiki, you know the difference,' Angel said wearily. 'This means he will be my constant escort while I'm here. And I am a married woman. It will be misunderstood by everyone. Especially by Mizrachi himself.'

'Oh, everybody understands these social alliances. Nobody thinks anything of them – a convenience, that's all. And you have to admit that Zev *is* a perfect gentleman. When we were in Vevey did he get out of line even once? Did he make one pass? He was the ideal, correct host, wasn't he?'

'Yes,' Angel agreed grudgingly.

'Well, then, what's there to worry about?'

'Plenty. What does he want? What is he after?'

'An affair, probably. Even marriage. But what of it? He can't marry you, because you're already married. And even if you weren't, he still couldn't unless you agreed. Isn't that right? Besides, is this place gorgeous or is it not?'

Angel cast an uninterested glance around the red-and-gold-velvet room. 'Ostentatious would be more like it. Or gaudy. Or vulgar. Except for that Utrillo.'

Kiki sighed in deep resignation. 'Please make an effort to be in a better mood. Try to be gracious. There's enough tension in the air as it is.'

'Angela!' Zev Mizrachi strode into the salon, meticulously groomed even though his attire was shipboard casual. 'Please forgive my delay in welcoming you. I was busy making some final arrangements.' He took both her hands in his. 'You have honored me by accepting my invitation.'

She smiled faintly. 'You have honored me by extending it.' *God! What baloney!*

'Come, let me show you around the rest of my *Venus*.' He took her arm, ignoring Kiki, who rang for the steward. She needed a drink badly.

Proudly Mizrachi pointed out the ornate appointments of the *Venus*, including the swimming pool with its beautifully intricate mosaic bottom. At a flip of a switch the pool was covered to form a dance floor.

'Where do you hide the orchestra when the swimming pool is in use?' Angel joked.

Zev looked at her blankly for a second. 'You do have a point there. I do bring an orchestra on board when I am planning a party. But I have been remiss. I should have engaged an orchestra for the week you will be here. Next time I will not be so neglectful. But I am imposing upon you now – you probably would like to retire to your stateroom for a while to rest up from your trip. Come, I will take you to it.' He led her to a suite that included a sitting room, bedroom, dressing room, and bath. All done in red velvet and gilt, with an El Greco over the mantel.

Angel chose not to look at the El Greco. *Those tortured eyes . . .*

'This is my personal suite but I wanted you to enjoy

299

it while you are here,' Zev confided.

'That wasn't necessary. I'm sure I would have been comfortable in any stateroom.'

'Ah! I couldn't take the chance.'

A maid was already unpacking her bags, putting her gowns on red velvet padded hangers.

'If there is anything you require, anything at all, please let me know immediately,' he said. 'Eva is here to help you with any service – your personal maid. I'll leave you now to let you settle in.'

Angel looked around the room. There were red roses everywhere, a bottle of champagne icing in a vermeil cooler, a bowl of fruit on the night table – fruit so large and so perfect and so waxen. There were small gold dishes of nuts and chocolates and dates. She smiled wryly. A first class hotel.

The maid finished hanging her clothes away. 'Is there anything else Madame wishes?'

'I will have a glass of champagne, Eva. Thank you.'

On the fourteenth, they attended the party Margaret and John Kelly were giving in honor of their daughter and her prince. Originally the party had been scheduled for the Hôtel de Paris, but since the press was becoming a problem and the casino was easier to secure, plans had changed and the party was moved to the cabaret of the casino. Liveried footmen stood guard at the elevator doors leading into the cabaret to ensure that each guest had an invitation, and that no member of the press crashed. All this security for the royal couple served to reassure Angel. She didn't want the attention of the press any more than the celebrated bride did.

Dancing with Zev Mizrachi to the mellow tones of Aime Barelli's orchestra, Angel noted only fleetingly that he was holding her tighter than necessary. She was reflecting instead on the manner in which he had introduced her to the prince and Grace in the receiving line: '*My* friend, Angela du Beaumond,' instead of 'Mrs

Richard Power, the governor's wife.' Maybe she was being silly to be disturbed. Was she mistaken about the stress Zev had put on the word *my*? Was it really as proprietary as it had sounded?

The following night, they attended the gala at the International Sporting Club. Angel supposed it was just as well they were staying on the yacht, so close to the festivities, since it was pouring outside. Still, there were some two hundred yards to maneuver. But she had underestimated Zev Mizrachi. For those two hundred yards he had arranged for a limousine.

Angel almost enjoyed herself that night – the ballet performed by Tamara Toumanova, the singing by Eddie Constantine, even the magician Channing Pollack. But the evening ended in a fracas. A photographer was knocked down by a policeman, and the inevitable free-for-all followed. Even though she was not involved, a chill coursed through her. Somehow she felt the incident boded ill, presaged something even more ominous to come.

The civil wedding ceremony was held at 11 A.M. in the Salle du Trone. The red-and-gold room was decorated with lilies and white lilacs, with a canopy bearing the crest of Monaco. Angel observed that the day was overcast. A bad omen? She laughed at herself. She and her superstitions. Hadn't the sun shone on her own wedding day? And what had that meant?

Anyway, for whom was she concerned? For herself or for today's bride?

As Angel finished dressing for the Opera Gala, she heard a knock on her door. The maid answered it, and Zev came straight in and sent the maid away. Angel, in a strapless off-white satin gown, stood before the full-length mirror contemplating the upswept hairdo that the maid Eva had just finished arranging.

'You'll have to be more careful, Angela, or you will put the bride to shame.'

'Grace has nothing to fear. She is . . . was . . . one of the most beautiful women in America.'

'She could never surpass you – in beauty or in grace.'

Angel wondered if that was an intentional pun. What did he want? Why had he come to her room?

'I see you haven't put any jewelry on yet,' he said. 'Good!' He took a gold chain from his pocket. Dangling from it was a large ruby. 'May I?' he asked, even as he fastened the chain about her neck.

Stunned, she gazed at her reflection in the mirror, then at his, standing so close behind her. The ruby lay almost but not quite in the cleft between her breasts. It had to be five or six carats.

'Zev,' she blurted out, 'I can't, it's sweet of you, but I simply can't. Really . . .'

'Of course you can. It's only a little gift, nothing more than a party favor. For a very special guest. I insist you accept it, wear it.' He placed an insistent hand on her bare shoulder.

His hand felt hot to her flesh.

'It's such a beautiful piece,' he said. 'Only you can do it justice. Or may I put it another way? Only a magnificent gem could do justice to your beauty.'

She lifted the ruby between her fingers. She loved the weight of it. She let it fall again against her breasts. It did look magnificent there, the vivid blood color against the whiteness of her flesh. Yes, she wanted the ruby. She could feel the excitement of possession surging through her body.

If Dick can give away diamond bracelets, I can accept a ruby. How many diamond bracelets has he given away in all the years we've been married?

Oh, yes, she would accept the ruby!

'Thank you,' she said. She brushed his cheek with cool lips, a totally nothing kiss, a kiss one gives an acquaintance on the street, a gesture. How many such meaningless gestures had she made through the years? Still, it might have been a mistake, for he asked, 'May I return the favor?' and without waiting for her consent he put his lips to hers in a soft, insinuating way, but pressed no further.

Angel wore a red velvet cloak over her satin gown. Kiki didn't see the ruby until they were in the Monte Carlo Opera House and Angel removed the cape. Then Kiki lifted the ruby between two fingers and rubbed it softly. 'Wow!' she whispered. 'Very nice,' and she smiled a very pleased smile. Then she said, 'Did you know that Caruso, Chaliapin, and Ruffo once sang here at the same time?'

The orchestra played 'The Star-spangled Banner,' then the Monegasque anthem. Angel looked to the prince's box, where he and Grace stood together. Grace seemed extremely happy and proud. And why not? Obviously she had gotten exactly what she wanted. The question was: *What do I really want, and will I ever get it?*

They were leaving the Opera House. The prince and Grace had already departed, but the multitude of photographers and newsmen were still there. The Aga Khan had been one of the scheduled guests that night – although he was reported to be ill – and Angel supposed they were waiting to catch him on film. Or was it Kiki they were after, or one of the other film stars from the States? Cary Grant perhaps?

There was a photographer on one knee, but aiming his camera right at *her*, at the both of them – Mizrachi with his arm halfway around her shoulder, guiding her through the crush of people. She gasped as the flash went off in her face. Could it possibly be Nick Dominguez? That was the first thing that popped into her head. *No, of course not!*

Then, did she only imagine that Zev raised his arm in the air, snapped his fingers? She saw four men come out of the crowd, seemingly newsmen themselves. They fell upon the photographer and dragged him away.

Without thinking, she pushed her way through the crowd, angrily shaking off Mizrachi's restraining hand, and ran after the four men as they carried the photographer off down the street. Kiki, Vic, and Zev rushed after her. In an alleyway, she saw the men beating the photographer, almost in cadence. Again and again their fists smashed into his face, and as he sank to the ground, they kicked him in the ribs.

By the light of a street lamp she saw that of course it wasn't Dominguez's face – not his nose or mouth that were covered with blood. Still, she screamed and flayed at the attackers with her fists, tried to pull them off. They fled, and Angel bent to the crumpled body on the ground. Kiki was at her side and said in surprise, 'It isn't Dominguez.'

'I think they've killed him!' Angel cried.

'No, he's not dead. He's moving. Vic and Zev are calling the *carabinieri*. Come, Angel, let's get out of here before they come,' Kiki urged as she tried to get her sister to her feet.

'Zev did it, Kiki!' Angel whispered fiercely. 'Zev! I saw him summon those men.'

'Don't be ridiculous! Why would he do such a thing?'

'Remember the incident the last time I was on the Riviera when he smashed the bottle of brandy that Nick Dominguez sent over to our table? He thought this man was Dominguez!'

'So did I.'

Angel was ineffectually dabbing at the man's bloodied face with her small square of handkerchief, and Kiki said, 'Please stop. An ambulance must be on its way by now. He'll be fine. Let's get out of here!'

When they were back on the *Venus*, a physician was summoned to give Angel a sedative. As she gave herself up to the drug-induced stupor, felt herself falling . . . falling . . . she realized, for just one clear instant, that from the moment she arrived, she had been expecting – no, waiting – for something terrible to happen, and now it had . . .

Everyone was to be in his place by nine thirty in the Cathedral of Saint Nicholas for the religious ceremony. At eight, Kiki came in to awaken Angel. 'Are you all right?'

'My head aches. I'm not going. You go on without me.'

'I'm not moving without you. You have to come. How will it be if you miss *the* event of the week? This is the main feature today.'

'I don't care. I'm sick of it all. The whole thing was a big mistake. Especially last night. Zev had that photographer beaten up. It was all so ugly! I can't look at that man again. He makes me ill.'

'But, Angel, he denies it. He had no men there.'

'I don't care. I just know he did it!'

'Even if he did, it was only to protect you. You can scarcely be angry with him for trying to protect you, to spare you grief.'

'My husband causes me grief. Is Zev going to have him beaten up too?'

Kiki laughed. 'Maybe he will at that.'

'I'm not amused.'

'Why trouble your little head about it? Just forget about it. Everybody's waiting for you. So get dressed like a good little girl, and don't spoil everything for everybody.'

It all had the appearance of a fairyland wedding. The pavement and steps leading to the cathedral were covered with a red velvet carpet. A white silk canopy floated overhead, supported by white columns. Inside the Cathedral, gold baskets of white flowers hung from the chandeliers, and the altar was banked with more flowers.

The bride entered on her father's arm. *No stepfather today. Not for a real princess.* Grace wore a gown of ivory satin and a little cap of lace and pearls. Next came the attendants, then His Serene Highness in military uniform. The High Nuptial Mass that followed seemed endless. Angel thought of all the Masses she had attended in her lifetime, infinite stretches of time. Now, for the life of her she couldn't conceive why she had endured them. *What for?* She was eager to leave the cathedral; more than ready to say good-bye to Monaco. Her head whirled. The television and movie cameras rolled; the aroma of the lilies, lilacs, and hydrangeas was overpowering; the glare of floodlights emitted waves of intense heat. *Will it never end?*

She was conscious of Zev sitting on her right, gazing at her with concern. She barely looked at him all morning, could not bear to. Kiki, on the other side, whispered, 'They say she dreamed of being a princess all her life.'

Yes, she had heard that, that Grace Kelly had always wanted to be a princess. Everybody seems to get what she wants out of life but me, she thought. *Are they so much smarter than I?*

Finally it was over. The royal couple exited first for the processional ride through the streets of Monaco to the palace in Monaco-ville. After a suitable wait, the guests were allowed to depart.

Angel tried not to think of last night; tried to focus on Kiki's stream of conversation; tried to avoid looking at Zev. Kiki took her hand and squeezed it hard. She kissed her and whispered, 'Don't you fret. Your turn will come if you let it.'

Now they were at the palace gates, manned by guards in scarlet plumed hats, and finally inside the Court of Honor. Only after the wedding party had started to partake of their separate buffet were the other guests permitted to start on theirs, set up across the courtyard. Angel wasn't hungry; she sipped champagne.

'Look, there's Ava! I'm going over to say hello,' Kiki said. 'Come, Vic. I want you to meet her.'

Angel, unwilling to be alone with Zev, started to follow them, but Zev put out a hand to detain her. 'I would like to apologize for the unpleasantness last night.'

Angel looked down at the cobblestoned floor of the courtyard. 'But you weren't responsible. You have nothing to apologize for.'

'I will make sure nothing like that happens on your next visit.'

Angel looked at him coldly. 'Are you so sure then there will be a next visit?'

'But of course.'

Her fingers played with the ruby dangling from the chain around her neck. She wondered if she could still, possibly, give it back.

The honeymoon couple sailed away on the prince's yacht, the *Deo Juvante II*, that afternoon. There were hordes of people by the sea wall watching the boat disappear over the horizon. Angel herself was leaving the next day on Zev Mizrachi's private jet, and she could hardly wait for morning.

Angel had been back in Sacramento but a week when she read in Tyler's column that Beebie was pleased to be the first to announce that Hollywood's own favorite, Kiki Devlin, who in the past few years had all but taken over the Italian screen, would star in an international remake of *War and Peace*. The proposed vehicle would be a Mizrachi-Rosa Production. 'Rosa, dear hearts, is Kiki Devlin's real-life husband, a count, and handsome enough to be a movie star himself,' the column alerted those not in the know.

Was this role Kiki's thirty pieces of silver? Angel asked herself, and did not answer.

6

Angel's day began like any of her routine days. At a quarter to eight, Anna, the maid, brought breakfast on a white wicker tray to her room: orange juice, toast and marmalade, one egg (which she did not always eat), and coffee in a small silver pot. Occasionally Angel would have the tray in bed. Mostly she would sit at the small table by the windows, facing the stand of trees to the west, and use the moments to daydream; to think, sometimes, of nothing at all. Then she would take note of the schedule for the day, bathe, and dress. By a quarter to nine she would be with her sons and would spend the next two hours with them, sometimes taking them out on the lawn to play ball with them, or to push them on the swings set up in the back, secluded from view by rows of evergreens. At a quarter to eleven she would go up to her small office on the second floor and go over her mail. She would be joined soon after by Helen O'Neil, her secretary. She and Helen would answer the mail, which consisted mostly of declining some invitations and accepting others, invitations of all kinds.

On this particular morning Angel's glance fell immediately upon the plain manila envelope marked PERSONAL, with no return address. In fact, the word PERSONAL was written and underlined on the envelope four times. Intrigued, she ignored the rest of the mail and slit the manila envelope open. Inside were several photographs. She took one quick look at the pictures, excused herself to Helen, who had just entered the room, and went to her bedroom and locked the door behind her, to preclude anyone's walking in on her. Then she went to the door separating her room from Dick's and locked that as well. Then she emptied the contents of the envelope onto the bed and counted. Ten pictures in all. No note.

Mouth dry, hands shaking, she lined the pictures up

meticulously, then examined each one carefully. All were of Dick. Eight with Gena Grant. One with an exotic brunette – possibly Eurasian. She couldn't be sure, because the picture was blurred. The tenth picture showed a young blonde, very fresh and very young.

She turned the pictures over. Each one was dated and had a place written next to the date. 'April 1956, Las Vegas.' 'January 1957 Chicago.' And so on.

Gena Grant had a beautiful body. There was no denying that. Her breasts were large yet upright, her rump high and tight. A flat stomach, incredibly flat all the way down to the crotch. From the two color pictures Angel saw that Gena was blond all over. Or was it bleached to match? That picture was particularly obscene. She could see Dick engorged, holding himself as an offering. And he was grinning.

The one with the brunette: she was kneeling as Dick sat in the motel-room chair, his head thrown back. Another looked like – what did they call it? – a Cook's tour? Dick's body was perpendicular to Gena's. His mouth on her abdomen. Low. His rear end high in the air. Flabby, Angel noted with grim satisfaction. And there were the two of them in the *soixante-neuf* position.

Nausea overcame her, and she ran for the bathroom.

Who had sent the pictures? She ruminated. Nick Dominguez? Had he hidden in closets, in bathrooms? Had he peeked through a motel drapery not completely drawn? Were the pictures really professional enough to be his work? Why had he sent them to her after having collected them for the last few years? Was Kiki right that his interest in her was a dark, sick thing? Was he simply trying to destroy her world? But that would be to conclude that she was ignorant of her husband's behavior, that her world was still a beautiful place and not one already in a state of irreparable decay. Or had he taken the pictures and sent them to her as a friend, arming her with weapons that she could use to fight her way to freedom? That would mean he *knew* that there was a battle and that she needed an ally. This, somehow, she could believe. There was much pained clairvoyance in those sad El Greco eyes.

And what was Dick thinking of to be so careless of his well-guarded reputation? Worried about the scandal of divorce, was he? What a joke!

She came out of the bathroom and went back to the bed to study the pictures some more. Her impulse was to tear them up, to destroy their ugliness. The pictures could destroy all of them – not only Dick, but all of them. But no – she couldn't tear them up. She had to use them. There was no possible way she could stay with Dick now and preserve her sanity. And he could talk about their sons and what a divorce would do to them till kingdom come. Nothing could deter her from leaving him now.

She picked up the picture of Dick with the blond girl. She was so young – looked so innocent. They were both on their backs, the girl on top of Dick, his hands coming up from behind her and clasping her breasts, a hand for each breast. Angel's mouth twisted in bitter derision. He had never been so playful, so innovative with her.

She swept the pictures up, put them hurriedly into a dresser drawer, shoved them under a pile of lingerie. She had to take a shower, she was perspiring so.

She adjusted the shower head so that the water shot out in a furious stream, and as it whipped her body she planned how she would reveal the pictures to Dick. Oh yes, she would do that: Reveal the pictures and watch him squirm.

Then it struck her – was it possible that the pictures weren't the work of Nick at all? That, instead, Zev Mizrachi had had them taken, had sent them so that she would— He had the power, the people, the ability to get anything he wanted. Had he presumed she wasn't aware of Dick's peregrinations? And that, once aware, she would leave Dick and— She was letting her imagination run away with her. That was dangerous!

She had to be careful, think things out carefully. It was one of the two men, she was sure. But which one? Had Nick sent them as her friend? Or Mizrachi as machinator? They were the only ones who cared enough. *Cared?* Yes, she was convinced that Nick Dominguez cared.

She dried herself with a heavy monogrammed towel. There was a knock on her door, but she ignored it. She was certainly not in the mood to talk to Helen or any of the staff. She had to plan her moves, had to keep a cool head. She needed to talk to someone, but outside of her mother and sister, who was there?

She could not possibly involve her cool, fastidious mother in such dirty proceedings. And she was angry with Kiki, had barely spoken with her since the Riviera. Her friends? They weren't the kind of friends she could possibly share this with. It had to be Kiki. There wasn't anyone else. And Kiki would come through for her this time, eager to make up with her, to show her that she really did love her, was sorry for what had happened the week of Grace Kelly's wedding.

Could she tell Kiki about the pictures over the phone? She had her own private line, separate from the official switchboard. Still, could she be sure she wouldn't be overheard? Maybe the line was tapped? Perhaps the transcontinental operator would eavesdrop? Telephone operators were known to pass juicy tidbits along to columnists for a price.

No, she couldn't risk that. She would use the pictures only to blackmail Dick into giving her her freedom, but she still had to protect her sons from scandal. The situation was delicate. She had to get Kiki to come to her without revealing anything drastic over the telephone wires. She would simply say, 'Come, I need you.' And Kiki would come, even if she was in the middle of a picture. She was sure of it.

There was a persistent knocking on the door again. Finally she called out, 'Yes?'

'It's Helen, Angel. I've been waiting for you to come back to the office. Is something wrong?'

'Of course not.' The efficient Helen was sometimes overbearingly concerned. How dare she knock over and over again?

'I thought we might go over some things now. It's almost eleven thirty.'

'Not now Helen, I'm resting.'

'Well, you do have the luncheon with the California Women for the Underprivileged at one—'

'You'll have to cancel.'

'But you were going to speak—'

'For God's sake, the speech is on my desk – give it to somebody else to deliver. I don't want to be disturbed for the rest of the day. And you can tell everybody else that, too.'

She heard the secretary walk away from the door. Too bad Dick was at the Capitol building or Helen could report her – get *him* to bang on the door and insist she attend the luncheon.

She went to the door and opened it a crack to make sure the secretary was really gone before she attempted to call Kiki. *Would* Kiki leave in the middle of making a movie? Was she really so sure about that? She placed the call to Milan. She couldn't bother to figure out the time there. Was it later? Earlier? She didn't care. Finally she got Kiki's housekeeper, whose limited English disclosed that Kiki was on location somewhere undecipherable. In a mixture of Spanish and Italian Angel asked that Kiki call her, if the housekeeper ever heard from her again.

With a sinking heart Angel told herself she would have to go it alone, choreograph the next scene. But at least she would have several hours to prepare. She knew that Dick wouldn't be home until late that night. He had an official dinner to attend.

She found a black lace nightgown left over from her trousseau. It had been worn just once. She had bought it in a foolish flight of fancy, then discarded it as obvious and trashy, something a mistress might wear, or a shopgirl, on her honeymoon. The truth was that wearing it had embarrassed her, as if she were offering herself up like some canapé which had to be dressed with pimiento and dusted with paprika to be rendered appetizing.

But it was perfect for tonight. She wanted to look trashy and tempting. And obvious. She took a lazy bath, buried herself in fragrant bubbles, patted herself dry, luxuriating in the plan she had devised for the evening. She rubbed her body all over with perfume – even her fingers and toes – then slipped into the nightgown. She thought now what a pity the gossamer gown had languished unworn all this time. It made her feel so lovely, so desirable. The lace molded her breasts, allowed the flesh to glow through, the pink nipples to peek out so provocatively. The slit in the skirt rose to just an inch or so of her mound. Perfect. She looked like a very high-class hooker.

She rummaged in a drawer until she came up with a red garter belt, a remnant of her teenage years, when it had seemed wicked fun to buy such things. She slid on the nylons and fastened them with the black garters attached to the belt. The final touch – a pair of high-heeled red satin mules.

She unlocked the door to Dick's room. Some light was necessary; one lamp left the room cast in shadow. Then she went back to her room and put a pile of records on the phonograph – old romantic ones that were her favorites: 'If I Loved You' . . . 'A Prisoner of Love' . . .

She even had a bottle of champagne cooling in a bucket of ice. She would put that in Dick's room. The ice had almost melted, but no matter. She hummed along to a record as she carried the bucket into his room and placed it on the table beside the bed, unconsciously trying to remember the words.

Flowers, she thought. We must have flowers. She

ran back again to her room, picked up the vase of tulips and daffodils that stood on her dressing table, carried it into Dick's room, and put it next to the champagne bucket. Tulips and daffodils weren't very sexy, but they would have to do.

She ran back to her room and took out the pictures and spread them out on her bed in a circle. Back to Dick's room once more. She lay down on the bed and waited.

After a while she heard a voice downstairs, Dick saying good night to someone. The maid? The housekeeper? Then he was walking up the stairs and down the hall. She heard him knock on her bedroom door, pause a moment, mutter something, and finally he came to his own door. He pushed it open and saw her on the bed. She saw rather than heard his gasp. He quickly closed the door behind him.

She smiled at him as she believed temptresses always did, and he grinned back, approaching her. 'What is all this?' he asked, incredulous.

His eyes took in everything – the lace nightgown, her breasts glimmering through, the legs encased in off-black nylon, the garter belt, a glimpse of her opening. She rose from the bed to meet him. She put her finger to his lips, signaling silence. She slid her arms around his neck and kissed him, her mouth open, her tongue probing his. His hands groped her body, his teeth bit her tongue. His fingers slid down to her parted thighs, reaching. She allowed him to put his fingers inside her. She sighed, groaned, growled.

She started undressing him slowly while he kissed her mouth, tongue, ears, neck, shoulders. She had his shirt off and his fly unzipped. She stuck her hand through the opening and massaged him gently. Ever so slightly. She didn't want him to become too aroused too soon.

He sat on the edge of the bed while she removed his trousers, his shorts. She sank to her knees and kissed his thighs, her tongue leaving wet traces on his flesh

314

but not quite touching his phallus. His head was thrown back as he emitted soft groans. He pulled her head toward him, his fingers enmeshed in her hair, trying to force his organ into her mouth, but she shook her head and laughed.

She spread herself out on the floor, legs apart, feet flat on the carpet, knees up. It was her turn. He was going to do to her all the things he had done to his other women. Her signature filled the air around him. He buried his face in her bush, his tongue in her opening. When she had gotten her fill, she pulled him away by his hair. She turned over and raised herself on her hands and knees. He pulled the nightgown up, and, seeing her buttocks thus extended, he frenziedly tried to mount her from the rear.

No! She indicated precisely what she wanted of him. Afterward, he again tried to enter her, but she crawled away from him, laughing delightedly. He chased her on his hands and knees, but his patience was near the breaking point. Soon he would take her by force.

She got to her feet and poured the wine. She handed him his glass as she sipped from hers. He gulped it down and she refilled it. He swallowed the second glass and took her glass from her hand. He pushed her down on the bed, but again she stopped him. For the first time she spoke. 'In the other room – everything is ready.'

She picked up a silk dressing-gown cord and indicated he should put his hands behind his back. He sucked in his breath as he allowed her to bind his wrists. With his hands firmly tied behind him, she touched him – insinuating, rubbing, cupping the testicles . . . He emitted low moans. Smiling into his face she said, 'Come.'

She led him into the other bedroom. He went with her eagerly. She led him to the bed and laughed wildly. 'Look at each one slowly and tell me which one excites you the most!'

He looked at the pictures as if unbelieving, turned to her in amazement and fury. He wrenched at his wrists, trying to tear them loose, but before he could manage this she gathered up all the pictures and held them behind her back. His hands free now, he came toward her. 'Give me those pictures, you bitch!'

'No, you won't have them. They're mine! If you take one more step toward me, I'll scream so that everyone in the house will hear. The door isn't locked. They'll come running and they'll see us like *this* and they'll see the pictures. Go on and try – I dare you to!'

His eyes narrowed, and he started toward the door. *To test it? To see if it is locked? Or to lock it?* 'The moment you touch that door, I start screaming! Go ahead! Try me!'

He stopped to evaluate the situation. His organ was no longer erect and he looked ridiculously naked, his penis shriveled and small. She laughed again, shrilly.

'Keep your pictures,' he said. 'What the hell good are they to you? You're not going to display them in any court. Not you,' he sneered. 'I always suspected you were screwing around with that greaser photographer Dominguez, Miss-Holier-than-thou. You had him do your dirty work. Well, a lot of good it's going to do you! You just try using those pictures against me. I've got a few cards up my sleeve, including a dossier on you and your hairless kike friend.'

'There's absolutely nothing between us.' But she had stopped laughing, caught up short.

'Get it into your head once and for all – you're not going any place. There's nowhere for you to go. Unless you're prepared to go there without your kids because you don't have the guts to use those pictures. And even if you did, I'd have ten experts to swear they were faked.'

He went to his own room, slamming the connecting door behind him. She raced to it and locked it. She could hear his bitter laugh as the bolt clicked. She sat down on the floor by the door, trying to hear what he was doing. She heard him on the telephone. Who was he calling for consultation?

Kiki, why don't you call? I need your help. I can't handle this all alone. Mother . . . Maybe Mother can help me? If only she's not afraid of the scandal. And Edward. Mother could make Edward help me. If only she would. I must make her see that she has to help me. Fastidious Marie. She will hate all this filth.

She got out her black alligator handbag, cut an opening in the silk lining, inserted the pictures; and sewed the opening closed again. When she was finished, no one could detect that the lining had been tampered with. She had been taught to sew a fine seam at the convent school in New Orleans.

Angel barely slept that night. In the morning she waited in her room until she heard Dick go downstairs to breakfast. Then she heard someone arrive. Pat Haggerty, one of his most trusted assistants. She heard Pat join Dick in the dining room. She prayed they wouldn't disappear into Dick's study after they ate, as they sometimes did. But after about a half hour, they left together in the chauffeured limousine. Thank God!

She hurried downstairs; she had been dressed and ready since seven. Without saying a word to any of the staff, she walked briskly over to the garages, demanded a car, refused the insistent offer from Horace, the second chauffeur, to drive her. With any luck and no problem traffic, she would be in Brentwood by three or four o'clock. Thank heavens her mother was currently in California.

She pulled into the brick courtyard, broke into a run as she approached the house. Why was she running now? A few minutes more or less wouldn't matter – she had come so far.

She found her mother in the garden room with a spray gun in hand, misting ferns. 'Mother!'

Marie whirled, her long gown moving in accompaniment. 'You're so pale, Angel! Where did you come from?' There was anxiety in her voice.

'I drove down to see you, Mother. I left early this morning.'

'And you didn't bring the children?'

'No.' She shivered. 'It's cold in here.'

'Yes, it's rather cool today. Come into the morning room. There's a fire lit in there.'

The morning room, furnished in a white glazed chintz with yellow and cream flowers, was cheerful, and the glowing fire warmed Angel a bit.

'Have you eaten anything at all today?'

Angel shook her head. 'I didn't want to stop for lunch. But I'm not hungry.'

'We'll have a high tea to hold you over to dinner.' She rang for the Swedish maid and instructed her to bring the tea, some sandwiches and little cakes.

'Well, what is it, Angel? I know there's something wrong. You girls are constantly in a state of despair, but I must say Kiki always manages to extricate herself to her advantage.'

'Oh, yes, she does. Oh, I wish Kiki were here now!' The tears rolled down her face.

'Tears are for children, Angel. Tell me the problem.'

'Mother, I want a divorce.'

'I'm not surprised.' Marie nodded solemnly. 'I wondered how long it would be. But you must be sure, Angel. Divorces are a messy business. Your children are involved. Your reputation. Dick's. Notoriety. Are you ready to face all the problems, the scandal, the gossipmongers, the press?'

'*You* faced those things, Mother. You divorced Father.'

'Yes, but my situation was much different. Remember, I wasn't a celebrity; my husband wasn't in government. Besides, I had no choice in the matter. I was abandoned with two children, with no money - thrown on my brother's charity. I could not do otherwise.'

'I can't do otherwise either, Mother.'

The maid knocked and came in with the tray – the tea in a silver pot, the Royal Copenhagen teacups, the sandwiches thinly sliced, crustless dark bread. Marie always said that white bread was an atrocity not to be suffered by the civilized person. Angel always wondered how her mother arrived at these dicta and then followed them to the letter. What tremendous self-confidence she possessed! Why did she, her daughter, have none? And why did Kiki, her other daughter, possess it too?

The maid left the room, and Angel slipped to her knees and put her head in her mother's lap. 'Help me, Mother, help me! I can't handle it alone!'

Marie remembered another girl who had done the same thing – fallen to the floor and clasped her brother's knees. How she had pleaded with Julian to help her . . .

'And whatever you do, Mother, don't throw the children up at me. I can't live for them alone. I can't stay with Dick just because of the children!' She burst out in a fresh outpouring of tears.

Marie stroked the wild, disarrayed hair. She wanted to lean down, bury her face in it, the hair that was much like the father's, that somehow always smelled of jasmine. All of a sudden the scent of New Orleans was in the room, deceiving her, overpowering her senses. How cruel that after so many years she should still be betrayed by a vagrant thought from the past, a scent, by her own daughter's wild, gypsy hair!

She made an effort to pull herself together. 'Well, if it's help you need, we'd best talk about it,' she said briskly.

Angel looked up, cheeks wet. 'You *are* going to help me?'

'Of course. You came to me for help and yet you thought I wouldn't?'

'I thought the idea of divorce would repel you – the scandal, all of it. I knew that you could cope with it in

Kiki's case, but in mine? I didn't know.'

'If I can stand it in Kiki's case then I can stand it in yours. I'm your mother, Angel, and nothing will keep me from doing what I have to. And I'm not afraid of Dick or his father, either. Only one thing frightens me – that you're so unhappy.'

And maybe I'm afraid that you will end up hating me as I did my mother for a while. Oh, she tried to help me, as I did you, but in the end she allowed me to marry Rory Devlin, and then sat all those years in silence as he humiliated me in the worst way a man can humiliate a woman. I tried to dissuade you from marrying Dick Power, but in the end I let you too. But I have sat enough years in silence. I will not wait, as my mother did, until the walls tumble down around us.

There were tears in Marie's eyes, and Angel was stunned, shocked. *Oh, dear God, Kiki will never believe this. Mother crying!*

'And Edward, Mother? Will he help, if he has to?'

'Edward's not too well these days – he's in Florida, as you know. Still, you can count on his support, I think. Edward will do what I ask of him. Now tell me, have you already discussed divorce with Richard?'

'Yes, several times. But he dismisses the whole thing as a childish fantasy of mine. He talks about the children and the Church. Oh, he doesn't give a hoot in hell about the Church, but he pretends to. He says a divorce will destroy the boys. But it's really only his image he's worried about. His public image and his career.'

'That would be his concern, of course.' Marie paused a moment, thinking. 'I want to be sure you are completely aware of all the ramifications. What you're going to give up. Being in the thick of things. Perhaps, even, going to the White House eventually. I, personally, would abhor living in that fishbowl, but you and Kiki . . . And of course, there *are* the children.'

'Mother, I'm desperate! At this stage I can't make dispassionate value judgments about what's good for the children. I have to think about myself. I'm so thoroughly miserable I . . .' Her voice trailed off.

'Is it the infidelities specifically?'

'Then you know about them. You've heard?'

'Rumors.' She made a moue of revulsion. 'But women do put up with infidelity. If they didn't, there'd be more divorces than wives.'

'I *have* put up with it by pretending it didn't exist. But I can't any longer. I won't. There are pictures, Mother, of *specific* infidelities. But I won't show them to you. They're too awful.'

'Pictures? But how did you get pictures? Did you hire a detective?'

'They were sent to me in the mail. I don't know by whom.'

Marie looked at her searchingly. 'Are you sure you don't?'

'I can only guess. But it doesn't matter. I don't really intend to use the pictures unless I have to – unless I'm left with no alternative. But it isn't the infidelities even – it's the coldness, the void, the lack of human contact. It's not even that I no longer love him, it's that he *never* loved me. No, never! And you knew it, Mother. You warned me. Oh, why didn't I listen? How can a person live without love, Mother?'

And then, thinking of Edward, she faltered, flushed. 'Oh, Mother, I'm sorry. Forgive me . . .'

'There's nothing to forgive. You see, when I married Edward I knew exactly what I was doing. I wasn't looking for love. At the time I had had enough of love.'

Angel touched her mother's face. 'You did love Father, didn't you? Very much?'

'Yes, I did. So much. Maybe so much so that I was, am, incapable of ever loving another man. But I know that this won't be true for you. *You* need love.'

'Oh yes, Mother, I do, I do! I'm so glad that you see that. I never even had my own home. I gave up my career and I have nothing really. You see that it's true, don't you? That I can't possibly go on any longer?' And she began to cry – dry, racking sobs.

Marie sought to soothe her, disturbed at how terribly, dangerously distraught Angel appeared. 'Yes, I can see that, Angel. Of course I can. And you don't have to go home tonight. You'll sleep here. Tomorrow you'll go home and get the children and fly back. Then I'll pick it up from there. That's all there will be to it.'

Angel pushed back her hair with nervous fingers. 'But if I go back for the children he'll never let me leave.'

'Of course he'll let you leave; he can't stop you. But what you can't do is leave the children there, thinking to pick them up in a few days. Then they could claim legal abandonment. Go back tomorrow, pretend everything is normal, that you've forgiven him. Then say that you're taking the children to spend a few days with me. Just pack a few things. You'll see. It will be easy. Right now, call home. Leave a message that you're here and will be back tomorrow.'

Her mother made it all sound so simple. Yes, it would be easier to pretend that she had forgiven Dick, to leave with the children without any further confrontation. Then after she was gone, she simply wouldn't talk with him again. She would simply, very grandly, say, 'Have him speak to my lawyers.' Oh, what bliss never to have to talk with him again.

'Oh, Mother, I can't believe how simple it is. That from this day on – no, from tomorrow on . . . So quickly!'

'If one is to do something, one must do it as quickly as possible. Take affirmative action. I learned that a long time ago.'

'You mean like the night we left New Orleans? Yes, I remember,' Angel said softly. 'I've thought about it often. How I was going away from my father – how the train was saying *a-way, a-way*, leaving my father far behind.'

'Only your father wasn't there; hadn't been there for a long, long time. *His* train had carried him away from you long before that.'

322

'I know, Mother, I know. I've thought about that too.'

'Well, that's the past, Angel. Soon we'll drink to your future. As soon as your divorce goes through, you can leave the children with me and take a long trip. Maybe visit with Kiki—'

'Oh, Mother! If I had only known that you could be this wonderful! I wish that Kiki were here so the three of us could be together.'

Was it really true? Did she want to share this moment with her mother with Kiki? Angel wondered.

'I tried to get in touch with Kiki last night, but her housekeeper said she was away on location.'

'Yes, I know. She's still working on *War and Peace*,' Marie said. 'She's in Yugoslavia. I spoke with her last week. I do hope this picture is the success she's been dreaming of. She told me that this movie should establish her as the biggest star in Europe and that Hollywood will be begging her to return. I think that's what she's counting on. I really do think she's had her fill of Europe.'

'I don't know what she would do about Vic and Nikki if she wanted to come back here to live,' Angel mused. 'But it would be wonderful if all of us could be together, wouldn't it? Little Rory and Nikki and Kiki and us – all of us – you and me and my boys . . .'

She didn't realize that she had included not one husband or father.

7

The minute she crossed the threshold of the mansion all the warm feeling of security she had absorbed from her mother evaporated. The housekeeper informed her that Mr Liam Power was there and staying for dinner. He and the governor were in the library and had asked to be informed the moment she returned.

So Dick's father is here, she thought, and then she was frightened.

Well, she was going to pretend the crisis was over, that things were back to normal, and that there was nothing special for Father Power to discuss with her. She started for the stairs. 'Don't interrupt them now, Mrs Peters. I'll see them shortly.'

'Mr Power said to tell him the minute you got in, Mrs Power.'

Damn her!

'All right, Mrs Peters. You can tell Mr Power I'm home and that I'll be down as soon as I change.'

'Yes, ma'am. I've told the kitchen there would be three for dinner tonight. Is that correct? Will there be anyone else?'

'No. I don't think so. If there's any change of plan I'll let you know.'

'I consulted with Miss O'Neil, and we thought Mr Power, the governor's father, that is, would enjoy a rack of lamb with the mint jelly. With small roasted potatoes and a purée of baby peas . . .'

Oh, Jesus, Son of Mary! Will you shut up?

'That sounds just fine, Mrs Peters. I'm sure Mr Power will enjoy the lamb. He always says that lamb is his very favorite.'

'And the purée of peas?'

Oh, my God! And a purée of arsenic on a bed of poisoned fig leaves for dessert.

'Just right.'

'Is there anything special you would like for dessert? Cook has already made a strawberry shortcake.'

'Wonderful. Just what I would have chosen myself.' She turned and mounted the stairs, ending any further discussion.

Helen O'Neil came out of her office. 'Oh, you're finally home. I've been waiting for you.'

The secretary's words were a statement of fact but sounded like a reproof. What made her think that Angela du Beaumond was accountable to her?

'I have some letters for you to sign, Angel. And I wanted to ask you a couple of things about the Oakland Day Care Center project. And there are three invitations you simply have to give a yes or no on immediately. Can you look at them now?'

'Tomorrow, Helen. You shouldn't have stayed so late. Why don't you go home right now and relax?'

'I really don't mind working another hour or so.'

'That's good of you, Helen, but not necessary. And we're having an early dinner.'

'All right,' Helen said reluctantly. 'I'll say good night then.' She turned to go back into the office.

'Oh, Helen, did my sister call by any chance?'

Helen turned around and cocked an eyebrow. 'To the best of my knowledge she didn't. Were you expecting a call from her?'

There she goes again, nosy bitch. 'It doesn't matter. Good night, Helen.'

Angel showered, taking her time. She put on a long white woolen skirt, topped it with a black sweater. She brushed her hair until it behaved and fell the way she willed it. She stopped in at the nursery. Timmy was already asleep and Dickie was having his bath. He complained that he hadn't seen her all day. She promised him they would spend the whole day together tomorrow. She spoke to the nurse, asking how the boys had spent the day. The nurse, too, seemed disapproving. *Do I have a whole household of people in league against me?*

She would have dinner served immediately. That would help to spur the old man on his way. They would eat and she would pretend there was nothing wrong, and hopefully he would leave soon after.

The meal was endless. Liam Power regaled them with stories of movie people she didn't know, of incidents that had happened twenty and thirty years before. Dick laughed loudly at the funny parts and asked pertinent questions about the tiniest detail. It still astounded Angel that his interest in the pettiest trifles was not feigned, his absorption genuine. But tonight she had the feeling that the two men were playing games with her, talking around her as she sat helpless, not knowing quite when they were going to pounce.

She was exhausted. The emotional wear and tear, the long drive, the fact that she had gotten very little sleep the past night had dimmed her faculties. She couldn't figure out their game, how long the foreplay would last, or when the climax would come, but she could endure it. Escape was near, the day after tomorrow.

They were nearly ready for dessert. Then she would excuse herself, leaving Dick and his father to their coffee, brandy and cigars. She had a plausible excuse – fatigue. Maybe she could circumvent talking to Father Powers, one-on-one, altogether. Had she convinced Dick that their conflict was resolved, that she had abandoned the notion of divorce, was ready to make up?

The maid served the strawberry shortcake. Angel didn't touch hers, but waited for the men to finish, for the coffee to be brought in along with the humidor of cigars on its silver tray, with the giant silver candlestick as a lighter. The inevitable charade would ensue. Dick knew that the smell of cigars nauseated her. He would light one and wait for her to excuse herself so that he could make his standard remark about his fastidious wife's abhorrence of smelly cigars. Angel's 'ways' were a recurrent source of amusement to him before guests. She knew the amusement was tinged with contempt; *delicacy* was not a virtue that particularly inspired his respect.

The houseman brought the coffee, the brandy, the cigars, the silver candlestick. She rose. 'Daddy Power, you'll excuse me, I'm sure. I'm tired and I'm going straight to bed. You two enjoy your cigars. I'll see you in the morning?' she asked as she bent to kiss his cheek. 'Or are you going back to Los Angeles tonight?'

Oh, please do say you're leaving tonight!

Before his father could answer, Dick got to his feet. 'I was planning on your entertaining Dad for a while, Angel. I'm going back to my office. Pat Haggerty is coming by for me in a bit. We have some work to finish up by Thursday.'

'Thursday?' she asked dully.

'Yes. I'm flying to Japan on Thursday.' He smiled. 'Don't you recall? That trade agreement we've been working on with the banks here and in Tokyo. And you're supposed to go with me. I told you that too. Have you forgotten? I see by the look on your face you have. Well, it doesn't matter. You'll have all of tomorrow to get yourself ready. So you stay here now and talk to Dad, and I'll see you both later.'

He expected her to go to Japan with him on Thursday. She hadn't even got the chance to say she was taking the children to visit her mother Thursday. What would she do? She had thought she had everything under control. What could she do about this new development? She could have sworn he had never said anything about her going to Japan with him before. But no, this couldn't hurt her. It might even work to her advantage. She would simply say she was sick Thursday morning, unable to rise from her bed. Then he would be forced to leave without her, and then once he was gone she would recover, pack a few things, and leave with the children. Why, it would be even simpler than she had planned. All she had to do now was get through this evening and tomorrow.

Dick left the room. Last night seemed never to have happened as far as he was concerned. They had parted with claws tearing at sensitive flesh, fangs bared for assault. Her last words to him were that nothing would stop her from divorcing him, still he had made plans for her to accompany him. Somehow he was sure that, no matter, she would go with him. So he had some kind of a plan too. He must be dealing from some position of strength. Was Daddy Power, sitting so calm and mellow, the source of his strength?

Oh, sweet Jesus, I'm in for it. It will not be so simple. No . . . I must be strong.

She turned to the old man smiling at her. 'Well, I'll stay for coffee with you, Daddy Power, then I'll just have to go to bed. Otherwise I'm afraid I'll yawn right in your face.'

He leaned back in his chair, lit his cigar. 'You should take better care of yourself, Angel. A young woman like you shouldn't be so tired all the time. I've been taking vitamin shots myself. Terrific stuff. Makes me feel like a young buck, if you know what I mean.'

I'd rather not think about what you mean. 'Would you like another piece of strawberry shortcake with your coffee?'

'No, I've had enough. But you're a thoughtful girl, Angel, arranging for my favorite dishes. I appreciate that. You're a grand hostess. I've always said that to Dick.'

She forced a smile, knowing that he knew she had not planned the menu. She waited for his shaft.

'Dick told me what happened last night.' His tone didn't change.

She smiled brightly. 'Oh, it was just a silly argument. It's all forgotten.'

'You're not leaving him, you know,' he said, ignoring her statement.

Her heart pounded in her chest. 'I told you, it was just a silly argument – it's all forgotten.'

His tone remained even. 'Don't play-act with me. You haven't changed your mind about anything. You've been pretending since you came home from your mother's. But you're right about one thing. You *are* going to forget it. We're going to put it all behind us. I guess you were just out of sorts to get so upset over nothing, a trifle that didn't mean a thing. Maybe you should take a little vacation when you and Dick come back from Japan. A vacation all by yourself. Without Dick or the children. Maybe go down to the island.'

She abandoned caution. 'A little vacation won't cure what's wrong with this marriage,' she spat out. Then she was sorry. She knew it wouldn't help to antagonize this vicious man further. It hadn't helped Kiki. It had ended her Hollywood career.

She softened her voice. 'I don't wish to offend you, Father Power, but this is a personal matter between Dick and me. I understand your natural regard for Dick, but it *is* so personal and so painful that I really can't discuss it with you.' She tried to give a note of finality to her words. She started to rise from her chair to indicate that there was nothing more for either of them to say.

'Sit down!' he roared.

And she sat from the impact of the violence in his voice.

'Don't you give me that shit about it having nothing to do with me! Like hell it doesn't! My son is me! *Me!* And I tell you, politics and scandal don't mix! So there will be *no* scandal!' He bolted his brandy and poured himself another. 'Now just you lighten up, little girl, and start behaving yourself and everything will be all right.'

She stared at him, frightened. He had spoken to her as he would to one of the starlets on his lot. But she wasn't his little starlet. *I don't have to listen to him, I don't—*

Aloud she said, 'But everything won't be all right. This marriage is insufferable to me. I cannot go on! I will not!'

'If you're talking about Dick's little peccadilloes, he's going to make amends for that. We spoke about it and he's prepared—'

'Don't you dare use the word *peccadillo* to me - your very use of the word is an insult! This whole marriage is an insult! I'm not going to discuss it with you another minute!' Again she rose from her chair.

This time he got up from his chair and pushed her down. 'Every man has a few skeletons of this sort in

329

his closet – that's what makes him a man. Dick is a healthy, virile young fellow. If you were more of a woman, he wouldn't have strayed. Don't look at me like that – you're no little girl from the country, so you can cut that act with me. Anyhow, all that is going to change. Dick's promised me there'll be no more—'

'I don't care what he's promised.' She was careful not to raise her voice, so that the servants wouldn't hear any more than they already had heard. 'This marriage can't go on for any number of reasons. One is, he doesn't love me. Two is, I no longer love him. Only third are his peccadilloes, as you have put it so charmingly. Oh, and there's more. I have never been treated like a wife, like a woman, like a real person. I've been some kind of very presentable concubine. I have never had a real home. I have never had a penny to spend that I didn't have to account for, beg for. Why, I'm no better off than I was when I was a schoolgirl. And yet, none of this would matter if only we had a real marriage. But we don't! There is no reason I have to go on with this charade. I know what Dick is getting out of it, but no one has shown me what I'm getting. Because they can't. Because there's nothing in it for me. No, this is no life! And I don't care what you say. You can't *make* me stay. I don't belong to Dick. I'm not some kind of slave labor for your son to exploit for his own gain. I'm going, and I *will* have a divorce,' she said in a low, controlled voice.

He sat there puffing on his cigar, smiling kindly at her as if she were some naughty, willful child. Finally he spoke. 'If there's anything else you'd like to get off your chest, Angel, go ahead. Get it all out.'

'I have nothing more to say except those pictures I have, which I *know* Dick has told you about, will *not* be used unless you absolutely force me to. And now, if you'll excuse me, I'm going to bed.'

He stopped smiling. 'One minute, lady. Now you listen carefully, because I don't intend to repeat myself. You're not going anyplace. Not if you want a shred of reputation left; not if you ever want to see those two boys again.'

This time it was she who smiled. 'Don't threaten me. I really will use those pictures if I have to, you know.'

He waved his hand. 'I'll have forty experts to say they're fakes. A hundred if I need them.'

'I'll have my own experts,' she said. 'My mother and stepfather are going to see that I get my divorce. They're standing behind me one hundred per cent. I know what counts in this world, Mr Power. Money. Money buys everything. You, of all people, ought to know that. And my stepfather is prepared to spend anything to back me. And the Whittiers, as you well know, had money when your father was only blinking his way out of steerage. If it's a fight you want, Edward will match you, blow for blow.'

'Good show, Angel Devlin.' He put the emphasis on the *Devlin*, which should have warned her what was coming. 'Of course you're snooty. Why shouldn't you be? Everyone knows what a proud name you bore. Just in case you're not up on the latest with your dad, let me brief you. He's no longer living off rich old broads on the French Riviera. I understand he's no longer presentable enough for that.'

Angel clapped her hands over her ears and ran for the door. With surprising alacrity, he jumped from his chair and forestalled her, his back blocking the door. 'I'm not finished yet. And I suggest you take your hands away from your ears so I don't have to holler for every servant in the house to hear.' He forcibly removed the trembling hands from her ears. 'What he does now for a living is pick up old fags and oblige them for five or ten bucks apiece. From what I understand about these things, old queens aren't as particular as rich old ladies. And I would imagine you'd be interested in the state of his health. I've heard various tales. One is that he's syphilitic; others say he's an addict. Morphine, I'm told. I haven't bothered to check which one of these stories is the exact truth, but I suppose it won't be hard to find out.'

He led her back to her chair, and she didn't resist. He pushed her down like a rag doll. 'Now I'm going to give you a lesson in money and power. I didn't realize how naïve you are. Take money first. You're right about that – money *is* power. The more money, the more power. But take power. Power is not always money. Sometimes power is the right connections, or a complete understanding of people and the rules of the game. *I* have the connections. From bottom to top and all the diagonals. You couple my money and my connections with my understanding of the rules and people and you've got an unbeatable combination.'

His voice dropped to a dramatic whisper. 'There's no game that exists that I don't know how to play. There's absolutely nothing I won't do to get what I want. I'll match my power and money against your stepfather's money, and I'll destroy the lot of you!' He paused for breath. 'You saw what I did to your sister. Drove her straight out of the country, didn't I?'

'I'll have a hundred people swear you're a bigger whore than your father is – honorable people, judges, senators, everybody whose name spells integrity. And they'll do as I say, because if they don't, they know I can destroy *them*. When we're through with you you'll be lucky if they don't only take away your children but put you in the nuthouse . . .

'You say you have some pictures? Well, *I've* got pictures – pictures of your very rich, very Mayflower stepfather – that would shake the foundations of his brokerage house. How about one of him having his cock sucked by another member of that great distinguished Devlin clan – your sister, Edward's stepdaughter, actress, socialite, countess, tramp – Kiki Devlin Rosa!'

But how could he possibly know about that? Some servant at the time must have seen, and later told. But a picture? He's lying about a picture!

'You're lying!' she screamed.

He held a finger to his lips. 'Hush, my dear, the servants, you know. They hear *everything*, and sometimes they spill the beans. I don't have to lie. I just have to know the right people. Would you like to hear some more family gossip? How about Marie du Beaumond Devlin Whittier? I have a really great story about her. A great lady. Everybody says so. Absolutely socially impeccable. Who just happens to get her dope from a very distinguished Palm Springs doctor and who peddles her ass to him for that very same dope. Fascinating, isn't it?'

She sprang up, hitting at him with her fists. 'You're lying, you evil man!'

He shook her off. 'You don't have to believe me. You can ask your mother. And if you hear words of denial from her, you still won't be sure what the truth is, will you? But everyone else will believe it. Everybody loves to believe things like that. And I have the ear of the biggest columnists in Hollywood. They owe me! They'll print whatever I say.'

They'll print whatever I say! Angel believed that. She knew that was no lie. She started to cry and then sobbed. She knew she was helpless against him.

'So, my dear, let's not hear any more about a divorce. I have to leave now – I have a plane waiting. I'm going back to LA tonight. You wipe your tears, pull yourself together, and go upstairs and have a good night's rest so you can go along with Dick Thursday. You don't want to let him down. But don't you worry, little girl, I've spoken to Dick and he's going to be a good boy from now on. He's promised *me* there'll be no more indiscretions. and just to show you that I'm not such a meanie, I'm going to see that you get a house of your own in Bel Air, right near us. How about that? You've always been a great favorite with me, Angel. Lots of style.

'Come on now. Pull yourself together before you let anybody in the house see you. You know how people will talk, especially servants. And you kiss those two little rascals for me tomorrow first thing. Damned if I don't think that Timmy looks just like me. Oh, I almost forgot – I brought along a little present for you. Picked it up a couple of days ago.'

He took out a bit of tissue from his breast pocket and withdrew a slim bracelet and held it up for her to see. It was composed of some twenty small diamonds with a few emerald chips centered in the middle. 'I picked it up at Cartier's,' he said, holding it out to her.

He smiled, shook his head. 'Did you really think we'd let you go? With the gubernatorial in '58 and the presidential race coming up in '60?'

God, why can't I kill him? Why? why? It's not fair.

When she didn't take the bracelet, he threw it into her lap. She looked at it dumbly.

'As soon as I laid eyes on it, I said to myself – just right for Angel . . . delicate, elegant, like she is.'

He left the room, and she sat there for some time. The maid knocked and came in. 'Shall I clear, Mrs Power?'

'Yes.' She rose from the chair with an effort, dangling the bracelet from one hand. She remembered to say, 'Good night,' although it took some effort. The maid looked at her curiously, but Angel turned her face away.

She started up the stairs, walking heavily, wearily. The housekeeper appeared at the foot of the stairs. 'Are you retiring for the evening, Mrs Power?'

Angel turned and looked at her dully. 'Yes, I'm retiring. Good night.'

'I had Clara turn down your bed. I *thought* you'd want to retire early.'

Did you now? Did you hear every word from the dining room, too? Sneak, sneak, sneak.

'What made you think I'd want to retire early, Mrs Peters?' she asked.

'Oh, your long day. You did have a long day, didn't you? Traveling up from Los Angeles? I knew you'd be fatigued.'

'I see. Yes, I am fatigued.'

'Good night then. Sleep well.'

The lamps in her bedroom were lit, the curtains were drawn, one window was open a few inches to admit the night air. The bedspread was removed and the satin comforter had one corner folded back in a neat triangle. The room looked warm, inviting, comforting. *What a laugh.*

Oh, God! What am I going to do? Well, one thing I'm going to do is replace Mrs Peters.

There was a knock on the door.

'Yes?' she inquired wearily. Apparently they were never going to let her be.

'It's Clara, ma'am. I wanted to know if there was anything I could do for you. Run a bath?'

'No. Thank you.'

'Good night, ma'am.'

She forced herself to say, 'Good night, Clara.'

She undressed and filled the marble tub in the old-fashioned white-tiled Victorian bathroom. She sank up to her neck in the suds, waiting for the hot water and steam to soak away some of her weariness and anxiety. But there was no relief to be found there. She dried herself slowly and put on a white cotton nightgown and a robe.

She would have to call her mother to tell her to forget all the plans. Her mother would want a full explanation, but she couldn't possibly go into it all with her tonight. She would have to tell her someday, but not tonight.

When her mother answered the phone, Angel could hear the worry and depression in her voice. *Poor Mother, I've upset her more than she let on.*

'Mother . . . everything we talked about . . . just forget it, just forget it all.'

'Angel! Why? What's happened to change your mind?'

'I can't talk about it.'

'Are you and Dick reconciling? Is that it?'

'No. Not reconciling. But I have to stay. Dick's father was with him when I got back.'

'So?'

'He flew in just to deal with me.'

'What of it? We can still go ahead with our plan.'

'No, Mother. He gave me a graphic description of power. And he has it, the power. I can't get the divorce. He has the power!'

'Stop saying that, Angélique, and explain to me what you're talking about.'

'I can't talk about it, Mother. Just believe me. He has the power and I can't get a divorce. Good night, Mother. Try not to worry.' She hung up the phone.

She didn't know if it was all true, the things Liam had told her about her mother and father. But he had known about Kiki and Edward, even if he didn't have a picture. Angel was convinced he could do anything he threatened to do. And he could have just about anything put in print, true or not.

She picked up the diamond bracelet she had tossed on the bed. Only a pavé of diamonds, not one real-sized stone there. A bunch of chips put together to look like something it wasn't. Just like her marriage.

A bitter smile appeared on her lips. Neither father nor son gave away very grand bracelets.

Oh, Father! No, I won't think about Father. Not tonight. Loitering on street corners looking for – I won't! And he just has to be lying about Mother! She's too strong to be an addict of anything, and she would never have relations with some horrible man . . . a doctor like that just to – He's lying, I know he is. Dirty, disgusting man! And using those women as his spies . . . that sneaky Mrs Peters. Damn her! And that Helen O'Neil!

If Kiki heard of the alleged picture of Edward and herself in a compromising position she would laugh herself sick. If Kiki saw the diamond pavé bracelet she would probably laugh even harder.

Angel broke into fresh sobs.

But one thing is sure. I will never, never sleep with Dick Power again if I live to be a hundred years and have to stay with him the whole time. I swear it!

She went to the bathroom and took two Valiums from a bottle. She poured a glass of water and swallowed them down. She deliberated a moment, took another, considered taking one more.

She lay down in bed and burrowed her face in the pillow. She thought about how pleasant it might be to sleep forever. Then she thought about her sons. That wouldn't be at all pleasant for them. She felt herself falling, sinking.

The phone rang beside her. She stuck out a hand, groped for the instrument. 'Yes? Hello?'

Some static, and Kiki's voice came on. 'Angel! How are you? I'm in Yugoslavia. We're having a gorgeous time. It's going to be a gorgeous movie. You'll never guess who I ran into – in the middle of Yugoslavia, mind you . . . Angel, are you there?'

'Yes. But I can't talk now.'

'Why not? Is someone there? What is it? You sound strange.'

'No, no. I'm too sleepy to talk now.'

She hung up, and in a few seconds she was dreaming.

It is on the television endlessly. Over and over again. The picture of Dick getting off the American plane with his beautiful actress wife. The governor arriving at a bank. A hodgepodge of people. Security guards, policemen, students. And then the picture of the American governor lying dead on the sidewalk.

Angel and Kiki sit upstairs in the house in Bel Air. They watch the TV endlessly. They laugh frequently and talk in whispers. A red-haired girl comes in and says, 'Why do you keep watching the TV? It's ghoulish of you.'

They laugh at her and make faces. Kiki says, 'Liam

Power is watching too. Downstairs. Why don't you make *him* stop.'

The red-haired girl walks away, shocked.

'She looks like a black crow in that black dress,' Kiki says. 'They all look like black crows.'

'Do we look like black crows too?'

'Don't be ridiculous,' Kiki says. '*We* look very elegant in our black dresses. I saw Nick downstairs. He looks very handsome in his black suit.'

Angel smiles sweetly. 'And Dick? Dick is very handsome too. Lying there so still. Don't you think Dick is handsome? Don't you think he looks so beautiful in his black box.'

'He does have a charming smile. And nice eyes. Only they're closed. But his eyelashes look very beautiful. But he isn't very good in bed.' Kiki whispers in Angel's ear, and they both go into gales of laughter.

Nick comes into the room, and Angel extends her hand. He kisses it. She winks at him, but he looks bashful.

'Come,' a man in a black suit says. 'Everybody. It's time to go. Hurry up and get in line. Who will be first?'

'I'll be first,' Angel says. 'Don't you think I should be first, Kiki?'

'Definitely. You should be first.'

'I will be second,' Sean, Dick's brother, says.

'Don't you think the children should be second? He is their father,' Angel reproaches him.

Kiki pouts. 'I want to be second and stand next to you, Angel.'

'All right, Kiki, you get the children and stand with them and all three of you can be second.'

'All right, then I'll be third,' Sean says.

'You're fourth. I have to be at least third,' Bonita, Dick's mother, says resentfully. 'You're only a brother, after all.'

Finally, everyone forms the conga line behind Angel and gets ready to march off. The line is so long it trails down the hall and down the stairs.

'We're ready to begin,' Liam Power says. 'I will be first.'

'No, I'm first,' Angel says.

'That's what you think! I'll be first, and that's that.'

'But wait,' Angel says. 'We can't bury Dick just yet. We have to wait for Daddy. Don't you know we have to wait for Daddy?'

Everyone choruses solemnly, 'Yes, we must wait for Daddy.'

Angel heard the phone ring. She strugged to come awake and find the phone. She heard Kiki's voice again.

'Angel? I was worried about you. I didn't like the way you sounded. What is it? What's wrong?'

She held the phone away from her ear. She had had a terrible dream, she thought, but she couldn't remember what it was.

8

Arriving for work that morning, Helen O'Neil noticed Clara, the maid, standing outside Angel's bedroom door, the breakfast tray set down on the hall table. 'What is it, Clara?' Helen glanced at her watch. 'It's ten to nine. It's late for Mrs Power's breakfast. Why haven't you taken the tray to her?'

'I don't know what to do, Miss O'Neil. I've been knocking on the door for a long time. I always knock before I go in. Sometimes Mrs Power wants to sleep some more and she tells me to come back later. But this morning she won't answer me. But I can hear her in there. She's not sleeping. I think she's crying . . .'

Helen put her ear to the door. She did hear crying. She knocked several times, but Angel still didn't answer. She hesitated only a moment, then said to maid, 'We'll have to get her up.'

She tried the door. It was open. They saw Angel lying flat on her back in the bed, crying convulsively. The secretary rushed in and ran to the bed; the maid followed slowly behind her. 'Shall I bring in the tray, Miss O'Neil? Should I call Mrs Peters?'

'Be quiet a minute, will you?' she said to the maid. 'Angel? Is something wrong? Are you ill?'

Angel stared straight ahead and continued to cry.

'Angel? Are you in pain? Can I do something for you?'

There was no answer.

'How about some coffee? That will make you feel better. Clara, bring Mrs Power a cup of coffee.'

The maid ran out into the hall. Helen sat down on the edge of the bed. She stroked Angel's forehead, spoke softly to her. The maid brought the coffee. Helen took it from her and urged Angel to sit up and take a sip. Angel ignored her. The secretary tried to put the cup to her lips, but Angel turned her head aside and closed her eyes.

Helen set the cup and saucer down and turned to the maid. 'Listen to me carefully, Clara. Go downstairs to Mr Power's study and tell him to come up here. Don't speak to anyone else. If Mr Power is with anyone, ask to speak to him alone.'

The maid seemed nervous, hesitated.

'Oh, never mind,' Helen said. 'I'll do it myself. You stay here with Mrs Power. Just sit with her and try to calm her down. Stroke her forehead or something.'

The maid, frightened, still hesitated.

'Go ahead!' Helen gave her a little push. 'Sit on the bed. Take her hand. There's nothing to be afraid of, for Pete's sake. She won't bite. I'll be right back.'

'Please hurry, Miss O'Neil. I don't know what to do.'

'Oh, God, just sit there! I don't think she even knows you're there.'

Dick Power came rushing into the room, with Helen at his heels. Clara jumped up and backed away.

'You can go downstairs, Clara, but don't say a word to anybody. You hear me? Nobody! And bring in that breakfast tray before you go,' Helen told her.

Dick stood a bit away from the bed, almost as if his wife were afflicted with a communicable disease. 'Would you mind waiting in the hall, Helen? And close the door, please.'

After Helen closed the door, Dick came closer to the bed. 'What kind of act are you pulling now? It's not going to do you any good, you know.'

Angel didn't answer him. She continued crying, her eyes shut.

'Will you answer, for God's sake? And stop crying! The whole household will know about this in five minutes!'

Still she didn't look at him, and still she didn't cease crying.

He ran a hand through his hair. 'Will you please get hold of yourself? You're going to make yourself really sick. You've got the children to think of.' Tentatively, he stroked her brow, pushing the wet strands of hair away from her face. But there was no reaction whatever. He watched her for several minutes, trying to decide what to do. He went to the door finally. 'Helen, step in here please. I think Angel's ill. Probably exhaustion. We'll have to call a doctor to give her a sedative. I think Dr Pintzer would be best. But first will you please call Pat Haggerty for me? Don't say what the problem is, just tell him I want him here immediately. Then call Dr Pintzer. Just tell him Angel's sick. Don't say anything more. Tell him to come immediately. Got that? When you've finished making the calls, go downstairs and wait for Pat and the doctor to arrive. I want you personally to bring them upstairs the second they get here. Got that?'

Helen started toward the door to go to her office.

'No, go in the other room and make the calls on my private line. Wait a minute. Before you call the doctor or Pat, try to get hold of my father. If you can't reach him, leave a message for him to call me right away.'

Helen picked up a piece of toast from the breakfast tray and nibbled at it as she went into the adjoining room. Dick would be running for the governor's seat, and after that there would be the run for the presidency. If she proved herself invaluable in this emergency, who knew what could happen?

'I'll give her a sedative, Dick, which will keep her asleep for a few hours. At least it will stop the crying and allow her to get some rest. I'll be back later when the sedative wears off and we'll see how she looks then. As you say, it might just be a case of nerves – exhaustion – and all she'll need is some rest. Or it might be a form of hysteria that will work itself out in a day or two. When I come back later, we'll know better. If the crying's stopped by then, maybe we'll be able to talk to her and I'll be able to judge better just how serious the situation is. Then we might have to decide on other steps. A nurse. Intravenous feedings, if we can't get her to eat or drink anything. Even a sanitarium, if this thing appears prolonged. But there's no sense in talking about it now. It'll probably turn out to be nothing more than a minor case of nerves. Angel's always been a bit high-strung. Just keep somebody with her today and I'll see you later.'

'Right, David. Thanks for coming over so quickly. I appreciate it. I'll leave Helen with Angel for today. I can count on her discretion. And she's fond of Angel. I'd like to contain this thing with the least amount of people involved. You know what I mean.'

'Surely. Of course. I'll see you around five or six. If the sedative should wear off sooner, call me.'

'I'll work here today, Helen, just in case. If Angel should awaken let me know right away. Otherwise, just sit with her and don't let anyone in. If you need anything, have Clara bring it up. I hope that little nincompoop can keep her mouth shut. I put the fear of

God into her, but you know servants. Everytime I say a word to her she looks like she's going to faint.

'And if any calls come through on Angel's private line, just tell whoever it is that she's out and you'll take a message. And that goes for her mother and sister in particular. Whatever you do, don't let her mother or sister suspect anything's wrong. One word and they'll come swooping down on me.'

Helen nodded. 'I'll take care.'

'I'm sorry, Dick, but now that the sedative's worn off, I don't see any improvement. She's crying hysterically, and not responding at all. I doubt if she even knows I'm in the room. I think I'll give her another shot just to get her through the night. In the morning I'd like an associate to have a look at her. Bob Pritchard. Good man. I think we need a psychiatric opinion.'

Liam Power, who had arrived only minutes before, growled, 'We don't want to start up with psychiatrists. Once you start with those guys, you're never rid of them. They'll drag the thing out for months. I say, let her cry it out. When she gets tired of crying, she'll stop.'

Dick listened, then turned to the doctor. 'What do you think, David. Can we put off calling somebody else in?'

'I don't feel I'm qualified to run with this alone, Dick. I think it's more serious than we first anticipated. We do have another alternative. I'm connected with a small clinic just out of town. The Stowe Clinic. They have a psychiatrist on staff, but it's not strictly *that* kind of place. I mean, even if word got out, we could deny a breakdown. We could always say it was something else – I'll think of something. We could take her there the first thing in the morning.'

'What do you think, Dad?'

'Why can't we keep her here a couple of more days and see what develops? Nobody cries forever. She'll get over it. There's no profit in getting involved with psychiatrists and sanitariums.'

The doctor shook his head. 'I'm sorry, but I can't allow her to go on this way. It would be totally irresponsible.'

'You can keep on giving her sedatives, can't you? That'll keep her quiet,' the elder Power grunted.

'I'm afraid I could not continue to administer sedatives without a consultation with somebody more qualified than I am on this sort of thing. I strongly advise you to call in a psychiatrist or take her to the clinic.'

'I don't think we want to keep her here, Dad. Everybody in the place knows something's wrong. And the longer we keep her locked in her room, the worse it's going to look when the story breaks. And it's bound to break – too many people involved.'

'All right then, get her the hell out of here,' Liam Power agreed. 'It's better than psychiatrists trooping in and out. But if you're getting her out, get her out tonight. There's less chance of a fuss. And then you can still leave for Japan tomorrow, right on schedule.'

The doctor went to the phone, relieved. 'I'll call the clinic and make the arrangements. And you don't have to worry. They have an unmarked ambulance. It looks like any dark-coloured station wagon. I'll give her another sedative and we'll get her out of here quietly.'

There was a knock on the door. Dick opened it. 'Yes, Helen, what is it? Did Angel say something?'

'No, Dick. It's just that Angel's mother called again. She knows something's wrong. She said to give you a message. She said if she doesn't hear from Angel personally in the next half hour, she's coming here tonight. She sounded a little hysterical herself.'

'What do you think, Dad? Should I call her and tell her what's happening?'

'Christ! *That* bitch! Get her on the phone and tell her anything. But not the truth. Stall her. Tell her Angel isn't feeling well and the doctor gave her a sedative. We don't need *her* here tonight!' Liam told his son.

'Convince her it's nothing but a cold.'

'I'll try. I'll try, but somehow I don't think it's going to work.'

The black station wagon came for Angel at nine that evening. At eleven, Marie arrived in her black chauffeured limousine. Dick and his father had been half waiting for her to show up. Dick went to let her in himself and ushered her into the library quickly.

Marie Whittier was regal in the long Russian broadtail coat hugging her slender body, the pale hair piled in a high knot. Liam Power thought with reluctant admiration, She's still a knockout. She looks hardly older than her daughter, and better-looking, if anyone was to ask me.

'All right, you bastards,' she said, still elegant despite the tough words, 'you tell me what's going on here. What have you done to my daughter?'

The elder Power chuckled appreciatively at her forthright approach. Dick cast an irate look at him, took a deep breath. It wasn't going to be easy. He explained the situation as delicately as he could, anticipating an explosion.

'So you've locked my Angel away, have you? In some institution where she'll be out of your way. Silent and unable to divorce you. What did you think you were going to do? Pretend she was crazy and let some quacks fill her full of dope until she really was? What do you think this is? One of your cheap movies? Did you really think I was going to stand by and let you do it? My poor baby! Who would dream that in this day and age you two filthy bastards would try to pull a stunt like this.'

Liam laughed as if Marie had made some kind of joke. 'Hold it, Marie, hold it! I can understand your being upset – it *is* mighty upsetting, believe me. I was here – I saw that poor child so . . . so unstrung that all she could do was cry. I was very upset myself, believe me. Here, Marie, sit down. Standing up all night isn't

345

going to help anything. Dick, get Marie a drink.'

'I don't want a drink. I want to see Angel! Now!' she added threateningly.

'You're talking nonsense,' Dick said. 'You can't possibly believe we would do anything so ridiculous as to pretend Angel's sick if she weren't. She's having some kind of breakdown. I'm sorry. Sorrier than you can imagine, but it's a fact. You can talk to Dr Pintzer. You'll believe him, won't you?'

'*Your* doctor?' she sneered. 'Why would I believe him any more than I believe you?'

Liam smiled broadly and shook his head in admiration. 'You're too much!'

'I wouldn't put anything past the two of you. I'll believe what I see with my own eyes. I want to see Angel now! Immediately!'

Dick struggled for control. 'You *can't* see her tonight. We can't go bursting into the clinic in the middle of the night and turn the place upside down. Can't you wait till tomorrow? You can spend the night here and see her the first thing in the morning. I give you my word. She's under sedation now anyhow. She's sleeping. You wouldn't be able to tell anything.'

'I'm going there now, with you or without you. I think you'd better call that clinic and tell them to expect me. And warn them that I expect to spend the night there in the same room with my daughter. If she's under sedation, I'm going to be at her side until she comes out of it. And to see what they're shooting into her veins. If you don't call them and tell them to admit me, I'm going straight to the police and ask them to escort me into the place. And in the morning I'm going to have a whole battery of lawyers here with a court order to have my daughter released. What do you say? Do you call the clinic or do I get the cops?'

Again Liam laughed. She was a pistol all right. You had to hand it to her, she knew how to fight. And she fought the way he did. 'You'd better call, son. I guess in their line of business, they're used to this. And while you have them on the phone, tell them to put another bed in the room for Marie. We want to make sure she's comfortable. And we'll go with you, Marie, just to see that you get everything you want at the clinic. After all, we're all family.'

After spending the night at the clinic, Marie had seen all that she needed to. Angel did not speak to her; Marie wasn't even sure she was aware of her presence. But she sat by her daughter's side while the doctors came and went. She questioned them, but all they would say was that they would have to wait and see.

The governor's limousine came to take her back to the mansion late in the day. Liam was sitting in front of the television set in the library, watching the early evening news. He rose from his chair to greet her. 'Glad you could make it back here to have dinner with me,' he said. 'I hate to eat alone. And it's nice to have a good-looking woman across the dinner table. Good for the digestion.'

'I didn't come back here to improve your digestion. Your clinic was good enough to give me whatever nourishment I required. I came back to talk to Dick, since he couldn't find the time to visit the clinic all day and see how his wife was doing. Where is he?'

Liam told Marie that Dick had left for Japan that morning, that he wouldn't be back for several days.

Marie smiled bitterly. 'Yesterday he parks his wife in a booby hatch; today, it's business as usual.'

Liam Power was tired, and he dropped his pose of geniality. 'Dick's the governor,' he said crankily, 'and he's got to do what he's got to do, go where his duty calls. The world can't stop because your daughter is spoiled so rotten that if she doesn't get her way she has a nervous breakdown.'

'Is that how you see it? As simple as that, is it? Well, since your son has no desire to cope with this problem, I'll have to do what I think best without consulting

347

him. I'm going to make arrangements to have Angel transferred to Payne Whitney in New York, where she'll get the quality of care she needs.'

'New York? Out of the question. And don't start giving me that jazz about getting a court order!' But despite his tough pose, he was worried.

'Yes. New York. They have the best doctors there for this sort of thing. You may be content with backwoods quacks, but I won't settle for anything but the best for my daughter.'

'If you ship her to New York, you know as well as I do what will happen. The reporters will come down on her like a swarm of maggots and ferret out the whole story. And what about the rags? Do you really want them to spread their usual *shit* about your daughter?' He used the vulgarity purposely, for greater impact. 'Do you think it's in her best interests to have *Secret* or *Whisper* spread her face across their front page looking like a raving maniac?'

He could tell from Marie's face that he had won. Having triumphed, he could afford to be genial once more. 'You can keep your own tabs on the situation. As *I* will, I assure you. You can come here any time you want to see how things are progressing. Dr Pintzer doesn't think it's a serious breakdown. He feels it shouldn't be long before Angel is back on her feet. But in a little while, if we don't see any improvement, why, we'll think about making a change. Maybe send her down to Los Angeles.'

Marie considered for a moment. 'All right. For now. But I'll be here constantly, I warn you. In the meantime, I'll take the children with me. With Angel not here and Dick away so much and so busy, I want to make sure they receive proper supervision.'

He thought that over for a minute and finally decided it would be a bad idea to lose control of the children. He shook his head. 'Dickie has his kindergarten class here and you know it's a bad idea in these situations to upset children's schedules. Bad enough their mother's not here.'

Marie considered. There *was* sense in what he said.

He continued, 'There's plenty of supervision here. Their nurse. Mrs Peters. And Helen O'Neil is a very capable woman. Everything will be fine, Marie. It will all turn out all right. I'll see to it, and that's a promise. Now, how about having a little dinner with me? I'd appreciate it.'

'I have decided to leave Angel at the clinic for the time being, and to leave the children here too, but don't misjudge me. I'm not taken in by you, you bastard! You've driven one of my daughters away and somehow you've driven my other daughter over the edge. I will never forget it and I *will* have my day in court. And that's my promise to you.'

Liam Power believed her.

PART NINE

Palm Springs, Sacramento, Brentwood
1958

'Hollywood was devastated by Angel's breakdown. Although she had never appeared in any movies, she was still thought of as one of our own. She had been an actress before she married Dick Power, and then had been the congressman's wife from *our* district, and then, of course, our own governor's first lady. Yes, Hollywood thought of Angel as one of its own daughters. Besides, she was always the sweetest, darlingest person you can imagine. Gracious and regal. Everybody said so, especially Nick Dominguez, who was probably the most prominent photographer in town. He had taken her picture many a time.

'Everybody speculated about the cause of her breakdown. I suppose I did my share, but *never* in print. Of course, I had my personal opinions about that. Everybody knew there was trouble in her marriage, but only Hedda printed anything along those lines.

'As for Kiki, her Italian career was going swimmingly until her husband got involved with that foreigner, Zev Mizrachi. Mizrachi put Kiki into a huge Italian version of *War and Peace*. Well, all I can say about that is, Russian literature is not an Italian cup of tea, if you get my meaning. Mizrachi's *War and Peace* became a synonym for a bomb in Hollywood. It was an international joke.

'But all Hollywood rejoiced when Angel was well enough to leave that sanitarium . . .'

1

'Kiki, will you please be yourself? Will you please treat me as you always have?'

'But, darling, what am I doing now that I haven't always done?'

'You're being extra careful, as if I were made of glass. You're not teasing me, or yelling at me, or telling me things for my own good like you've done since we were children. I'm just the same as I've always been, or almost.'

'I know you are. In fact, you look extra-specially good. Your skin is marvelous, your eyes are clear and sparkling, and your figure is yummy, if a bit on the thin side.'

'Well, all that bed rest is supposed to be good for you. Goodness knows, I've had my share of sleep. And I've been here in Palm Springs for three weeks already, soaking up this sun. Mother hasn't let me move from this chaise. Even last week, when the children were here.'

'Why didn't the children stay longer? I mean, only one week when it's been almost a year . . .'

'Dickie does have his school. And in a couple of weeks I'll be going . . . home, if you want to call it that.'

'Does it scare you terribly, baby? Going back?'

'Yes, it does . . . a little. A lot. But Dr Preston says I mustn't anticipate. I shouldn't think about next week or next month. I have to go it one day at a time.'

'And what does Dr Preston prescribe for your marriage? What does he suggest you do about Dick?'

'Kiki, Dr Preston is not a marriage counselor, but he told me he did suggest to Dick that in the interest of my mental health we be divorced but he was not able to persuade Dick to let me go.'

Kiki sat on the edge of her chair. 'How did Dick have the nerve—?'

'Dr Preston said that Dick implied that after he ran in 1960 for the presidential office, he would let me go if he lost. I myself didn't really believe that. I think he'd still want me because he'd still be the governor, but that's what he implied. And he also implied that if he won the presidency he would let me go after the four or eight years of office.'

'And suppose you don't agree?'

'Dr Preston inferred from Dick that they would take my children away from me because of my mental instability . . .'

'That bastard! That son of a bitch! That fucking, rotten no-good— What did Dr Preston say to that? Wasn't he shocked?'

'No. It seems psychiatrists are never shocked. They're used to people with all the emotions . . . even when those emotions are horrid. So Dr Preston said that if I can't undo the marriage *at this time*, then I have to accept it, live with it, for the time being. He did strike a sort of bargain with Dick in my behalf. The marriage is to be in name only. I don't mean just not sleeping with Dick. All I have to do is live in the same house with him and make a few public appearances with him. No personal conversation. Nothing like that. And I can lead my own life as long as I don't do anything that is publicly embarrassing. Dr Preston's a wonderful man, warm . . . compassionate.'

'This Dr Preston sounds too good to be true. Tell me, did you fall a teeny little bit in love with him? It's normal, I understand, to get the hots for your shrink.'

'Kiki!'

'All right, I won't mention it again. I won't say another word.' She clapped her hand across her mouth, but in a second dropped it. 'Can I ask you just one little thing? Is he dark-eyed, dark-haired, olive-skinned, and mustached?'

355

Angel rose from the chaise. 'I think I'll have a swim. Will you join me, sister darling?'

'You know I hate to get wet . . . on the outside, that is.'

Angel shook her head in mock desperation, drew on a bathing cap, and dove into the pool, swam a few laps, and climbed out. She belted a terrycloth robe around herself and lay back on the chaise again.

'Seriously, Angel, I have to ask you one more question.'

'Yes?'

'I just want to know if you discussed Father with him.'

'Of course I discussed Daddy. But I'm not supposed to discuss it with you,' she said pointedly.

'And Nick Dominguez? Did you talk about him?'

Angel stared at her sister coldly. 'Why should I talk about him?'

'Then you didn't?'

Angel stared straight ahead, not answering. They sat in silence awhile. Then Kiki said, 'If you'd like me to stay awhile and go back to Sacramento with you, I will.'

Angel jumped up and hugged her. 'Would you? Could you? It would make all the difference. I was dying for you to do just that but I thought maybe it would be too much to ask.'

Kiki smiled provocatively. 'Perhaps you want to ask Dr Preston first. I mean, if it's all right.'

'No. I'm not going to ask him. He might say I was using you as a crutch and that I have to learn to get along without crutches. So I just won't ask him! But I don't know that I can let you make such a big sacrifice. I know how painful it is for you to be here in California and not see Rory. Kiki, why don't you?'

'No. It's just not worth it. Seeing her would just make me feel worse. It would kill me to see her and know I can't have her.'

' And Brad? Do you ever hear from him?'

'Yes. He drops me a note every now and then and

tells me what Rory's doing. He sends me pictures.'

'And what about Vic and Nikki? Won't Vic be upset if you stay in Sacramento?'

'Oh, Vic's too enmeshed in his career problems to know I'm gone. He's back in Israel again making matzo-ball westerns, would you believe? After our *War and Peace* fiasco, Vic's like a whipped dog.'

Angel said nothing. Her mother had told her that the big picture had failed miserably.

'I sometimes wonder,' Kiki said, 'if Mizrachi wanted the picture to bomb.'

'But that's ridiculous. Why would he? It was his reputation at stake, after all, and it must have cost millions.'

'Twenty-eight, to be exact. But the man is so devious. Who knows what's in his mind? Maybe he *needed* a tax loss. All I know is, from the very first moment we got involved with the man, everything's turned to shit. Everything! My career, my marriage. I even allowed him to manipulate me into— Oh, forget it. What's the use of talking?'

What had Kiki started to say? Angel wondered. That she had even allowed him to manipulate her into using her own sister for some kind of gain. But why? What for? Ah, but it was all water under the bridge . . .

Kiki gave a short, bitter laugh. 'He was absolutely furious about your illness.'

'What do you mean, he was *furious*? That's a curious reaction. And what concern is it of his?'

'He *thinks* it's his concern. He thinks he's your very good friend. He's furious with Dick. He thinks Dick drove you to a breakdown. He thinks Dick's a monster who mistreats you.'

'Really,' Angel said drily. 'I wonder where he could possibly have gotten that idea. Kiki, how could you discuss my marriage with that man?'

Kiki flushed. 'I'm sorry, Angel. He has a way of worming things out of one. Really, I never meant to . . . And then he was intent on going to visit you at the clinic. I talked him out of that, but just barely. He insisted he was going to remove you from the clinic and take you to *his* doctors in Switzerland. He was barely dissuaded from that idea, too.'

Angel couldn't help laughing. 'I can't believe this conversation. Where did he think he was going to get authority for such a move? Why, he's practically a stranger . . .'

'Well, if you saw Mother and Zev with their heads together, you wouldn't think he was just a stranger.'

Angel paled. 'Mother and Zev Mizrachi? How did that happen?'

'Well, you know, I was shuttling back and forth between the clinic and Europe while you were ill. And Zev insisted I use his private plane. Well, that's the way it is with him. You accept a favor, and before you know it, he's taking over your life. Before I knew it, he insisted on coming with me. And he met Mother. Mother was actually the one who talked him out of pushing his way into the clinic. She told him it would be indiscreet. Zev was very impressed with Marie. Marie charmed Zev and Zev charmed Marie. Stanley and Livingstone – instant rapport. Marie even invited him to stay with her in Brentwood.'

'What are you saying, Kiki? That Mother and Mizrachi . . . ?'

Kiki laughed delightedly. 'That would really have been a gas! But no, nothing like that. At least I don't *think* so.' She paused, thoughtful. 'I think Marie sees in Zev a match for Liam Power.'

'I'd really like to know what's going on,' Angel said agitatedly. 'Mother hasn't said a word about any of this.'

'Now, don't get upset. If Marie is playing some kind of power game with Zev, who are we to interfere? I'll put my money on Marie. I do know that she told him he couldn't come here to Palm Springs to see you.'

'Oh my God! Did he want to?'

'Yes, he tried. But Marie said it wasn't a good idea. They've become such good friends that Zev listens to her. Maybe she could persuade Zev to let Vic out of his clutches. Marie could do it, if anyone could. Oh, but she probably wouldn't bother with my problems right now. I mean, she does have you to worry about right now. I don't think she could think of anyone else but you right now.'

'Oh, Kiki, are you starting again'

But she wasn't really thinking about what Kiki had said.

I won't think about Mizrachi and Marie becoming friends. Dr Preston says I must think only positive thoughts. Only good things. I'll think about how good it is to lie in the sun. How good it is to have Kiki here. That she's going home with me. How good it will be to be with Dickie and Timmy again! What fun it will be to shop for new clothes with Kiki. How good it is that no one will dare yell at me for spending too much money. How good it is knowing Mother is really on my side. I will not think about Daddy. I will not think about Dick. I will not think about – No, I won't even say his name to myself. I will not think about Zev Mizrachi. I will think ahead only one day at a time.

2

Dick came out of the house to welcome her home. It seemed to Angel that he had aged. He was getting a bit heavy in the jowls, and there were lines around his eyes she hadn't noticed before.

This was a public welcome, to be sure. All the household staff was lined up by the door to greet her as well. Dick kissed her on the lips. He must have planned that. To the staff, a kiss on the ckeek for a wife who had been gone for so many months might have seemed a bit restrained. He even pecked Kiki perfunctorily. The staff all told her how good it was to have her back, and Helen O'Neil told her she looked marvelous. She went upstairs quickly to where the boys were waiting. She had seen them only two weeks before, in Palm Springs; still, it seemed like a long time.

The housekeeper had prepared a room for Kiki at the far end of the hall. It seemed like a mile away from her own room, and the nights were still frightening, even now that she was supposed to be getting well. No, *getting well* was the wrong term. *Improving* was the correct word.

Dr Preston said that she wasn't to brood about things; she was to verbalize her wishes, to speak up for herself. So later, when they were in the library having before-dinner cocktails, just Kiki and Dick and herself, Angel brought up the sleeping arrangements. Pat Haggerty and his wife, Celia, were due to join them for dinner – obviously Dick had invited his longtime friend and associate to help ease the tension of their first evening – and Angel wanted to broach the subject before they arrived.

'I'd like Kiki to share my room with me during the time she'll be here. I thought I would tell you about it before I spoke to Mrs Peters, so there wouldn't be any misunderstandings.' She didn't know exactly how to say it – it was difficult for her to talk to him at all. More difficult than ever before. She had avoided speaking directly to him since she had come home. Even now as she spoke, her body trembled. She had thought she would be able to control the loathing she felt for him. Dr Preston had told her to try for a feeling of indifference. He said there were any number of couples who maintained marriages by remaining indifferent to each other.

Dick flushed, the red spreading quickly to his ears. 'I don't want to upset you, Angel. I'm trying to make this as easy for you as I can. But it would be embarrassing, to say the least, to have Kiki bunking down in your room. How would it look to the staff for you to come home after such a long time and have your sister sleeping with you? And that brings up something else I want to talk to you about . . .' He looked at Kiki as if

360

wondering whether to speak in front of her.

'I'm staying right here,' Kiki volunteered, 'so spit it out.'

Angel felt herself on the verge of tears. He was violating the unspoken terms of the their agreement, that there be no intimate talk of any kind.

Dick flushed again. 'It's not *that* kind of talk, and I wasn't about to ask you to leave, Kiki,' he said huffily. 'I just wanted to tell you, Angel, to explain really, that there's a conference of governors in New York. I'm scheduled to speak—' He broke off. 'I'm supposed to leave tomorrow. Under the circumstances, I wouldn't go, except that I *am* giving the principal address. You understand. And maybe it's just as well. It will give you a chance to get acclimated again while I'm gone. And there's no reason after I leave tomorrow that Kiki couldn't move into my room. *That* would look all right.'

Relief flooded through Angel, such relief that it left her giddy. He would be gone for a few days – a reprieve. She knew she wasn't supposed to feel this rancor – hatred was a self-defeating emotion, Dr Preston said – but she couldn't help it. She couldn't control it. But now Dick would be gone for a few days. It was more than she had hoped for.

'How long will you be away?' she asked quietly, still not looking directly at him as he paced nervously back and forth.

'Probably about five days. I could still make arrangements for you to accompany me if you felt up to it,' He said politely, looking at Kiki. 'Kiki could come too.'

'Oh no I can't,' Kiki said. 'I'm staying put, and so is Angel.'

Angel looked at Kiki with gratitude before saying, 'Oh no, thank you. I can't leave the boys – I've barely seen them.'

'I think I hear Pat and Celia now,' Dick said, happy for the chance to rush out of the room.

Later that night, after everyone had retired, Kiki

sneaked into Angel's bedroom. They giggled in the dark. 'Makes me feel like I'm a schoolgirl again, having a party in someone's room after lights out. Where's the wine? Do you think we could sneak a light just to pour? And guess what I brought?'

'Chocolates?' Angel guessed.

'Meanie! How did you guess?'

With Kiki beside her, Angel got through the night. She only wakened once from a dream. It wasn't such a bad dream. She and Nick Dominguez, both dressed in black leotards, were doing some kind of dance. Ballet. A modern ballet.

After Dick left for New York, Angel was already nervously contemplating his return, Kiki's eventual departure, the beginning of the electioneering once more. How would she be able to face it? Dr Preston's theory was one thing, reality another.

'Suppose I can't hack it, Kiki? Suppose the whole situation gets too much for me again? I'm terrified I'll have another breakdown.'

'You yourself told me that Dr Preston told you to take it one day at a time. Right? Well, that's what you're going to do. And who knows what will happen? Sometimes fate does, kind of, take a hand. Maybe Dick's old girlfriend will get pregnant and make such a public scandal he'll have to divorce you to marry her. Maybe I'll be the little birdie to whisper the suggestion in her ear.'

'Oh, Kiki! I'm serious.'

'We'll try to work something out. One day at a time, okay? Now let's get your mind off that motherfucking son of a bitch. How about flying down to Los Angeles to do some shopping?'

'No, Kiki. I want to stay with the boys.'

'Okay. How about we go to San Francisco just for the day.'

'No, Kiki. I'm really not in the mood.'

'Okay. How about we jump off the roof in our

panties and scandalize the neighbors?'

'Oh, Kiki, you are dear . . . very, very dear. Really. I'll try to cheer up. Really I will.'

When Marie arrived for the weekend, Kiki took her aside.

'We have to do something about Angel, Marie. She's trying, but it's an uphill struggle. They let her loose out of that place but she's really not all that well. And if we don't do something, I'm afraid she really will break down again. Dick Power is a monster, an absolute monster, to hold on to her with the threat of taking the children away, of having her declared mentally incompetent. My God! I tell you, I'm just sick of sitting around and doing nothing to help her.'

'We're going to do something. Be assured of that!'

'Marie! You do have an idea then? You do have a plan?'

'I did promise Angel I would help her, and I'm going to keep my promise. But you have to do one thing for me, my dear Kiki.'

'Yes, Marie? What is it?'

'Stop calling me Marie. I'm your mother.'

Maybe I would call you that if you'd remember that you are my mother and not just Eddie and Angel's . . . precious Angel's.

Oh shit! The trouble was, Angel *was* precious.

3

Angel waited impatiently for Kiki's arrival. She had wanted to go along with Marie and Henry, the chauffeur, to the airport, but her mother had insisted she wait at the house in Brentwood and take a nap instead. Angel had arrived only that morning from Sacramento and her mother still insisted on treating her like an invalid, insisted she must have her rest.

It had been three months since she had seen Kiki.

When Kiki had received that offer to do a picture in Czechoslovakia while she was staying with her in Sacramento, she had leaped at the chance and left in a hurry. 'Oh, it's a shitty little picture,' Kiki had said, 'and probably will never make it out of Czechsville, but what can I do? I'm washed up everywhere else after the big bomb. It was all war and no peace.'

'Why can't you just wait until Vic is ready to make a picture with you?' Angel said.

'Oh, I think I'd have to wait until my hair turned gray. Zev won't *let* Vic make a picture with me. Marie says she's working on Zev. It seems they keep in touch. But who knows what will come of that unholy alliance?'

Kiki came bursting through the door with Marie behind her, and Henry following them both, juggling five pieces of matched luggage. Kiki had a new hairdo – a wild mass of curls and waves.

'I adore your hair!' Angel said, touching it. The hand trembled, Kiki noted.

'Isn't it just too, too wild? It's called the Italian cut. Liz Taylor is wearing it too.'

Marie excused herself, and Angel said, 'Let's go upstairs. Mother's put us in a bedroom together. We'll pretend we're teenagers. Wouldn't it be wonderful to be sixteen and seventeen again?'

Angel threw herself down on the bed. 'This *is* a cheerful room, isn't it?' The sun streamed in on the yellow-and-white room, confirming her words, but Kiki found her sister's voice colorless, listless.

'Me for the spa in the dressing room. Join me?'

'Right now?' Angel asked wearily.

'No time like the right time,' Kiki answered, discarding her clothes, running into the dressing room, turning on the faucets in the big, yellow-tiled Jacuzzi, watching the jets spit out the foamy water.

'Come on in. Last one in is a rotten egg,' she declared, already in the water, submerged to the chin

Angel stepped in gingerly. 'You never play fair.'

'All's fair in love and war and between sisters.' She studied Angel's body, thinking how thin she was. Another few pounds and she could actually be called wasted. 'So how goes it, little sister?'

Angel smiled wistfully at the use of the old name. 'It's kind of lonely with Dickie away at school. Just Timmy and me ... And Timmy is in nursery school for half the day. Of course, there's Helen O'Neil, my constant companion.' Angel rolled her eyes. 'But she's lost a lot of her starch. Dick's running for reelection this year, you know, and she was hoping to get in on that, I think. Not that I blame her. It's a lot more exciting and fun for a single lady to be traveling around the state with lots of men around than to be stuck in Sacramento in a drafty old Victorian relic, playing watchdog to a crazy lady. But she'll have her chance in '60. Dick's going to try for the presidential nomination, and everyone seems to think that the Democrats have a very good chance with Eisenhower out of the picture.'

Kiki was thoughtful. 'You mean there's a chance that *you* might really be the First Lady?'

'Oh, please dear God, I pray not! There's the possibility, but there's the primary and then the election. Even Dick's people say that Jack Kennedy is the party's fair-haired boy for '60. But who knows? By that time, there'll be dozens of others who'll be running ... Anyhow, I'm out of it. Our agreement is that I don't have to campaign. Not ever. Not then and not now. As a matter of fact, Dick's in town this weekend for campaign appearances. He's at the Bev Wilshire.'

'And what does Dr Preston say to this?'

'He agrees that I should have nothing to do with the campaign. Even if I had the strength. He thinks I should develop a life of my own. That I should think about going back to acting.' Angel laughed mirthlessly. 'He doesn't see what a ridiculous proposition that is.

How could the governor's wife, or, more ridiculous yet, the President's wife, be an actress? Not to mention that I'm not strong enough, physically or mentally, to be *anything*. The doctor's not in the real world. He doesn't understand how much stamina it requires to be an actress. He's a serious man, you see. To him medicine is serious and psychiatry is serious. Everything else is only a game. Acting to him is only being a star, the enactment of fairy-like dreams.'

'Some dreams! What does the big man, Mr Dick, have to say to Dr Preston's idea?'

'Oh, I never discussed it with him. We don't discuss. The only time we ever speak to each other is publicly. Just every once in a while he throws me a look – sort of a warning look, as if to say, better behave yourself, lady, or it's back to the asylum for you.'

Kiki's face mirrored her contempt. 'Who would believe that *even* Dick could be that crude?'

'Never mind about me – tell me what's happening with you. How are things between you and Vic?'

'Oh, great. Just great.'

'That didn't exactly register very high on the enthusiasm scale.'

'Well, we do spend a lot of time apart and nothing is exactly the same when we do get together again. You know – things change. People change. I really *owe* that Jewish Hitler,' she said, her eyes glinting with viciousness.

Angel's own eyes filled. *We're star-crossed, Kiki and I. Why did it all go wrong?*

'How's my niece? I wish I could see her.'

'Unfortunately, physically she hasn't changed a bit. She still looks like a little chimp. Bigger, of course, and climbing around like a monkey. Smart as a whip, though.'

'I wish you had brought her along.'

'Oh, Vic won't let me take her anywhere. He doesn't even let me take her with me when I'm in my apartment in Rome.'

'Your apartment in Rome? I didn't know you had an apartment.'

'Oh, it's just a little *pied-à-terre*. I slip away for a couple of days now and then. Why don't you bring the boys to San Remo this summer? We'll be there with the little monkey and we'll do everything with the kids.'

Angel gestured excitedly. 'I know what! Why don't you ask Brad to let Rory go to San Remo too? And I'll bring her over when I come!'

Kiki appeared betrayed. 'You promised not to mention Rory. I don't want to talk about her, you hear?'

'But you haven't seen her since that time in Texas. It's ridiculous. She's six already. You can't just—'

'I know what I can and can't do. I can't see her and that's that. Conversation finished!'

Marie knocked, then came in. 'Are you two going to sit there submerged all afternoon and leave me to my own devices?'

'Why don't you strip, Marie, old girl, and join us?'

'Thank you but no thank you, Kiki.' She appeared distracted. 'I was just wondering . . . I think I'd like to go shopping. Why don't you two get dressed right away and we'll go?'

'I just got off the plane, for God's sake, Marie, and Angel here looks like she's collapsing. Can't we go shopping tomorrow?'

'There are a few things I must get.'

'Well, why don't you toddle along without us and we'll see you later?'

'No, I want both of you to go with me. I insist—'

Kiki and Angel exchanged looks. Their mother had never before insisted on their company for a shopping expedition. But before the sisters could answer, they heard an insistent knocking on the bedroom door.

'My goodness,' Kiki declared. 'More traffic. Why don't you invite whoever's at the door to join us in here? I think we have room for a few more.'

Marie opened the door to the housekeeper, Gladys. She saw that Gladys was crying, and she stiffened. 'Yes, Gladys? What is it?'

'You'd better be coming out here, into the hall, Mrs Whittier . . .'

'Yes?' She stepped into the hall and closed the door carefully behind her. 'Yes, Gladys?' Her voice was carefully modulated.

'It's about Mr Power, Mrs Whittier . . . the governor,' the woman sobbed.

Marie put her hand on the housekeeper's shoulder. 'Softly, Gladys. What about Governor Power?'

'I was taking my afternoon rest in my room—' She seemed unable to continue.

'Go on, Gladys.'

'It came over on the TV . . . a special report . . . I was all set to watch my show . . . I always watch—'

'What about the governor?'

'He's dead, Mrs Whittier! The poor man's dead!'

Marie's expression didn't change. Putting a finger to her lips and gesturing to the door, she said, 'Quietly, Gladys. What happened?'

'I'm not sure, Mrs Whittier. They said he fell off a balcony. I didn't hear all of it. I wanted to come up here and tell you. All I heard was that he was in his room at the Beverly Wilshire Hotel in Beverly Hills waiting to go downstairs for a press conference and he fell twelve floors to his death!' She took out a large handkerchief from her dress pocket and blew her nose hard. 'I thought you'd want to tell Mrs Power yourself. That's why I rushed up here. That poor little thing, and herself not well.'

Marie put her arms around the housekeeper. 'Yes. We must all be brave for Angel's sake.'

'And for those poor little tots. Their father dead and him so young and handsome—' She sobbed uncontrollably.

'Yes . . . yes. I must go to her now, Gladys. Please

try to control yourself.' Marie took out her own handkerchief, a small linen square and dabbed at her eyes. 'Oh . . . did they say if anyone was with Mr Power, Gladys?'

'I don't know, Mrs Whittier. I told you all I heard.'

'I suppose we'll get the details soon enough,' she said sadly. 'I must go now and break the news to Angel. And would you please bring that little TV from my dressing room?'

'Yes. And tell Mrs Power . . . tell her that I'm so sorry.'

'Of course, Gladys. Of course.' She patted the woman's shoulder. 'Would you bring some tea too, Gladys, and the decanter of brandy, if you will?'

She straightened her linen skirt, and was about to open the bedroom door again when the sound of the telephone filled the hall. 'And we won't take any calls for a while, Gladys. Unless it's about the children, of course.'

She went back into the bedroom and then into the dressing area and broke the news of the tragedy to her daughters.

4

The Power family, along with the governor's staff, took over the first floor of the governor's mansion, receiving callers, while Angel, with Kiki beside her, received in the second-floor sitting room. Marie was everywhere, seeing to the children and the domestic arrangements, a veritable watchdog.

'Will I be glad when this thing is over and done with and we can get the hell out of Sacramento,' Kiki said, between callers. 'I still don't understand why if the funeral is going to be in Los Angeles, everybody is sitting around here.'

'You know everything has to be done properly,'

Angel reproved her. 'Dick is . . . was,' she corrected herself, 'the governor. It's only proper that his body lie in state at the Capitol building, and of course we all have to receive here officially. And I do so want everything to be right . . .' She started to cry. 'For the sake of the boys, Kiki. He *was* their father, and I want them to be proud . . .'

'Sure, sure,' Kiki said quickly. God, Angel was a bundle of nerves, the way she broke into tears every few minutes. One would think that the goddamn accident wasn't the best thing that had ever happened to her.

'I must say, those Power women are one set of bowwows! I declare, they look like a bunch of crows,' she smirked, trying to get Angel to laugh.

But instead of laughing, Angel looked at her in the most peculiar way. 'Why, that's what you said the last time, Kiki.'

'What do you mean, the last time? I don't remember ever saying that before. When did I say it?'

'I don't know . . .' Angel wrinkled her brow. 'Oh, yes I do! I remember! It was a dream!' she said, relieved to have remembered. 'You used almost the exact same words.'

Kiki sighed a breath of relief. 'Well, forget your dreams of old. You're going to have only good dreams from now on. Star dreams . . .'

'It will soon be over. Tomorrow they'll celebrate the High Mass. And then the next day will be the burial. You do think I was right about deciding on his family's mausoleum in Los Angeles?'

'Absolutely. Just where he belongs.' Then, once again trying to get Angel's mind off things in general, she said, 'I think Sean looks terrible. He used to be so handsome. Personally, I always thought he was the better-looking brother.'

'But Dick *was* very good-looking,' Angel defended her deceased husband.

'I guess,' Kiki granted. 'He did have a winning smile

– if you didn't know how phony it was.'

'I used to love that smile. It really used to make me melt . . . in the beginning. Dick was getting paunchy of late. Did you notice that when you saw him last?'

'Yes. But it was predictable. He *always* had the hint of a prospective pot in his belly.'

Angel looked at her suspiciously. 'When did you see his bare belly?'

Kiki considered. 'I must have seen him in his bathing trunks.'

'Kiki, is there anything you haven't told me? Is there something you'd like me to know now?' Angel tensed.

Kiki looked sheepish. 'It was a long, long time ago – long before you ever started going with him.' She giggled. 'God, I was only about sixteen . . .'

Angel was angry, even though she knew how foolish it was now. Peeved. Irritated. 'How could you not have told me, Kiki? I think that was despicable of you.'

'Which was despicable? Doing it with Dick? Or just not having told you? If I *had* told you, you would only have been upset. To no purpose. As for going to bed with Dick when I was sixteen, how did I know you were ever going to be so dumb as to marry him?'

'Well, thanks a lot,'

'I did try to warn you what he was like, didn't I?' Kiki demanded, but she saw that Angel's mood was changing even as they spoke.'

'This is a terrible conversation to be having now. Please, Kiki, let's just drop it. I want to think only the best thoughts about Dick now.'

'Why? How can you? After what he did to you? I mean, why be hypocritical? Death doesn't change anything.'

But Angel wasn't listening. Kiki saw that her sister's eyes were closed now, her hands clasped, her lips moving in a silent prayer. Angel's unpredictable moods were beginning to be a worry. Was she starting to crack?

The visitors came and went.

'What do you think of Greg Lane?' Angel asked Kiki after the Power family attorney arrived and paid his respects.

'Nice-looking but pompous.' Kiki made a face in imitation. 'He looks like he takes himself so seriously, he never screws at all.'

Angel chuckled. 'He has two children.'

'So what? Two screws – two children. That's all it takes.'

Angel chuckled again. 'He's the executor of Dick's will, you know.'

'Oh dear. Then you can bank on a lot of trouble. He's not about to make things easy on you, I can tell you.'

'I won't think about that now.' Then, distractedly, she demanded, 'Did you ever go to bed with Sean? You did deal with him at the studio, didn't you?'

'Really, Angel, do you think I went to bed with *every* man I ever met? And besides, I wouldn't have gone to bed with Dick's brother, not after you decided to marry Dick. It would have been . . . *incestuous*, for God's sake!'

Angel giggled a bit at her sister's reasoning, saw her mother frowning at them from across the room. 'Ssh!' she reproved Kiki. 'Mother's making faces. People will think I'm terrible . . . that I'm not really mourning.'

Am I? Of course I am. For the children's sake.

But exhilaration flooded her whole being. *Free . . . free . . . free!* She was ashamed of her feelings, but still, there they were.

'Uh-oh! Here comes Greg Lane again, speaking of the devil. I think I'll cut out for a while.'

'No, Kiki, don't go. Don't leave me alone with him.'

'I'll just sneak a quick peek at what's going on downstairs.'

'Do you think I have to talk to him? I suppose so,' she answered herself. 'I must be gracious. I am being gracious, aren't I, Kiki?'

'You bet. You've been terrific.'

Greg Lane nodded to Kiki. 'Would you excuse us? I'd like to speak to Angel alone.'

'I hope you're not going to talk to her about money now. This is a hell of a time to talk about money.'

He was offended. 'I had no intention of discussing finances at this time.'

'Well, see that you don't. Angel's on the verge of collapse. I'll be right back, Angel darling, just in case you need me.' She cast a burlesque of a dark glance at the lawyer, and Angel wanted to laugh but didn't dare.

'How is Mother Power bearing up, Greg?'

'She's going to be all right, but they're considering not letting her attend the funeral.'

'That's too bad.' She started to cry.

The attorney appeared pained. 'You've been so brave. Hold on a little longer, won't you?'

'Is there any more information on Dick's . . . death?'

'Well, it's not conclusive, but we think the coroner's office is going to call it an accident – that Dick opened the window wide in his room because it was hot and stuffy and then got dizzy and fell . . . or somehow tripped and fell. But the thing is, he was only alone in that suite for about *five* minutes. Liam won't accept that contention – he says that it's too much of a coincidence that it happened at that particular time, the *only* time he was alone. Liam's pressing for a further investigation. He claims' – Greg lowered his voice to a whisper – 'that it was a political assassination.'

'Oh my God!' Angel's hand flew to her face. 'But why? Who? It doesn't make sense!'

'It makes as much sense as those who are claiming he jumped deliberately.'

'You mean committed suicide?'

Greg nodded. Angel slumped suddenly, and Greg caught her. Marie came running over. 'What's going on here?' she asked accusingly. 'What did you say to her?'

Marie wanted Angel to go straight to bed, but Angel refused. Greg Lane, anxious to get away now, quickly explained what it was he wanted before he got into the discussion about the cause of Dick's death. Would Angel change her mind and permit the children to attend the funeral? Liam and the rest of the family thought it was the right thing, considering their father's eminence.

Marie said that it was out of the question. Children that young did not belong at a funeral. They would, however, attend the Mass. Angel wanted them to do that.

Suicide? Angel wondered. It was inconceivable. *No, it has to have been an accident. Nothing else makes sense.*

Sean Power came up to speak to Angel. 'Will you excuse us, Kiki?'

'Why?' she asked belligerently. She certainly didn't owe this son of a bitch the right time. He was part of PIF, wasn't he? 'How personal is this conversation going to get, anyway? I think I'd better stick around. I think Angel may need my protection.'

Angel flashed Kiki a look that implied she was going too far. To Sean she said, 'It's all right. You can say whatever you have to say in front of Kiki.'

'We . . . that is, Dad . . . understands that you and the children intend to go to your mother's house in Brentwood after the burial. I . . . we . . . are a little upset to hear that. We thought we should all be together at the Bel Air house after the services. There are going to be a lot more people wanting to pay their respects after the funeral – those who weren't able to come before – and we . . . Dad . . . thinks that it's important for us all to receive together.'

'I'm sorry, Sean, but I'll be more comfortable at Mother's.'

'We were hoping you'd consider the second house on the estate as your home. You and Dick and the kids always stayed there. Dad and Mother want you there, with the children. It's been your home . . .'

Oh, they do have incredible nerve!

'No, Sean, it was never my home. We stayed there frequently but it was never my home. And now, well, it's over, isn't it?'

'But they want you there, Angel – they'll look after you.'

Angel shook her head. How could they not know how eager she was to get away from them? Didn't Liam know how much she hated him? Did he believe that she could have forgotten, or forgiven, the conversation she had with him the night before she got sick? Did he believe she didn't blame him, partially at least, for setting her breakdown in motion? The arrogance of him!

Still Sean persisted. 'Stay at the house for a couple of weeks then. It's awkward to have a mourning period in two different places, Brentwood and Bel Air. Look, Angel, you have a responsibility to us.'

But Angel was resolute. It was an oddly tranquil resolution. She smiled, shook her head in a negative rhythm. Finally Sean stormed off, and Kiki said with relish, 'Oh, good! You really stuck it to him. I want Liam Power squealing like a stuck pig!'

'Kiki, would you please see if Angel is ready? I'll check and see if Nurse and the children are set,' Marie said, ticking things off in her head and at the same time mentally checking Kiki's appearance. 'Wipe off some of that lipstick, please. We wish to appear well groomed but hardly flamboyant.'

'For Christ's sake, Marie! This business of the train down to LA is absolutely ridiculous! Us and a coffin on a train caravan at six in the morning and us sitting there in our weeds like characters in a bad movie! By the time we get to LA we're going to look like warmed-over oatmeal.'

'Stop whining, dear. Black becomes you. There's nothing like black to set off a blonde.'

375

'I'll take white, thank you.'

'You'll have all summer to wear white. You will come East and spend some time with Angel and me at Southampton this summer, won't you?'

'Maybe for a couple of weeks. I was counting on Angel and the kids coming to 'Remo. It'd be nice if you came too.'

'Well, we have time to think about that. In the meantime, please check on Angel. The cars are waiting to take us to the train. They're expecting us to board in about a half hour.'

'I still don't see why Angel can't make it easier on herself and all of us by taking a plane. Or at least using limousines, like ordinary people. The railroad – really! This staging seems more like Liam Power's creation than Angel's.'

'No. The train caravan was Angel's own idea. You know that. She thought it would be picturesque and fitting. Personally, I feel it's a rather corny – as you girls used to put it – gesture, but Angel has always been a romantic. So would you please go and see if she's all set? *Now!*'

Kiki sighed heavily, dramatically. 'I'm going, Marie, I'm going. And you don't have to push!'

She entered Angel's room but found it empty. She went into the bathroom, but Angel wasn't there either. Then she heard a cry from Dick's room, next door. Kiki hurried in and found her sister sitting on the floor by the row of bookcases, an open book in her lap. She was rocking back and forth and sobbing softly, rhythmically.

Oh, God! What now?

'What are you doing on that floor, Angélique Devlin? Get up! It's time to go.' Calculatingly, she spoke sharply.

Angel looked up. 'But Kiki, King Richard is dead!'

She's going to pieces again, Kiki thought. She feels guilty to be relieved now that Dick's gone. But of all the lousy times to crack up! How am I going to handle this? *Please, for God's sake, don't go to pieces on us now, Angel!*

'Richard is dead, Angel, but he *never* was a king.'

'Oh yes, he was. I used to call him that. King Richard! When we were engaged we used to quote Shakespeare to each other and I always called him my King Richard.'

'Oh, shit, Angel, that was a long time ago. He hasn't been a king for a long time. Just another lousy two-timer.'

'But look at this poem, Kiki. It's from *King Richard the Second.*' She held the book up to Kiki, and when Kiki didn't take it, she started to read.

'"For God's sake, let us sit upon the ground,
And tell sad stories of the death of kings."'

Kiki interrupted. 'Get up, Angel! I don't want to hear that crud.' But Angel went on:

'"How some have been deposed; some slain in war;
Some haunted by the ghosts they deposed;
Some poisoned by their wives . . ."'

'Did you hear that? "Some poisoned by their wives"?' she howled.

Kiki got down on the floor with her. 'Shut up, do you hear? Shut up! Don't you dare go to pieces on us!' She shook Angel by the shoulders, hard. 'Get hold of yourself or you're going straight back to the funny farm. Do you hear me?'

Angel's howl subsided into thin, low cries, but she persisted, 'There's more to the poem. I want to read it to you.'

'If I let you read it, will you promise to pull yourself together? I'm warning you. Old man Power is dying to get his slimy hands on your kids. Give them half a chance and they'll salt you away and grab them. Do – you – hear – me?'

377

'Let me just finish. Please, Kiki!'

'All right, but then I want you to go into the bathroom, wash your face, put on some makeup, and go downstairs. That damn train is leaving in a few minutes. And you have to be on it doing the Grand Lady bit for the peasants. Have you got that? If you break down now, all is lost. If you hold on just a little while longer, the whole world is yours. It's up to you!'

'I'll do everything I have to, Kiki, I swear. Just let me read this poem to you:

'"For God's sake, let us sit upon the ground,
And tell sad stories of the death of kings:
How some have been deposed; some slain in war;
Some haunted by the ghosts they have deposed;
Some poisoned by their wives; some sleeping killed;
All murdered: - for within the hollow crown
That rounds the mortal temples of a king
Keeps Death his court . . ."'

By the time she finished reading, she was calm. She got to her feet and put the book back on the shelf. She smoothed the skirt of her black dress and smiled at Kiki. 'I'm all right, really I am. I'll be ready to leave in a minute.'

She washed her face and put on makeup. Not too much. Foundation. A touch of eye shadow. A bit of mascara.

'What do you think, rouge or not?'

'A touch.'

She put a dab on each cheek and blended.

5

Angel, dressed in black, sat in her mother's exquisite pale yellow drawing room and received a flow of visitors while her family surrounded her, trying to

378

divert her from unpleasant thoughts. Her mother managed things, Kiki kept up a stream of constant chatter, her brother, Eddie, offered to play chess, and her two sons ran through the rooms, playing, yelling, squabbling. All the while, she was preoccupied with one question – what would she do with herself when the mourning time was over, when Kiki went back to Italy, as she daily proclaimed she must, when even Eddie and her mother would leave to pick up the current of their lives in the East? Oh, her mother insisted that she and the boys would come East too, to summer in Southampton. But after the summer was over, what then? Kiki demanded that she come to Italy. They would play together – San Remo, Rome, whatever. Kiki had time on her hands too. There seemed to be a very large hiatus in her career.

'But, Kiki, I can't spend my life being a nomad, wandering from place to place. I need a direction. I need something meaningful in my life. I need—'

'Give it time. My God, it's only been a tiny while since you got rid of that—'

'Kiki! Don't. Once I loved him, and now that he's gone I don't want to—'

'Okay. It's only a little while since you've been widowed. Is that better?'

'Kiki, I think I'd like to go back to the theater.'

'I see.' *So it's going to be like that again.* 'It's not going to be as easy as you think. You think you snap your fingers and Angela du Beaumond will be resurrected? It's been quite a while, you know, and now you're almost thirty. Maybe you've been away from it too long. Maybe you're over the hill for the theater.' Her tone was grim. 'Maybe we're both over the hill. One way or another, the bloom is off the rose . . .'

And then Kiki herself didn't cheer up until a kind of miracle in the form of a visitor materialized.

'Angel, Kiki – we have a caller!' Marie called out, coming into the room, obviously pleased. 'And here he is—'

Kiki fell upon Brad, draping her arms around his neck, pressing her body against his. 'This is the nicest thing that's happened since Dick died,' she whispered in his ear.

Brad, accustomed to his ex-wife's excessive behavior and speech, laughed. 'I hardly know how to take that remark.'

'It all depends on how you look at it. In the meantime, I'm looking at you, and you're the best thing I've seen in years – at least in the past month.'

Brad kissed Angel. 'I'm sorry I couldn't make the funeral, but I came as soon as I could.'

Then he turned back to Kiki, who hung back now, avoiding the question that was on her lips and trembling to be asked. He grinned at her widely, the bearer of gifts. 'I have someone outside. I thought she would cheer everyone up.'

Kiki paled and sat down, silenced for once.

'Well, do I bring her in?'

'You *are* a shit, Brad, doing this to me without any warning.'

'Brad, for heaven's sake,' Angel said, tears coursing down her cheeks. 'Don't stand there – go get her!'

Kiki sat stone-faced as Brad went out. In a couple of minutes he was back with his daughter, a small replica of Kiki: pale blond hair falling in waves to the waist, green eyes tilted slightly upward, nose tiny but already finely chiseled. She wore a long-sleeved pink dress covered with a starchy, ruffled white pinafore.

'Brad, you horse's asshole, why are you dressing *my* daughter in all those tacky ruffles?' Kiki exclaimed in a voice touched with hysteria.

Brad grinned. 'Rory, kiss your grandmother,' and the little girl dutifully put her face up to Marie, who bent down to embrace her. 'And now Uncle Eddie,' and Uncle Eddie hugged her. 'And your Aunt Angel.'

Rory reached up to receive Angel's kiss, then approached the seemingly petrified Kiki. 'Mommy!' she said, and climbed into Kiki's lap. 'I know you're my mommy because you look like your picture.' She put her arms around the still motionless Kiki. 'Do you have a picture of me too, Mommy?'

Kiki squeezed the child to her and released, finally, a dam of tears. She rocked back and forth, holding the little girl as if she would never let her go. 'God, Brad! You *are* a son of a bitch!'

After a while, Angel went and fetched Dickie and Timmy. It was a day to remember, Angel thought, wishing she could freeze it in place, to have and to hold forever.

Marie asked Brad to stay at the house for a few days, but he demurred. He offered to leave Rory with them, though, until Kiki was ready to return to Europe.

'No.' Kiki shook her head, and everyone looked at her as if she wasn't to be believed. 'I'm going to go home with you, that's what I'm going to do. You, Rory, and I are all going home to Rodeo Drive for a lovely visit.'

Brad merely looked surprised. Marie raised her eyebrows but said nothing. Angel let out a little sound of anguish, but her mother put her hand on her shoulder. 'Let her go, Angel. You'll be fine.'

Her mother thought that she was thinking of herself, Angel realized, but it was not so. She was thinking of Nikki in Milan, waiting for her mother's return.

Marie found Angel in the lanai, watching Timmy and Dickie playing hide-and-go-seek with their Uncle Eddie. 'You don't have to see him, you know. One doesn't *have* to see journalists.'

'What are you talking about, Mother?' But as soon as Angel spoke the words, she knew exactly what and whom her mother referred to. 'Is . . . is it Nick? Nick Dominguez? Is he here?'

'Yes, Gladys says he's here. But you don't have to see him. In fact, you shouldn't see him.'

Not see him? But she had been expecting him, had known that he would come. Had been sure. Had been eagerly awaiting this moment.

'But I want to see him, Mother! He's my friend.'

She walked quickly to greet him, to take his hand. She murmured that it had been a long time since she had seen him. He agreed. Then he smiled that infrequent smile that lit up his usually somber face, and there was recognition in his eyes of the communion between them.

'I've thought of you often,' he said. '*Think* of you often,' he corrected himself. 'I've come to extend my sympathies.'

And why else?

'I know,' she said. 'Thank you,' and she thought of the pictures she had so recently recovered from her purse and burned. She had been so sure that it was he who had sent them, thinking perhaps they could be of some use to her. But now she wasn't that certain. The pictures were so ugly, and Nick Dominguez was a gentle soul, was in his own way an artist, a poet. Oh, how Kiki would sneer if she were here and knew what she was thinking! *Nick Dominguez a poet? Indeed!* Ah, but what did Kiki know of poets?

But still, she was so glad that Kiki wasn't here. Somehow, Kiki would have managed to spoil this afternoon for her, as she had done before.

'I was approached to do a photojournalistic essay on the governor – a study of his entire life, including pictures of you and your sons – but I declined.'

'Why?'

'I was afraid you might be offended. That you might think it exploitative . . .'

'No, I wouldn't have been offended. I'm sure that whatever you did would have been in fine taste, would have been only a source of pride to me.'

He laughed ruefully, and she thought, My God! He's so attractive when he laughs.

'Actually, I wasn't being completely honest when I said I declined only because I didn't want to offend you,' he said. 'The real reason I declined was that I didn't *want* to do a photographic essay on you with the governor. I'd much rather think of you without him.'

Now he was confusing her. Was he trying to tell her something in particular or was he just being bold? Bold after a decade of reverent reticence?

They talked through the afternoon, of this and that, about nothing of consequence. That which was of consequence was silently transmitted. The air between them vibrated with a certain tension. At last he rose to go, not without an obvious reluctance. And she didn't want him to go. But what could she do? She was a widow of but a couple of weeks.

'I'm glad you came,' she said.

'I wasn't sure that I should, but I decided that maybe it was time I took a chance.'

'Will you come back?' Now *she* was being bold. Her body ached toward his. It was all she could do to control it.

He held her hand and his eyes questioned hers. He wasn't sure of her, she could tell. 'You'll tell me when,' he said. 'And if there's anything I can do, you'll let me know. Please!'

Gregory Lane came to talk about money.

'I know it's a bit early to be discussing your financial picture but I understand you're going East for a while, and since we all know how things stood between you and Dick, there's no sense in forestalling this talk out of any sense of false delicacy. I thought we might as well get it over with so you would know just where you stand.

'Roughly speaking, Dick left an estate of a little less than eight hundred thousand dollars.'

'But there must be some mistake. That's approximately what we . . . what Dick said we had before Timmy was born, and then I clearly remember Dick

383

saying that Liam . . . that his father was making us a gift of a million dollars as a present for the baby . . .'

Greg Lane shook his head. 'You must have misunderstood. Liam allotted you and Dick the annual *income* from a million dollars when Timothy was born, but the actual million was never transferred.'

Angel said nothing, permitted herself a tight, bitter smile.

'But there's no reason for you to be concerned about your sons' futures. Besides sharing in their father's estate, they are included in Liam's will, too. As for Dick's estate, it's divided equally between you and the children. You each get a third. All of it in trust. You'll have the income from the principal. The children's expenses will be paid out of their income from their trusts. You can't touch your own principal or that of the children. If you remarry, or upon your death, your share will revert to the children.'

Angel realized then that she had been had.

'What you're saying, Greg, is that I'll only be getting the income from one third of the estate. Since I can't *ever* touch the principal, it's not really mine.'

Greg Lane's expression didn't change. 'If you choose to put it that way. The estate will be reduced by taxes, but the insurance policies will make up the difference. I would say that you personally will have in the neighborhood of between twenty thousand and twenty-five thousand dollars a year. But as all the children's expenses, their schooling, nursemaids, food, and other upkeep, will come out of the income from their own trusts, your money will be more or less free and clear. You'll submit all the children's bills through the office and we'll work out some kind of budget.'

Angel was shocked to learn how little money she would end up with. Bewildered, she asked, 'If I can't touch the principal, I can't even buy a house. Where are we supposed to live?'

Greg was not thrown by her question – he was prepared for it. 'You do have a choice, Angel. You *can* live in the house on the Power estate where you and Dick and the boys have lived from time to time. It is there, being held for you. Of course, if you don't choose that option . . .' He spread his hands.

She shook her head.

'If you choose to rent, I suppose we can make arrangements for part of the rent to come out of the children's income.'

'I think perhaps I'd better consult with my own attorney, if you will forgive me, Greg. Would you be so good as to send me a copy of the will and whatever else I should have? I have a feeling I'll be able to break your will so that the money can be mine free and clear. I'm sure you can understand how inconvenient it would be for me to have you and some trust officer doling out a yearly allowance.'

'And I'm sure you'll understand, Angel, that it's my duty and obligation to protect and carry out my late friend and client's wishes.' He rose and extended his hand. When she did not take it, he observed, 'Many people would be overjoyed with over twenty thousand dollars a year to spend just on themselves. Before taxes, of course. If you do elect to go to court, you'll put yourself in the dubious position of fighting your own children for that money, since they are the only other beneficiaries of the will. I doubt very much if you would like to institute proceedings reading *Angel Power* v *Timothy and Richard Power*.'

He picked up his briefcase and started to leave. He turned back for a parting shot. 'In any case, when you speak to your attorneys it would pay to bear in mind that there are a lot of intangibles involved. Just bear that in mind before you decide to go to court.'

Was he talking about her breakdown?

Threats. Another lesson in Power power.

Angel repeated the conversation to Marie, who said simply, 'We'll break the will. At the very least I would think you're entitled to that third of the estate free and clear.'

'No, Mother, I'm not going to fight it. Greg was right. I refuse to put myself in the position of fighting my own children.'

Marie's silence signified her tacit agreement.

'Still, I really don't know how I'll manage. Even if they give me enough money to rent a house or an apartment, I'll need staff. A maid, a cook. They'll pay for a nursemaid, but I still won't have money left over for cab fare.'

'Well, you needn't worry. I'll see to it that you have everything you need.'

'As if I were still a child. But I'm an adult, a woman. I need to be in charge of myself, take care of my own children. Not with an allowance doled out to me. Movie-and-popcorn money. I didn't want to have to take anything from anyone – I wanted only what I had coming. I earned it!'

'Oh, Angel. We all end up taking from someone else, one way or another. Sometimes we take only so that we can give.'

Then Kiki came back without any warning and announced that she had to leave for Italy immediately. When pressed for further information about what had happened with Brad and Rory, all she would say was that Rory was any mother's dream. And as for Brad, well, he was a dream too. An elusive one.

'What does that mean, Kiki?' Angel asked, puzzled.

'For the love of God! Leave me be! Don't you know when to let go? I know and I'm getting the hell out of here, and I suggest you do the same. You can come with me to Italy if you like. Or you can go back to New York. But do *something!* The California dream is over, don't you see that?'

She would say no more, and Angel decided what she would do. Yes, she would leave California. She would go back to New York and try to get back into the theater. She could live in her mother's townhouse in the city, or in Kiki's. It would really be a fresh beginning.

So Kiki left for Italy and Angel prepared to leave too, for the summer in Southampton. And there was one last caller. Zev Mizrachi arrived at Marie's Brentwood doorstep one afternoon when Marie was doing some last-minute shopping in Beverly Hills. Zev Mizrachi arrived unheralded to extend his sympathies on Angel's loss, and, always highly verbal, and with a good command of the English language in spite of his foreign birth, he had a lot to say.

PART TEN

Palm Springs, Milan, Paris, London
1959–1960

'Well, you can imagine how Hollywood took the death of Dick Power. Liam Power was so crushed he stepped down from the presidency of PIF and let his son, Sean, take over. He became obsessed with finding out the real truth about the circumstances of his son's demise, he never accepted the official theory of an accident. You can imagine the stories that circulated! I stayed out of it. I never got involved in political things in my column, as Hedda did. She was death on communists, you know, and she was always seeing pink through her keyholes, if you get my meaning. And Louella! She always saw things the way her boss, Willy Hearst, did, if you get my drift. Naturally, *he* was political. But he couldn't talk about scandal – not with his own personal life . . .

'But all our hearts went out to the poor darling widow, Angel, and to her dear little boys. Kiki was a tower of strength to Angel in those hard times, as was Marie, of course. They were very supportive, and what followed later was shocking, to say the very least.'

1

Marie sat on her terrace in Palm Springs, which overlooked the pool that she used infrequently, and ate her breakfast. The morning mail was brought to her, and, seeing nothing else of interest, she picked up the copy of *People in the News* and turned the pages idly. The magazine arrived every week, and although it was of a higher caliber than the exploitation tabloids, Marie never admitted to anyone that she read it. In fact, if anyone were present when the magazine arrived, she would pretend she hadn't the slightest idea where it had come from. Suddenly she sat up, sloshing a bit of the Sweet Almond herbal tea from her cup on to her pink crepe de Chine morning gown. Out of the pages of *People in the News* a familiar face smiled out at her – a face that she was, still, making an effort to banish from her mind. Rory Devlin!

Her stomach lurched, her heart pounded, and deep within her loins there was an urge she could not bear to admit.

Oh, the gossipmongers were wrong! This Rory Devlin was no seedy has-been but a man in the prime of his life! The picture showed a man still strikingly handsome in top hat and formal morning clothes, a flower in his lapel, smile flashing, and the dark eyes sardonic as ever, as he stood in the winners ring at Longchamps alongside his filly, New Orleans Belle, winner of the Grand Prix de Paris.

Breakfast forgotten, Marie hungrily read the text. How adroitly the journalist had managed to include so many facts in the two paragraphs allotted to him. Hollywood star of the thirties, war hero, former husband of Marie du Beaumond Whittier; father of the Italian movie star, the Countess Kiki Devlin Rosa, and of Angela du Beaumond Power, ex-actress and widow of the late California governor. The former idol of the silver screen was married to the Countess Jean Claude La Charbonne, née Alice Mazursky of Scranton, Pennsylvania.

Married!

The couple now commute between their Paris apartment and their Château du Bois in the countryside east of Paris, when they are not in residence at their château in Cap Ferrat or traveling with their racehorses to the Irish Derby, to Epsom Downs, Churchill Downs, or the Queen's own Ascot in England, or currently, as pictured here, to the Bois de Boulogne to win again at Longchamps . . .

A mixture of feelings: bitterness, the taste of it on her tongue, nausea rising up in her throat; a sense of loss so strong she felt weak; and still there was pride. Like the phoenix, Rory Devlin had risen from the ashes of his debacle to triumph once again. And then the physical fire that had been lit thirty years before in a virginal innocent, and banked prematurely, glowed again within her, and she burst into tears with the aching frustration of it all.

She retired to her bedroom and, with a mental image of a coupling thirty years old, brought herself to climax. She cried again. The desire was gone, but a sense of futility remained.

The phone rang. She picked it up, heard a foreign operator announce a call from Paris.

Paris? She could think of no one it could be . . . except for Rory Devlin . . .

'Hello?'

'Mother, it's Angel.'

'Angel! I thought you were in New York! What are you doing in Paris?'

2

Kiki had just returned to Milan from Rome, and as usual after an absence of a few days, the housekeeper besieged her.

'Nicole has had the fever three days already, Contessa.'

'How high? Oh, never mind. I'll take it myself. Did you call the doctor? The *dottore?*'

'*Si*. He said it was only *un raffreddore*. But she's been crying for her *madre*.'

'All right. All right. I'll see her in a minute.'

She looked over the pile of accumulated mail. The usual crap. The magazines from America, *Vogue*, *People in the News*, *Life*, *Time*; the magazines from France, *Paris Match*, *Elle*, *L'Oeil*; the London newspapers.

'And here is the list of the *telefono* calls.'

Kiki took a fast look. 'The *conte* called? And my sister?'

'*Si*. The *conte* in Haifa. The *sorella*, Signora Power, in Paris.'

'My *sorella* – she called from Paris? Are you sure?'

'*Si*, I sure. I told her you in Roma. But she call back. She say she no find you in Roma. She left number in Paris. She say you call her there.'

'Paris? Are you sure, Amelia?'

The woman was insulted. '*Si*, I sure! The number there!'

Kiki started to dial, then stopped. Better check on Nikki first.

She started for the stairs, then remembered to ask, 'Did the *conte* leave a message?'

'*Si*. He say you don't call. He coming home.'

'He's coming home? You're sure?'

'I sure!'

Kiki saw that the housekeeper had been exaggerating,

as usual. Nikki had a case of the sniffles, nothing more. Enraged, Kiki yelled down to the househeeper, 'Amelia, I want that bunch of mail up here and I want it fast! And that list of telephone calls! Right away! Do you hear me, Amelia?'

'Si!' she yelled up the stairs. 'Not deaf!' She dispatched a maid with the requested items, not wishing to speak with the contessa again.

Kiki placed her call to Paris and was told there would be a delay of thirty minutes. So what else was new? She sighed heavily and settled down to wait. It was obvious that Alexander Graham Bell hadn't been an Italian, even if Don Ameche was. She looked over the list of phone calls again. Her mother had called from Palm Springs. But she would wait until she was finished with Angel before she called her mother back.

She looked through the pile of letters and threw them aside unopened. She reached for the copy of *People in the News*. An expatriate, she was always eager to see what was going on in the States, even if she wouldn't admit it, even to herself. She turned the pages rapidly, looking only at the pictures. And then her father's image popped out at her. For a moment she thought, Jesus! I'd better lay off that white stuff. But no, it was her father! Damn him! From the day she had spotted him in Monte Carlo with that old, horrid bag she had tried not to think about him at all. But here he was again! He still lived on! Big as life!

She poured herself a brandy from the tiny bar, sipped, and studied the picture. *Well, Father, you're certainly looking good. Handsome as ever, you bastard!*

As she read the text she started to smile. When she finished, she was laughing, and tossed off her drink. So he had married the rich old horror, had he? Still, it was a comeback. He was in gravy, but solid. He was probably screwing the old harridan to death, counting on her to drop dead, whereupon he would be a real winner. *Good for you, Pop. You've been a bust as a father, but as a survivor you're tops!*

Maybe blood would tell. Maybe, if her father could triumph after his decline, so could she! Maybe she could survive all her mistakes; maybe even her marriage would survive the mess that son of a bitch Mizrachi had made of it. She would lay off the drugs, cut down on the drinking, stop making those crummy pictures Gino had talked her into . . .

Dammit! She would come back too! Just like her father, she would prevail!

The phone rang. Her Paris party was on the line.

'Angel? Angel! What the hell are you doing in Paris? You never mentioned that you were coming to the Continent?'

At first Kiki thought she heard incorrectly, but Angel repeated herself.

'I'm on my honeymoon, Kiki. I married Zev Mizrachi yesterday.'

3

Marie had barely walked through the door of the apartment when she turned on Angel.

'Why did you do it? How *could* you do it? How could you marry a man like Zev Mizrachi in the first place, and so soon after you were rid—? I couldn't believe you on the telephone. I thought you were teasing me. I thought I was asleep and in the middle of a nightmare. Tell me that it's a nightmare, Angel . . . a ghastly joke.'

'You tell me, Mother. You know more about it than I do.'

'I don't know what you're talking about. Start at the beginning.'

She could begin with the day Zev came to pay his condolence call. Oddly enough, it had been one of the few occasions Marie had been out, had left her alone. At first she had thought how kind it was of Zev

Mizrachi to come all the way from Europe, or wherever he had been, just to say how sorry he was to hear of Dick's death. But only minutes later he had proposed marriage. She had been absolutely shocked, shocked that he would even think that she could possibly consider marrying him. Shocked that an apparently civilized man would bring up the subject just days after she had buried her husband. And she was repelled. Oh, so repelled . . .

'I find this conversation distasteful, Mr Mizrachi,' she said.

He laughed. *Laughed!* 'I propose marriage and you revert to addressing me as Mr Mizrachi?'

'My husband is dead only a few days, Mr Mizrachi, and I find this conversation extremely distasteful – extremely offensive.'

'I agree, Angela. And if I had more time I would certainly wait for what would be considered a respectable passage of time – certainly until next week. But I am a very busy man and my time is limited. In fact, I must be in Bucharest tomorrow morning. So you will forgive me if I bypass some of the amenities.'

'I think that if you must be in Bucharest in the morning, it would be best if you left immediately. I have no intention of discussing this with you any further.'

'I have no intention of taking my leave before we set a date for the wedding.'

She looked at him incredulously. Haughtily she said, 'What can possibly make you think I would *ever* contemplate such a step, and particularly now, when I am in mourning?'

'My dear, it is completely unnecessary for you to pretend with me. I know that you are *not* mourning your late husband. If anyone would know that, it would be I, *I, your mother, and you.* We three, after all, are the principals in this covenant. My help with your . . . problem, requested by your mother, in return for your hand, if you will pardon the use of such an old-fashioned expression . . .'

Her first impulse was to run to her mother, confront her, see her horrified reaction, hear her denounce Zev Mizrachi for a lying scoundrel. She would beg Marie, 'Is it true? Did you really ask this dreadful man to dispose of my children's father? Did you offer my hand in marriage to this horrible man?' And her mother would reassure her so completely that they would both laugh at the ghoulish, preposterous story.

But only moments later all her instincts told her that the story was true. Her mother *had* struck a bargain with the devil. Kiki had told her that Marie and Zev had become close friends, had had tea and drinks together, dinners and conversation, throughout all the months that she had been at the clinic. Her fastidious mother and Zev the Terrible! It was the only possible explanation for the friendship.

Still, she had to disavow her belief. It was the only thing she could possibly do.

'What a ridiculous story! If it weren't so malevolent, so sickening, I would laugh. You must be mad, Mr Mizrachi. I think you had better leave before I call the police. They surely would lock you up as a madman.'

He only sat there and smiled with a show of infinite patience.

'Even if your story were true, even if my mother did that – which I don't believe for a moment – all I could say was that you were both most terribly . . . misguided . . . if you assumed I could countenance this – this – Oh my God! I can't believe it! I admit I did not love my husband, but a million women have been in my position without resorting to— He was my children's father. I . . . I am appalled even to contemplate—' Finally her voice broke and she could not go on and she wept, but still he sat.

She knew that she must stop crying. She must let him know that she was strong, in command of herself.

398

She must retain icy control, let him know that there was no way in God's world she would consider his proposal. She had to impress this upon him and get him out of the house before her mother returned. She couldn't bear for this to turn into a three-way confrontation, with her mother in the middle. Now she had to protect Marie. She had to get Mizrachi out of that chair, out of the house.

'I knew nothing of this covenant, this alleged bargain, Mr Mizrachi, if it did indeed exist. Knowing nothing of it, even if it did exist, I would feel no obligation to honor it.' *Such foolish, formal words. Nineteenth-century words.*

'So please, Mr Mizrachi, go now, immediately – and we will both forget this conversation ever took place. Frankly, I find it difficult to believe it myself. I keep thinking it's a bad dream.'

He laughed, almost good-naturedly, and the laughter chilled Angel. She would have understood anger. Their conversation reminded her too vividly of another, the one she had with Liam Power the night before her breakdown.

'Do I strike you as the sort of man who would make a bargain, uphold his end, then crawl away like a dog with his tail between his legs when the other party did not fulfill her obligation?'

No, of course not, Angel realized with sickening apprehension. How foolish of her to think that Zev had come without aces up both sleeves. Now he proceeded to lay his cards before her.

First, there was her mother. She was not without implication in this affair, and he, Zev, had worked it out that she, and only she, could and would be implicated. And then there was her father. Zev Mizrachi would see to it that all the world knew of Rory Devlin's problems and dissipations – the most sordid details. He would not only blow Devlin's cover, so to speak, but would see to it that all the members of the family suffered from this disclosure. After all,

Devlin had four grandchildren growing up, did he not? And then there was Kiki. If Angel complied with his wishes, he would release Kiki's husband, that fool and weakling, from their partnership without ruining him completely.

In the end, Zev and Angel set the date for their wedding.

'It was *you*, Mother, who made the bargain with Zev. I simply honored it.' Angel lit a cigarette with shaking fingers.

'And when did you find out? About this bargain?'

'When Zev made a condolence call right after Dick's funeral. Fortunately, or unfortunately, you weren't home that day.'

'But still and all, you didn't confer with me! That's unbelievable! How could you not?'

'Oh, Mother! How could *you* do such a thing to me in the first place? And even so, having done it, how could you not have told me about it? Didn't you know that Zev Mizrachi would come to collect?'

Does the guilt never stop? Marie asked herself in despair. *For how long, God, are the sins of the parents visited upon the child?*

She sat down now for the first time since entering the apartment, a crumpled figure.

'I put it off – I thought that Zev might realize that a marriage between the two of you was preposterous and that he'd never come to you – that you would never know . . . Yes, I was wrong not to tell you, Angel, but you were so terribly wrong to go ahead with this thing without consulting me. I never actually promised him that you would marry him. I *hinted, implied* – as I hinted, implied, that he should do something about . . . I never actually said anything definite about either matter, don't you see? I never intended for you to . . . I always intended for you to renege. Deceitful? Yes! Ruthless? Of course. But I had no compunctions about being ruthless to rid you of—

400

And I felt no qualms about being dishonest with the likes of Zev Mizrachi. You *use* men like him, Angel, you don't marry them!'

No, Mother. You don't use men like Mizrachi. They use others, always.

'Mother, you don't fully understand. *You* were implicated. He said that he would see to it that you were brought to justice if I didn't acquiesce. He said he would be in the clear and that only you—'

'Oh, Angel, Angel . . .' Marie quailed. 'There was no way he could have done that! He did everything. I only made vague allusions. I never actually asked him to do anything. He talked. I listened. He implied. I inferred. Or the other way around.' Marie touched her lips with a handkerchief, and then her throat. 'With my silence I implied certain things – perhaps my approval of his plan. From my silence, he inferred certain things – my acquiescence. That was my only complicity.'

Silent complicity. Angel wistfully wondered how many worlds had been toppled by unspoken compliance, but it was all beside the point now.

'The thing is, Mother, *I* believed him. And I believe him now. He could do it to you, Mother. He could implicate you and keep his own skirts clean. He can do anything. I see that.'

There was no point in revealing to her mother the rest of what Zev had said – her father, Kiki and Vic. After all, as they said in the comic books of her childhood, the dastardly deed was done. And *her* life was a comic book, one of those horror epics with green-eyed monsters and long-taloned creatures.

The sound of the telephone filled the apartment as mother and daughter sat in silence facing each other. The maid entered the room. 'Monsieur Mizrachi is on the line, madame.'

Angel went into another room to take the call. When she returned, Marie plucked at her arm. 'It's not too late yet. Fly back with me, Angel. We'll try for an annulment, and failing that, for a divorce.'

'No, Mother. I told you. I believe Zev can do to you what he has threatened. And you know what he's like. He'll never let me divorce him. The only way I'll be through with him is when he's ready to be through with me. The only thing I can do now is pray that that time comes quickly.'

Her poor mother was so crushed, so broken, that Angel pitied her. She stroked her mother's hair. 'It's all right, Mother. I'll make it. Really I will. I won't have another breakdown. I promise.'

'I wanted so much to help you. I wanted so much for you to be happy. And now you're even worse off.'

'Please, Mother, don't. I know you only wanted me to be happy. I know, I know . . .'

Marie laughed as she cried. 'And you married a man who isn't even Catholic,' she said foolishly. 'Little Angel, who clung so to her Catholicism. Remember when I first married Edward and wanted you and Kiki to become Protestants? You howled like a wounded dog.'

'I remember, Mother. That was a million years ago and I was a child. That was Zev on the phone just now. I told him you were here. Seems he's been expecting you. He said he'd be along soon and take us to Maxim's for dinner.'

Marie appeared not to hear. 'What about the children, Angel?'

'What about them? They're in school in New York.'

'My God! Timmy's only five.'

'They take five-year-olds too, Mother,' Angel said, and started to cry.

'Will you bring the children here?'

'No. Not here. We're just staying in Paris for a few weeks. I think we'll be going to Switzerland from here.'

'Then you'll put them in school there?'

'No. I don't know. I'll have to see. Don't worry about the boys, Mother, I'll see them. Vacations, holidays. And I'll be back and forth constantly. I expect I'll be spending a lot of time traveling from now on.'

Marie made an effort to pull herself together. 'There doesn't seem to be anything more to be said. Would you ask the maid to get my coat?'

'Where are you going, Mother?'

'To a hotel. To rest up. I'm flying back in the morning. Edward is not well – my place is at his side. I owe him that.'

'Yes, I suppose you do. You too made a bargain, didn't you?'

'I needed security. For myself, my daughters. I suppose we're always making bargains, trading. I liked to think that I made my bargain so that my daughters wouldn't have to bargain, trade themselves. I wanted so much for you to have a good life . . . love. And Kiki too, of course, if that was what she wanted for herself. But I *knew* that you, Angel, needed the right kind of love . . .'

'Please don't go yet, Mother. Must you go to a hotel? Stay here with me, please . . .'

'I cannot stay here, Angel and see you with that man.'

'Please, Mother . . . just a little while. I haven't even shown you around the apartment yet. It's so beautifully decorated, not overly formal, as so many French interiors are,' she cried. 'And the things I got at the salons . . . my chinchilla coat . . .' She sobbed. 'Please, Mother, stay just a little bit longer . . . kiss me . . . wish me well . . . Oh, *Maman*, I'm frightened . . .'

4

'I was hoping to catch Mother,' Kiki complained. 'She could have at least stayed until I arrived. I told her I was coming as soon as possible.'

'It was too terrible for her being here with me. And she was eager to get back to Edward.'

'Well, I certainly can understand about her not wanting to stay here, seeing you and Zev together.'

'Oh, please, Kiki, don't *you* start.'

'What did you think I was going to say, *mazel tov*? Congratulations on being the dumbest broad the twentieth century has produced? You were lucky! You got over the nervous breakdown and you got past Dick Power. You had it made and it was clear sailing ahead. And then to go and do a dumb thing like – no, not dumb – a *criminal* thing like this. If they hadn't let you out of that asylum I would say you should have your head examined. And such unseemly haste – the body was hardly cold, my dear. For myself I wouldn't give a fucking damn, but I thought you cared about appearances.'

'Zev was in a rush.'

'I'll just bet he was! Before you could think it over and realize the big mistake you were making!'

'What makes you so sure I made a mistake? After all, I'm a rich lady now,' Angel said, self-mocking. 'Wasn't it Kiki Devlin who told me, "If you're rich, you may be a bitch, but if you're poor, darling, you're a boor!"?'

'Yes, I said that. But I could add a word to that, and it also rhymes with *boor*.'

At first, Angel was puzzled. When she figured out what the word was, she was furious.

'How dare you? You can say that to me when *you're* one of the reasons I married Zev? I did it for you, Kiki Devlin Rosa, among others!' she blurted out in a blind rage.

'What do you mean, for me?'

'He said he'd release Vic if I married him! He said he would let Vic off the hook! You kept saying how Zev Mizrachi was ruining your marriage, keeping the two of you apart. I wanted you to be happy.'

'Oh, Angel, you little fool: Didn't you know it was too late to save my marriage? It had already fallen into too many pieces. And like Humpty Dumpty, nothing is going to put it back together again. I'm just clinging to the pieces now, but only the pieces. Angel, you poor darling, you married Zev Mizrachi for nothing if you married him to save me!'

Angel stared at her stony-eyed. 'No, not for nothing. Not really. I'm sorry if I was too late to save your marriage, but you were only part of the bargain. Zev proposed marriage a few days after the funeral. He told me what he had done for me, how—' She couldn't bring herself to say the words. 'And how he had done it with Mother's blessing.'

Kiki tried to speak, but Angel went on, 'With Mother's promise that I would be his when it was . . . all over – *fait accompli*. He said Mother was implicated. He said he could arrange to have Mother indicted while he remained completely in the clear. I believed him. Mother says no, but I still believe him. I know from experience how men like him operate. And he said that the day I became his bride, he would send Vic home to you. Is that true? Is Vic free of him?'

'Yes, for all that's worth,' Kiki said bitterly.

'But there was more . . . about Father. He told me Father was on the Riviera, a drunk, a dope addict. That he sells his body to *men* for a few dollars. He threatened to expose all this . . . filth. I couldn't let him do that. For my own sake, for yours, for Mother's, and for the sake of my sons and your daughters. Even for Father's sake. I couldn't let him suffer this final humiliation.'

Kiki covered her face with her hands. 'Oh, Angel, that's not true either! Father's all right.'

Angel's face filled with a new rage. 'What are you saying? First Mother tells me that there's no way Zev could have implicated her. Then you tell me that it was too late to save your marriage. And now you're saying Father is all right? That I sold myself for nothing? I *know* it's true about Father.'

'How do you know?'

'Because Dick's father told me the same thing. He too threatened to expose Daddy when I wanted to divorce Dick. It has to be true. Zev and Liam Power both said exactly the same things about him!'

Kiki went to her suitcase and took out the copy of *People in the News*. 'Here. I brought this to show you because I thought it would please you. Some joke!' She turned the pages until she came to the one with their father's picture. 'See for yourself.'

Angel practically tore the magazine from Kiki's hand. She studied the picture, read the text twice.

'We can go see him now, if it will help, Angel.' Kiki said softly. 'If he's in Paris and—'

Angel looked at Kiki with blazing eyes. 'Go see him?' she screamed. 'I'll kill him if I see him.'

Kiki was taken aback. 'I thought you'd be happy to see that he's okay. For myself, he can go fuck himself. But I don't understand why—'

'I hate him! Oh, Jesus, help me, I hate him so! All these years I loved him and forgave him for never seeing us, for never making the slightest effort to get in touch with us. I assumed he loved us too much to let us see that he wasn't handsome anymore, or successful. And then when Liam Power told me all that filth about him, my heart went out to him. I forgave him for being what he was, I felt sorry for him. My heart went out to him. But look what it says here – he married this woman in '56. He was already out of whatever mire he'd been in when Dick's father threatened to expose him. He was well off, racing horses, traveling, being handsome and dashing all over the place, most probably having affairs, enjoying life – and *still* he didn't contact us! It never occured to him that maybe we still needed him – we would have rejoiced to know that he was alive and well and sitting on top of the world!'

'You mean you could forgive him when he was down and out but not now, when he's climbed out of the slime?'

'Don't you see what he's done to me? If he had been a normal father, if he had maintained some contact with us, I could have thrown Dick's father's lies right back in his face. Because then I would have known that *everything* the old man said was lies. I would have found the courage to resist his threats. I might never have suffered a nervous breakdown. Mother wouldn't have had to go to Zev for help. I would be free now – free . . .'

For once, Kiki had no words to offer.

'And you,' Angel went on, 'maybe you could have found happiness with Brad if only you hadn't been chasing after somebody that reminded you of—'

'Shut up! I don't want to hear that Freudian crap. I'm not blaming my mistakes on Father. He's made enough of his own. I'll accept the responsibility for my own screwing up, just as I don't want my daughters blaming me for their mistakes.'

'Oh, but they will – they will! And they'll be right, too! You are responsible for what they grow up to be. And it all started with *him!*' She held her hand flat on the magazine page, tore it loose and crumpled it all in the same motion. 'Don't ever mention his name to me. If the world suddenly went mad and appointed him God, I still wouldn't want to hear his name again!'

Kiki sat down on the couch next to Angel and put her arms around her, hugging her to her breast. They sat there like that without speaking. Finally Kiki said, 'Let's go to lunch and try to lighten up. That's all we can do now.'

'Yes, that's all we can do now.'

They went to the Ritz for lunch, and although they had no reservation they were immediately seated, the maître d' immediately knowing who he was dealing with, the famous and beautiful American sisters – the new Mrs Mizrachi and the international movie star, Kiki Devlin. The restaurant buzzed with their presence. Even here among the rich and the famous, the elegant and the beautiful, the Devlin women caused heads to turn.

'It will have to be your treat, Kiki. I don't have any money.'

'Fine thing. I thought you were the rich sister now. Where are all those Mizrachi millions?'

'So far I've only charged things. I haven't seen a dollar in currency. I don't even know if Zev carries any cash. But I'm sure I can charge our lunch if you don't have any cash either.'

'Don't bother. It gives me a special kick to treat a billionairess, but I do hope you're not going to turn out to be one of those rich old skinflints.'

'Skinflint maybe, but old – never!'

They laughed in a desperate effort to be gay. The wine steward brought a bottle of wine and showed the label to Angel, who nodded absentmindedly. He uncorked it and poured a little into her glass. She tasted it and nodded again. He served them both and withdrew.

'After that little show, I *am* going to let you charge this meal. I don't see why I have to pay for that extravaganza,' Kiki said, drinking her wine in gulps. 'Tell me, Angel, speaking of money, did you and Zev sign a prenuptial contract?'

'You mean how much I'm to get if we divorce or—'

Kiki nodded.

'No.'

'You little fool! That's the very least you should have demanded.'

'I assure you, Kiki, under the circumstances, that was the last thing I was thinking of. My whole life turning into a nightmare and you think I was capable of dickering over money?' Her voice started to rise.

A waiter came to mix the salads at their table and they grew silent, waiting for him to finish. When he was done, Kiki asked, 'How has it been so far?'

'You mean the marriage?'

'What did you think I meant, the appetizer?'

'Well, in the few days I've been in Paris, I've bought five furs and a stack of dresses and Zev's presented me with a really remarkable diamond-and-emerald necklace. Is that what you meant?'

'I'm being serious and you're being sarcastic. Why are you turning on *me*?'

Angel drained her wine glass for the third time.

'Maybe I can't help thinking that if you had never introduced me to Zev Mizrachi in the first place, I wouldn't be in my present predicament – tied to a man I detest – and Dick would still be alive.'

'But you detested Dick too, didn't you?'

The waiter brought another bottle of wine and proceeded to display the label, preparing to go through the pouring ritual once more.

'Just pour,' Kiki commanded, and the steward did so and disappeared.

'You detested Dick too, didn't you?' she repeated.

'Oh, Kiki!' Angel wailed. 'I didn't want him *dead*! What do you think I am? And do you really think I'm better off now?'

'Oh, Angel, if I had only known what it would all lead to, I would never have done what I did, believe me. You do believe me, don't you? Besides, I've been more than just touched by that monster's hand myself. I wish to God neither one of us had ever met him.'

They sank into a morose silence, not eating but drinking more wine.

'And how is the sex?' Kiki finally asked.

Angel blushed a pale pink. 'Please . . .' she demurred.

'*Please*,' Kiki mimicked. 'We've talked about sex a zillion times before. Why are you turning all girlish on me now?'

'Because I don't want to talk about it.'

'Why not?'

'Because I *can't*! It's too godawful. Especially that first night.'

'My poor Angel. What did he do?'

'What do you think?' Angel asked resentfully. 'He's an animal.'

'What did he do?'

'He made me do things I've never even—' She looked down at her uneaten food. 'Over and over . . . on and on . . .'

'Did he keep coming?'

Angel looked all around to see if anyone had overheard Kiki. 'Yes,' she whispered. 'I told you. Over and over and over again.'

'Then it was drugs,' Kiki said knowingly.

'He did have cocaine. He made me snort some too. Kiki, he even sprinkled some on . . .' She bent her head closer to whisper in her sister's ear.

Kiki nodded her head.

'You?'

'Yes,' Kiki answered, turned sullen.

'The next night he had some ampules he broke under my nose. I tried to refuse, but he wouldn't listen. It made me feel like I was exploding all over, inside my head, down there. It made me . . .' Again she bent over and whispered into Kiki's ear.

Kiki nodded gloomily. 'Still and all, it had to be more than that for a man his age to keep getting it up. I'll bet my ass he's getting injections too,' she said thoughtfully.

'You mean those injections that—'

'I know a lot of people who get them. Like that story I told you about his ex-girlfriend, Lisa, and her husband. Remember? Some kind of speed. He wouldn't be able to keep it up at that rate unless he was.'

'He told me he's only fifty-nine.'

'Sure. So's Grandma Moses. Well, that's one consolation. Fifty-nine or sixty-nine, at this pace he's not going to last, and you'll be a widow again before you know it.'

They went back to the apartment, and Angel brought out her new acquisitions.

'Pretty soon you'll need special rooms to hold all these duds.'

'Zev is having a room twice this size designed for me at the house in Vevey, just as a wardrobe room. All the walls are going to be lined with shelves for bags, shoes, sweaters, and stuff like that. The rest of the room will e filled with revolving racks for dresses and coats.'

'Isn't that peachy?' Then: 'Angel, are you sure this shit about Mother and Father and me is *really* the reason you married Zev? Are you sure you weren't just using us as an excuse to convince yourself? Something you can't admit even to yourself – that you married him for all this?' She spread her hands.

'How *dare* you? After what you did to me? Introducing me to Zev in the first place? You get me into a situation like this and then you have the nerve to belittle me, to imply that I married him for money – you Judas!'

Kiki started to cry. 'I never meant for you to *marry* him! I swear it! I thought you'd string him along, that we'd string him along. Who would have thought you would become a widow and marry him? If you had only consulted me before you did this, do you think I would have allowed it? Not in a thousand years. I would have killed him myself before I would have. Don't you know that?' She picked up the empty brandy bottle and waved it in the air. 'Get another one of these!'

Angel rang for the maid. After she brought the new bottle and left, Kiki said, 'Angel, you must leave him now! There's no reason why you can't now. He lied about Daddy. It doesn't matter anymore about Vic. And you've got to realize that that *merde* about implicating Mother in Dick's death is sheer bluff. Why, for all you knew, Zev himself might have had nothing to do with Dick's death – maybe he just took credit for the turn of events. I bet that's it. Angel, leave him!'

Angel smiled sourly. 'You're always accusing me of being such a naïve dumb bunny, but you're the fool now. Don't you realize that Zev is capable of anything and everything? Maybe he didn't get rid of Dick, but *I believe* he did. I believe he's capable of getting rid of anybody he wants. It doesn't matter anymore about why I married him, whether the reasons were valid or not. It's the future I'm afraid of – what he would do if I left him. And I was afraid of Liam Power! Afraid of *his* threats! How silly all that seems now in the face o what Zev Mizrachi can do! I should never hav listened to Dick or his father. They were babes in th woods compared to Zev. All bluff, and I believed them But Zev Mizrachi! He's no bluffer . . .

'But while I can't leave him, I tell you I *will* last him out. Until he's sick and tired of me. I'm going to stan up – I'm not going to crack! I'm going to fight! I'm going to find a way out!'

Kiki ran to her and held her hard. 'I'll help you, I will I swear it! Hold on! We'll find a way . . . somehow.

'We're going to the Tour d'Argent for dinner. When told Zev you were here, he said he would make reservation and bring along a dinner partner for you a lawyer, Paul something or other.'

Kiki was somewhat drunk. 'I told you I couldn't stay Angel, didn't I, Angel? I told you my poor littl marriage is in tiny pieces. Shouldn't I go home and tr to glue it back together? I should go home, shouldn't I To my little girl?'

'You will, Kiki. Tomorrow. You can wait til tomorrow. Tonight we'll have fun. Please, Kiki. Th Tour d'Argent is the finest restaurant in all Paris. From the top-floor dining room you can see across the Sein to Notre-Dame.'

'Oh, Angel, who cares?'

'Kiki, you said you would stand by me! I'm jus asking you to spend one little evening with me.'

Kiki sighed. 'All right. One evening. If I could jus get hold of some arsenic, I could slip it into his soup. only I knew a pharmacist here!' Then she giggle 'Wouldn't it be funny if we could give him som Spanish fly?'

Kiki was sober but surly by the time they went t dinner, a very restrained affair. The lawyer Zev ha brought along as Kiki's escort said almost nothing. It was as if he were along only to take mental notes. Angel sat with her eyes cast down, as if she could not bear to look anyone in the eye. Only Zev was at ease, affable, garrulous, he carried the conversation all by himself. When Kiki, with an air of some defiance, said something about Angel coming to visit her, Zev answered, 'But Angel will be much too busy for visits.'

'Busy with what?' Kiki demanded.

'Making pictures, of course. All over the world.'

Kiki stared at him, as did Angel herself, his words as much a surprise to her.

'Angela du Beaumond is going to be the biggest star in films. Bigger than Loren. What Ponti can do, I can do ten times better. She is going to be bigger than Garbo. Her first picture, in fact, will be *Anna Karenina*. After that, we shall see. Perhaps we will do *Madame Bovary*. She will star in only the greatest stories written about women. She will have her own company: Angel Productions. What do you say to that for a wedding present, my dear?'

Angel shook her head. 'I don't know what to say,' she answered finally, thinking only about her sons.

Zev turned to Kiki. 'And what do you say, dear Kiki?'

Kiki smiled tersely, staring at Angel. 'I would say that my sister has made a brilliant marriage.'

Zev stood naked before Angel. It was hard for her to gaze at the hairless body with the huge bald head and grotesquely enlarged phallus without showing her deep revulsion. He pinched the nipple of her right breast until she gasped in pain.

'You have not properly thanked me for the great future I am making for you.'

'When will I see my sons if I'm going to be making pictures all over the world? I have to see my boys.'

'You will see them between pictures. Would I stand between you and your sons?' He laughed, pressing her

413

face to him with a soft but insistent gesture.

She drew away to the other side of the huge bed.

'Why did you have to have me? I can't believe it was just to turn me into a great star. *Why* did you make me marry you?'

He laughed, reaching for her again. 'Have you not heard of the magnificent obsession? Why did Caesar want Cleopatra? Why did Edward abdicate the throne? Obsession, my dear, obsession.'

Obsession? That's what Kiki once said about Nick Dominguez – that he was obsessed with me. Tears filled her eyes. *Nick Dominguez – such a gentle man.* What did he think of her now. Probably he was thinking much the same thing as her sister Kiki was.

'Whom do you cry for, Shatzie?' Mizrachi asked as he forced her mouth open to take him. 'Is it for me, my angel? Ah, ah, yes . . . for me with my magnificent obsession . . . yes . . . yes, ah . . . yes!'

5

'Oh Kiki, Kiki, it's so good to see you.' Angel hugged her almost desperately. 'It seems like ages. How long will you stay with me here in London?'

'I'm not sure. It all depends. A couple of days maybe. How long will Zev be away?'

'Wait a minute.' Angel closed the double oak doors. 'I know it sounds paranoid, but I'm sure the servants eavesdrop. I know they do at Vevey. Zev will be gone for four days. That's what he told me, anyway. I'm just grateful that he didn't insist I go with him.'

Kiki sat down on the chintz-covered sofa and looked around. 'This place isn't anything like I imagined. I thought it would be sort of art deco. I didn't expect the English countryside in a Mayfair flat.'

'Why not?'

'I don't know why not. I just expected it to be more citified.'

'Well, it's the English manor fashion. The style was codified by Lady Sybil Colefax, I believe. The Axminster rug was originally made for—'

'Okay, okay. Why are we going on at length about interior decoration, for God's sake?'

'Why not, Kiki? Why can't we ever have a plain, normal conversation like other people?'

'Well, for one I don't give a damn about your flat or how it's decorated. Do you?'

'No. I can't say that I do.'

'So let's drop it. How do you like London?'

'Like. Not like.' Angel shrugged. 'I never realized before, but one place is like another if you don't belong. And nothing in Europe will ever feel like home to me.'

'Home is where you hang your diaphragm, baby,' Kiki said out of the corner of her mouth, but obviously her heart was not in it. 'So how was it – being presented at court?'

Angel shrugged. 'Boring. Her Majesty asked me, "And how do you like London?" And I said, "Oh, very well." And she said, "Oh, jolly good!"'

'So you were not impressed with the queen?'

'What does she mean to me? The only people I want to see are my sons. Do you realize, Kiki, I haven't seen them in five months. After we finished in Finland I thought we were going to go to the States. Then Zev said we had to do some retakes in Yugoslavia. Oh, why am I going on this way? You know the story. Cannes . . . Rio . . . and now London. Mother keeps going to see the boys, thank God, but she won't come and see me. She said she can't bear to.'

'You really do complain so much. You really shouldn't. It's very unbecoming, you know.'

Angel couldn't believe her ears. After all the years she had listened to Kiki complain, on and on.

'I've heard that all Hollywood is going gaga over you in *Anna*,' Kiki said with a touch of mockery in her voice.

So that was it, Angel thought. Kiki found her

success in *Anna* difficult to accept.

'But I don't care about that, Kiki. It means nothing to me. I never even wanted to be in films particularly. I was interested in acting, in the theater, but even that was just something to do with my life. All I care about now are the boys. About going home. Oh, Kiki,' she pleaded, 'don't you see that it doesn't mean a thing to me? That I'm miserable. What can anything mean if I have to live with Zev, endure his lovemaking, night after night? What can anything mean if I'm not free? Nothing means anything. Nothing! Not being a star! Not the clothes, the jewelry, the homes. Now Zev says he's buying a house for me here in England, in the country. An estate in Lincolnshire so that we can keep horses. Who cares? I'll be there for a few days and then what? I won't be there long enough for the boys to be with me. Before I get a chance to bring the boys over, I'll be someplace else. I'm starting a new picture next month.'

'Really. What?'

'*Camille.*'

'Who's doing Armand?'

'You haven't heard a word I've said, have you? Kiki, I'm drowning! I'm dying! And you want to know who's playing Armand . . .'

'Oh, baby, I was just trying to distract you! My heart is really breaking for you! I'd like to kill him, really I would!' She hugged Angel fiercely. Then she was thoughtful. 'Where are you going to be filming *Camille*?'

'Why?'

'No reason. Who knows, maybe I can think of something to help. I'll want to know where to reach you.'

'Well, I'm not sure. Some of the scenes are going to be shot in Switzerland, I think. In that case we'll stay at the house in Vevey. If we do, will you come stay with me awhile? Please! You can, can't you? Do you plan to start work on anything?'

416

Kiki chuckled ruefully. 'The little quickies I've being doing of late are usually completed in about three days, so that's no problem. But Zev's made it pretty clear that I'm not welcome in his households. What will we do if he orders me out?'

'We won't listen. You *must* come, Kiki. I'm so lonely. And do you know what else? Wherever I go, if Zev's not with me, he has people spying on me. I'm always escorted. His people are *always* with me. I feel like a prisoner instead of a star.'

'It does sound like everything has gone from bad to worse, doesn't it? And we thought Liam Power was such a horror. Look, can we get a drink around here, or does Zev Hitler lock up the booze when he goes away?'

Angel smiled through her tears. 'The liquor things are over there. Make us a pitcher of martinis, Kiki. You make them better than anyone else.'

'Sure thing. I do do things better than anyone else, don't I? I even screw better than anyone else. *Everyone* says so.'

Angel laughed brightly, eager to laugh. 'Oh, Kiki, it is good to have you here. But I have gone on about my troubles without asking how things are going between Vic and you. Or how Nikki is.'

'She gets smarter every day. She's a positive genius. Which is fortunate, considering she still looks like King Kong's daughter.'

Angel protested, but Kiki laughed. 'I'm only kidding. She's not as bad as all that. Not beautiful like Rory, but not terrible. But lovely as Rory is, she's no dummy either. Didn't you think she was very bright that time you saw her at Mother's?'

'Yes. Exceedingly bright. And beautiful manners, too. She's really a well-brought-up young lady. You must be so proud . . .' Angel's voice died off when she perceived how tactless she was being. 'You know that time when you left with Brad and Rory and didn't return for five days? I thought for sure you two were

417

going to reconcile.'

Kiki gave a short, mirthless laugh. 'I almost though so myself.'

'I've always wondered what happened, what wen wrong.'

'We had a gorgeous five days. And it was heaven to be with Rory. But something was missing. At first I thought the trouble was with Brad. That he just didn' feel the same way about me, that he really would never forgive me for leaving him for Vic. But then I realized part of the trouble was with me, too. I couldn't quite give up on Vic. And Nikki, of course. I kept thinking about how great it had been with Vic - the sex and how the very look of him had thrilled me so - that next to him Brad was a pretty loaf of white bread. I kept thinking that maybe we could still make it.'

'And now?'

Kiki handed her a martini. 'It doesn't look like we're going to make it at all. And that's the understatement of the year. So what else is new? What else do you have to show me in the way of acquisitions? Any new fur coats? Have you bought out all the jewelry store in Switzerland and London and wherever?'

'No, I'm not allowed to buy my own jewelry.'

'Is Zev turning miserly too, along with all his other attributes?'

'No. I can spend all the money I want, providing it's for clothes, furs, furniture, servants, services – any thing but jewelry or paintings. He says he wants to make jewelry his personal gifts to me. Well, I can understand that. But it's the paintings that mystifies me. He insists on buying them personally, too. If I see a painting I like, even if it's only one of those tiny interiors, I have to tell him about it and *he* buys it. It's really puzzling, because I know it's not the money.'

'For a smart girl you can't see the nose in front of your face. It's obvious what he's doing. And it *does* have to do with money. You can charge all the clothes and fur coats in the world, hire ten full-time hairdressers, or whatever. At the end of a year, what are all these things worth on the open market?' Kiki held up a thumb and a finger to form a circle. 'A five-thousand-dollar dress is worth five cents once you put it on your back. No matter how much you've spent, you're still worth zero in tangible assets. But jewelry, paintings, antiques are *investments*. They constitute appreciable assets. If Zev buys all those things in his name and insures them in his name, they're gifts to you in name only. Legally, *he* owns them. What he is doing is making sure you remain a poor woman. You don't even get an income from the trust from Dick's estate anymore. And poor is weak.'

Revelation illuminated Angel's eyes. 'Of course! You're right. I never see any *real* money.'

'My God, don't you even get cab fare or a few francs for the washroom attendant?'

'Yes. A few francs for the washroom, but I never take cabs. Zev says it isn't safe for me to use public transportation. I suppose that's more or less true, but I'm never permitted to drive myself, either. I have a chauffeur, who's also my bodyguard. Yet Zev drives all over – he won't have a driver for himself. But I think the real reason I have a chauffeur is so Zev always has a report on where I go when he's not around.'

'Life with Mizrachi certainly sounds charming. Let's get out of here for a while. Let's go to lunch. We'll talk about your problem some more. And then we'll go shopping. I'd like to pick up a couple of Hartnell chiffons while I'm here.'

Angel wrinkled her nose. 'Only dowagers wear Hartnells.'

'A Hartnell might look "old lady" on an old lady, my dear, but on Kiki Devlin see-through chiffon without a bra is absolutely irresistible!'

Angel kissed her. 'I *knew* when you showed up everything wouldn't seem so bad!'

'Eventually, things *won't* be so bad. You'll see. And

you know what else? We're not going in your fucking chauffeured car.' With your sister Kiki along to pay the tab, you're going in style – in a cab! Did you ever hear of such luxury?'

The taxi driver asked for Angela du Beaumond's autograph, and she happily complied. When they emerged from the cab Kiki gave him exactly the cost of the ride. 'Kiki, you didn't tip him,' Angel cried.

'Of course not. He didn't ask for *my* autograph, and I've been around longer than you. No matter what you think, my sweet, I'm still *the* Kiki Devlin.'

As they were about to enter the restaurant, a crowd of teenagers flocked about Angel, asking for her autograph, wanting to touch her, declaring their admiration, calling her 'Anna.' Angel graciously signed autographs, answered questions, conversed with the girls.

Kiki, standing ignored, muttered, 'Apparently, one picture a star makes.'

Trying to direct the girls to Kiki, Angel enthusiastically cried, 'I'm sure Kiki Devlin would give you her autograph too, won't you, Kiki?'

The group of fans all looked at Kiki, trying to figure out who she was. A redheaded girl asked, 'What picture were you in?' and another said, 'I remember her. Weren't you in *Red Sands* a couple of years ago?'

The Mirabelle's head waiter jumped to attention. 'Miss du Beaumond! Our pleasure!' He led the way to the restaurant's prime seating.

Kiki sulked. 'I'm not hungry.'

'Try the *ris de veau* with sauce *périgourdine*, Kiki. I had it here a few nights ago and it was divine.'

'No, thanks, I lost my appetite.'

'But, Kiki, the Mirabelle is one of the fines restaurants in the world.'

'That may be their reputation, but what's in a

420

reputation, after all? Next week a new dive may open up and the Mirabelle will be last week's newspaper, no matter how big they were formerly. Just try to keep that in mind when you're acting like the big star!'

'Kiki! You're being unfair!'

'Who cares? Are they going to pin a medal on me if I'm fair? Two years ago, Kiki Devlin was the fairest person in the world.'

'Kiki, I told you. None of this matters. It's only personal happiness that counts.'

'The hell you say. I'll have a lamb chop. That's the only thing the English know how to cook properly.'

Angel consulted the wine list. 'What do you think of a Le Chevalier-Montrachet?'

'You're the star. You order it and I'll drink it. How's that for amiability?'

'Really, Kiki. Is that all you're going to do all afternoon? Make cracks about me being a star? You said you'd talk about my problem, what I can do about Zev . . .'

'All right. We will talk about your problem. How's your sex life these days?'

'Kiki!'

'Tell me about your sex life. It's important!'

'It's the same. Horrid. Well, not exactly the same. It's not as frequent as at first, but it's still awful. Sometimes I feel so desperate I want to kill myself.'

'Not as frequent as before, eh?'

'Well, at first it was constantly. Now it's down to four or five times a week.'

'And how is it then?'

'Oh, God, Kiki! Have mercy!'

Kiki pouted. 'I'm asking for a specific reason, not just out of prurient curiosity. I want to gauge the situation. Does he keep it up? More than once? Does he go on for great lengths of time?'

'Yes! For hours! Until I want to roll over and die!'

'I see. That means he's still getting injections, but since he does it a little less frequently than before, he's cutting down on the shots. Obviously he doesn't want to overtax himself.'

'I haven't analyzed it. I try not to think about it at all.'

They stopped talking while the steward served the wine. As soon as he turned away, Kiki said impatiently, 'I'm telling you, that's what it is! He's getting himself shot full of happy juice so he can play the stud. And that's the crux of my plan.'

'Plan?'

'You're going to . . .' Kiki lowered her voice dramatically and then waited while the waiter served them, then waited again as the busboy whisked away the soiled ashtray and replaced it with another. 'God!' she muttered as another waiter refilled the crystal water glasses. Then: 'You're going to' – again she paused for effect – 'fuck him to death!'

Angel was disappointed. 'You said something like that last time and nothing's happened. Besides, if you ask me, *he's fucking me* to death!'

Kiki looked at her sister amazed. 'You actually said the word. It must be a first! The thing is, he may be fucking you to death but *you* can take it. All you have to do is lie back and endure. And the last time I mentioned this I was just joking. Now I'm earnestly serious. In order for Zev to get it up and make it wiggle, he obviously needs those injections, just like his old girlfriend, Lisa Olmsburg's, husband. She was so insatiable that he was forced to get those injections I'm talking about – the injections that are supposed to be vitamins but are really speed – until he dropped dead from a heart attack. That's what you must do to Zev. Screw his balls off – figuratively speaking, of course.'

Angel was unconvinced. 'He must know that story about Lisa's husband better than you. If I start suggesting he get those injections, won't he know what I'm up to?'

'You're not going to suggest anything. You're too naïve to even know about such things. It's just that you're going to be so fresh, so tantalizing and tempting, that Zev is going to turn into a stallion, more so than now. You're going to wear only the sexiest lingerie. You're going to be more inviting, receptive, and sexually aggressive, so that Zev's manhood is challenged. He'll have to satisfy his sweet young wife's appetite for the sake of his pride, but the young wife will never get enough. You get the idea? It'll work if you take an active part. You have to put your heart into it.'

'I don't know if I can. My God, how will I bear it?'

'You can. Just think of the rewards. You'll be free! And you'll be rich! What could be better than being rich and free?'

'Just to go home. To go home and be with my sons again. And, of course, to be independent, mistress of my own destiny . . . That's my dream.'

'And, just incidentally, walk off with an Oscar for your next picture, Miss Star?'

'Ok, Kiki! You are impossible! You have a one-track mind! You really *are* impossible.'

PART ELEVEN

Rome, Vevey, New York
1961–1963

'Nobody could understand Angel marrying Zev Mizrachi. For one thing, he was much older than she. Another thing were his credentials. When she married Dick Power one had to say that he was a match for her in every way – socially, financially, attractiveness. But Mizrachi? Here in Hollywood there were two schools of thought on the marriage. Some thought she did it for the money. After all, she didn't have very much of that after Dick Power died. And there were those who thought she did it for the sake of a career. Mizrachi did make her into a great star. Her very first picture, *Anna Karenina*, did that for her. Sometimes it only takes one picture, you know. She was nominated for an Oscar for *Anna*. I think it was '61. But she didn't win. I think Sophia did that year. I remember the earlier years so much better. Little Janet Gaynor won in 1928 . . .

'Everyone said that Kiki's nose was out of joint about Angel's success. Well, one can't blame her for that. Her own career was on the skids, as was her marriage to that Italian.

'Marie, I heard, was beside herself about Angel's marriage. I don't think she ever went to visit Angel in Europe. But she was very close to Kiki at that time. And she was taking care of her own sick husband and keeping an eye on Angel's children, because Angel didn't get to see them very often herself.

'That was a puzzle. She had always been so devoted. She lost a lot of public sympathy over that, but perhaps it couldn't be helped. I always say that often no one knows what goes on behind someone else's door. If anyone knows that, I do, after forty years in dear old Hollywood.'

'How did you manage to get away?' Kiki asked, almost as if her sister had escaped from behind the Iron Curtain.

'It wasn't easy.'

'Well, before you tell me all about it, let me get the drinks.'

'Are you still drinking as much, Kiki? I thought you told me that—'

'Hey! Remember? *I'm* the big sister. I don't want to hear about my drinking. What are you going to have?'

'Nothing,' Angel said primly, a reproach.

'Well, I'm only going to have a Campari. That's not too bad, is it? So tell me.' She joined Angel on the low-slung white couch. 'How *did* you sneak away?'

'We just finished shooting *Camille* and I was supposed to be resting at Vevey, but of course there were a series of press interviews scheduled. With Zev on hand, doing the orchestration. But then he had to leave suddenly for Israel. At first he insisted I go with him, but I started to cry hysterically, pleading physical exhaustion. After he was gone I packed the one bag, put on my dark glasses, and ordered Jan, my driver-bodyguard, to drive to Milan. As simple as that. I didn't give him a chance to call anybody. I just said get in the car and drive. Anyway, when I got to Milan and you weren't there, I simply told Jan to keep on driving. And here I am!'

'And where is Jan now?'

'I told him he could have himself a little vacation. I told him to go off and have some fun, but I suppose he ran to the nearest telephone and is now probably hanging around outside, not letting me out of his sight. Not that I really blame him. It *is* his job and he will get hell as it is, allowing *the* Angela du Beaumond to be all by herself for a few hours.'

Kiki got up to refill her glass. 'And *Camille*? How did it go?'

'Fine. The rushes looked marvelous. I really think it's going to be a big hit.'

Kiki downed her drink in one gulp, still standing at the black-and-chrome bar, then poured another. 'But of course' – she turned and smiled – 'Angela du Beaumond doesn't *make* a movie that isn't a hit.'

'Kiki!' Angel protested, wounded.

'What did I say? Only the truth. And what's wrong with that? *Anna Karenina* is a tremendous success, isn't it? It's been running all over the world for months and months. And *Camille* will too.'

'I told you, Kiki, I could care less. My life isn't a tremendous success. It's a disaster, and that's all I care about.'

Kiki sat down next to her again. 'Well, then, tell me, how is our little plan progressing?'

'I'm doing exactly what you told me to, but I don't think anything's happening.'

'What's not happening? He's not fucking you or it's not having any effect?'

'I've done everything you said. I've offered myself like a whore on toast, and he's eaten every bite. He's delighted with my appreciation of his manly prowess. But it doesn't seem to be doing him any harm. He's like a bull and showing no signs of weakening.'

'I can't understand it! You'll just have to do better. Speed things up. He won't be able to keep it up.'

'I think I'll break down before he does.'

'No you won't! You come from healthy stock. You can do anything you have to!' But she wasn't as positive as she sounded. She reflected a moment. 'I guess Mother was right at that.'

'You're always talking in riddles,' Angel complained peevishly. 'Mother was right about what?'

'She once told me that only a fool sends a girl to do a man's work.'

'Apropos of what?'

'Apropos of that it's time somebody takes a more

active, to-the-point hand in this matter.'

'I suppose it would be useless to ask you what that means, too.'

'Just remember, my angel, all riddles have answers. Or they're supposed to—'

'Who are you calling?' Angel asked as Kiki dialed a number.

'My producer, Gino Rinaldi.' The line was busy and she hung up. 'I thought we'd go out for the evening. Gino will be thrilled to escort us – the biggest star in the cinematic firmament, Miss Angela du Beaumond, after all. As long as you're in Rome you might as well do what the Romans do. And you haven't heard anything until you've heard Italian rock!'

She tried the number again. 'Still busy,' she said, hanging up.

'Kiki, why, exactly, are you making pictures for this Gino Rinaldi? Why aren't you working with Vic?'

Kiki's laugh had a hard, brittle edge. 'For one thing, my darling, Vic is a chicken running around without its head. After Zev was done with him he only had the remnants of a studio left. So Vic is making these Italian beach bingo party things, desperately trying to make things he *knows* will make the box office register ring. Anything of higher quality is too chancy, he says. And who do you think plays in these teenage romps? Sixteen-year-old whores in two inches of bikini. Even I have to admit that I can't fill the bill. Oh, I was after Vic to move the goddamn studio back to Rome, and he's going to do that. But I wanted him to make some flesh-and-blood movies. Pictures of social significance that make a statement! Italy is ripe for that. Pictures that could give Vic a name again, not to mention his wife. Or even an important comedy, a Fellini or a de Sica. Something for an actress to sink her teeth into. But he's lost his balls.'

'So you work for Gino Rinaldi, who does—'

'Sexual farce,' Kiki finished for her.

Angel wet her lips before speaking. Kiki was so touchy when it was her career that was being discussed. 'Kiki, they're only one step above . . .'

'Pornography? Is that what you were going to say? Well, they're not. Well, maybe they're what you could call *daring*, but they're the wave of the future. Gino is really avant-garde. There's nothing really wrong with them. A little peek of the old vj is no crime. That's what all the movies are going to be in a couple of years. Frank statements. Big deal! Besides, do you think I would be making that shit if I had any better offers? Nobody's begging *me* to do remakes of Garbo. Nobody's kicking millions of dollars into making *me* an international star.'

Angel was silent. There was no adequate answer.

Kiki picked up the phone again.

'Jan will certainly follow us,' Angel said. 'He'll tell Zev where I went and with whom.' Not to mention the *paparazzi*, who would be sure to catch her smiling at someone she shouldn't. But she didn't mention this to Kiki, who would be miffed at the implication that the photographers would snap Angel and not her, even here in Italy, on her homeground.

'Fuck Jan and fuck Zev! Fuck everybody, but especially fuck Zev! . . . Hello, Gino? Kiki. Guess who's in town and ready for a big night?' she enticed him. 'My sister, Angela du Beaumond, the star!'

2

There were about thirty for dinner, mostly Europeans, with a few Americans thrown in to spice up the pot. Not too many from the world of cinema. Zev didn't particularly like to mix with them socially. But tonight's dinner was to be followed by a screening of *Ninotchka*, and the assemblage included Orson; Charlie and Oona, who were neighbors; Bill Holden; Suzette Delain, the French model; and Greta Thomberg, who was taking the treatments at one of the clinics. The rest were the usually flotsamed titles that drifted across the continent from resort to resort: Princess Ava Gonzales; Baron von Wolfe; the pale, emaciated Duke of Waterbury and his equally pale, thin wife; Francis Anthony, one of a vanishing breed of international polo players . . .

After the brandy and liqueurs, the guests were ushered into the theater occupying the sublevel of the villa. 'There's a double bill tonight,' Angel told Greta Thomberg. Angel was regal in ruby velvet that matched the ruby-and-pearl necklace Zev had given her the night before to commemorate the completion of *Ninotchka*. '*Ninotcha* will be shown after another movie, which is going to be a surprise to me, too.'

Everyone took his seat, and Zev signaled for the film to begin. The moment the title, *The Intruders*, flashed on the screen with the producer's name below it – Gino Rinaldi – acute anxiety gripped Angel. She directed a questioning look at Zev, who only smiled and took her hand.

The credits rolled, revealing the female star's name: Amorata. Quizzed by Francis Anthony, Zev said only that he had been advised that she was a new, most striking personality and a great beauty. Finally, after a long list of credits embellished with the most fanciful names, too fanciful to be real, the picture began, and with a sickening realization Angel saw that her apprehensions were well founded – Amorata *was* Kiki!

Now she knew without a doubt what kind of picture would unroll on the screen, and it would not be just another of Gino Rinaldi's run-of-the-mill smarmy extravaganzas.

Murmurs of recognition came from the rest of their small audience as the opening scene revealed Kiki in a lavish bedroom setting, leisurely undressing. Then the scene shifted to disclose what was apparently the ground floor of an enormous Italianate palace. Stalking into the house was a band of what appeared to be thieves – human grotesques, for which the Italian film industry had such a fondness: dwarves, a one-eyed man, a fat woman with a face eaten away by what one assumed to be leprosy, freaks of all sorts in various stages of debility, and finally the oversized Negro – an African prince complete to turban and tribal attire. Instinctively, Angel knew what was coming. She started to rise from her seat, but Zev held her fast. The others knew too, since a wave of giggles and whispers ensued.

First the thieves ransacked the downstairs, hurling silver, bronzes and other valuables into sacks. This was accomplished swiftly, with no wasted motions or subtleties. Soon the horrible crew was on its way upstairs. They entered bedroom after bedroom, snatching treasures, until, inevitably, they came to the bedroom occupied by the star of the picture, now lying nude on a satin upholstered bed, stroking her breasts and sighing with voluptuous yearning.

Sighting the sighing mistress of the house, the band approached the bed, grinning and leering with relish, while the poor lady expressed her dismay in a shriek. The Negro drew ropes, chains, and whips from a satchel. They spread-eagled the screaming Amorata and bound her to the bed, revealing the lipsticked gash of her anatomy. Angel thought she would surely retch.

The black man tore off his robe, exposing a superbly muscled and oiled physique complete to a gargantuan organ. Left with only his silken turban now, he raised the black braided whip while the other monstrosities took stations at each of the helpless woman's exposed orifices.

Now Angel *knew* she was going to be sick. She broke loose from Zev's grip and fled from the room.

Kiki! Kiki! Goddamn you! How could you do this to me?

But of course Kiki had not done anything to her. Not really. Poor Kiki had only done it to herself, as some sort of self-punishment. And Zev had done it to both of them, had shown the revolting film to punish them both – but for what?

3

The first thing Kiki said as she walked into the Mizrachis' Swiss villa was 'And how is my favorite brother-in-law? I take it he hasn't dropped dead yet from all the fucking?'

'Ssh!' Angel looked around to see if anyone had overheard. 'He's in Zurich, but he'll be back soon. What do you want to do about your chauffeur? Is he taking your car back to Rome or what?'

'No, Milko's going to hang around awhile. *After* he takes me to the airport for the final lap of this fateful journey, then he'll take the car back to Rome. In the meantime, have him put up somewhere. I *was* thinking of taking Milko to the United States with me, but I decided it would get too complicated. Wasn't it Thoreau who said, "Simplify! Simplify!" Or was it Emerson?'

'I don't understand you. Why would you ever think of taking him back to the States with you?'

'He's a handy chap to have around. He does so many things really well.' She winked at Angel.

'Oh, for heaven's sake,' Angel said, half in dismay, half in digust.' 'Haven't you had your fill of these sordid—'

'Oh, come off it, Angel. You're an international star now. You don't have to be Miss Goody Two Shoes anymore. I told you – Milko is a handy man to have around. He can do lots of things. He's positively marvelous with cars.'

'He looks nefarious.'

Kiki laughed. 'Nefarious is as nefarious does.'

'Where did you find him? You had a different chauffeur last time I saw you, didn't you?'

'I picked Milko up in Trieste. He's a Yugoslavian. They're a very talented people.'

'I'm sure,' Angel said curtly. Ever since she had witnessed Kiki's fling at pornography she was far less tolerant of her sister's interests and amusements than she had been in the past. But she shook off her annoyance. This was Kiki, after all, and, after her sons and her mother, the person closest to her, her best friend.

'I was shocked when you called me. I still can't believe it. You're really going home for good?'

'Yes. This is it. In fact, all my stuff's been shipped already. I only have a couple of bags in the car.'

'But what led to this latest development? I thought you and Vic had patched things up.'

'Before you grill me, do you think I might have a little drinkie? And where in this fucking place can we talk? I mean *really* talk.'

They went to Angel's dressing suite, which was outfitted with a solarium, a sauna, a terrace for private sunbathing, and a round sunken tub approached by a tiny flight of stairs. 'We can talk here. I read several books on the subject, then spent two complete days checking the place out for bugs. It's clean. By now I could probably qualify as an expert debugger.'

Kiki was delighted. 'Great! I'm thrilled that you've become so resourceful. Hey! I think I'll take a bath while we talk.'

She undressed while Angel filled the tub, sprinkling and spilling various lotions and powders into the steaming water. 'Mmmm . . . good,' she murmured as she lowered herself into the scented bubbles. 'Why don't you get in with me? We can do each other's backs.'

'Why not?' Angel took off her lounging gown and joined Kiki in the tub.

'It was Zev, you realize, who did me in completely. First he destroyed the foundations of my marriage when he kept Vic and me apart, forcing Vic to make pictures without me. Then he finished the job with a sledge-hammer.' She sighed. 'The sledgehammer was my debut as Amorata in *The Intruders*.'

'No, Kiki.' Angel shook her head emphatically. 'Oh, I know it makes you feel better to be able to blame *The*

Intruders on Zev too,' she said, scrubbing Kiki's back almost viciously with the lufa, 'but it really doesn't play. *You* and Gino made that filthy thing. All Zev did was show it in our house, which was a vile thing to do, but he didn't produce it and didn't make you perform in it. I'll never understand why you did it. You're a legitimate actress with a name. It was bad enough that you were in all those other Rinaldi epics, but *The Intruders*? That piece of filth?'

'Before you get carried away, let me explain something. It's easy for you to talk. As an actress you've got it all. You're riding a crest' – Angel tried to protest, but Kiki continued – 'but I was flat on my face. Then Gino said he was going to do an art film, one that would revolutionize moviemaking. If I gave him carte blanche in shooting, would do everything he asked, then afterward he would judiciously edit the whole thing, cut out all the stuff that was strictly prurient, and what would emerge would be a study of a woman and what happens to her *after* she is raped, sodomized, etc., eventually leading to her complete demoralization and disintegration as a human being. Don't you see? I thought the picture would be in the style of maybe Ingmar Bergman – strong stuff but an artistic study, not a dirty picture! But whatever Gino's intentions before the fact, your husband found out about the picture, and then, of course, he found out Gino's price and he paid it. The Ginos of this world always have a price. As a result, what ended up on the cutting-room floor was the art, and what was left in, completely unedited, was the filth.'

She reached for a bath sheet and stepped out of the tub. 'I was a victim of Gino's greed and Zev's machinations . . . not a participant.'

Angel got out of the tub and wrapped herself in a robe, hugged it to her, feeling so cold. 'Kiki, Kiki,' she mourned, starting to cry.

'I think I want to go in the sauna now,' Kiki said. 'Steam out some of the poison.'

They stretched out on the wooden benches, Kiki on the upper level, Angel below, still crying.

'Now Zev's distributing the film throughout Europe. I only hope it doesn't get to America, but that's probably too much to hope for. It's probably playing on Forty-second Street in New York this very minute. Well, anyhow, Vic said to me, "Your excesses have become too excessive, even for me." Can you believe it? After it was he who chased after Zev in the first place. Do you see? If he hadn't gotten involved with Zev, then I wouldn't have gotten involved with Gino.'

Through her tears, Angel said, 'You should have explained.'

'Oh, I did. But he was *so* disgraced. And it was all rotten anyhow. Our marriage is over! *Fini!*'

Then she took note of how terribly hard Angel was crying and she grew frightened. That was how the breakdown had started last time. She lowered herself to the first level, bent over her. 'Don't cry, Angel. It will be all right.'

'No. It can't be. It's bad enough what he's done to my life, but to ruin your marriage too . . . It's too much, too much . . .'

'It's all right, Angel. Vic really wasn't so much, you know. He really wasn't such a big deal,' she said softly and sadly.

Angel stopped crying. 'He wasn't?' She couldn't believe that Kiki had said that.

'No, he wasn't . . . Not like Brad . . . Now Brad's really *somebody!* I was fooled by . . . Oh, hell! I was fooled by a lot of things.'

Angel sat up. 'There's still one thing I don't understand. Before I married Zev, you said Zev was using you and Vic – pressuring the two of you into pressuring me. That he was after me. Now he *has* me, God help me. So why was he still out to ruin you and your marriage? Why did he buy Gino's picture and distribute it? Did he want to discredit you and humiliate Vic out of sheer malice?'

Kiki was surprised. 'You haven't figured it all out yet have you? Zev *wanted* Vic to throw me out so that I would go back to America. Don't you see? He wants you here in Europe all alone, without any of us, me, Mother, or the boys. He wants you to have no one but him!'

'Oh my God!' She was frightened, more so than she had ever been. 'Kiki, don't go! Can't you live in Paris? I bet you could make films in France. You know the French. They wouldn't care about *The Intruders*. You could work there.'

'No, I can't stay in Europe. That's part of my agreement with Vic. He can't divorce me in Italy. I've promised to go back to the States and divorce him there.'

'And what if you didn't?'

'Then he'd get a legal separation from me in Italy and I'd get nothing. Not a red cent. I'm better off taking my settlement and splitting. What's the use of holding on to a dead horse? And to tell you the truth, I've had it up to here with the Continent and the fucking Continentals. I'm really ready to go home. I miss the hot dogs and the apple pie and the purple mountain majesty.'

'But what about Nikki? You haven't said a word about Nikki.'

'I haven't, have I?' She stood up. 'I've had enough of this hot box. My pussy is withering.' Without waiting for Angel, she stepped out of the sauna and into the shower. Angel followed her in. 'Kiki!' she yelled over the noise of the water. 'You can't give up your daughter! You just can't. Not again!'

Kiki left the shower, put on a terry robe, wrapped her hair in a towel. Angel followed suit. 'Kiki?'

'Oh, Jesus, Angel! Don't you ever understand anything? There's nothing I can do about it, not a damn thing. Nikki's an Italian citizen. And Vic's an Italian, with an old family name, still fairly important. And *I*, the American divorcee, have committed the immoralities. I don't have a chance in hell of getting custody. All I can do is pick up my marbles, which is whatever money I can get my hands on, and screw off!'

'So you're leaving me and Nikki behind . . .'

'Nikki? . . . Yes.'

'Why do you put it that way? You're leaving me too!'

'Maybe not. I *have* to leave Nikki, but you're not necessarily expendable. Just don't ask too many questions and don't cry, for God's sake, I don't want you getting sick on me, you hear? As long as the solarium isn't bugged, let's go in there and sit awhile. You can give me a drink and *I'll* do the crying for both of us.'

'Does Zev still do all his own driving?'

'Yes, but—'

'And he leaves the villa to do business in town, without taking you with him.'

'Sometimes. Why all these questions?'

'He's coming back today, you said? Will he be leaving the house tomorrow?'

'I'm not sure. I don't know. Yes, I do know. I remember – he does have an appointment in Geneva tomorrow. At a bank. I heard him confirming it.'

'Good.'

To Angel's inquiring look she said, 'I'm just planning on staying out of his way, is all. If he were going to stay home all day, I intended to stay in bed the whole time. I'm afraid that if I saw him I might be tempted to claw out his eyes.'

'Oh, Kiki, what am I going to do?'

'We'll see. We'll figure it out after all the votes are in. I did get you into this mess, and I'm thinking about how to get you out. But think of one thing – if I hadn't gotten you into this mess with Zev you wouldn't be the great big movie star you are, either.'

Early the next morning, a white-faced, bathrobed Angel came into the bedroom where Kiki lay sleeping, a peaceful look on the still delicate face. Angel shook her awake. 'Kiki! Wake up! Wake up!'

'Christ! What is it? A fire?'

'Kiki! *Zev is dead.* The police were just here. Zev's car

439

went off the road about three hundred yards from the gatehouse. It's so weird. Four security guards sitting in that gatehouse and only three hundred yards away Zev died. I just can't believe it! Zev dead!'

Kiki smiled sleepily. 'I'll take you home again, Kathleen,' she crooned.

'Kiki?'

'Yes. Only one thing. You'll have to stop saying my name like that, over and over again. It's becoming boring . . .'

4

They arrived in New York on Angel's thirty-fourth birthday, and moved immediately into Kiki's townhouse, which had been quickly readied for their homecoming. Since it was Angel's birthday and Kiki was eager to start seeing people, she insisted they celebrate that very night at El Morocco. Angel protested. She was hardly in the mood for partying. Besides, she would be mobbed as usual and how would it look? She was a widow of only two weeks. So Kiki called up some people and went without her.

Angel stayed at home by herself and wondered if she had done the right thing in coming back to New York and moving in with Kiki. Perhaps she should have gone straight to Los Angeles as she wanted to – she had moved her sons to school there only a year before, and she could have moved into her mother's house in Brentwood until her financial situation was straightened out. And she had had all kinds of offers in the two weeks since Zev had died – from managers, agents, studios, independent producers. It was much too soon for her to think about any of that, although she might have to, shortly, for financial reasons. Although the laywers in Switzerland had said they could not give her any information at that time about Zev's estate, she already had the distinct impression that she was not about to be his principal beneficiary. She might have been Zev Mizrachi's great bright star and magnificent obsession, but she certainly had not been his great love, and his lawyers had given off a distinct odor of pessimism as far as she was concerned. Kiki had already engaged a battery of attorneys on her behalf; still, Angel had the strong feeling that she had to get to work soon unless she was content to live off her mother and Kiki.

It was quite ironic that she, who had been the wife of a man whom the world suspected of being one of its richest, should end up with trunks full of clothes and a few trinkets – only those pieces of jewelry that had not been locked up in Zev's vault – and not much more. She didn't even know what had become of the money she had earned in *Anna Karenina*, *Camille*, and *Ninotchka*. Thank God, that the last movie she had made for the Angela du Beaumond-Mizrachi Production Company, *Hedda*, would soon be ready for distribution. Surely she would realize some money from that. But yes, she would have to get to work very soon, and the best place for that would be California. Yet Kiki had been so insistent that she move in with her.

'It's the only practical solution as of the moment. Of course you have to visit Dickie and Timmy, but leave them in school in California while you acclimatize yourself to being a free woman. Of course you're going to be inundated with offers from Hollywood, but you have to take your time, pick and choose. Don't forget, you're not exactly used to making decisions for yourself.'

'But now that I'm free I have to make a real home for the boys.'

'You will, you will. You can even make a real home for them here in New York. You can put them in school here, can't you. There's plenty of room here for everybody, God knows, and I don't want to be alone. We've always wanted to be together, haven't we?'

'But why New York? Why not Los Angeles? Rory's

there, and now that you've . . .'

'Go ahead, say it. Now that I've lost Nikki . . .'

'Well . . . yes. And there's Brad, too. Didn't you almost reconcile that last time? Think about it, Kiki. It would be so wonderful!'

'I've thought about it, but I can't go back there now. Not when I'm a failure. In disgrace. And nobody will touch me with a ten-foot pole out there. I've heard that *The Intruders* has made its presence well known there. It's all over the place, like shit on a blanket. And you know how provincial they are in Hollywood. Beebie Tyler and her crowd would be after my ass like a bunch of churchgoing vigilantes. The New York theater is much more sophisticated. They don't give a shit what you've done. If I have a chance at being an actress at all, it's here. When I've redeemed myself, I'll go back, see Rory . . . and Brad . . . Now *you*, of course, can do anything you want – the screen, the theater; you can pick and choose. And I'm not going to beg you to stay with me. If you want to go back to LA and leave me in New York alone, then go,' she said spitefully. 'Maybe you just don't want to move in with me because of my notorious reputation. Guilt by association?'

'Oh, Kiki, notorious or not, I love you.' Angel hugged her.

'Then it's settled. We'll stay in New York until we get our lives together, okay?'

Of course she couldn't leave Kiki all alone, not when she was spiritually down and out. Not after what Kiki had done for her, or what she suspected Kiki had done for her. Coward that she was, she couldn't, wouldn't, ask, and Kiki never exactly said – not in so many words.

Any regrets about Zev's death, or any feelings of guilt about her lack of regrets, were quickly obliterated when Angel heard further from the lawyers in Switzerland. Even in death, Zev had played a last malicious joke on her.

Other than for a few specific bequests to his wife, all of

442

Zev Mizrachi's holdings and interests throughout the world were left to the Mizrachi Foundation, with its largesse to be dispensed to Swiss and Israeli charities – educational, medical, and cultural. Even personal property was to be included, with all the Mizrachi art treasures, including those housed on the *Venus*, to form the basis of a museum, to be called the Mizrachi Fine Arts Museum, to be erected in Haifa. The apartments in London, Paris, and New York had been leases, but the house in Vevey was to become the Mizrachi Institute for Medical Research. The house he had bought for Angel (but not in her name) in Lincolnshire, England, was to become the Mizrachi Institute for the Advancement of Irish Culture, a kind of Mizrachi joke. That he had a fine sense of humor was further established by the clause that his home outside of Madrid become the Mizrachi Institute for the Advancement of the Marrano.

As for the bequests to his beloved wife, there was a copper mine in Mexico that had been abandoned, a South American airline that was on the verge of bankruptcy, and oil wells in Persia that had not produced oil in years. The most amusing joke was his bequest to her of the *Venus* minus its appointments, considering that its annual upkeep was somewhere in the posh neighborhood of a million dollars. The only thing Angel could hope for was to unload the yacht quickly before it deteriorated from lack of maintenance. Finally, there was a yearly income of ten thousand dollars 'to assure my beloved wife of a comfortable existence as she contests this will in the courts.' Yes, that was Zev – grinning at her from the grave.

When she inquired about her jewelry that had been kept in the Mizrachi vaults, she was told that the jewelry belonged to Zev and not to her, and therefore was considered part of the estate. They did add, however, that whatever pieces she had taken with her she would be permitted to keep. Since she had been allowed to keep them in her own bedroom safe, they would be willing to interpret that as Mr Mizrachi's implied consent that

443

possession was hers.

She was also informed that while her latest movie, *Hedda*, had been readied for distribution and would be released shortly, all rights to the movie belonged to the Mizrachi Foundation, as did the Mizrachi Studios itself, its complete library of films, and the Angela du Beaumond-Mizrachi Production Company. If Miss du Beaumond had any claims for salary or recompense for her performances in any of the four pictures she had made for the company, she should have her laywers present her contracts or agreements as proof of her claim, and appropriate compensation would certainly be made.

Of course she had no such contracts or agreements. Zev had told her to perform and she had performed. She had assumed vaguely that the production company was hers and somewhere there were accounts in her name. Of course her lawyers would sue, about the will and about her share in the movies she had made, but it would take years to go through the foreign courts, and it was an extremely difficult case. If individuals had constituted the main beneficiaries, an equitable arrangement might have been worked out, but charities that were in effect nationalistic . . . well, it was most difficult. Meanwhile, the lawyers wanted huge retainers.

'Of course,' Kiki said. 'Of course it will take years, between their lawyers and your lawyers. They figure by that time you'll be so exhausted, they'll be able to walk away with most of your money and you'll be too pooped to peep. What did Shakespeare say about lawyers? Didn't he say something clever?'

'Yes, in *Henry VI*, I think. "The first thing we do, let's kill all the lawyers."'

'Mmm . . . that's something to think about, isn't it? Well, there's nothing to be done but to let the fuckers work on it, and while they do, forget about it. At least you've got one legacy from Zev – he left you a star. And one more comforting thought – Zev screwed you, and he screwed me, but in the end, who screwed whom the most? He's dead and we're alive . . .'

444

PART TWELVE

Hollywood, New York
1964–1966

'It was shocking to all of us when Angela du Beaumond was widowed again. And when the business about Zev Mizrachi's will came out, people's tongues certainly did waggle. I can't tell you how many phone calls I received wanting to know the real story about that. But whatever I knew, I wasn't telling. Not even when I received pressure from my dear boss, Adolph Guttenheimer, the publisher of the *Los Angeles Dispatch*. Some secrets *are* sacred, although I always contend that my first responsibility is to my reader.

'The movie colony was hurt and disappointed when Angel went to New York to live instead of coming back to Los Angeles, which really was her home by this time. It was Kiki who wanted to go to New York, and Angel went along with her. And to tell the truth, it was no wonder Kiki didn't want to show her face here, what with that disgraceful movie that was being shown all over in certain select theaters, and in all the private screening rooms from Beverly Hills to Malibu. And she with two young lovely daughters. That was one time I did spank her bottom in print.

'It looked like Kiki was washed up in the industry. A lot of people think Hollywood is all sex, scandal, and drugs – wanton living – but we're just like any other American community when it comes to these things. We too have high standards, and we expect our people to act like decent, law-abiding citizens, and when they don't, we chastise our own.

'Well, New York or Hollywood, Angela du Beaumond was still a very important star, and she was inundated with offers. It seemed that she was going to be very much in demand, very busy indeed. The only problem seemed to be with Kiki, who really was a wonderful actress. What was she going to do next?'

447

1

Very soon after they settled in New York, Angel flew
out to California to take her children out of school there
and move them East too. It was an incredible joy to see
her boys daily. Since it was near the end of their
semester, she decided to wait in Los Angeles for the
school term to end. She moved into her mother's house
in Brentwood. Marie was at Stoningham now, taking
care of Edward, who had suffered a stroke and was
nearly totally paralyzed.

From the day she moved in, with only a maid in
attendance, she was besieged with offers and was forced
to hire help – a secretary to take care of the calls and mail,
a press agent to handle all the requests for interviews, a
reader to go through the scripts that poured in, and
finally an agent to represent her, to help her consider the
various offers. Friends called, she was invited to parties,
and she was sorely tempted to remain where she was and
accept one of the more attractive film offers. But Kiki
called repeatedly, demanding to know when she would
be back.

She thought of Nick Dominguez almost daily, debating
whether to call him or not. She remembered that he had
said that he would wait for her call, but that was right
after Dick had died, and before she had married Zev. Had
the right time come and gone? she wondered. And then
he called *her*, but she was out and her secretary gave her
his message: he was leaving the country on assignment,
he would call upon his return. She was so disappointed
she could have wept. Had the right time come and gone
again? And dammit, if he was really drawn to her, why
had he waited so long to call? He didn't have to wait until
she called him. Was he afraid of her? She, whom no other
man had ever feared?

*

While she was waiting to go back to New York she was talked into doing a cameo in a picture an old friend, Harry Grixby, was directing, and as soon as Beebie Tyler reported it in her column, she heard from an irate Kiki.

'What a crazy thing to do! You're a big star, they tell me. So why did you take a bit part?'

'As a favor to Harry, who said my name would help him immeasurably, and because it was fun, and because they gave me a hundred and fifty thousand dollars for three days' work. Believe me, I was glad to get it, even though no one here suspects that I really need the money desperately.'

'*Desperately?* Are you sure you want to use that word? I'd give you whatever you needed. So would Mother. Are you sure you're not using this just as an excuse because you couldn't bear to be out of the limelight for even a few weeks?'

'Kiki,' Angel reproached her softly.

Poor Kiki. She must be having a terrible time of it in New York, not getting any response in her quest for work.

'Any luck, Keek?'

'Well, I've been auditioning. And you know – "don't call us . . ." In general, I would say nobody's taking my calls.'

'I'm going to see what I can do for you here. I have an agent, Pát Drey—'

Kiki cut her off in mid-name. 'That son of a bitch? Why did you get him? And thanks but no thanks.'

'Well, things will change. You'll see.'

'Sure. Any more fairy tales?'

'Kiki, I went to see Brad and Rory . . .'

'Who asked you to?'

'Why, Brad did. He invited me to dinner.'

'Oh, really? Was it candlelight and roses?'

'Kiki, you *are* impossible! Brad and I are friends, and I did want so much to see Rory.'

'So?' Sharp.

'She was delightful. Just delightful. A darling. And unspoiled. and, Kiki – she asked a thousand questions

449

about you. And I told her – I told them both – that you're coming out to see them, and soon.'

'Why did you do that?'

'Because that's what I think you should do. Brad still says only the nicest things about you. I think he's still in love with you.' Actually, Angel wasn't sure whether it was really love or merely Brad's innate niceness. But let Kiki find out. It couldn't hurt for Kiki to find out. At the very least, she would see her daughter, and at most . . . oh, what a happy ending.

'I'll think about it. In the meantime, when are you coming back? I have a lot of new friends who'd like to meet you.'

'Oh? Who are they?' Why did the hair on her nape bristle.

'I've been having a ball. Andy Warhol, Edie Sedgwick . . . Baby Jane, Mario . . . he's too much, really. And Viva . . . they're all a barrel of fun.'

'I'm sure,' Angel said drily.

'Ho, ho. Do I hear a superior note there?'

'Of course not. But I did hear that Edie's heavily into drugs. She has family out here, you know. Santa Barbara . . . Kiki, I hope you're being careful.'

'You *are* being superior. God, you're sickening with that ramrod up your ass.'

'I think I'll say goodbye now, Kiki. I'll be seeing you really soon.' She would control herself with Kiki, no matter what the provocation.

'Andy Warhol is a great artist, no matter what you think!' Kiki yelled into the phone. 'Art with a capital *A*, more of an artist than that greaser friend of yours, Dominguez.'

'Try to control yourself, Kiki. You're completely out of line.'

'Oh, come off it, Angel. Do you really think I swallow that crap about you staying until the end of the boys' term? You could just as soon have waited here. It's a man that's keeping you there, and his name is enough to make me puke!'

Angel hung up and counted to ten, and *then* she did what she usually did – she cried. It was all she could do to try to rationalize Kiki's behavior to herself. How could she say such rotten things, especially about such a lovely man as Nick? In the future, if Kiki brought up his name, she would tell her the truth, dammit! She would say: I haven't seen Nick Dominguez in a very long time. But I think about him quite a bit. Currently, and in the past. All the time I was married to Zev. Sometimes when Zev was making love to me I would only endure it by forcing myself to think it was Nick . . . And let Kiki make something out of that!

Impulsively she picked up the phone and dialed Nick's studio in Hollywood, asking when he would be back. A secretary informed her that Mr Dominguez's date of return to the United States was indefinite. However, he planned on going to New York first. He did divide his time between the two coasts. Would she like a number in London where he could be reached?

Angel hesitated a moment, then hung up. But that night, sleeping in Marie's peach satin-and-silk bedroom, she dreamed about him. Or at least in the beginning of the dream, Nick was its star. But suddenly, he turned into Rory Devlin! And then she woke up. It was so peculiar. She had thought about Nick often in the past months, but about her father not at all.

2

Angel brought the boys back and enrolled them in a school near Tarrytown. At first she had planned on putting them in a school in Manhattan, but considering Kiki's present mood, it was not the best of ideas. The Ruddy School would be near enough for her to see them often, and for her mother to visit them, too.

Angel came back from her lunch date with Myles Porter and found Kiki sitting in the living room, drinking, still in her dressing gown. 'What have you been up to?' Kiki asked.

She was reluctant to tell Kiki her good news while she was so obviously depressed, but there really wasn't any way to avoid it. 'I've been out to lunch with Myles Porter. He's asked me to do *The Little Foxes* and I've accepted. It will be a real change of pace for me . . . an exciting challenge. I—' She was stopped in mid-sentence by the look on Kiki's face. It was almost . . . menacing.

'I've been after that part for weeks.'

Angel was appalled. 'But I had no idea. Myles didn't say.'

'Maybe Myles didn't know it, but I doubt it. *I* was working on Thornton White, the money man. Obviously, times have changed' – Kiki smiled, her mouth twisted – 'and it's not whom you sleep with these days that counts. Or have you been sleeping with Myles?'

Angel was beside herself. 'Of course not! Today was the first time I've seen him in years. Kiki, why didn't you say something? I didn't know you wanted that role. If you had, I never, not in a million years, would have agreed to— Wait a moment, I'm going to insist you play in it too. I'll—'

Kiki laughed drunkenly. 'What part would you have me play? The teenage daughter? *Your* teenage daughter? No, of course not. I know – Birdie, the old broken-down lush. Is that the part you had in mind for me?'

'Oh, Kiki, of course not. I wasn't thinking. Well, I won't do the show at all. I'll call Myles and tell him I've changed my mind.'

'Don't bother. After *you*, why would they settle for me? *I'm* not a big star. Besides, I really don't want your charity.' Kiki smirked. 'Who knows? Maybe you'll win the Tony. With a Goody Two Shoes like you playing a character like Regina, a lady with balls, *anything* can happen. Anyway, I've been sitting here thinking. I'm going to head out for the Coast. Maybe my luck will

452

change out there. Maybe somebody will offer me a porno. After all, Hollywood is still Hollywood, and Italy isn't the only place for dirty pictures, is it?'

Kiki wasn't sure whom she was trying to wound – Angel or herself.

'Don't do this to yourself, Kiki. Things are bound to change. You know they always do.'

'Ah! But they don't always change for the better. Of course, *for you* they do.'

Angel said nothing more; Kiki's bitterness toward her, while understandable, was hard to take. She was glad that Kiki was going out to the Coast for a while.

'Will you be staying at Mother's house?'

'Don't be ridiculous,' Kiki answered. 'Rory and Brad are still living in my lovely house on Rodeo, aren't they? Why would I stay anywhere else?'

Well, Angel reflected, everything wasn't *all* that bad. If Kiki was still scheming, she wasn't completely down for the count.

3

Angel went into rehearsal for *The Little Foxes*, and Kiki stayed away for almost two months. She was back after the holidays.

'Did something go wrong, Kiki? When you didn't come back right away and I stopped hearing from you, I assumed that everything was going swimmingly . . . that maybe you and Brad were . . .'

'Well, for starters, not soon after I moved into my house, Brad sold it right out from under me. Imagine! He traded that lovely house that I had decorated and practically rebuilt for a fucking ranch in Malibu. Now the big hero is going to raise horses. And he has Rory, my absolutely gorgeous, doll-like daughter, decked out in jeans and plaid shirts.'

Angel frowned. 'What's so terrible about Malibu? And

what kind of a reason—?'

'We're not talking about an estate on the water, like Sara Gold Ross's. Now *she* has a Southern mansion, for God's sake, that looks like something out of *Gone with the Wind*. Brad's ranch is in the hills.'

'So what? Don't you know yet that you can be as happy on a ranch as in a fancy house in Beverly Hills? And Rory's not a little girl anymore.'

'Wait. You haven't heard the worst of it. Brad's changed toward me. He's not sure he can put his trust in me, he says. What the son of a bitch won't say is that he no longer lusts for my body. I'm no longer in my prime, after all.'

'You talk more nonsense, Kiki. It sounds to me as if Brad was saying that he had been hurt and wanted to take his time . . . to be sure about you . . .'

'How the hell do you know what he was implying? Were you there, for Christ's sake?'

'Why didn't you stay out there a while longer? Rory's future is at stake here too.'

'Rory is her father's daughter. She prefers him to me.'

'You didn't ask her to make a choice, I hope. Of course, *now* she would choose Brad. He's been with her, while you—'

'Shut up! Do you hear? Just shut up! You don't know what the hell you're talking about. I'm not going to sit around waiting for that bastard to make up his mind about me. Not Kiki Devlin! Nor will I suck up to some snotty little kid who has to ask her daddy's permission before she decides to love her mother. Goddammit! She's supposed to love me, not wait to be told!'

'You have to give both of them time. Look, my own Dickie and Timmie are still miffed at me for leaving them here in school all the time I was married to Zev. And frankly, I don't blame them. We have to be there for our children – earn their love.'

'Oh, is that so? And when do they earn the love we give them?'

'Now you're being plain silly. You're hurt. I know. Give it all time.'

A few days later Angel found Kiki playing with what appeared to be two rag dolls. 'Those look like the homemade dolls we played with when we were little. Where'd you get them?'

Kiki smiled a bit sheepishly. 'I made them myself.' She held one up. It was made of some kind of white sheeting, stuffed, with a painted face and yarn hair, and crudely sewn clothes. The doll had black hair and a black mustache.

'Who did you make them for?' Angel asked, puzzled.

'Ninny, don't you recognize my handsome ex, Vic Rosa? And this one?' She shook the other doll. It had yellow wool hair and blue circles for eyes.

'Brad!'

'Give the lady a box of Crackerjacks,' Kiki cried. 'And here is my little box of pins. See?' She opened the box, withdrew one, and plunged it into the Vic doll's hand.

Angel laughed uncertainly. 'Now you've done it, Kiki! You've gone stark, raving mad!'

'I know there's some kind of mumbo-jumbo I'm supposed to recite, so I'm making up my own incantations. It's fun. Do you want me to make a doll for you to stick pins in? Dick's gone, as is old Zev. But how about Nick Dominguez?'

Angel turned on her heel and walked out.

Two days later Kiki phoned Rome and talked to Nikki. After she hung up, she hunted Angel down in the bathtub. She was almost hysterical with laughter. 'Guess what? Nikki said her father went skiing just yesterday and – get this—'

'Don't tell me he broke something?'

Kiki was laughing so hard she could hardly get the words out. 'He broke his arm! What do you think about that?'

Angel gasped.

'Oh, God!' Kiki wiped away the tears from her eyes. 'I haven't had such a good laugh in I don't know when. Well, since I've been so successful with my first venture, I think I'll go to work on my Brad doll.'

Angel gasped again. 'Oh, Kiki, no! Not Brad!' she pleaded.

Kiki laughed. 'Oh, my goodness, I've really made a believer out of you.' Then she sobered. 'No, Angel, not Brad. Not Brad.'

It was with relief that Angel found both rag dolls in Kiki's wastebasket the next day. But she wondered. Had Kiki thrown them away because she was tired of the childish game, or was she really a believer who had frightened even herself?

4

Kiki did not attend the opening of *The Little Foxes*. She was working on a movie, an underground movie that her new friend Andy was filming. Angel had argued with Kiki fiercely.

'What do you expect to get out of this, Kiki? It won't do a thing for your career. Don't you know that?'

'It's publicity, isn't it?'

'But it's the wrong kind.'

'It will enhance my reputation.'

'With whom? Where?'

'At the discotheques, darling. We all can't do Regina in the *theatuh*, so we do the best we can.'

Angel looked at Kiki in her black tights and green sequined mini-dress, her white-painted face with electric-blue eyelids – the eye shadow extending in wide arcs into her hairline – and wondered what their mother would think of Kiki in her new incarnation.

'But must you work tonight, Kiki?'

'We *always* film at night.'

'But couldn't you skip tonight, just this once, so that you can be there at my opening?'

'No, I can't. Alan says the moon is right tonight. And everyone will be angry if I put *your* play before their movie. But don't worry – you'll have all your hundreds of friends and supporters and admirers and fans around you, I'm sure.'

'But I won't have any family, Kiki. And you know what that means to me.'

'Well, you could have brought Tim and Dickie down, couldn't you?'

'They're coming Saturday night with Mother. I didn't want to interfere with their school schedule.'

'Oh, I see!' Kiki smiled sweetly. 'We can't interfere with the boys' school schedule but we *may* interfere with Kiki's filming schedule. You're getting mighty selfish, *Regina*. But don't feel too bad. Maybe old Nicky will show up to take your picture. Or then again, maybe he won't . . .'

Opening night and she was nervous, tense, almost sick to her stomach. But she received a reassuring ovation upon her entrance on-stage, and took seven curtain calls before she ran back to her dressing room to see who had come backstage to visit. But it was not Nick, whom she had rather expected, but Johnny Dunham, and it was Johnny who escorted her to the opening-night party at Sardi's.

5

Angel found John Dunham's presence at the party reassuring. He was a familiar figure out of her past, a thoroughly nice man who had befriended her during a dark period of her life.

The reviews that night were excellent, and it seemed

457

to be the consensus that Angela du Beaumond could do a creditable job on the stage as well as on the silver screen, where her beauty and glamour counted for so much more.

After that evening, John escorted her everywhere: to private parties, supper clubs, to the April in Paris Ball at the Waldorf, and, when her schedule permitted, to the opera and to other plays. They didn't make love, but only because John didn't initiate it, for Angel had made up her mind that when he did, she would be receptive.

She had not heard from Nick Dominguez and she was hurt. He could at least have called to congratulate her on her success in the play, or come to see her in it. She didn't know what to think anymore. Had her marriage to Zev cancelled out whatever feelings he had for her? Or did he think, now that she was a star, that he certainly wasn't good enough for her? It was really time, she told herself, to put him out of her mind, since it was clear he was not a real presence in her life. She should forget him, as she had her father.

She was ready for a real affair, a flesh-and-blood one. She had known only two men, and had felt love for just one, for a brief while only. She didn't think she was in love with John. She didn't feel the rapture that she had felt for Dick in the beginning, but she had been hardly out of her teens then, and rapture was for the young. She didn't think of him constantly, as she had Nick Dominguez. But at least he was real and not a romantic dream. And he was a suitable suitor – one could even say a *desirable* suitor. Even her mother approved of John, and even Kiki didn't have anything *bad* to say about him, except that one could really hope for a bit more pizazz.

When John asked her to go away for a couple of days, she said yes.

'My friend has a cottage upstate. It's called Moon Lake. How does that sound to you?'

'Romantic,' she said. 'Cold but romantic.'

'I'll keep you warm.'

She was delighted. Wasn't that what eighteen-year-

ld boys said when you complained you were cold? It was
like being young again. 'When will we leave?'

'Right after your performance Saturday night. That
way we can have Sunday and all day Monday.'

'There are horses here too! You didn't tell me that! I'm so
excited. I haven't ridden in ages. How good of you to plan
his surprise.'

'That was the general idea. To show you how good I
was.'

'When can we ride?'

'Well, it's about two in the morning. Do you think you
can wait until tomorrow?'

She laughed. 'I think so.'

They went inside the cabin. It was rustic but
comfortable, with a fur rug in front of the fireplace and
deep sofas, and there was a fire burning in the hearth.

'Who lit the fire?'

'There's a couple who take care of the house and the
horses, but they don't stay here.' He took both of her
hands, kissed first one, then the other, and drew her
over to the fireplace.

She stretched out on the rug. 'Nice,' she said.

The room was shrouded in shadows illuminated only
by firelight. He brought her a snifter of brandy, and they
sipped and kissed. Warm, and heady with the brandy,
Angel said, 'My sister would say this was a very shmaltzy
scene.'

He leaned over her. 'But what does Angel say?'

'Angel says lovely. Lovely, lovely, lovely . . .' And it
was.

Gently he undressed her, then himself. Gently,
slowly, exquisitely, he made love to her. His flesh
yielding to hers, hers yielding to his. Loving, yielding,
giving, receiving. After, John said the classic, 'I love you,'
and she said, 'Thank you.'

'I guess now is the time then when I ask you to marry
me so that we can live happily ever after.'

She had thought that perhaps he *would* say, 'I love

459

you,' but she was unprepared for a proposal of marriag
so soon. Unprepared, not ready.

'I wish that I could say yes.'

'Why can't you?'

'I guess that I'm not ready, John. And I'm not su
when I will be. I'm not even sure that I ever will.' She w
filled with sadness. Oh, how she had loved his phrase '
that we can live happily ever after.'

'But I felt love emanating from you—'

'Oh yes, I am not without love for you. But I dor
think it's the right kind of love, you see . . .'

She *knew* that it wasn't – it was not the kind of love sh
had dreamed about all her life.

Later, she thought often about what she had said
John. Many times afterward she asked herself why sh
hadn't said yes. It would have been so easy, and life wi
John would have been good. Not perfect, but good. Wh
not perfect? she asked herself, and had no answer. W
she, too, like Kiki, unable to find complete satisfaction
anything, in any person? Was it that they were both st
looking over their shoulders? Were there still too ma
ghosts in their lives?

She wanted to remain friends with John, wanted the
to be lovers, but he could not accept less than a on
hundred-percent commitment, and she could not fau
him for that. She had accepted less than one hundr
percent in her relationships and it had left her with
very bitter feeling in her soul, a bitter taste on t
tongue.

6

Kiki's underground film was released, and it was n
that it didn't get good reviews – it was as if no one saw t
picture at all. No one whom Kiki found relevar
anyway. And there were *no* reviews. Not in a

460

publication of consequence. There were some in underground newspapers and magazines and in subsidized avant-garde magazines publications that admired Warhol, but for the most part the movie disappeared without making even a tiny ripple. As far as the public was concerned, the antics of that whole gang were far more interesting to read about than to watch.

'Just one more fiasco in the lives and loves of Kiki Devlin,' Kiki said, hanging away the sequined minis and tossing the tights into the trash. 'So what else is new?'

She stopped going to the Factory where the action didn't start until midnight. 'It better behooves a girl to think about her beauty sleep,' she announced, and for a while she cut down on her drinking. Then she announced, 'I think I'll go to Europe. It really is time for a face job. Thirty-five is really the dividing line when middle age begins and we're both *over* thirty-five,' she said, obviously very nervous, drumming her fingers on the coffee table. 'Come with me, Angel.'

'I can't now. But if you wait until *Foxes* is over, I'll keep you company.'

'No, I can't wait. I have to go now.'

There was an urgency in Kiki's voice and Angel wondered what caused it.

'While I'm in Europe I might as well go see Nikki.'

'Of course. Nikki. Why didn't you just say you wanted to see Nikki and not give me all this nonsense about face lifts.'

'I can do both, can't I?' Kiki asked, smoking a cigarette, and trying to still the trembling of her hands.

Angel picked Kiki up at LaGuardia in a rented limousine. The face lift was barely discernible and her mood seemed only slightly elevated.

'Did you ever feel like excess baggage?' Kiki demanded.

'I'm sure. But how do *you* mean?'

'Well, first there was Vic. He wasn't interested in even a friendly little screw. He lit out for San Remo

practically the moment I arrived, leaving me alone wit
Dr Frankenstein.'

'And who's Dr Frankenstein?'

'My eleven-year-old daughter, Nikki. She has a littl
laboratory where she conducts experiments. Frankly,
was afraid to ask what kind. I was scared she migh
decide I should be her next guinea pig. God! What a ki
What a brain! She spoke to me condescendingly in a
English a Harvard professor would envy. We went t
restaurants and she did all the ordering because sh
didn't trust *my* Italian. If anyone looked at us, she ducke
her head – her American not-too-bright mother bein
such an embarrassment. We went shopping, and when
ever I picked out something for her or for myself sh
rolled her eyes to heaven. *She* made all the final choices

'She sounds adorable. Why can't you admit you ha
the time of your life with her?'

'Yes. It was kind of fun. If you don't mind bein
tolerated.' Kiki laughed.

'And it sounds like she enjoyed you. You're lucky, Kik
that she doesn't resent you.'

'Resent me? Why the hell should she? What did *I* do?
was her father who kicked *me* out. I like that – resent me
Who the hell does she think she is anyway? That littl
snip!' She smiled, shaking her head.

She looked out the window at the city street
'Everything looks gray and depressing, doesn't it? Go
I'd like to go back to California. I wasn't depresse
there . . . was I?'

'Sometimes. Just sometimes.'

'Well, tell me, what does the star have on the agenda
What are *you* going to do next now that you're out c
Foxes?'

'I've been asked to do *A Doll's House.*'

'On the stage?'

'Yes.'

'And? Are you going to do it?'

'Kiki, if you want to go back to California, I won't do i
We'll both go back.'

Kiki put her hand on Angel's. 'That's good of you, sis. You are good, you really are. But I'm not ready for Hollywood. Not yet.'

She looked out the window again. 'God, it's so gray out there. You know, drugs can take care of that little problem. Gray depression. I don't even know why I even went to that sanitarium in Switzerland to break the habit. Did you know that was the reason – the real reason I went?'

'I think maybe I guessed that. I suppose I didn't want to face it. That was cowardly of me. I might have helped, Anyhow, I think it was courageous of you to face your problem and do something about it, all by yourself.'

'Shit! Now I'm not at all sure that I'd rather be off the stuff. I don't know if I really want to see the world without those rosy-coloured glasses.'

'Oh, Kiki! Things will be better.'

'For you they'll be better. For me? We'll see . . .'

'Kiki, we're not even forty. Life isn't over . . .'

Kiki smiled. 'You want to bet? Hey, you haven't even noticed my lift.' She posed in profile. 'What do you think?'

'I noticed. It was just the green-eyed monster that kept me from saying anything. Why, you've lost twenty years!'

Kiki howled with laughter. 'That would make me jailbait. Even my sweetie-pie sister wouldn't dare to go that far. Do you mean to say I look sweet sixteen?'

'Sweet sixteen!'

'And boy, have I ever been kissed!'

If only there was some way I could find for us both to go forward. All it should take is a big hop, skip, and a jump! why does it all have to be so complicated?

7

When finally the offer came from television's *Night at the*

463

Theater, Kiki never knew it was Angel who had instigated the whole thing, that Angel had bartered with the executive producer, Tom Hopper: give Kiki the part of Patricia in the original teleplay *Golden Evening* and Angel would consent to do *A Doll's House* for them after she did it on the stage.

Kiki made a big fuss over whether to accept the offer, but Angel could see that she was delighted.

'Well, I don't know if I should do it. Patricia is rather a shallow character, don't you think?'

'It's up to you to give her more depth by shading your performance. If anybody can do it, you can. You know the scene where the mother dies and Patricia talks about how her mother's hacking cough was always so irritating? Well, you can show there that although her words seem uncaring, how affected she really is underneath.'

'Yes, I suppose . . . I suppose that's the tack to take – that she's a shallow person on the surface, but underneath – well, still waters run deep. I only wish that Hurd Phillips wasn't directing. He's such a jerk.'

'Not really. He won an Emmy for *Take the Shortcut.*'

'I don't remember that.'

'Well, he did.'

'I don't know. Maybe it's a comedown to do television after the stage and features.'

'Everyone's doing it, Kiki.'

'I don't know. Most people start *out* in television these days, then move on to features. George Scott . . . Reynolds. Even some of the people on the soaps.'

'Well, good. You'll do so well in *Golden Evening* that they'll be begging you to do features again.'

'I suppose it *could* happen.'

'Of course it could.'

There was trouble right from the start. The whole production, from start to finish, was supposed to take only three weeks. Kiki immediately balked and was told 'This is television, this is how we work.' There were no

464

star dressing rooms, no special treatment, no acquiescence to temperament, or to complaints of how many of the best lines went to this one or that one. There was no special hairdresser or make up artist assigned to Miss Devlin. And finally someone sneered, 'Maybe that's the way they work on Mr Rinaldi's sets in Italy, but we don't do things that way here.'

The day following the airing of *Golden Evening* some television critics reviewed it, and some covered *A Special Evening with Fred Astaire* instead. That was the way television was covered. Space *was* limited. Mr Phillips's direction was praised, and everyone agreed that Kiki Devlin was still a treat for the eyes, even though she seemed to be miscast.

Kiki brooded for a day or two, then decided it was time for her to visit the West Coast again. An old friend (he *had* been a friend in better days, anyway) had been made a vice-president of production at Columbia and what did she have to lose? Besides, she wanted to see what Brad and Rory were up to.

'That sounds like a good idea,' Angel said. 'When will you leave?'

'Oh, in a couple of weeks, I guess. Anxious to be rid of me?'

'Oh sure. I wish you were leaving tomorrow.'

In retrospect, Angel would wish that it had been so.

8

Kiki said she wanted to attend Truman Capote's masked ball before leaving for Hollywood. She couldn't miss that. It was going to be the party of the year.

Angel wasn't sure she wanted to attend, but Kiki insisted. 'You've hardly left the house since you broke off with Johnny. You may be Saint Angela, but you're not a nun yet, for God's sake. You have to start seeing people again. Didn't anyone ever tell you that if you don't use it, it petrifies?'

There were more than five hundred people at the Black-and-White dance at the Plaza, and everyone was in a costume that was either black or white or both. There was a large contingent from the West Coast. Exactly who it was of that Hollywood group – Frank and Mia, or the Fondas, or the Vincent Minnellis, or the Matthaus – who told Kiki that Brad had a young ladyfriend, a very young ladyfriend, she didn't recall later. It didn't matter. She was consumed with anxiety, and then anger. She was going to go out to the Coast as soon as she could get on a plane, and she was going to tear *somebody's* hair out. In the meantime, she got drunk the better to bear it.

The rest of the evening was mostly a blur to Kiki. Did J. K. Galbraith really dance around with a candelabra in his arms? Did Mia do a practically nonstop twist all night? And had she herself danced with Bill Buckley? She thought that she had, but did Buckley *really* rock and roll? Had the Secret Service men really searched all night for Lynda Bird Johnson's lost mask? She thought she remembered drinking Taitinger champagne, oodles and oodles of it, and eating sherried chicken hash and spaghetti Bolognaise. But of one thing she was absolutely certain – she saw her sister Angel sitting at a table with Norman Mailer, Philip Roth, and Arthur Schlesinger, and yet deep in conversation with Nick Dominguez! She couldn't believe it! Everyone after her, everyone making a tremendous fuss over her, and she sat staring like a lovesick dove into Dominguez's eyes. Well, she was going to fly to Los Angeles tomorrow, but before she did, she was going to take care of Dominguez once and for all!

Kiki never went home that night. When she woke up the next morning in a hotel room next to an unknown young and pretty boy, she didn't even stop to ascertain who he was. It wasn't until she donned her costume of the night before, a black twenties gown embroidered in white beads, and went down to the lobby that she discovered that she was at the Waldorf. She remembered that she had to fly to California that day, but first she had something else to do – *she had to go see Nick Dominguez!* She knew his New York studio was at Fiftieth and Madison, and somebody had told her that his private quarters were upstairs above the studio and gallery. Why, she had spent the night practically on top of him! Or was it her sister who had done that? That stupid, naïve Angel! She had to save her from herself; she had to keep Angel from making another mistake.

It was early and the gallery was empty. Kiki asked the receptionist to see Mr Dominguez. The receptionist stared at her . . . as if she were some kind of an eccentric, just because of the way she was dressed. Hadn't the little ass ever seen someone in a party dress before? Didn't the little ass know to whom she was talking? *And you don't mess with Kiki Devlin, my little friend.*

Kiki smoothed her bouffant hairdo with one hand as best she could – she had forgotten to brush it before she left the hotel room.

'I'm sorry, madam, Mr Dominguez is not in at present. Would you like to call back later in the day? Or would you like to leave your card?'

'Do I look as if I have a card on me?'

'I'm sure I don't know. Here—' The young lady shoved a pad at her. 'Why don't you leave your phone number and I'll be sure to give it to Mr Dominguez as soon as he comes in.' And she rose and excused herself, going into one of the back rooms.

Kiki had spied the black wrought-iron spiral staircase to one side of the gallery as soon as she had come in. Now, congratulating herself on her cunning, she called out toward the back room, 'Thank you. I'll stop by later in the day,' and, removing her pumps, ran up the staircase.

It was dark upstairs. Trying to adjust to the dimness, Kiki made out two rooms. The room in which she was standing was a living room she supposed, or a study. The room beyond it, a bedroom. Was he sleeping there, curtains tightly drawn against the light? Was Angel in there with him? Should she barge in, pull back the covers, denounce Angel for a fool, and him for a slimy, filthy mole unworthy to see the light of day? Men! They were all unworthy, the lot of them, starting with Rory Devlin . . . and then Edward Whittier . . . Power and Mizrachi . . . Vic Rosa and Brad Cranford . . . especially Brad Cranford and Nick Dominguez!

She groped for a light switch, found one. The sudden light blinded her for a moment and her head whirled. The room was minimally furnished: a white couch, white chairs, black pillows, and all around her, *Angel* – pictures of Angel in all sizes and forms. Black-and-whites, huge ones on white lacquered walls, the most beautiful photographs she had ever seen! The pictures were all radiance and shadows, daggers of light, darks of razor-blade sharpness cutting across the brilliance of a white cheek, tonal graduations, a black cloud of hair, a sinous white-satin-sheathed body carved out of a background of ebony. They were more than art – they were poetry . . . odes. Where, when, had he taken these pictures? Could such beauty be fashioned from snips and pieces and bits of candid photos taken while the subject was unaware? Could they have been fashioned without the subject in the flesh before him? Of what magic was he capable in his darkroom? What miracles could he work? What had possession wrought? For surely he was possessed. This room was an altar to a goddess.

First came the terror. Was Angel safe in a world where a maniac stalked? A madman possessed with her image?

Then there was anger, contempt. How dare he? This upstart from the East Bronx, up from the sleazy depths of slimy publications – how dared he aspire to her sister a du Beaumond, a Manard, a Devlin?

468

And then the terror, the anger, and the contempt subsided and the *why* of it became imperative. *Why* had Dominguez chosen her sister as the object of his monomania, his *idée fixe*? And as the grandeur of this passion infused her, the excitement growled deep within her.

She ran into the bedroom but it was *empty*. Disappointment coursed through her. Here too, in this chamber of monastic simplicity, were more photographs. And then she heard the outer door open and close, and she swung around to face him. There was no inkling of surprise on his face, not even alarm that she had penetrated his alter. Not anger. He didn't speak, just nodded toward the door, indicating that she should get out.

Her anger rose again, fired by his lack of anger, an anger the situation demanded. Without anger, she was only something beneath contempt. He insulted her by not speaking, as if she were some low creature who didn't deserve words. He infuriated her by his lack of interest. What would he have done, this man who fashioned gods from paper, silver nitrate and black and white, if he found her sister here instead of her? Would he have crawled to her on hands and knees and kissed the hem of her gown?

The rage engulfed her, threatening to drown her. And then along with the rage came desire – naked, raw lust – and she didn't know how to refuse desire; she never had.

She stripped herself of her twenties dress now, let it drop to the floor, black lace bra discarded, silken panties thrown aside. But Nick Dominguez's eyes were not on her body, but only on her face, his dark eyes boring into hers. What were they saying, those eyes? She could not read them.

She sank to her knees and came to him, standing there in the doorway between the living room and the bedroom. She buried her face in his groin, mouth groping through the material of his trousers, but his hand came down on her head and pushed her away, not hard. Still, she lost her balance and fell backward. Before he turned and went out the door she felt his gaze. Was it disdain? Compassion? Damn him to eternity!

She remained on her knees staring at the closed door for a minute or two. Then she donned her clothes almost as quickly as she had discarded them and fled down the spiral staircase and out the gallery's front door.

She hurried home. She had to fly out of New York today and she had to warn Angel about Dominguez. There was no telling what the man might do. A man so possessed might go beserk at any time. She ran through the first floor of her house calling out her sister's name, and Angel came out into the upstairs hall. 'Kiki, I'm up here. What's wrong?'

Kiki started to run up the stairs but faltered as if unable to go on. Angel ran down and helped her the rest of the way. 'Kiki, what is it? Where did you go after the ball last night? Are you ill?'

'I've been to see him – your Nick Dominguez!'

'But why? We settled everything between us last night.'

'I went to see him to tell him to stay away from you.'

'But why did you want to interfere? What *right* did you have to interfere? How dared you?'

'Because he's not right for you. And I saw the two of you together last night. You were looking at him as if he were the second coming.'

'What business is it of yours? Who are you to judge?'

'I'll tell you what business it is of mine. I've seen you make a mess of your life with two men, two wrong choices. You are so besotted with him you don't know what you're doing!'

Angel tried to speak, but Kiki yelled over her, beside herself with fury. 'I had to help you out of one mess, didn't I? And now you want this . . . this . . . crazy man . . . with his mania! He's not for you! You're Angela du Beaumond, Angel Devlin, and he's a nobody!

He's less than a nobody! He's a third-rater just like your—'

'Oh, Kiki, he loves me the way no one has ever loved me. Not Dick, not Zev, not anybody. He adores me, don't you see? Oh, Kiki, isn't it every woman's dream to be placed on a pedestal? He loves me beyond anything I ever dreamed of. And, Kiki, I want that love! I yearn for it, oh, how I yearn! I will have it!'

'Oh, you think *you* can have everything, don't you? Stardom. Romance. But you can't! You can't have *everything!*'

'*Oh Kiki,*' Angel whispered. 'Do you really think I've *had* everything? You, of all people, can you say that to me?'

'Oh, yes, you want *everything*. Everything that I've ever had! First it was Daddy. You tried to take him away from me. And then, when he was gone, it was Mother. You *always* had to come first with her, too. Then I went on the stage and you made sure to best me there. And then I became a movie star but you became an even bigger one. And him! You just want him because he reminds you of your father. Well, *you* can't have him! And you said it yourself: you *can't* fuck your father!'

'Kiki!' Angel grabbed her by the shoulders. 'Kiki! What happened there?'

Kiki's rage seemed to have dissipated itself, and she stood listlessly now, averting her face from Angel.

'What, Kiki?' Angel's voice rose. 'What happened?'

'Nothing. Nothing happened, for God's sake. We hardly spoke.' She still wouldn't look at Angel.

Angel, still holding her by the shoulders, shook her sister. 'You look at me, Kiki!'

'I was upstairs . . . in his living quarters. And it was sick. Pictures of you everywhere . . . blow-ups . . . it was sick!'

'What did you do, Kiki? What happened between the two of you? What did you do, Kiki?' Angel screamed.

'What do you think I did? What do you think happened? Are you afraid that *I* fucked your precious Nick?' She shook herself loose from Angel's grip.

Angel looked at her dully, still not sure what

471

happened between them. 'I think I would like to kill you . . .'

'Oh, don't be a fool! You've always been a fool, always, always. I told him to stay away from you. I told him it was a matter of class – that a woman like you could have nothing to do with a man like him. And I meant it, no matter what. I acted in your best interests—'

'I don't believe you. I don't believe you, and I don't think I'm ever going to want to talk to you again. When you come back from California I won't be here, Kiki . . . not ever again.'

True to her word, Angel moved out of Kiki's house into her own apartment. She didn't know what to believe. Had something happened between Nick and Kiki? Or had Kiki just told him to stay away from her, as she had said? She wanted to go to him and ask him, but she couldn't bring herself to do that. Why didn't he come to her, reassure her, tell her that he loved her? Was his silence indicative? Or was it that he had taken Kiki's words to heart, believed too that he wasn't good enough for her? She would wait and see. She would be patient. But then she wondered – if Nick came and told her an ugly story about Kiki, whom then would she believe? Perhaps she really didn't want to hear the truth.

She counted the months as they passed. One month . . . two months . . . three months . . . Still, she had not heard from Nick, and not from Kiki, either . .

9

Angel found her mother in the solarium, staring through the expansive glass windows at the day-old snow. 'How about some lights in here?' Angel asked, snapping on a table lamp.

'Angel! You startled me. Did you drive up here all b

472

yourself with that snow on the ground?'

'No, I didn't drive. I took the train this morning to see the boys. Then I cabbed over here. Why were you sitting in the dark?'

Marie smiled. 'I hadn't even realized it had gotten dark. It wasn't when I came in here about an hour ago. So you took the train up? Weren't you recognized? Mobbed?'

Angel shook her head, laughed. 'For one thing, I wore this hat – my Greta Garbo hat – and my dark glasses. And the train was almost empty. Besides, I've been on *the stage* of late. It's not exactly the same exposure one gets in the movies. What were you doing, Mother? Just sitting there and looking out at the snow?'

'Yes. I was thinking of the angels you girls used to make in the freshly fallen snow – how delicate they were.'

'How is Edward?'

'The same. Always the same.'

'I don't understand why you don't take him to Florida or California. You seem depressed, Mother. A little sun would cheer you up.'

'Edward likes it best here.'

'And you, Mother?'

'I don't like Stoningham in the winter as I used to. Perhaps I've really outgrown Stoningham.'

'So why don't you just leave?'

'Just like that? Walk out on Edward?'

'No, Mother, not walk out on him. Put him in a nursing home, where he can probably get better attention than here. He is, to all extent and purposes, out of it, Mother. It wouldn't be an abandonment, you know.'

'It still would be . . . rather. This is Edward's home. He loves it here. Even if he is, as you say, out of it, I'm sure it still gives him a sense of security and sustenance.'

'But what about you, Mother? You've been tied here for the last couple of years almost like a prisoner. It's not fair. You're still a young woman. Why, look at your

473

hair – it's still the same color as Kiki's.'

Marie laughed. 'Shame on you, Angel, for being such a *naïf*. And you an actress. My hair has been colored once a month for a long time now.' Then she became serious. 'I'm paying back a debt, Angel. I will be sixty this year, past the time for dreams and desires ... but I do have my pride and my honor. A lady of pride always pays her debts.'

'What do you possibly owe Edward that you haven't paid for, over and over again?'

'When I married Edward we made a bargain. He would give me what I needed; I would give him what he wanted. I never really did. I never loved him, but when I married him I led him to believe that I did. That was false – as false as— No matter, now. But still, Edward did keep his side of the bargain – gave me all sorts of things I contracted for. So now I must pay him back, give him comfort and sustenance and faithfulness. It's that simple.'

No, Mother, not as simple as that.

A scene flashed through her mind: that early summer afternoon ... Kiki kneeling at Edward's chair ... Where did that scene balance out? on which side of the ledger? Where was *his* faithfulness?

But now, twenty years later, wasn't the time to speak of this. There had been so much bitterness in their lives – enough bitterness already for all their years.

'And you're just going to sit here, year after year?'

'Yes. I think so. Until my debt is fully paid. Or until it's impossible for me to care for Edward any longer. You see, Angel, I'm also repaying another debt too. There was a bedside at which I should have kept vigil and didn't. Any which way, you make it sound so awful.' Marie tried to laugh. 'It's hardly that. This *isn't* a prison. And I've had more than a lot of people have, you know.'

'Material things! You never had—'

'Love? But I had my love for you and Kiki and Eddie. And the kind of love you're talking about ... well, I had that for a little while too. You see, *I* felt it, even if your father didn't . . . Besides, not everyone is meant to have a *great* love, Angel. Not everyone can handle that kind of love. Can you? Do you have everything you want, Angel?'

Such a straightforward question. It deserved a straightforward answer.

'No, not everything, Mother. There's somebody I think I want very much, but I don't think you'd approve.'

'Is that what's keeping you from this man, *my approval?*'

'No. Not just that. Not exactly. It's more complicated than that.'

'Is this love . . . this man . . . is it Nick Dominguez?'

'But how did you know?'

'It was a guess. But I had a clue here and there.'

'So you see, Mother, you *don't* approve. You've always talked about suitable matches. Well, I suppose no one would call Nick Dominguez suitable. Certainly not Kiki.'

'Kiki? Is Kiki mixed up in this?'

Angel sighed. 'I'm afraid she is. Kiki told me he was unsuitable. That he was crazy, sick – just because he worshipped me from afar.' She gave a little laugh at the words.

'Ah! how romantic! To be worshipped from afar. I remember thinking that about your father. That he worshipped me from afar before he ever met me. But I was wrong.'

'At this point, Mother, I would much rather be worshipped face-to-face.'

'I would think so. So that's the problem then. Kiki. Because she thinks he is unsuitable.'

'Partly. Kiki's always implied that I was drawn to him because he resembles my father.'

'Does he?'

'That's right. You've never actually seen him, except that one time at Kiki's coming out party, and that's a long time ago. He does, somewhat, physically. I don't think in any other way. But how would I know? I don't know anything about my father except for some silly

475

childhood memories that probably aren't accurate,' she said with self-derision.

'So he looks something like your father? Then he must be very handsome. Your father was the most beautiful man I've ever seen, to this day. I've always thought you married Dick because he was so *unlike* your father, physically and in all other ways.'

'That's what Kiki said too.'

'But I think it was because subconsciously you realize that your father was not a man to be counted on – for security, for stability – so you thought if you married someone unlike your father, well then, presto: security, stability. But your marriage certainly didn't give you happiness, did it?'

'So what are you saying, Mother?' she asked impatiently.

'All I'm saying is that the looks of the thing don't matter. What matters is if *inside him* he's the man that you want, that you need. That's the test of the man, isn't it?'

'Mother, are you saying you *do* approve?'

'Angel, soon you'll be forty. And any month now I'll be sixty. You've had a terrible time of it. Two godawful marriages. And you sit there and tell me that you love this man and he loves you – worships you – and you think I'm going to tell you to sit around another twenty years and wait for someone with a better background? I remember saying to you years ago that what I wanted for you was a sweet, sensitive man – a poet. Dammit, Angel, is this man a poet?'

'Oh, yes, Mother! I think he is!'

'Well then, Kiki was right about you. You *are* a ninny! And you must think me a bigger one than you.' And she blew her nose into a tissue.

The world *was* coming to an end, Angel thought. Her mother had just put her stamp of approval on Nick and for the first time in her life was using a tissue instead of a linen or lace handkerchief.

'Shall we get ready for dinner, Angel, or is there anything else that should be discussed?'

'Yes Mother. I'm afraid there is. You see, Kiki and I went to Truman Capote's ball the night before she left for California. And I saw Nick there and I thought that after that evening we would . . . But something happened, something terrible happened after that – the next morning, when Kiki went to see him to tell him to stay away from me.'

Marie closed her eyes wearily. 'What did Kiki do?'

'I'm not sure but I think I know . . . I *feel* it.'

'Didn't you speak to Nick about it? Ask him what happened?' Marie's voice was harsh now.

'No. I couldn't. And I never heard from him again. His silence convinces me that—'

'Perhaps he was waiting for you to come to him, Angel . . . to demonstrate your faith in him . . . your belief.'

'I couldn't do that, Mother. You see, I didn't believe Kiki when she said nothing happened. But at the same time if I went to see Nick, took his word over hers – why, that would be to deny *her*, my own sister, my own Kiki. I couldn't do that even if I can't forgive her.'

'Haven't the years taught you anything, Angel? To believe in somebody else is not to deny Kiki. Of course Kiki has faults, many, many faults . . . she's a troubled woman. But she has many wonderful qualities too. We have to accept her faults and forgive her. She's not completely responsible. It's been hard on her. It was very hard for her without her father. She loved him so.'

Angel sat up. 'I know it was hard for her, Mother. It was hard for me too!'

'No, not *as* hard. Kiki was never as strong as you.'

Angel stared at her mother unbelievingly. 'But I always thought of Kiki as the strong one, Mother. She *was* . . . for me.'

Marie shook her head.

'It's *his* fault, Mother. If only he had come to see us when we were young, then we wouldn't have fantasized about him so. But we both yearned for him so that he became bigger than life for both of us . . . that it

477

distorted everything for us.

Marie's eyes filled with tears. 'Then that must be my sin. You see, your father did try to see you girls when you were young. It was I who kept him from you then. Oh, I rationalized that it was for your own good, but it wasn't really so. I acted out of spite and revenge . . . and hurt the two of you. Maybe, so much that you both can't be happy adults.'

Angel closed her eyes in pain, could only think of what might have been if she and Kiki had had a normal relationship with their father. Then she thought of Marie's pain and spoke: 'Don't blame yourself, Mother. Where was he when we were grown up, when you couldn't stop him from seeing us any longer? We still needed him, maybe even more than when we were young.'

'Ah, by then he had been brought down, an eagle who could no longer soar. He was on hard times, and I think he was ashamed. He could not bear for the two of you to see him like that.'

'And after that? When he was on his feet? After he married that woman?'

'Who knows? Maybe he was still ashamed. Maybe it was too late. Maybe too many years had passed.' She cried bitterly.

Angel leaned forward to caress her mother, to comfort her. 'Don't cry for him, Mother, please.'

'I'm not, Angel. And not for myself, either. It's Kiki, my poor child . . . how she has suffered because of the two of us, your father and me.'

Angel was startled. 'But I've suffered too. And you're not crying for me? Kiki always said that I was your favorite, and I must confess I thought so too.'

'I've loved you both . . . equally. But a mother has to treat different children differently, according to their needs as she sees them. You as a mother must realize that. And Kiki is still in need and is still suffering. And you, Angel, I'm proud to say, have come through everything well and strong. You're standing on your own two feet and coping. Go see your Nick, Angel. Don't wait for him to come to you. He might be waiting for *you* to demonstrate your faith in him. See him, believe in him. And Kiki . . . forgive her and try to help her.'

Angel reached out her hand to touch her mother's. 'I will. Where is she? With Brad and Rory?'

Marie stared at her. 'Is that where she's supposed to be? I haven't heard from her since she went out to California . . . what is it? . . . three months ago. I didn't think anything of it. That's not unusual behaviour for Kiki. But the thing is, I did speak to Rory on the phone, and she didn't say a word about Kiki being with them.'

10

Angel went back to her apartment at the Dakota. She wandered through the huge, high-ceilinged rooms trying to think what she could do. Then she got on the telephone, called first Brad and then almost everyone else she and Kiki knew. It was funny how even here the past played its part. Sara Gold Ross, one of Kiki's best friends from Chalmer's, led her to Ginny Furbush Finkelstein, another girl from Chalmer's, and it was Ginny who gave her the number of the House of Cosmos on Sunset Boulevard, where Kiki could be reached.

Would Kiki talk to her? Well, if she didn't, she would rush out there on the next plane, would tell Myles that she was sorry, that she couldn't possibly start rehearsal on his new project right away, that she would have to have a week or two delay. But Kiki came to the phone as if nothing had happened between them, as if there had never been any harsh words. That was Kiki's true spirit of generosity, Angel thought.

'Kiki, I've called everywhere! I can't believe the name of that place you're staying. Is it a hotel?'

'Not, it's a temple. I'm getting in touch with myself. With the real me. With all the shit stripped away. I'm getting to the core of my soul, and I'm exorcising all the devils that have plagued me for years.'

'What happened with Brad and Rory? All this time and I thought that you were with them.'

'They didn't want me, Angel. That's the simple truth. That rumor I heard about Brad and that girl was true. She's only eighteen. Can you believe it? She's not only a child but a back-to-the-earth flower child. She wears long dresses and braids. She's got this *shtick*. She's into earth and growing your own food, and Brad is going along with the whole idiocy. He's buying some kind of spread in Oregon. They're going to raise organic veggies, or whatever. And he's going to marry her! My Brad!' Kiki began to cry. 'My Brad! As soon as *her* divorce comes through. How do you like that?' She stopped crying. 'A nature girl and already divorced at eighteen. It seems her husband was a materialist and that's a terrible thing to be. It's enough to make me throw up! And now they have Rory into the whole thing. She eats only vegetables and some kind of nutty eggs – fertile ones – and she's wearing braids and ankle-length dresses too. Christ! That's what hurts – seeing Rory looking like a freak. That's when I had it and I told Brad I was suing to regain custody. Do you know what that bastard said? That since Rory was fourteen she was old enough to exercise free choice and he would allow her to choose for herself. He asked her right then and there with whom she preferred to live. And she said, "Kiki" – she called me Kiki, not Mother – "Kiki, you're my mother so I love you and respect you, but I really don't know you very well. So it would be hard to tell if I wanted to live with you. I'm sure you're a good person and an interesting one, but I feel that my place is with my father and Callie." Callie is that hippie bitch. Then she said something about hoping to get to know me better. Would you believe that?

'Well, nobody has to hit me on the head to tell me when I'm not wanted. I picked up and got out. And for a few weeks I really hit the bottle. I was bombed out of my skull. I didn't even know where I was.

'I woke up one day in Sara Ross's house out in Malibu. She said she saw me walking on the Pacific Coast Highway looking like something the cat dragged in and she stopped her car and picked me up and took me home. I stayed with her for over two weeks. I don't know what would have happened to me if Sara didn't pick me up that day. I probably would have ended up dead on some beach or—'

'Oh my God! Thank God for Sara!'

'Of course, now Sara's mad at me because of Ginny. You remember Ginny from Chalmer's?'

'Yes. She's the one who told me where to reach you.'

'Oh. Well, after I was feeling better I left Sara's and went to stay with Ginny. And Sara says Ginny is into all the wrong things. Weird shit! Kinky stuff! But it's Sara who's weird . . . she's changed . . . she's just not with it anymore. Anyway, Ginny said I should try the House of Cosmos, that they would help me. And, Angel, you wouldn't believe it. In the time I've been here I'm another person. I've found peace of mind! And believe me, in today's world, that's not easy.'

'Kiki, how long are you going to stay there?'

'I'm not sure right now.'

'Look, Kiki, I'm flying out to see you as soon as I can get a flight. Okay?'

'Sure. Why not? I *want* you to come here and find some answers. It will be a rebirth for you as well.'

Angel tried to joke, although she was desperately worried. 'I really don't think I'd care to go through all this again.'

But Kiki took her seriously. 'That's because you've made so many cosmic mistakes. They weren't your fault, you see. It was always outside forces driving you, cosmic forces . . .'

11

The House of Cosmos was an old dilapidated mansion in Hollywood, a relic of another era, a leftover from some long-forgotten star's heyday. Kiki herself came to answer the door when Angel turned the bell handle. Kiki hugged and kissed her repeatedly. 'I'm so thrilled you're here.'

With relief, Angel saw that her sister looked well. Her eyes were large and bright, and there was a luminous quality to her skin.

'Angel darling, come in and meet Veronica, the founder of the House of Cosmos.'

Veronica, a statuesque redhead of spectacular proportions, wore flowing chiffon, as did Kiki herself and several other young women Angel saw floating in an out of the rooms. 'I don't see any men,' she remarked to Kiki.

'No, of course not. They would interfere with the purification of the spirit.'

Kiki without men? That was a first, Angel thought with increased anxiety.

'We're going to open a branch of the House of Cosmos in New York too!' Kiki said excitedly. 'Veronica will be the Mistress and I'm going to be the first assistant!'

'But what is it you do?' Angel asked, bewildered. 'I mean, exactly.'

'We get in touch with our real selves and we exorcise our harmful vibrations. You would never have had any of your problems if you had been more aware of the spirits of the reincarnation that are trying to harm you.'

Oh my God! Kiki! Angel deliberately laughed. 'Spirits of reincarnation?'

'I'm not kidding, Angel. I'm deadly serious. My stay here has been a revelation. Veronica has opened up a whole new world for me.'

'We were only the instruments, Kiki. It was your vibrations, your own karmas drawn from the Cosmos, that restored you,' Veronica lulled.

'See?' Kiki turned to Angel with delight. 'Things are going to be different for us both from now on. I've discovered the secret. All this time I thought that my mistakes, all my problems with men, were caused by me. Myself. Now I know that everything that happens to us doesn't come from within but from outside forces, vibrations, spirits of the reincarnation that are intent upon doing evil unto us for reasons we don't even know – for events that happened maybe centuries ago. We have to break their spell and control *them*.'

Mother of God! Angel couldn't believe this was Kiki taking!

'Control the spirits of the reincarnation?' she mocked. 'Really, Kiki.'

'Exactly. Once we control those spirits poisoning our vibrations we gain control of ourselves. Until we expel these forces, Angel, we are their victims – they control us, do evil unto us.'

Angel tried to gather her own forces of energy about her to answer Kiki, to break the spell that Veronica had woven about her. As she was about to ask that Veronica leave them alone, Veronica, as if reading her mind, floated over to Angel, sat down on the sofa to her right, and took her hand in her own cool, strong one. 'We're going to help you too, Angel. We know what you've gone through. We're going to free you.'

Angel removed her hand from Veronica's deliberately n what she hoped was a show of strength. 'What do you know of what I've gone through?' she asked coldly.

Veronica and Kiki exchanged commiserating glances. 'Of course we know. We've meditated on your problems, your past mistakes. Do not chastise yourself. We'll help you resolve all your problems.'

'I have no problems I can't handle myself. I accept the responsibility for my past mistakes, you see, but they are n the past. I've learned from them and I, only I, am in control of my destiny.'

Veronica and Kiki shook their heads, smiling as if Angel were a not quite bright child. Veronica raised an arm and pointed a finger at Angel melodramatically. 'You have within you an incubus!'

Angel laughed out loud. 'An incubus? You mean a demon?'

'And that incubus is – Nick Dominguez!' Kiki finished triumphantly.

Angel felt like getting up and walking out, but she hadn't come across the country to walk out on Kiki in disgust, as much as she wanted to.

'And sometimes that incubus takes the form of Rory Devlin!' Kiki pronounced.

'You mean the incubus is both of them? Nicky and Daddy?'

'If you think you can be quiet long enough, I will continue,' Kiki said shrewishly.

Well, at least that sounds like Kiki.

'Your incubus is Abigor. And Abigor is a demon, the Grand Duke of Hell. He usually reveals himself as a handsome horseman. But he can take other shapes and forms. First Rory. Then Dick. And then Zev. It didn't matter whom you married, don't you see? It could have been any Rory, Dick, or Zev. Now he is Nick. The black shadow! And you have to be set free . . .'

Angel wondered how much money Kiki had given Veronica. Well, it was probably too late to worry about that. She had to get Kiki out of here before any more damage was done. Break the spell Veronica had woven. But how?'

She had arrived when the California sun was high. It was dark now, and no one moved to put on any lights. Then a few candles were lit and the disciples came bringing liquid refreshment, bestowing glassy smiles of love.

'Sip this,' Kiki said, 'and it will help you see things more clearly. You will see colors that you have never seen before . . . shapes and sounds and—'

'Kiki!' Angel said sharply 'Just a few months ago you said you wouldn't take anything again – that you—'

Kiki's eyes opened wide. 'Oh, but this is not the same ~~t~~hing. This' – she held the glass up – 'is only a voyage on ~~t~~he sea of enlightenment.'

~~A~~ngel was really frightened now. This whole thing – ~~C~~osmos, Veronica, whatever it was that Kiki was ~~i~~mbibing – was all too much for her to contend with. She ~~h~~ad to get out of this place – to think, to plan, to get help. ~~S~~he had to get Kiki out of here, one way or another.

She called a cab to take her to the Beverly Hills Hotel. ~~S~~he leaned back in the taxi. It had been a very long day, ~~o~~ne of the longest she could remember. What was it that ~~K~~iki always said to her on New Year's Eve every year, ~~e~~ither in person or by telephone if they were separated: ~~I~~t's a New Year, sis. A new beginning. Come on – let's ~~m~~ake it a biggie!'

'A biggie,' Angel whispered. 'This year, the biggest, ~~K~~iki!' she promised.

~~A~~s soon as the bellboy left, Angel stripped off her clothes ~~a~~nd let them fall to the floor. She crawled into the big ~~b~~ed, too tired even to put on a nightgown. She didn't see ~~h~~ow she was going to talk Kiki out of this. She had been ~~a~~t it all day and had made no headway at all. Maybe it was ~~a~~ psychiatrist that Kiki needed. But Dr Preston had said ~~t~~hat one must be willing for a psychiatrist to help, before ~~a~~nything could be accomplished. Their mother! Yes. ~~M~~arie could help, if anyone could. But Marie had asked ~~h~~er to do this job, and *she* wanted to do it for Kiki, if she ~~c~~ould. It was important to her. She would call on Marie ~~o~~nly if everything else failed.

There was Brad. He too would most probably respond ~~t~~o Kiki's need. He was a good person. But would Kiki ~~r~~espond to him at this time? She was full of hostility ~~t~~oward him, and contempt, too, now that he was ~~c~~ontemplating marriage to that eighteen-year-old.

She thought of Vic. Would he respond to an appeal on ~~K~~iki's behalf? She was not at all sure that he would. Or ~~t~~hat Kiki would value his judgment. Their relationship

485

had so deteriorated that neither had any respect for th
other.

But there was Rory. If there could be some kind o
reconciliation between Kiki and Rory . . . and Nikki . .
Yes, that was it! If she could pull that off. Angel laughe
with exhilaration. She just knew that was the answer
All she had to do was convince Brad and Rory. She woul
go see them as soon as it was light. Oh, if she could jus
pull this off, help Kiki, who had helped her through s
many times, nothing would ever be too difficult for he
again, not even her own life.

Angel awoke from a dream in the unfamiliar surround
ings, tried in vain to remember what she had dreamec
She looked at her wristwatch on the nightstand. It wa
only seven. She had lots of time – she couldn't go to se
Brad and Rory before nine. She picked up the phone an
asked for room service, then sat in bed feeling wonderfu
about the solution she had worked out the night befor
Today she was going to deal with Kiki's problem and sh
was going to win, she felt it deep inside. And then sh
would go back and deal with her own life.

Kiki had been right about one thing – there *were* tw
shadows in her life, Nick and her father. Nick was nc
only the past but the present. She would go back and tal
to him about their future. As for her father, he was onl
the past. Her mother had told her to forgive him – that
would be better for *her*. Well, she would try, But she ha
forgotten to ask her mother a question. Someday sh
would. *Had Marie herself forgiven Rory Devlin?*

She saw Rory and Brad, and after she was finishe
talking with them she made a call to Rome. And after th
call, she was so sure how things were going to b
resolved that she made a reservation for herself on th
afternoon flight to New York for one final confront
tion. The resolution of Kiki's life was no longer i
question – only her own was, but she felt rathe
optimistic about that too.

*

Angel turned the bell handle for the third time and still nothing happened. Damn! Where were they? Why didn't anyone answer? Finally, in exasperation, she tried the door handle and the door swung open. *Please, Kiki, be here!*

She looked into the big white room. Sheer white curtains stirred slightly in a gentle breeze. Some of the disciples were in there, dancing and swaying in their flowing gowns in some graceful rite, completely oblivious to her. Had they been there all through the night?

'Kiki!' she called out. There was no answer.

The dancing women didn't turn around. Were they sleep-dancing? In some kind of a trance?

Kiki was probably still sleeping upstairs, she decided. She dashed up the stairs quickly. She ran down the hall, looking into each of the rooms. *Kiki, for God's sake! Where are you? Please, Mother of God! Please! Let Kiki be here!*

Sickeningly, a feeling of *déjà vu* came over her. She had done this once before . . . long ago . . . run up a flight of stairs, run down a hallway, looking into rooms.

Yes, it had all happened before. Dear God, yes! A tangle of bodies in a bed. White skin. White bodies. Thus it had been when the nightmare had started for her – when her life had first fallen apart. Then there had been two dark heads upon the white pillow. Today there was one pale blond head, and another – a magnificent spill of red, wild hair . . .

Kiki! Kiki! But the screams died in her throat.

Thus the nightmare had begun, thus the new dream would die. She ran down the hall, down the stairs, out of the House of Cosmos.

12

Angel snatched her two suitcases from the cab herself, not waiting for the driver. She slung her coat over her

487

shoulder and ran into the terminal. At the ticket counter, the young man in attendance took the bags and wrote out her ticket, and she scribbed out a check. The clerk, smiling, looked up to wish Miss Angela du Beaumond a good trip, and to caution her that she had only about five minutes to board. He stopped smiling when he saw the tears coursing down her cheeks.

She sprinted from the gate, but just as she was about to hand her ticket to the flight attendant, she stopped short. What *was* she doing? Running away? From what? From Kiki? Kiki, who had sustained her and cherished her and comforted her through so many bad times? So Kiki wasn't perfect . . . and who had promised her perfection anyway? She thought of the young girls dancing in a semi-trance in the big white room of the Cosmos house, their eyes fixed on some distant dream that did not exist, their smiles unreal and vague. For God's sake, where were *their* sisters?

She did an about-face and started back toward the entrance. The man at the gate yelled after her. 'Miss du Beaumond, your plane is leaving—'

She turned, gave him her brilliant stage smile, waved 'There'll be other planes later today, won't there? Today . . . tonight . . .'

Nick had waited for so many years. For Kiki, he could wait a few more hours.

This time an angelic fair-haired girl answered the door welcomed her ceremonially, ushered her into the white room where Veronica and Kiki sat drinking tea, talking their heads close together.

Kiki waved Angel to a chair. 'I was wondering when you were going to show up. Veronica and I were just talking about you. We've decided that—'

'Kiki, I have to talk to you alone.'

'Oh, Jesus!' Kiki complained. 'Are you starting that again? I told you, Veronica can hear anything.'

'Kiki, I have some news to tell you and you're not goin,

to hear it until we're alone. Have you got that straight?'

'Well, somebody is certainly getting masterful in her old age. All right then.' Kiki finally smiled, and turned to Veronica beseechingly.

Veronica reluctantly rose. 'Call me, darling,' she said to Kiki, 'if you need me. I'm only here to serve . . .'

'You certainly know how to break up the good karmas,' Kiki grouched. What's the big news that Veronica can't hear?'

'I've been to Malibu, Kiki. I've talked to Rory.'

'You what? Why the hell did you do that?'

'Because I wanted to talk to my niece. Is that so terrible?'

'Okay. Okay. So what's new? Did Brad break his fucking neck? Did little Miss Callie drop dead?'

'Boy, your new spiritual awareness has improved neither your disposition nor your vocabulary.'

'Look, Angel, if you have something to tell me, please do so. I tried to help you. I wanted you to find peace of mind and liberation from the past here, as I have, but you don't want to be helped. So tell me what you came to tell me and get off my back.'

'Kiki, I had this wonderful conversation with Rory. She's so lovely and she has so much character – she's so mature.'

'So I've noticed. But she's not interested in being my daughter . . . She's only—'

'Kiki, shut up! For once, shut up and listen! Rory told me that the most wonderful thing that could possibly happen to her would be if you, her sweet, lovely mother, would come and get her and take her to Rome so she can meet and be united with the sister she had never known . . . and that the three of you, you, Rory, Nikki, could all be together for a while, loving each other—' She broke off as she started to cry. *Damn!* This one time she had promised herself she wouldn't cry!

Kiki stared at her, her mouth hanging open, speechless.

'Kiki, this might be your last chance,' Angel sobbed.

'Please don't blow it!'

Kiki, her hand covering her mouth, her eyes huge in her face, slipped off the sofa to her knees and crawled over to her sister. 'Angel, do you mean it? Are you sure? She said that she would go with me? And Brad said that he would let her go?'

Angel nodded her head. 'She's waiting for you . . . right this minute. And somebody else is waiting too . . . in Rome.'

Kiki buried her head in Angel's lap.

'Are you going to help me pack or are you going to sit there grinning like some fucking Cheshire cat?'

'What about Veronica, Kiki? And the House of Cosmos? Are you going to drop them, just like that?' Angel wanted to hear her say it.

Kiki looked at her and dropped her eyes. 'It was just something to do,' she muttered, embarrassed, 'until something else come along.' Then she perked up. 'Besides, you can't imagine how bored I was getting with these goddamn robes.' She kicked the chiffon garment across the room. 'Oh, what a relief to be chic Kiki Devlin again!' She adjusted the collar of her white suit. She looked into the mirror and her eyes met Angel's. 'Hey! How do I say thanks?'

'You don't. You never have to say thank you to a sister. We're two sides of the same coin, you and I.'

'Oh, Angel . . .' The tears welled up in eyes huge with emotion. 'Why, then, why?'

'I read in a book, Kiki, that the relationship between sisters is probably the most difficult and complex of all human relationships. And we had problems, you and I, that most sisters don't have to deal with. Rivalry over a father is not uncommon, but then he left us and we, in our insecurity, were forced into competition for our mother's love. She told me that she always loved both of us equally, but how could we know that? And then it got so mixed up. When I was attracted to Nick Dominguez

490

and he to me, to you it was as if I was going to end up with Daddy after all. And I never really liked Vic, I always resented him, but I just didn't realize why. I thought it was because he replaced Brad, whom I adored. But it was for the same reason you didn't want me to have Nick.

'Then it all got carried over to our professional lives and . . .' Angel smiled entreatingly.

'How'd you get so smart, little sister?'

'I always had a good teacher.'

'Everything you say is probably true, Angel, but I have always loved you, in spite of it all. You know that, don't you?'

'You have proved that, too, over and over again.'

'Good. I'm glad. Hey, by the way, do you have a car waiting, Big Star?'

'No, Kiki, I don't. We'll have to call a cab. Two cabs.'

'Two cabs? Why? Aren't you coming with me to Malibu?'

'No. I think you can handle this alone – without the big star's help.'

'Get a load of her. And where is the big star going?'

'I've got a plane to catch back to New York. I have a rendezvous of my own.'

'Him?'

'Yes, him.'

Kiki smiled tremulously. 'I'm glad.'

'And, Kiki. I have a message for you from Marie.'

'Yes? What does Marie say?'

'She said that while you're in Europe, why don't you look up *somebody else?* She seems to think it would be good for your psyche. You know the line, forgive and forget?'

'Does Marie mean who I think she means?' Kiki asked incredulously. '*Him?*'

'Yes, Kiki, him. And there's something else I want to tell you. Mother told me that there were times that he attempted to see us and she wouldn't allow it.'

'I see. I always suspected as much.' She was thoughtful for a few seconds and then said, 'And how about Marie?

Does *she* forgive him?'

'I'm not sure. One of these days I'm going to ask her.'

They were anxious to be out and away from the House of Cosmos, so they waited for their cabs out on Sunset Boulevard. The sun was starting to go down in the west.

Kiki smoothed her hair nervously. 'How do you think I look?'

'I think you look like . . . a star!'

Kiki smiled brilliantly. 'You better believe it. And you know, all this sentimental crap aside, I was always a son-of-a-bitchin' better actress than you.'

Angel laughed. 'Wanna bet?'

A cab pulled up.

'You take it, Kiki. I'll wait. I have plenty of time to make my plane.'

'Are you sure?' Kiki asked as she walked to the cab and blew Angel a kiss.

The cabdriver jumped out to open the door. 'Hey!' he said. 'I know you. You're that Italian movie star . . .'

'I'm afraid not, pardner,' she said as she winked at Angel. 'I'm just a little old gal from New Orleans!'

EPILOGUE

Hollywood
1970

My goodness,' Beebie Tyler says to her guest. 'It's
rowing late. The Awards start early here, you know, to
ccommodate the television viewers in the East. I must
egin dressing.'

'Oh, but you haven't told me how it all turns out – if
here's a happy ending. I know who Angela married,
ut . . .'

Beebie Tyler smiles grandly. 'I think you should find
ut for yourself. Do you know what I'm going to do? I'm
oing to take you along with me tonight.'

'But how can you? Don't I need an invitation?'

Beebie Tyler laughs. 'We'll squeeze you in. *No one*
uestions Beebie Tyler.'

'But I'm not dressed for the Awards.'

'Ah! But Hollywood is the land of miracles, is it not?
Vhat size are you? All I have to do is call up my favorite
alesperson at my favorite shop and a selection of
resses will be here in a half hour.'

t's a typical Oscar night in Hollywood, folks, and
veryone is here,' Ralph Donalds, the emcee of the
vening, reports, as the limousines draw up to the front
f the theater.

Donalds introduces the stars, one after another, as
hey hurry into the theater. Taylor . . . Grant . . .
Vayne . . . Brad Cranford with his wife, Callie. It is
etting late, but still some of the nominees have not yet
rrived. And then one more limousine pulls up to the
urb and two young men emerge, and then a very
andsome man in his forties with a full head of wavy
lack-and-gray hair. The three men turn to help Angel
u Beaumond out, handling her as carefully as if she
vere a rare, fragile flower.

She is not eager to speak with Ralph Donalds, but he
rowds in on her with his mike. 'Just a few words for our
udience, Miss du Beaumond,' he pleads.

She laughs. 'Considering my state' – she holds her

stomach, which is prominently extended – 'you'd better call me Mrs Dominguez. This is my husband, Nick' – she draws him forward from the background – 'and these are my sons, Tim and Dick.'

'Mr Dominguez is Hollywood's foremost photographer,' Donalds explains to the TV audience. 'Tonight is a particularly big night for you, Angela – both you and your sister competing for the Best Actress award.'

Holding her stomach again, Angel du Beaumond smiles. 'I'm going to have *my* big award in about three months,' she says, seemingly making light of the competition for the Oscar, but still she squeezes Nick's hand to make the tension more bearable. Tonight might be her very last chance for the prize. Roles like the one she played in *Audrina* did not come along very often for actresses in their forties. How long could she go on playing glamorous but vulnerable women in love? And was she really the actress Kiki was, able to play a role such as Kiki had been nominated for? A woman of the streets, in her fifties, ugly, scarred, and hopeless. Was she courageous enough to undertake such a role?

They are seated around a big table with the still vacant chairs, and Angel is visibly nervous now. Her husband puts his hand over hers and says, 'I spoke to the airlines. Their plane landed about ten minutes ago and they should be here soon, and you know you're not supposed to excite yourself.'

She feels like a fraud. Nick thinks that she is only nervous about the safe arrival of Kiki and the girl and . . . *him*. And although the excitement of finally seeing him is almost too much to be endured, that alone is not all of it. Winning tonight means more to her than she has disclosed to Nick, and she is ashamed to admit how much it does mean, considering how blessed she already is with Nick and her sons and with the new baby coming, after they almost gave up on

496

er conceiving.

'I promise to go to bed the minute this thing is over,' she says now, to reassure him. 'Did they say if he . . . ? I'm so afraid that at the last minute he changed his mind.'

Nick shakes his head. 'All they said was that Miss Devlin and her party were on their way here.'

'I'm glad that Mother isn't here tonight. I wouldn't want her to have to, you know . . . see him, with everybody watching.'

And she thinks of her mother in New York, watching the Awards on television. *Who is she rooting for tonight? Me or my sister?*

Then, watching the entrance, she says ruefully, 'I just know Kiki is going to rush in here looking every inch the star, in gold lamé probably, and dripping white mink, while I sit here in my Mother Hubbard preggy outfit.' Nick and her sons tell her she looks ravishing.

There's a buzz in the crowd and everyone turns to the entrance, where a stunning woman and two young ladies rush in. One young lady is strikingly beautiful, the blond one. The dark-haired girl is 'interesting'-looking. All three are wearing not evening gowns, but midis with polished boots.

Angel searches desperately with her eyes, but that is all there is to the party – Kiki with her hair hanging straight down from a middle part, a new hairdo again, and the two girls. Kiki is laughing and waving to everybody in the room and throwing kisses as she makes her way to her sister's table. The daughters smile at each other knowingly, watching her mother act the star. Brad Cranford runs over, kisses his daughter several times and hugs his ex-wife.

Angel is crying with disappointment now, disappointment and tension. Once more he has not shown up. And to top it all, she just knows she is going to lose tonight to Kiki. Through her tears she says to Nick,

'Trust Kiki to make a big entrance.'

And then Kiki and her daughters are at the table and everyone is kissing. Tim and Dick are making a big fuss over their cousins and Kiki is hugging her brother-in-law and whispering in her sister's ear, 'Don't cry, littlest Angel. *He is here!* He just couldn't bring himself to come here tonight, but he's waiting for you . . . back at your house!'

And then Angel really starts to cry, and the crowd wonders what the one sister had said to the other to cause all that. And Kiki turns to Nick, who is alarmed at his wife's fresh outburst, and shrugs. 'I just told her that if she beats me out tonight, I'm going to beat the hell out of her.'

Beebie Tyler goes up for her award and makes a lengthy speech extolling the legend of Hollywood and the 'tiny' part she played in its evolution. Then she sits down again, proud and moved by her own role in the night's proceedings.

'Whom do you want to see win for Best Actress in a Leading Role, Miss Tyler?' the young woman next to her asks. 'You never told me. Kiki, Angel . . . or one of the others?'

'Kiki Devlin, of course!'

'But why? I thought you were crazy about her sister. You told me how sweet she was.'

Beebie Tyler looks at the girl indignantly. 'This is not a contest for sweetness. This is an award for *performance*. Kiki Devlin delivered the performance of the year, an acting job without peer. Here she is a beautiful woman, even though she is in her forties, glamorous, and with a divine figure, and in the interest of her art she allows herself to appear as an ugly, disfigured woman, and does it convincingly with an artistry that no one believed her capable of. understand that in order to play the role she went out into the streets of Rome, slept on benches, exposed herself to the elements and the dangers of the street

What dedication! I doubt very much if her sister would have done that. Not that I'm taking anything away from Angel. She's a capable, efficient, charming actress. But Kiki – the word is *inspired*. I think acting was . . . is . . . her life. It always meant more to her than it did to Angel. And she had to overcome a lot of obstacles. She had a lot of bad luck and she made a lot of mistakes. But she was . . . indomitable! You have to give her credit for that. Both girls deserve a lot of credit. They've both matured and grown and are women I'm proud to have in our industry. Why, *Cry of the People*, the picture Kiki is nominated for – which is also nominated for the Best Picture of the Year – would never have gotten made at all without her. Why she— Oh, there's the Duke now . . . Ssh! We'll talk later.'

Kiki and Angel look at each other across the table, their smiles fading. Kiki finger-combs her hair. Yes. She wants the prize . . . at anyone's expense . . . yes, at Angel's expense. Winning tonight means redemption in the eyes of the whole goddamn world, and she has that coming.

Angel fidgets in her chair. She averts her eyes from Kiki's. Her stomach is in knots. She *needs* the prize tonight. For years, despite her cinematic triumphs, in her heart she had doubted her own abilities as an actress. Tonight could be her vote of confidence.

John Wayne is onstage to present the award for the Best Actress in a Leading Role. He is making the usual pleasantries, but the air is very tense, maybe more so than is usual. Finally he is tearing open the envelope.

Again Kiki's and Angel's eyes meet.

'And the winner is . . .'

Angel grips Nick's hand and Kiki stares into her lap.

'Glenda Jackson! For *Women in Love!*'

The sisters look at each other in bewildered disappointment – it was as if they forgot that anyone

499

else was in the running besides the two of them. Then, suddenly, they burst out laughing. And they laugh and laugh until everybody at their table is laughing uncontrollably.

'Oh, I am disappointed, I wanted so much for Kiki to win,' Beebie Tyler says to her young friend.

'*She* doesn't seem to be that disappointed. Look over there. She and Angel are laughing up a storm. But please . . . tell me about the movie, *Cry of the People*.'

'Kiki did the whole thing for her ex-husband, Vittorio Rosa, even though they were not on the best of terms. He was in trouble, you see. He hadn't had a hit picture in years. Kiki had the vision to see the possibilities in the film. It's all about social issues – divorce and abortion and the problems of the working woman. Strong stuff for a movie today, and especially for Italy. And Vittorio was scared to do it and he couldn't raise the money. But Kiki pushed. She even agreed to take the title role, although it was such a complete departure from anything she had ever done. Well, Kiki got Brad Cranford, who has his own production company, to back it, put up the money, so actually it's an Italian-American film, produced by the Cranford-Rosa Film Company – a one-time thing, I think, just for this film. And after the picture was in the can, she went all over selling it, plugging it. No matter that she lost the Oscar – she's *proved* what a trouper she is!'

The night is almost over and the last award of the evening is to be presented. Jack Lemmon comes up to make the award for Best Picture and he makes a few jokes and the audience responds. It's that kind of an evening. Jack tears open the envelope and announces, '*Cry of the People* . . . Cranford-Rosa Productions. Vittorio Rosa, producer. Mr Rosa couldn't be present tonight. Accepting for him will be Kiki Devlin!'

There is a standing ovation for Kiki as she goes on stage. She, is, after all, Hollywood's own, come home

She accepts the golden statue and holds it high over her head, waving it. 'Who says Kiki Devlin couldn't pick up an Oscar?' and the audience roars.

'See my sister over there . . . laughing? Do you know why she's laughing? Because she's managed to top me again. Imagine! Having a baby at her age! And she's ten years older than I am, honest. And she's . . . *thirty-nine!*' And the audience claps.

'Well, Vic told me to say, just in case this happened, thank you to you all. And I want to thank Vic for letting me appear in his most beautiful picture. Vic, as you know, is my ex. And they make the most wonderful kind of husband, you know, these exes. If you doubt me, take a gander at Brad Cranford over there, without whom this picture would never have been made. He's another ex, and *he's* pretty wonderful, isn't he?' The audience applauds wildly. Brad Cranford is a favorite.

'And as long as I'm up here and as long as I'm holding Vittorio Rosa's Oscar, I might as well thank Vittorio Rosa's daughter, my own Nikki. And what the hell, I'll thank Nikki's sister too, Rory Cranford. And I want to thank *my* sister for being there when I needed her . . . and for just *being.*' Kiki's voice cracks, and the audience is very still. Then she says, 'And I'm *not* going to mention her name. I'm not giving *her* any free publicity.' The audience laughs wildly.

Nick Dominguez presses his wife's hand. 'She lost the Oscar,' he whispers to her, 'but she's turned the evening into a triumph . . . for both of you.'

'And lest I neglect to thank a very important, loving lady, let me do so at once. My friend Beebie Tyler, who pushed the hell out of *Cry of the People* in her column and accounted for a great deal of its success. The funny thing was, I thought she did it for me, out of friendship, and to make up for all the times she took potshots at me.' The audience claps in appreciation. 'But when I said as much to her, she was insulted. She told me she would never use her column for personal reasons – that she praised the picture only because she *believed* in it. Well, be it friendship or the spirit of truth, thank you, Beebie Tyler.'

Beebie Tyler raises her head high, blinks back tears, nods solemnly.

'They're signalling me to get off but this is such fun and God knows when I'll ever be up here again, so I think I'll thank my mother, Marie du Beaumond Whittier, and my dad, who has come home tonight . . .' Her voice breaks. '. . . Movieland's Rory Devlin!'

Kiki Devlin leaves the stage amidst thunderous applause, and many in the audience rush forward to congratulate her. Finally, after that is all over, Angela du Beaumond comes forward to take her sister's hand. 'Let's go home, Kiki, and see Daddy.'

I have loved you, Kiki, I have hated you, but I have never, never been so proud of you. I have never been so proud of myself. The past is at last done with, and yes, I'm proud to be one of the Devlin sisters . . .

The Debutantes
June Flaum Singer

They are the golden girls. A quartet of blue-blooded beauties whose names and faces fill the society pages. Poor little rich girls whose glamorous exploits make international headlines – but whose tortured private lives are the hidden price of fame:

Chrissy, survivor of a notorious custody battle between her mother and her grandmother, with a fatal weakness for all the wrong men . . .

Maeve, daughter of the celebrated Padraic, and Daddy's little girl in every sense . . .

Sara, whose father could hide his Jewish origins from the world, but couldn't hide his taste for lechery from his blackmailing daughter . . .

Marlena, Sara's poor cousin from the South, swept into a world of affluence she couldn't quite handle . . .

0 552 12118 5

CORGI BOOKS

THE MOVIE SET

BY JUNE FLAUM SINGER

They were young, beautiful, talented, and they all wanted to make it into the fastest set of all – the Movie Set, which fed on scandal, glamour, sex, and raw emotion.

Buffy she fell in love with a hero, then found herself a victim of the ultimate degradation.

Suzannah breathtakingly lovely, who mutilated her body and nearly destroyed herself on her own burning ambition.

Cleo who was dazzled by her clever intellectual lover, and spent the rest of her life trying to keep up with him.

Cassie who married to spite her mother, and was trapped in a nightmare of sadistic cruelty.

Suellen she knew all the secrets, but still hoped for a happy ending.

They all made it into The Movie Set – and no one but them knew the cost

0 552 12636 5

SEX IN THE AFTERNOON

BY JUNE FLAUM SINGER

She was the most beautiful and alluring woman he had ever seen. She was also the most elusive. But Jonathan West was a millionaire and knew how to get what he wanted. And he wanted her – the mysterious woman in the luxury suite on the *Q.E.2*. He set his vast organisation to find out who she was, where she came from, but even as he tried to subdue her, possess her, claim her as yet another of his conquests, he found himself drawn into a web of sexuality and mystery. All he could discover was her name – Andrianna DeArte.

As their devious and curious relationship grew, the secrets grew stranger. For Andrianna DeArte had many names and many lives. And no one knew the real life, the life that had begun as the daughter of a Mexican girl and the ruthless man who had bought her, the life that had shattered into violence, lies, and passionate sexual betrayal until there was no man she trusted, no man she would not use.

Between her and Jonathan West exploded a raw sexual hunger, a passionate obsession that threatened to shatter both their lives.

0 552 13503 8

A SELECTED LIST OF FINE TITLES FROM CORGI BOOKS

☐	13395 7	The Naked Heart	Jacqueline Briskin	£4.50
☐	12850 3	Too Much, Too Soon	Jacqueline Briskin	£4.99
☐	13558 5	Ambition	Julie Burchill	£3.99
☐	12486 9	Riders	Jilly Cooper	£4.99
☐	13264 0	Rivals	Jilly Cooper	£4.99
☐	13266 7	A Glimpse of Stocking	Elizabeth Gage	£4.99
☐	12867 8	Between Two Worlds	Monique Raphel High	£4.99
☐	13502 X	Next of Kin	Carly McIntyre	£3.99
☐	12689 6	In the Shadow of the Castle	Erin Pizzey	£2.50
☐	12462 1	The Watershed	Erin Pizzey	£4.99
☐	13268 3	Hot Flashes	Barbara Raskin	£3.99
☐	13022 2	The Markoff Women	June Flaum Singer	£3.50
☐	12636 5	The Movie Set	June Flaum Singer	£4.99
☐	13333 7	The President's Women	June Flaum Singer	£3.99
☐	13503 8	Sex in the Afternoon	June Flaum Singer	£4.99
☐	13522 4	Daddy	Danielle Steel	£3.99
☐	13524 0	Message From Nam	Danielle Steel	£4.99
☐	11575 4	A Necessary Woman	Helen Van Slyke	£3.50
☐	11779 X	No Love Lost	Helen Van Slyke	£3.99
☐	12240 8	Public Smiles, Private Tears	Helen Van Slyke	£2.95